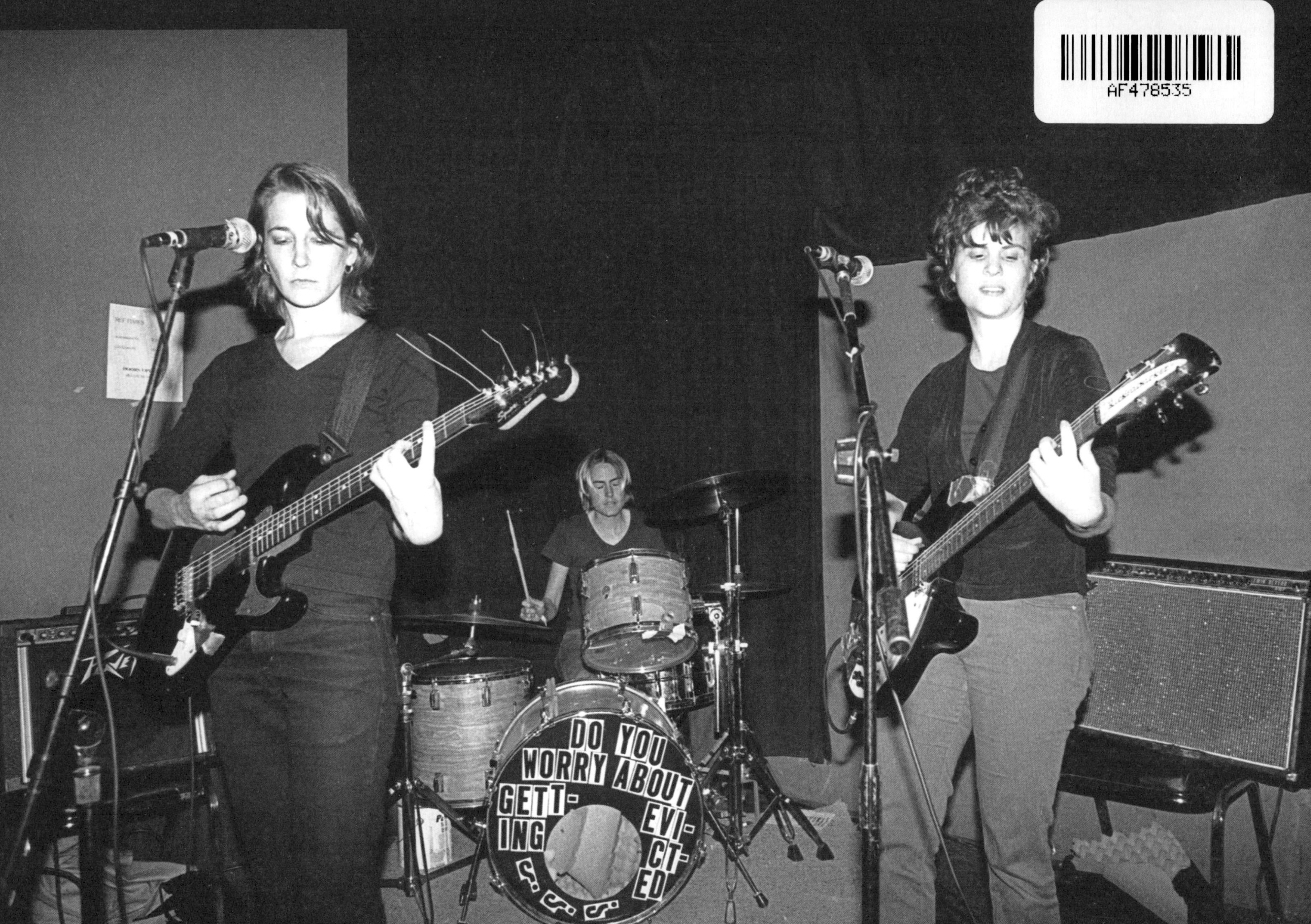
DO YOU
WORRY ABOUT
GETT-
ING
EVI-
CT-
ED

ANTONIA TRICARICO

FRAME OF MIND | PUNK PHOTOS AND ESSAYS FROM WASHINGTON, DC, AND BEYOND | 1997–2017

FOR ALL OF US

Published by Akashic Books

ISBN: 978-1-61775-719-8
Library of Congress Control Number: 2018960612

Photography: Antonia Tricarico
Photo editor: Nichole Procopenko
Design: Vida Russell

Front cover: Jennifer Finch, L7, 9:30 Club / WDC, 2016
Front endpapers: left: Scaramouche, backstage, Black Cat / WDC, 1998;
right: Kazu Makino, Blonde Redhead, Black Cat / WDC, 1998
Back endpapers: Babes in Toyland, Black Cat / WDC, 2015
Back cover: empty stage, Black Cat / WDC, 2015

Printed in China

Antonia Tricarico has been taking photos since 1997. In recent years she has worked as a photo archivist for Lucian Perkins (Pulitzer Prize–winning photographer for the *Washington Post*) and collaborated with Tolotta Records, Dischord Records, Kill Rock Stars, and Youth Action Research Group. Her work can be found in the private collection of the Smithsonian Institution's National Museum of American History and the Special Collections Division of the District of Columbia Public Library. Her work appeared in *Photo Review* from 2006–2013. For more information visit www.antoniatricarico.com.

Thank you.

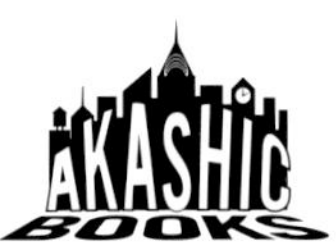

Akashic Books
Brooklyn, New York, USA
Ballydehob, Co. Cork, Ireland
Twitter: @AkashicBooks
Facebook: AkashicBooks
E-mail: info@akashicbooks.com
Website: www.akashicbooks.com

CONTENTS

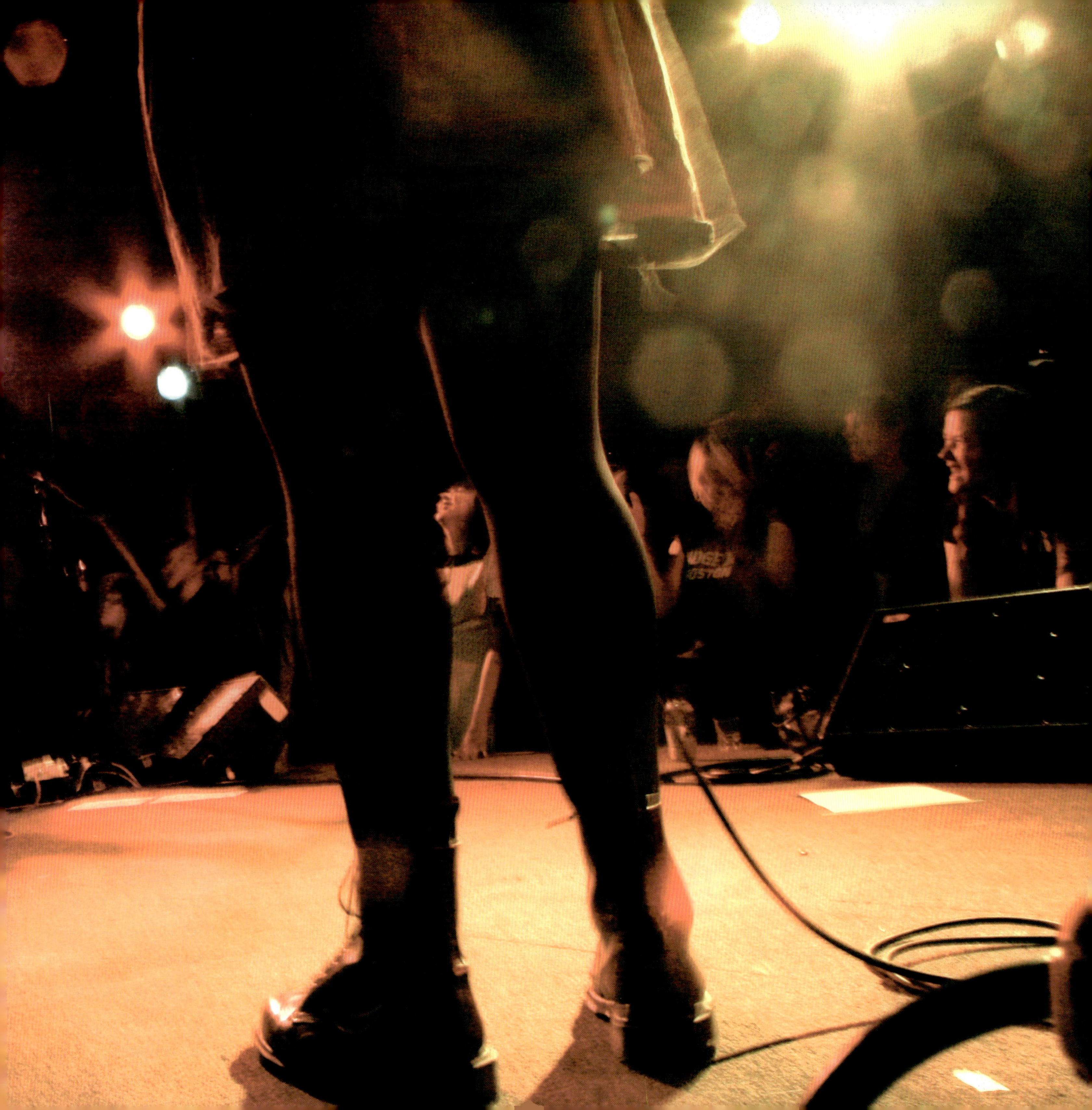

ANTONIA TRICARICO

It was love at first sight. The visceral and passionate, the no-doubts-at-all. It was the music. Not just any music. Lyrics and notes bound in a cycle of personal matters that in time became political, grounded in social issues.

When you are thirteen years old, hungry to know about bands playing on the radio and concerts that you probably won't see anytime soon, you need to convince your parents to buy you some music. That's when I got my first imported 7" single in my hands.

The Beatles, with "Come Together" on side A and "Something" on side B, made my days, in a small town located in the south of Italy, bright as a thousand flashlights in a cave of miners.

Then came the uncomfortable doubts threading into my life—all related to being a woman.

When you are sixteen years old and suddenly unmask the reality that your privileges are bordered, you need to free yourself first from institutional patterns and open your eyes fully. Fathers, brothers, priests, and politicians transmitting harmful beliefs and behaviors from generation to generation.

Truth gets revealed in everyday moments, in ordinary gestures, in corporeal, verbal, and domestic violations. For me, liberation came via meetings, marches, theater, and music.

The family crashed, relations were questioned, love was discussed and broken. Music was played with acoustic guitars, sit-ins were held in the main plaza, shouting against repression, singing of new perspectives, the personal becoming political, and we learned to question authority.

When sisterhood rises up, it never goes back.

Though it did slow down at a certain point. So I flew to a bigger city, started a hardcore band, played drums, dissolved the band, and began working in music production. Best job ever. My English was poor and I was shy, but it didn't matter. Musicians loved Rome like their mothers and nothing could disrupt the vibe.

I had the fortune to work with two of the best people in the local underground music scene. Without them, Italy would never have had the pleasure to host so many visitors, and I would never have gotten to know some of the great human beings hidden behind instruments and microphones, with hearts full of love for their music.

Dressing rooms filled with laughter and cigarette smoke, jokes and stories from all over the world, music spreading in venues, clubs, theaters, and small arenas, crowds filled with energy and joy. I was too lazy to be a musician myself—I couldn't handle the tolerance for pain required—but that was the place I wanted to be, to get involved, to participate. Many years later, I crossed the ocean with my camera, the only old friend involved in "I don't know what I am doing"—the friend who gave me direction during what became one of the most interesting periods of my life.

In 1997 I moved from Rome to Washington, DC. I was going out to shows nearly every night, taking photos of the local music scene. I saw bands like Fugazi, Lungfish, The Make-Up, Deep Lust, Quix*o*tic, and Spirit Caravan. There was a sense of community that made me feel as if I belonged here, like years before in Italy. Having dinners and pajamas parties, going to see movies, visiting backstages crowded with the band's closest friends, sometimes touring together—I had to document all of this, to honor the friendship, the action, and, most of all, the bands' control of their own music without compromise.

Today, underground music is still so alive, and women are constantly in motion; the commitment to fight for human rights still runs deep and many of the struggles are the same, but now we are a million stronger, not just cisgender women but people of all marginalized gender identities.

Everybody in my photographs deserves a place in *Frame of Mind* because it is all about music. However, since the majority of the writing in music books has been done by men, I wanted to highlight the voices of women. The essays here are presented in alphabetical order by the author's name, and each of them is unique and powerful; together they offer paths to follow, stimulation for the detached or ignored or unaware, showing how music can become a home for everyone.

When I realized that I had enough good photos to publish a book, I didn't know how to organize it. But when I reviewed the negatives and digital files, they made me think that the beginning should be my very first shots after I arrived in DC, followed by the others, chronologically from 1997 to 2017. So many memories to share that I didn't want to break up the natural flow.

Babes in Toyland, Black Cat / WDC, 2015

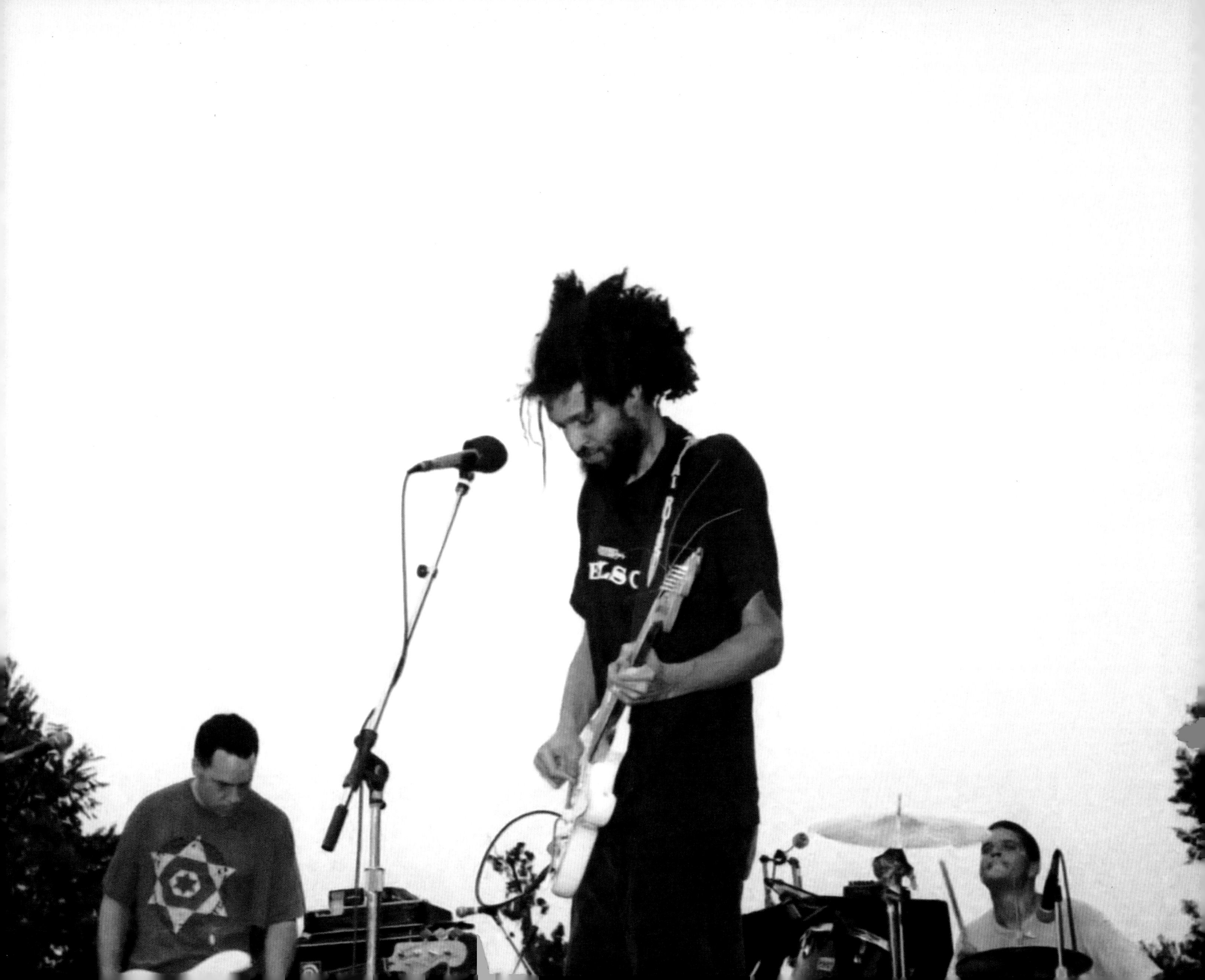

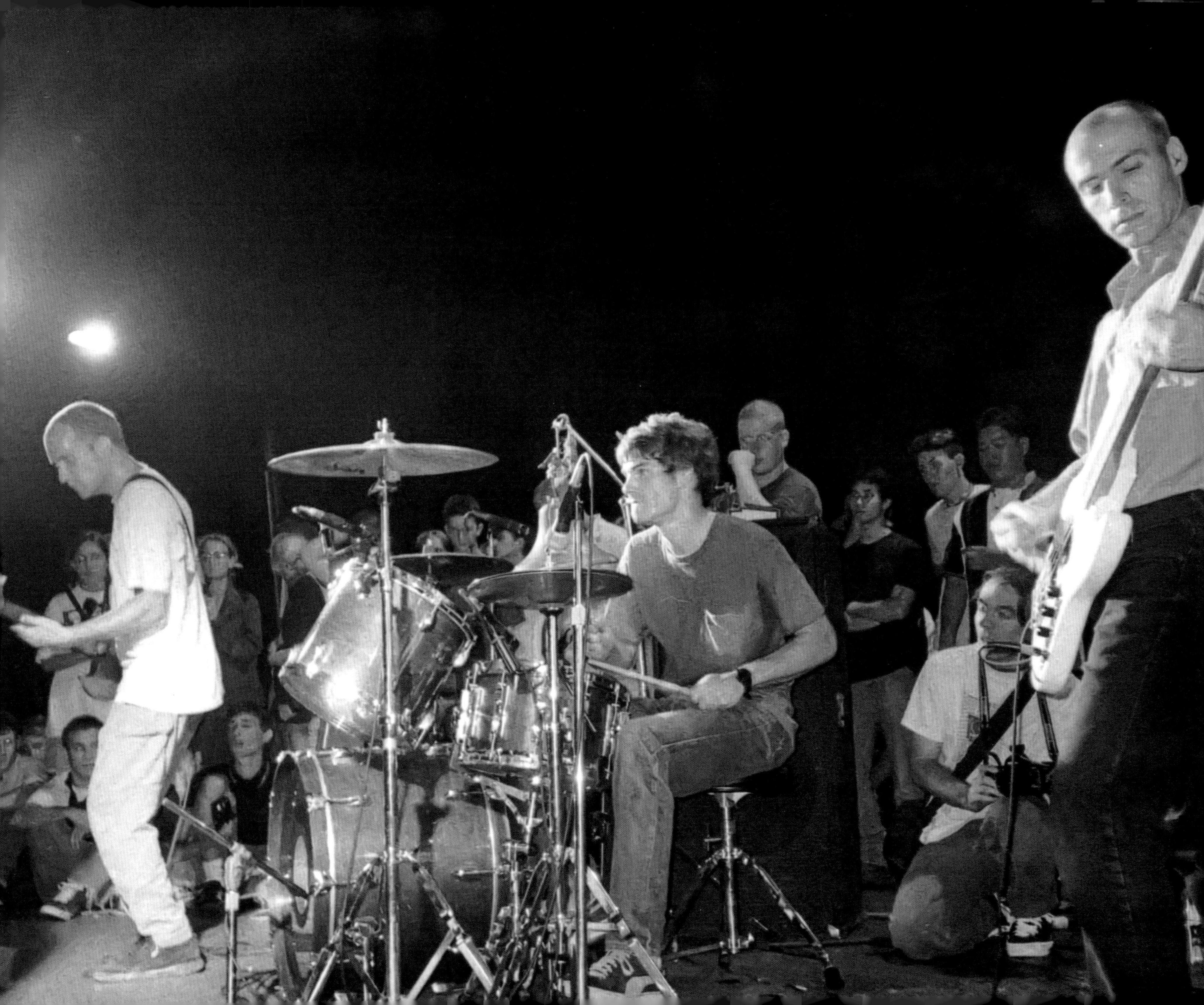

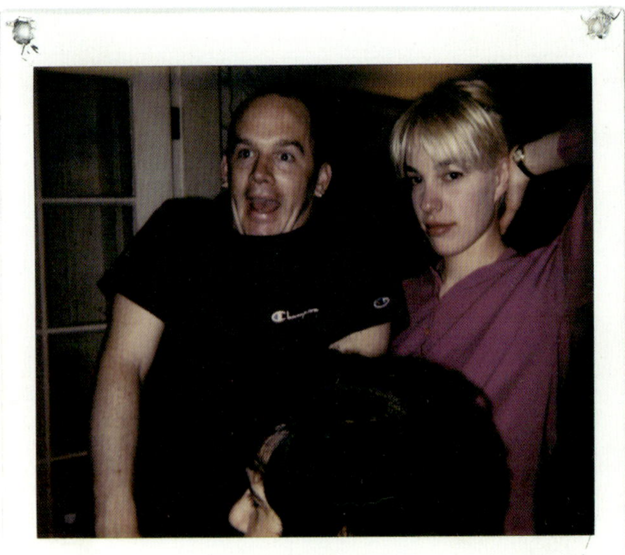

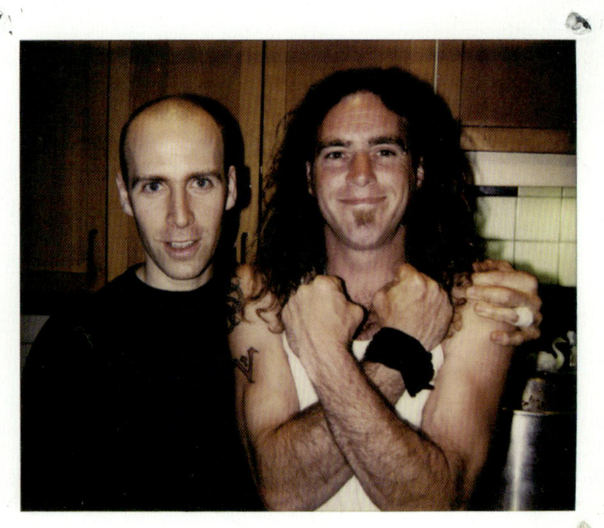

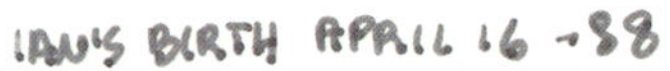

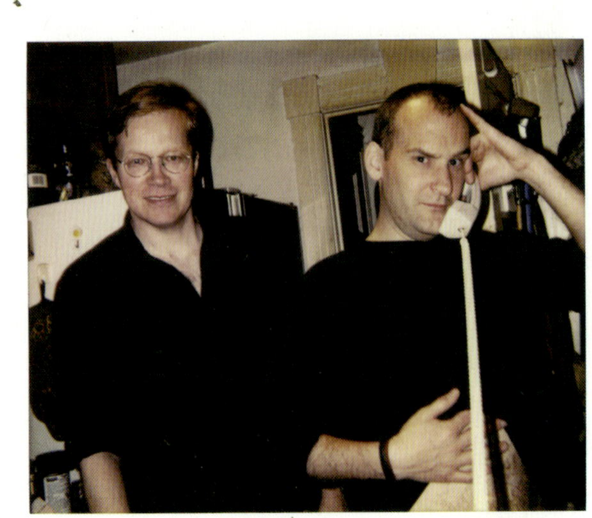

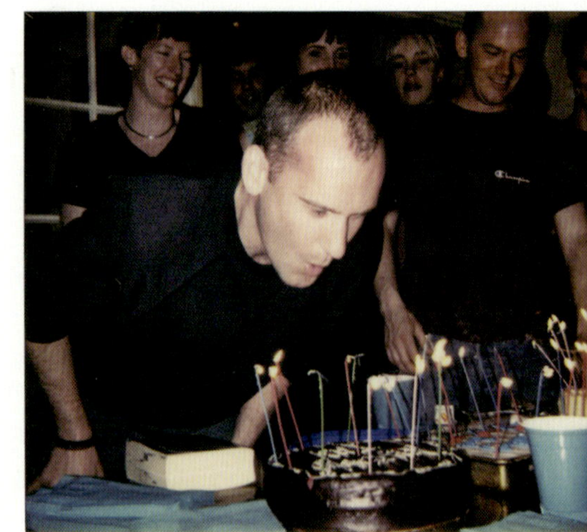

Ian MacKaye birthday party / WDC, 1998
Opposite: Giovanna Cacciola, Uzeda, Black Cat / WDC, 1998
Previous spread, from left: Branch Manager, Fort Reno / WDC, 1997; Fugazi, Fort Reno / WDC, 1997

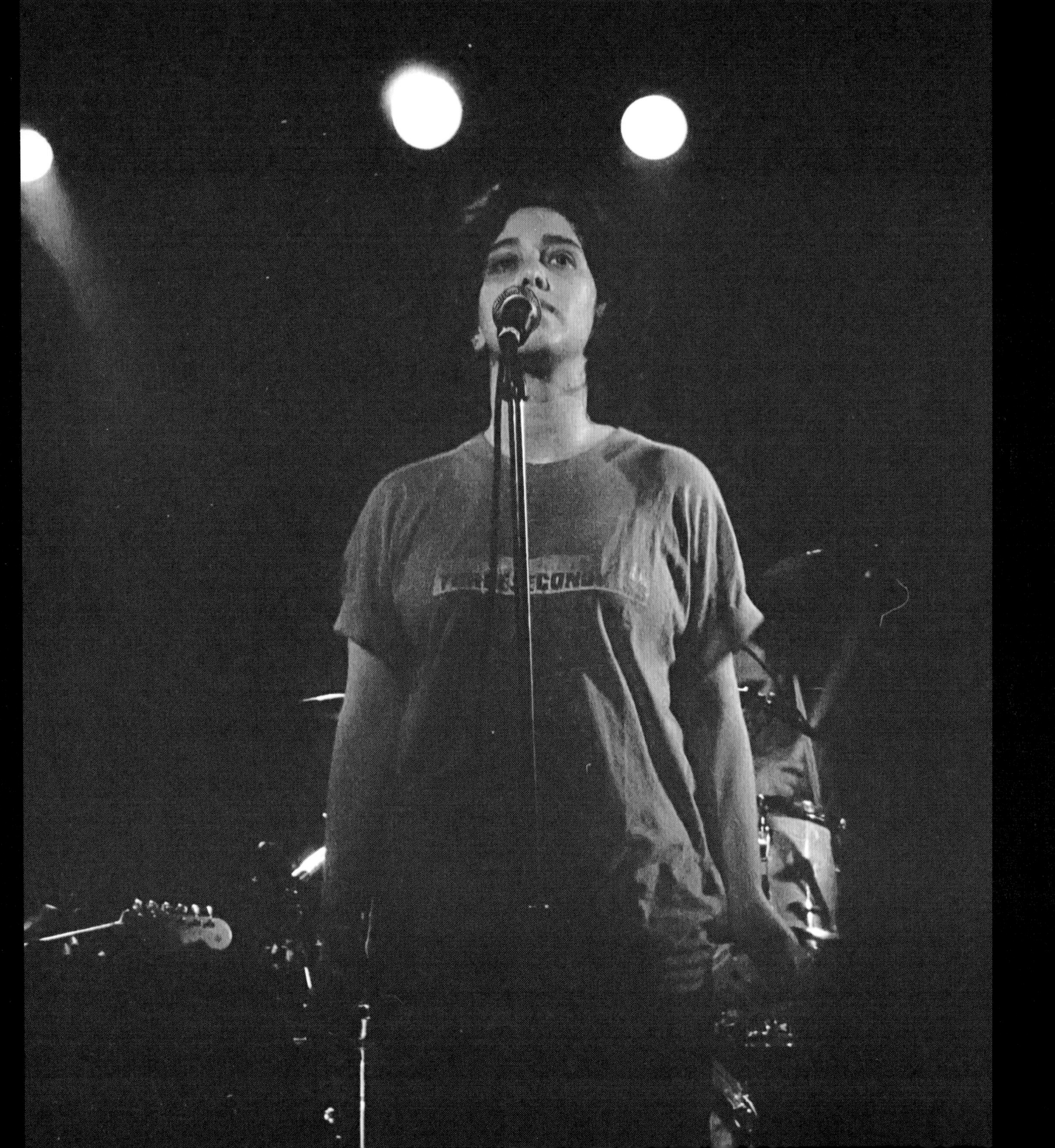

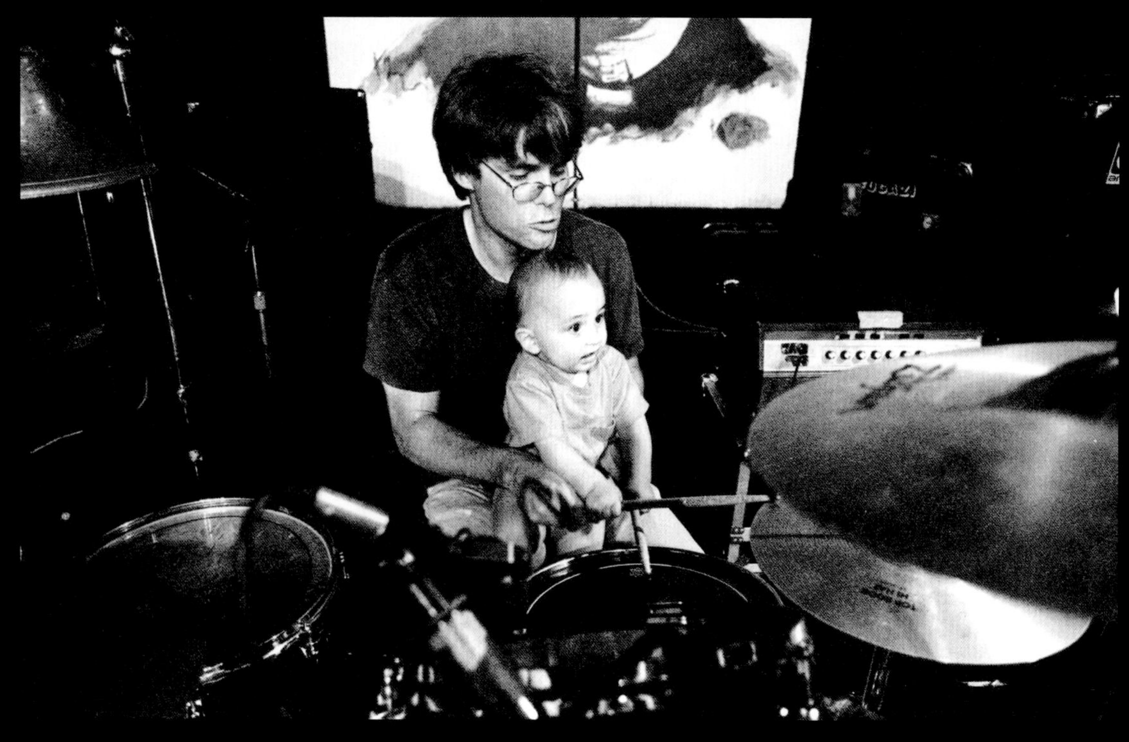

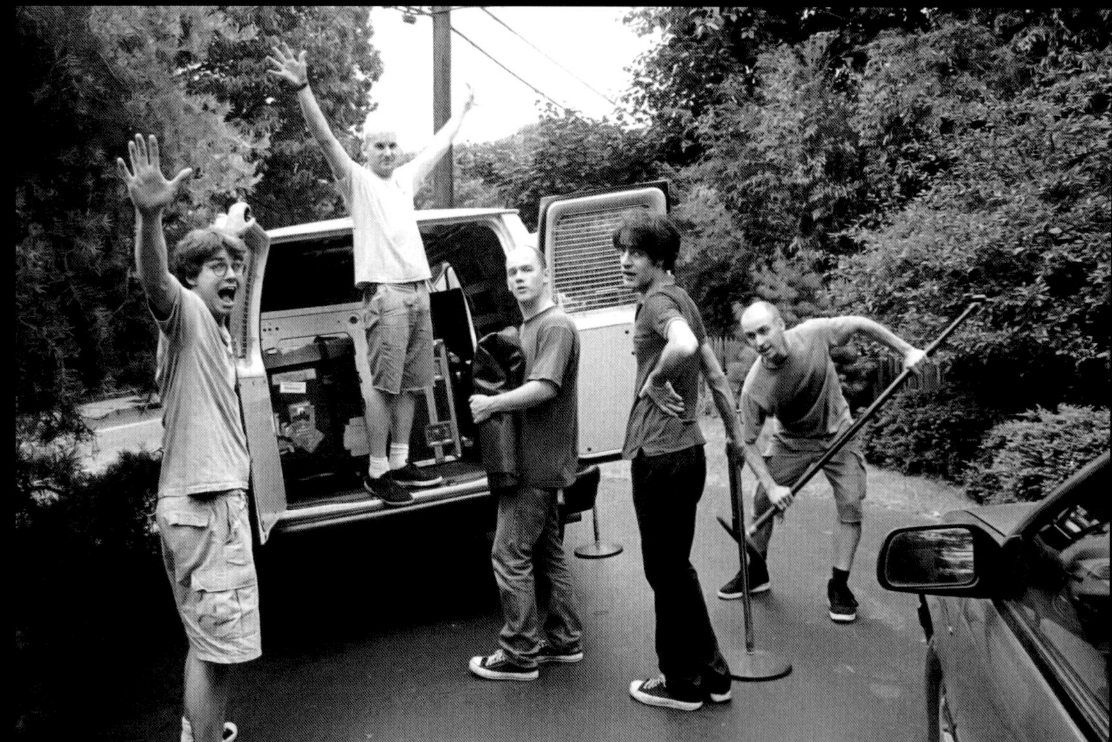

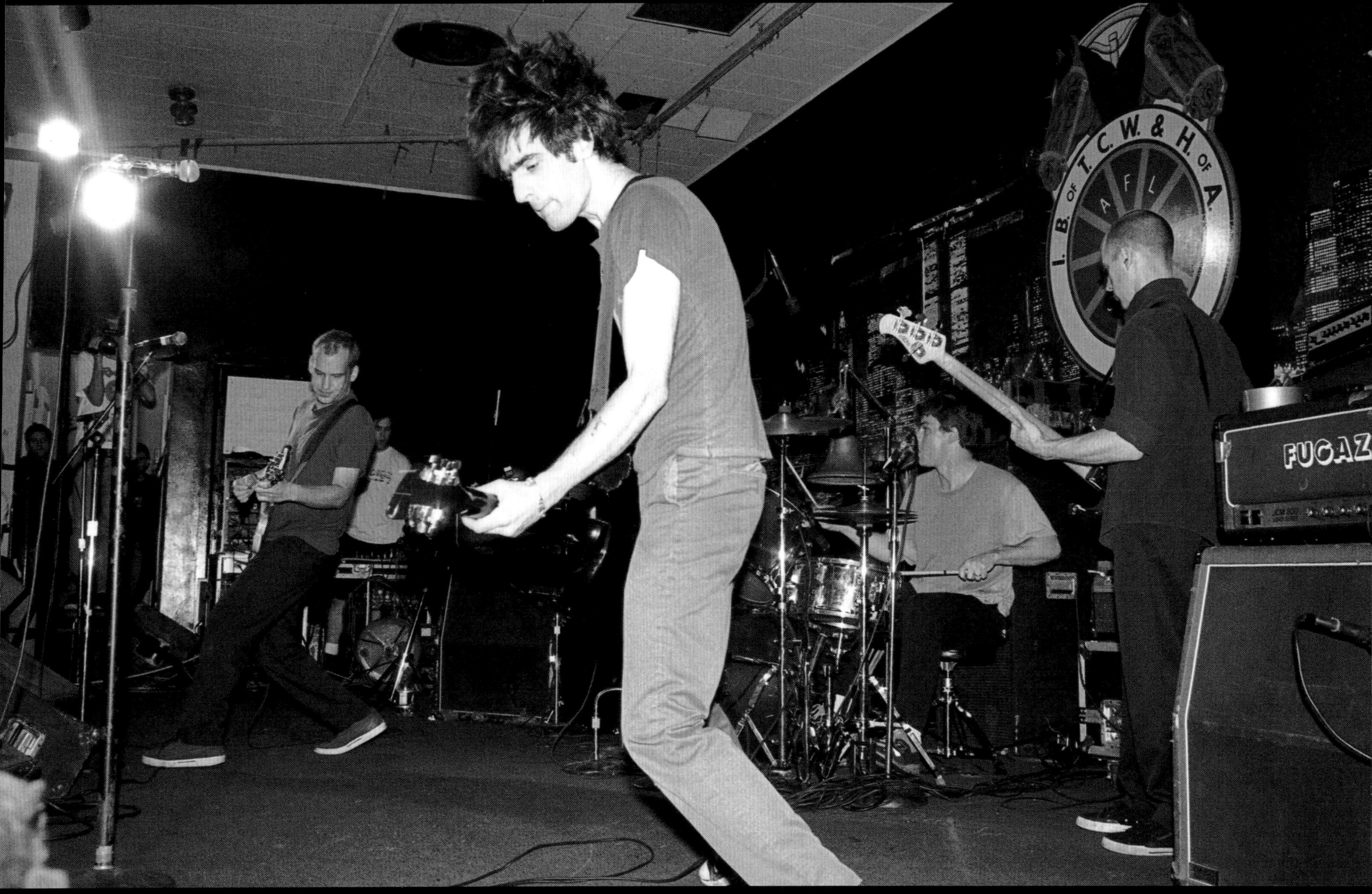

Fugazi, Teamsters Hall / Baltimore, MD, 1998
Opposite (from top): Brendan Canty and Asa Canty, Sanctuary Theater / WDC, 1998;
Fugazi leaving for tour, 1998

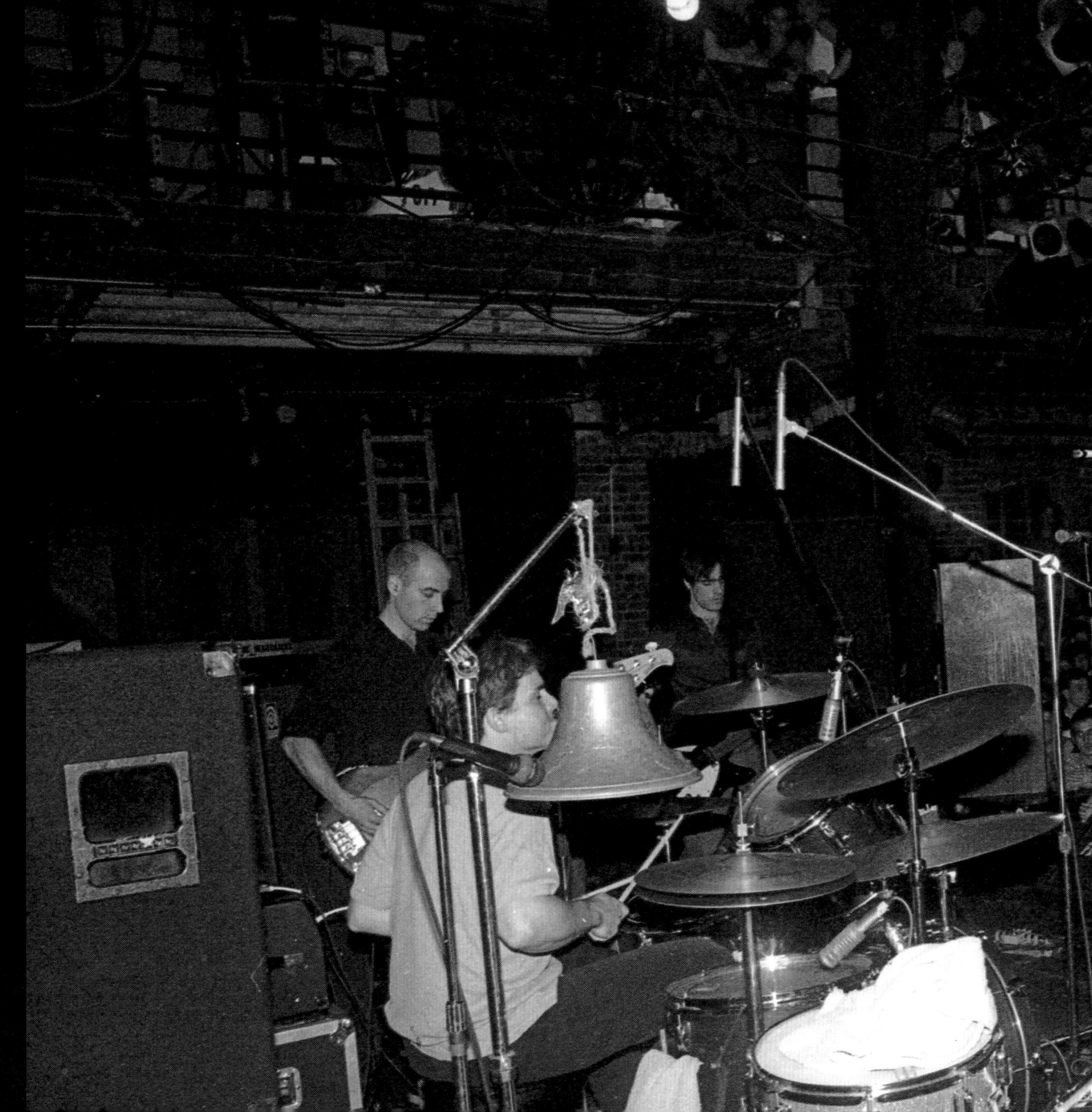

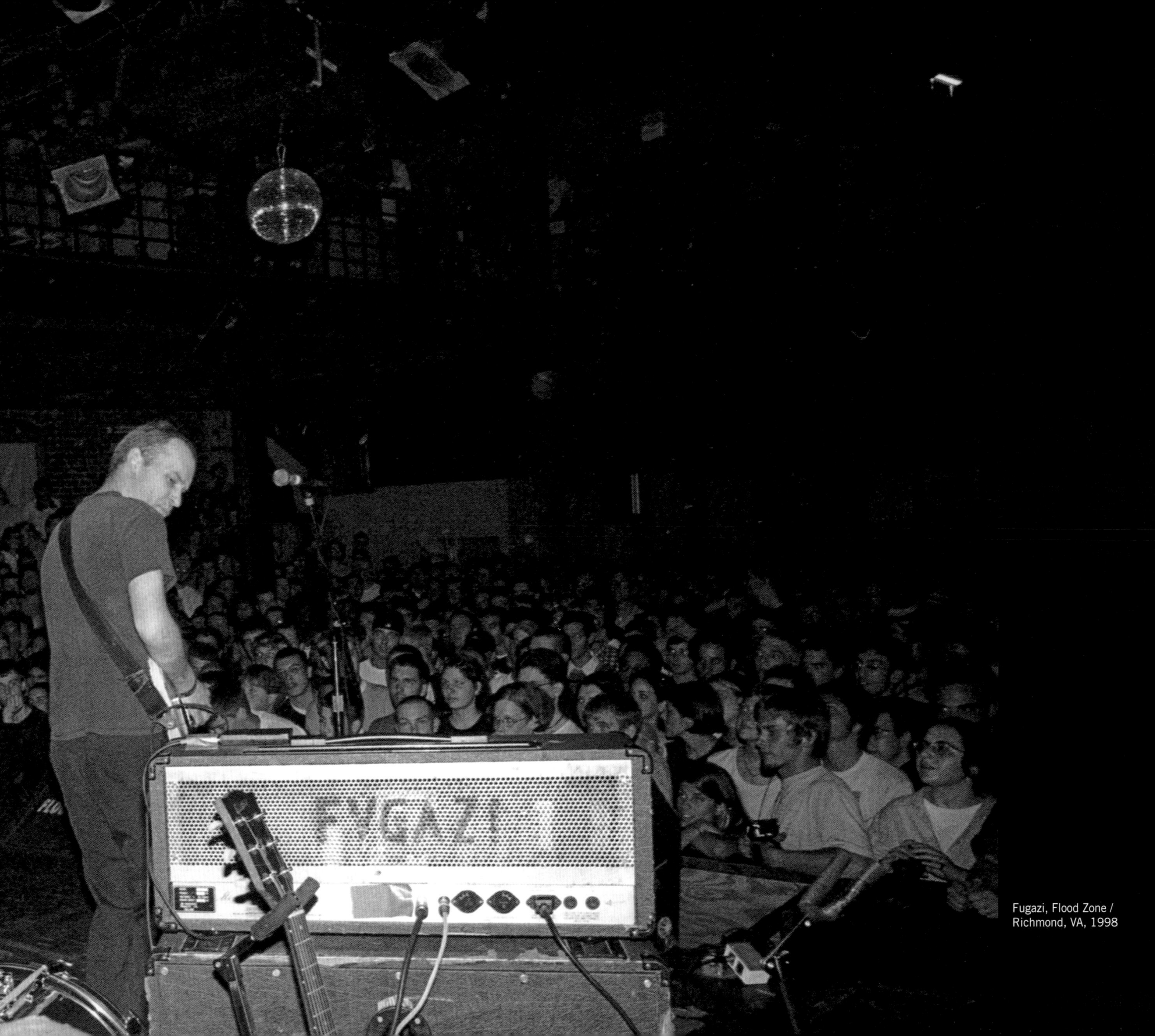

Fugazi, Flood Zone /
Richmond, VA, 1998

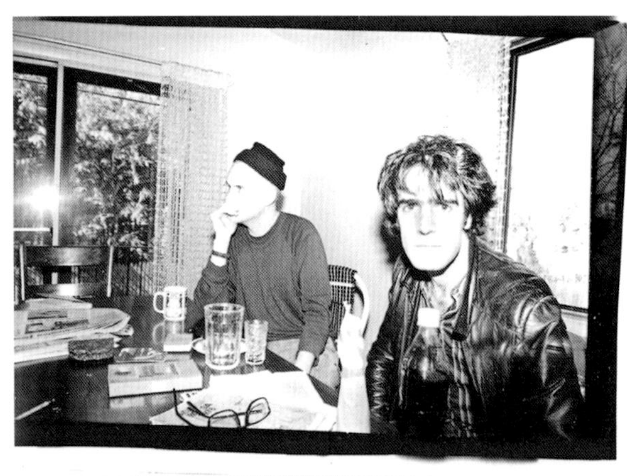
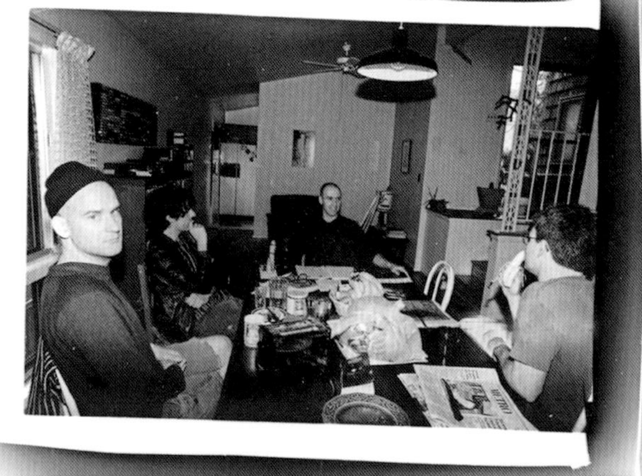
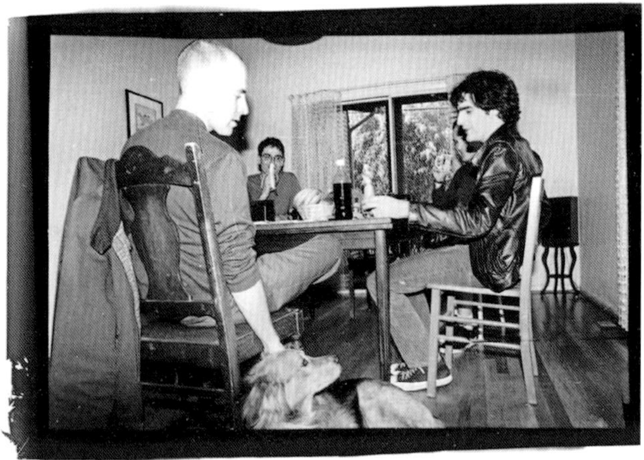
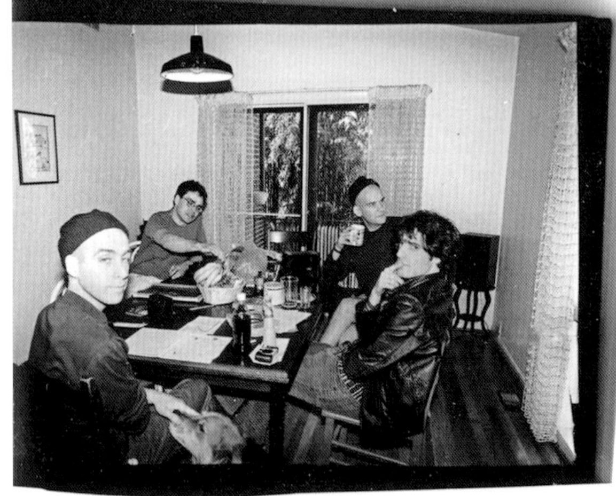
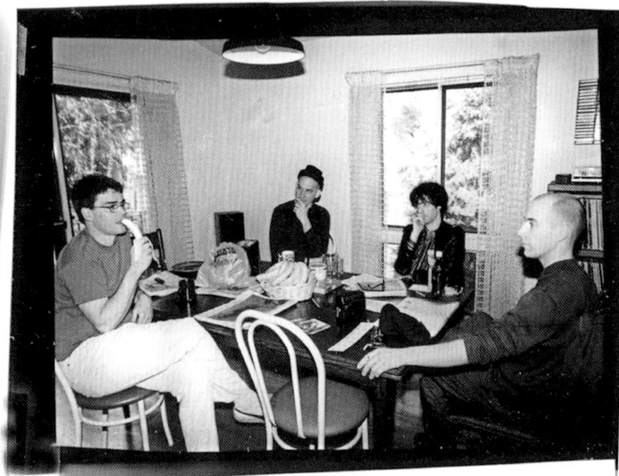
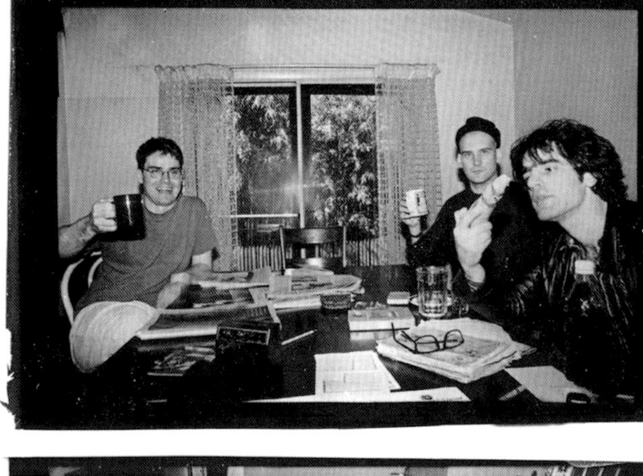
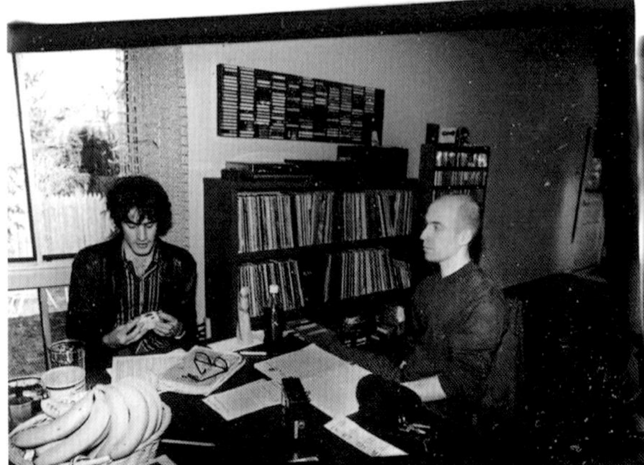
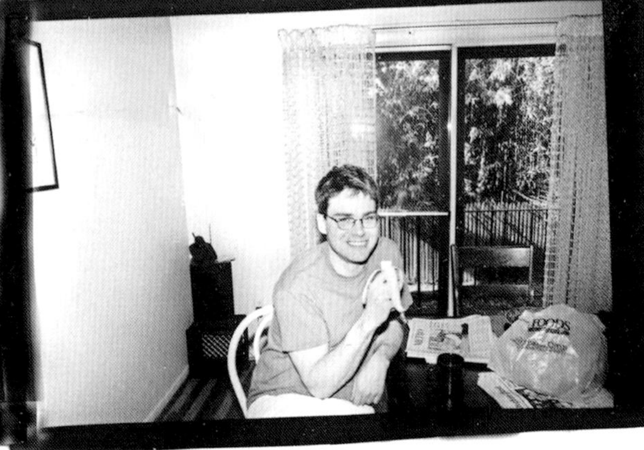
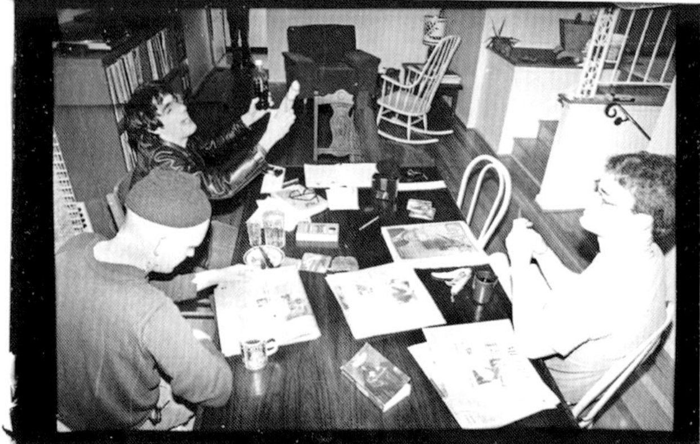

Fugazi, Fillmore Street / Arlington, VA, 1998
Opposite: Ian Svenonius, Black Cat / WDC, 1998

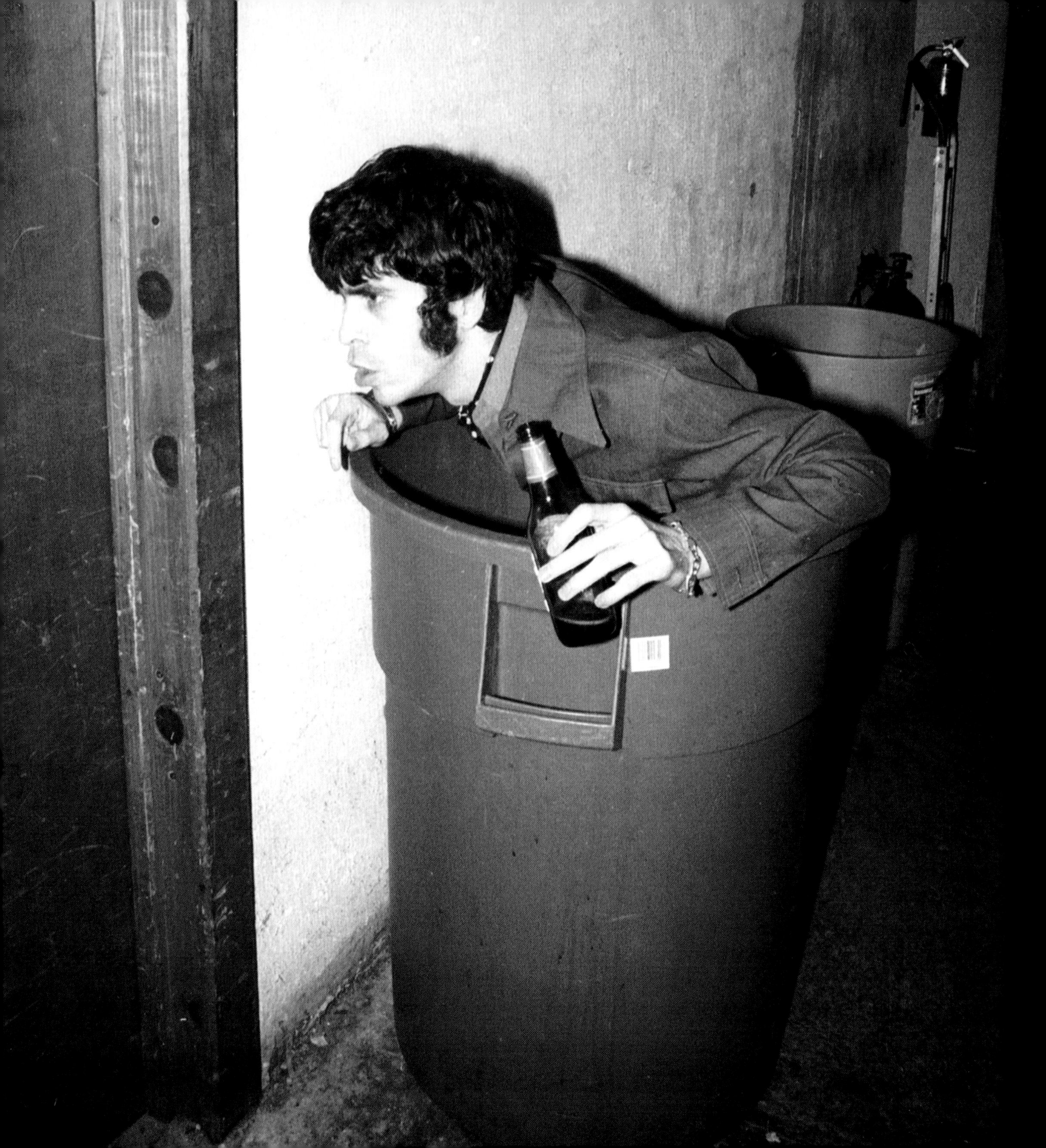

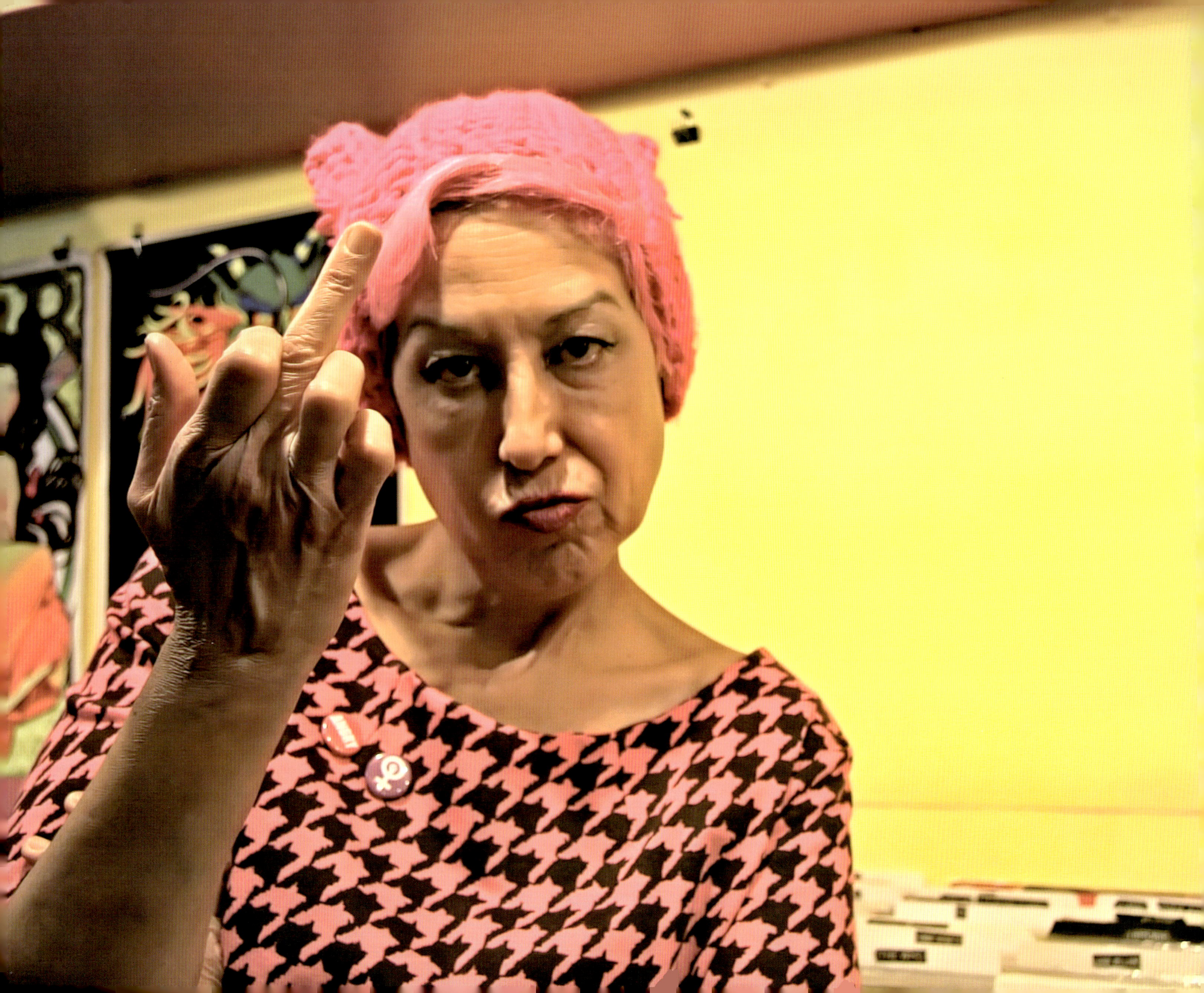

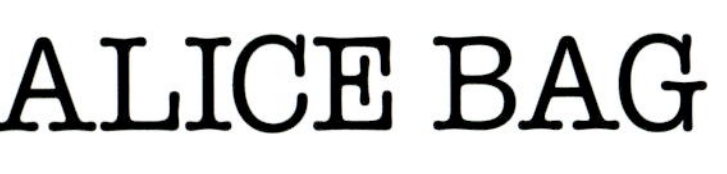

ALICE BAG

How did I get into music? Well, in elementary school I was a chubby, bucktoothed, unpopular kid with a bad attitude. My only shining moment in an otherwise miserable day was the half hour once a week when the music teacher would come into our classroom and make me feel like I was special. Miss Yonkers believed in me. She would often single me out to lead the class in a round, or ask me to play the autoharp while she sang. She definitely fueled my love of music.

Around this same time, I was reading a lot of comic books and watching Saturday-morning cartoons. These gave me the idea that one day I would have an all-girl band like Josie and Pussycats. Of course, I never told anybody about my plans. Instead, I told my parents and teachers and anyone else who would ask that I planned to be a pilot, or a brain surgeon, or some other acceptable profession—but deep down in my heart, I always wanted to be a singer in a band. Of course, it wasn't always a rock band.

I grew up steeped in my family's musical tastes. I loved belting out Mexican rancheras. I pretended to duet with Spanish child star Joselito; I'd sing while doing the penguin to "Want Ads" by the American vocal group the Honey Cone. I was raised on a diet of soul, rancheras, and Mexi-pop.

It wasn't until middle school that I got into rock, and not just any rock—I discovered glam. I discovered David Bowie, to be precise. I remember listening to *Hunky Dory*, feeling like I could be the "girl with the mousy hair" in his song "Life on Mars?" Aside from his music, Bowie brought with him all kinds of new and exciting concepts. He cultivated and celebrated androgyny; indeed, at times he seemed more like a genderless extraterrestrial than a boy or a girl. But genderless is not asexual, and Bowie exuded sexuality that appealed to both boys and girls. It was through Bowie that I would discover the concept of bisexuality and learn to accept it in myself. It was also through him that I would learn that I could present my own gender in whichever way I pleased.

The problem with glam was that there weren't a whole lot of women represented in the genre, and my Josie and the Pussycats fantasy felt more unattainable than ever. Rock magazines rarely wrote about female musicians. If they wrote about women at all, they were portrayed as muses or groupies, and I for one started to believe that being a groupie was the only way a girl could get close to rock and roll. I was so wrong!

In high school, I put on some tall, glittery platforms and tried to play the role using the groupie name Alice Phallus, yet I wasn't cut out for it. Not only was I still a virgin, but I quickly got bored trying to feed the hungry egos of male musicians. I realized that I didn't want to cater to the rock star, I wanted to *be* the rock star.

Fortunately for me, punk came along right around that time. In 1976, I was a senior in high school

Alice Bag, SMASH! / WDC, 2017

and I was going crazy trying to figure out what I would do after graduation. My love of music had led me to forge friendships with two girls from other schools who I had met while stalking rock stars. My two girlfriends had similar dreams of being in an all-girl band. While others were preparing for SATs, we decided to take guitar lessons. After a few weeks of lessons, we decided that one of my friends would play bass, the other would play guitar, and I would be the singer. We wanted to play "Bohemian Rhapsody" but could barely get through "Louie Louie." Nevertheless, we bolstered each other's egos and cheered every time one of us made any progress. We were groupies for ourselves.

Then one day we heard the Ramones, and a little bit later we heard the Runaways. Glam was morphing into punk. The simpler structures of the songs these two groups were performing helped move the finish line closer. In the past we had felt like it would take years of lessons and practice before we'd be able to play. Now, we started shopping for amps!

To be a girl in the mid-1970s out shopping for a guitar amp was an exercise in sexism that started the minute you walked through the door of the music store. Some dude would come up to you and ask, "Are you shopping for your boyfriend?" My friend Patricia would never stand for this and quickly asserted herself as a competent bassist. I, on the other hand, have to confess that I sometimes worked these situations to get free labor.

"Can you show me again how to bend my knees while you lift my amp?" Then I tried to smile sweetly, which is really hard for me because I'm not sweet, which is probably the main reason I gave up this technique. That smile must have looked fake as hell. Plus, I have the kind of face that gets blamed for things . . . but I digress.

My two friends and I called our band Femme Fatale. We actually had the name before we even knew how to play. One night in 1976, we were out in Hollywood seeing a local band when we ran into the Mayor of Sunset Strip, Rodney Bingenheimer. The word around town was that he liked young girls. I was seventeen, so my friends sent me out on a mission to tell him about our band. My mission was successful and I said goodbye to Rodney with his reassurance that he would help us in any way he could. A few days later, I got a call from Rodney's friend Kim Fowley. At the time, there were rumors flying around describing him as a Svengali—at best unhinged, and at worst abusive—so I answered his call with a mixture of excitement and suspicion. He said he was looking for some female musicians to put together a new band which was going to be called Venus and the Razorblades. He asked me if my bandmates and I would like to audition for this group. I accepted the invitation for the whole band.

The audition consisted of Fowley calling up different women in different configurations to play together. Those he liked stayed on longer and went on to play with others. Those who didn't cut it were sent outside. I was immediately cut and sent outside, where something thrilling and unexpected was happening. All of Fowley's rejected female musicians began talking to each other and making connections. Instead of feeling depressed, we all left the audition feeling jubilant because among the rejects was our future drummer. We now had bass, drums, guitar, and vocals—we were ready to go! We didn't need Kim Fowley!

It was still a few months before Patricia and I would form our first punk band. That happened in 1977, the year punk exploded.

Alice is the author of *Violence Girl* (Feral House, 2011) and *Pipe Bomb for the Soul* (Alice Bag Publishing, 2015).

THE BAGS • CASTRATION SQUAD • CAMBRIDGE APOSTLES • FUN HOUSE • THE SWING SET • THE AFRO SISTER • CHOLITA • LAS TRES • GODDESS 13 • STAY AT HOME BOMB • SHE RIFFS • ALICE BAG AND THE SISSY BEARS • SCORPIO SCORPIO

Alice Bag, Black Cat / WDC, 2017

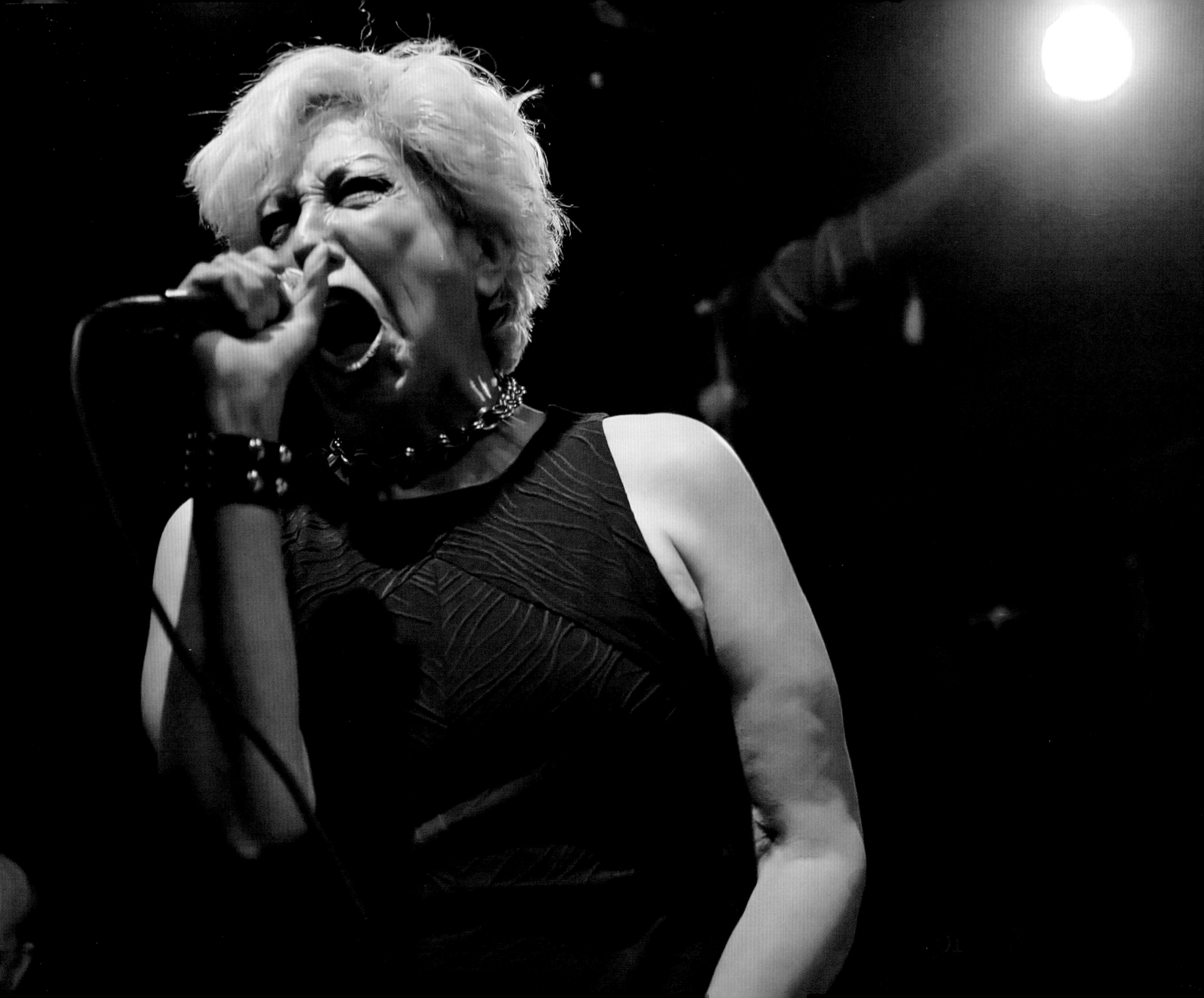

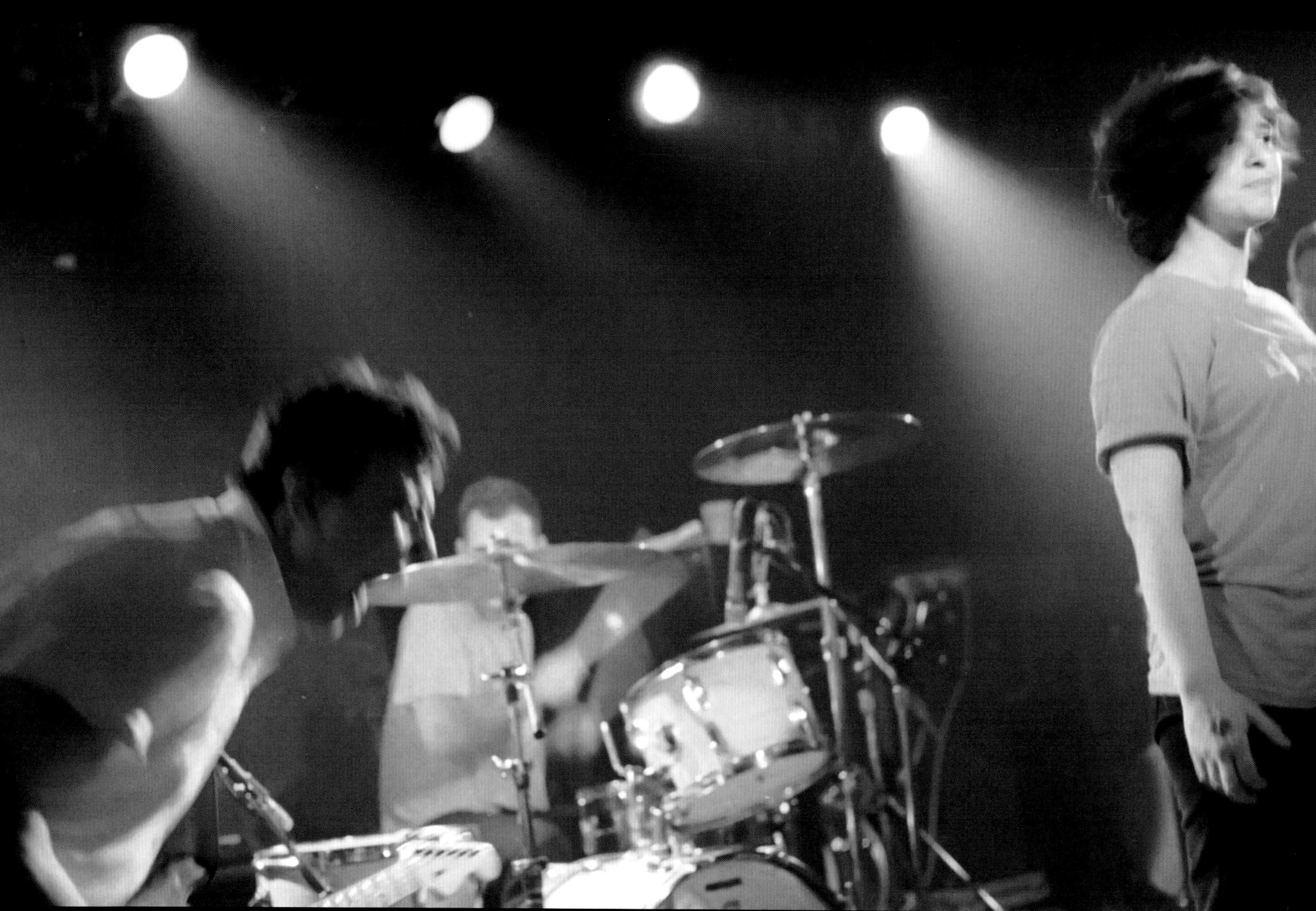

Uzeda, Black Cat / WDC, 1998

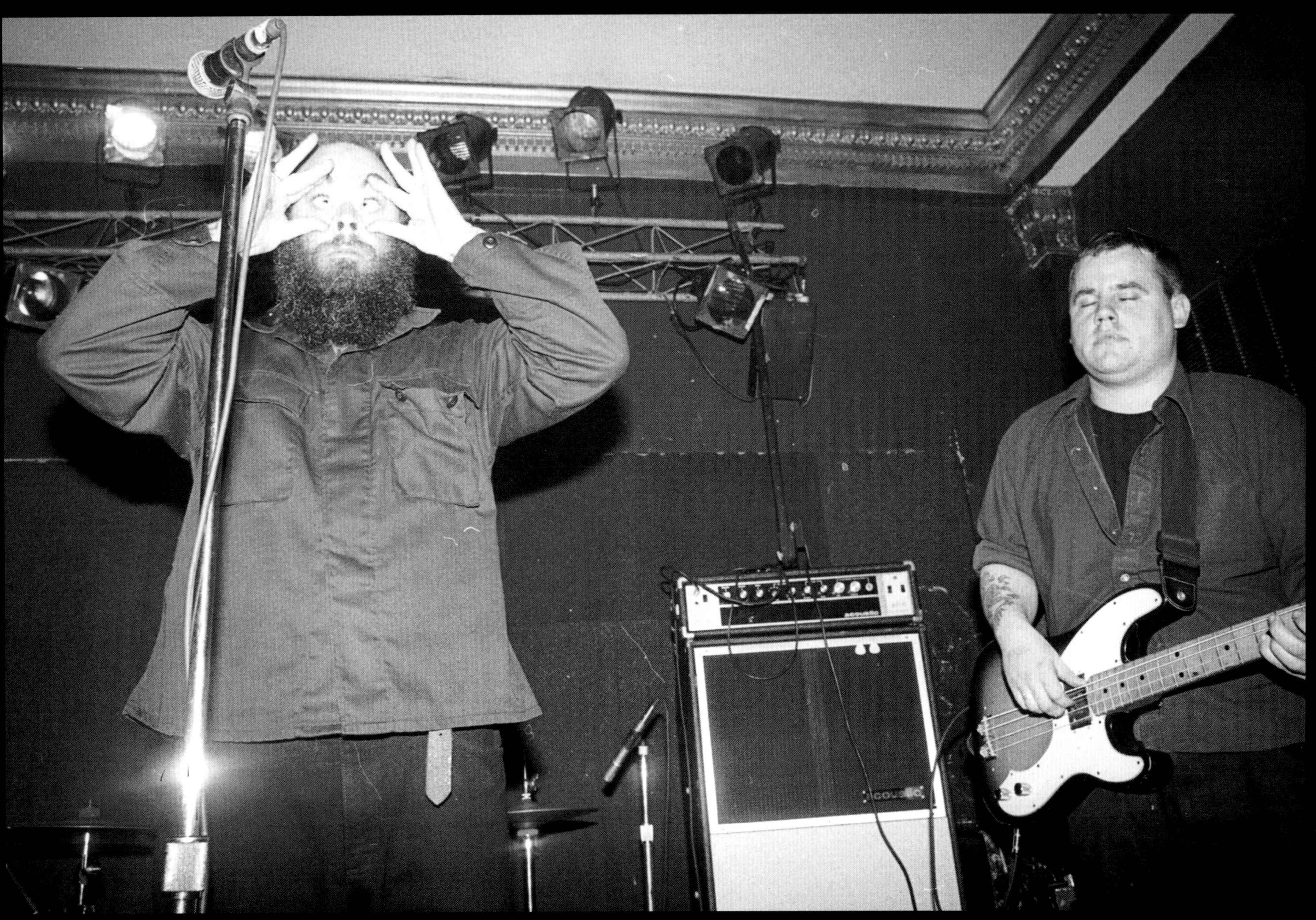

Lungfish / Baltimore, MD, 1998

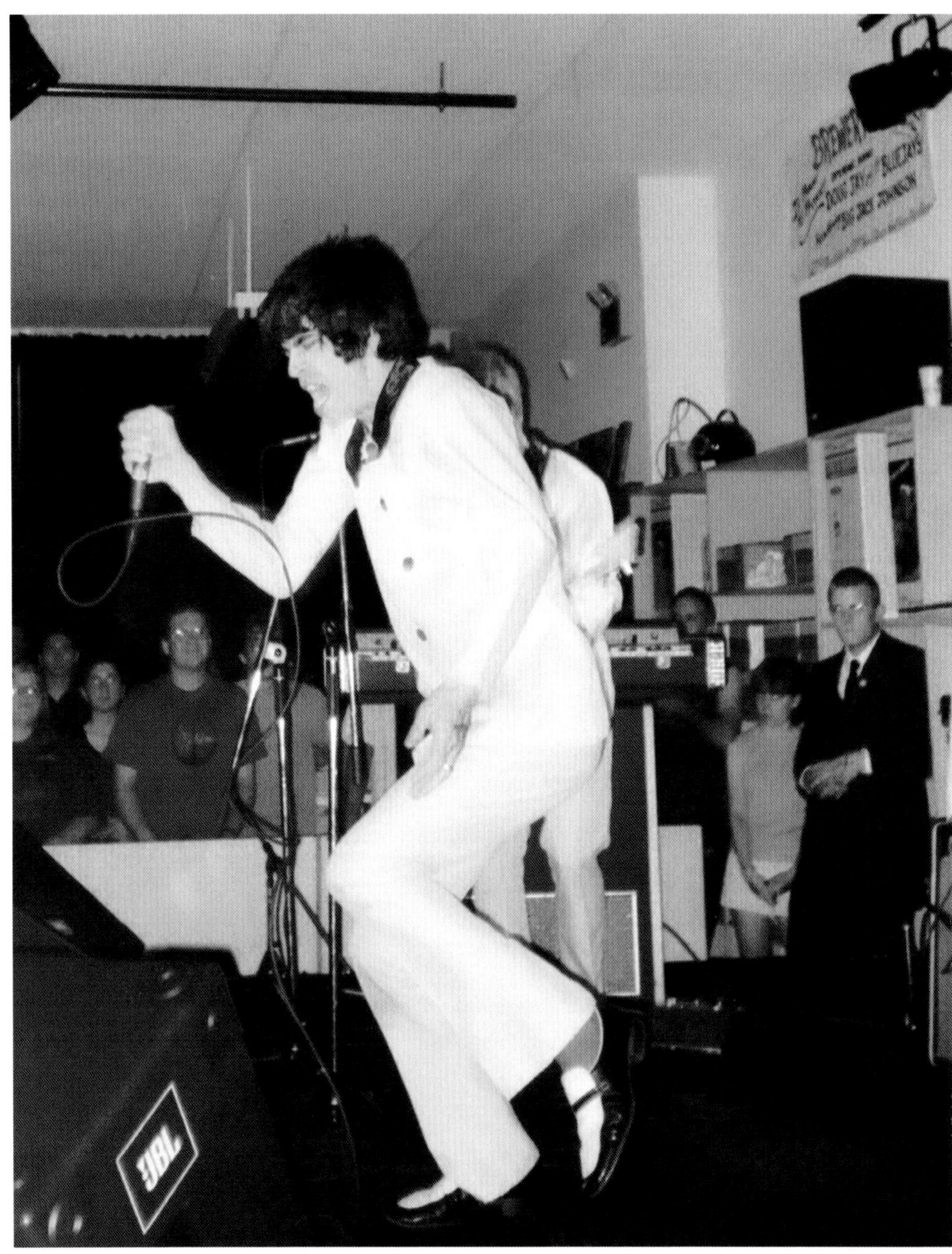

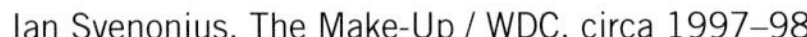
Ian Svenonius, The Make-Up / WDC, circa 1997–98

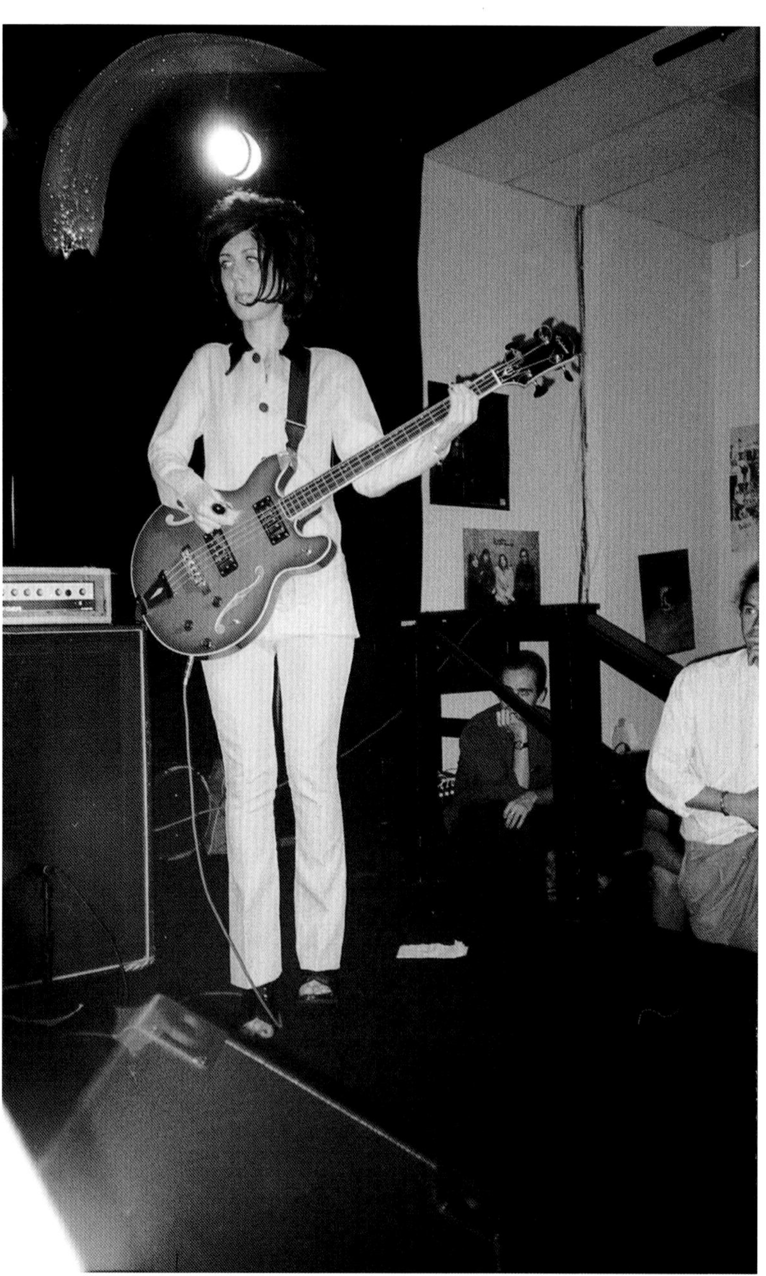

Michelle Mae, The Make-Up / WDC, circa 1997–98

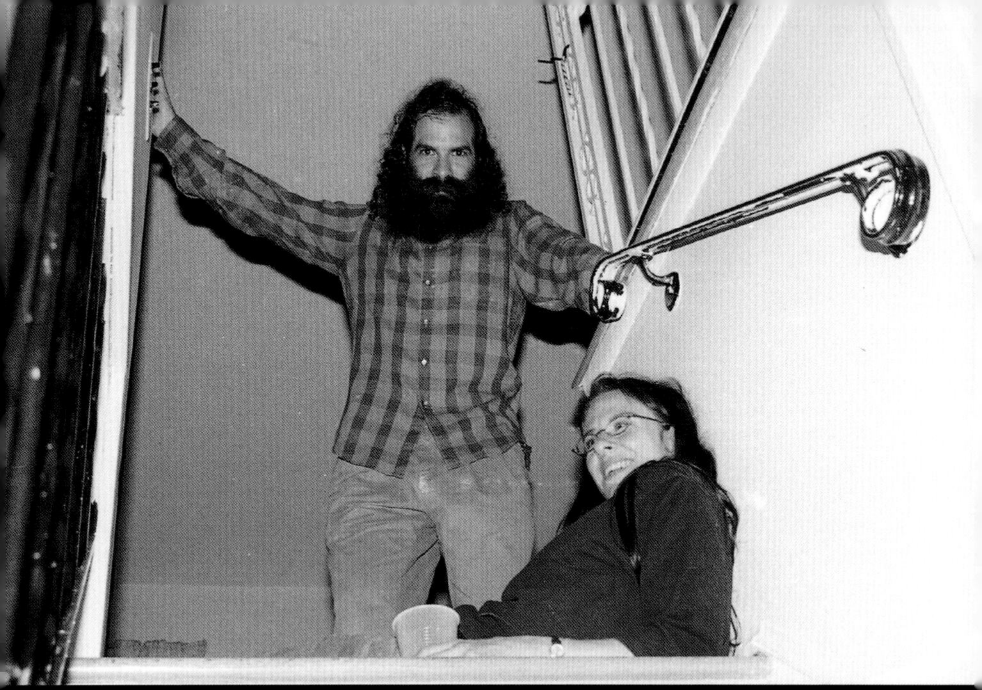

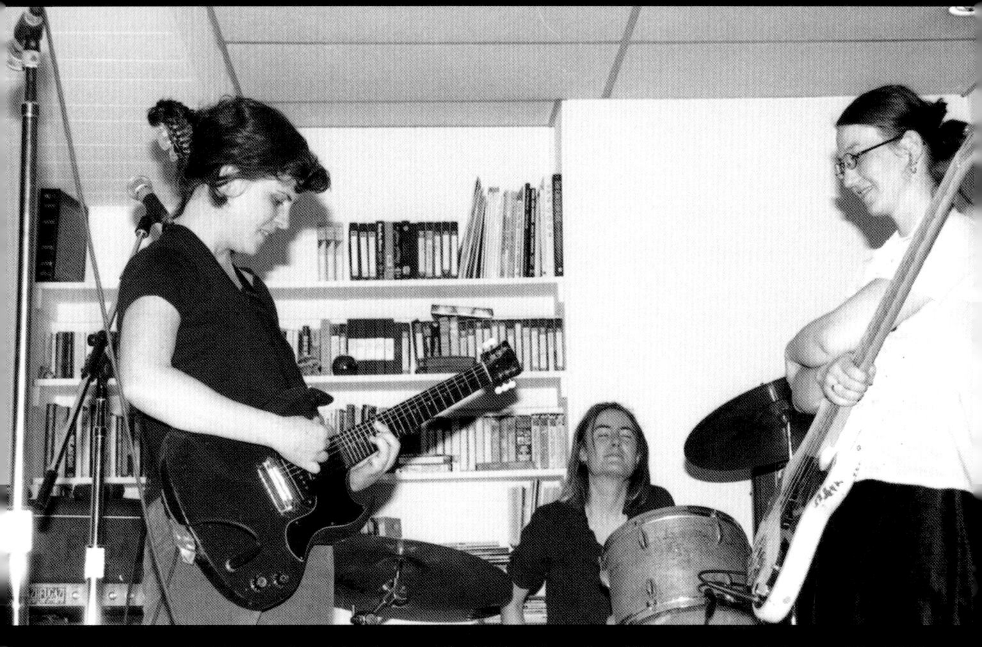

From top: wedding party, Fillmore Street / Arlington, VA, 1998; Stigmatics, Fillmore Street / Arlington, VA, 1998

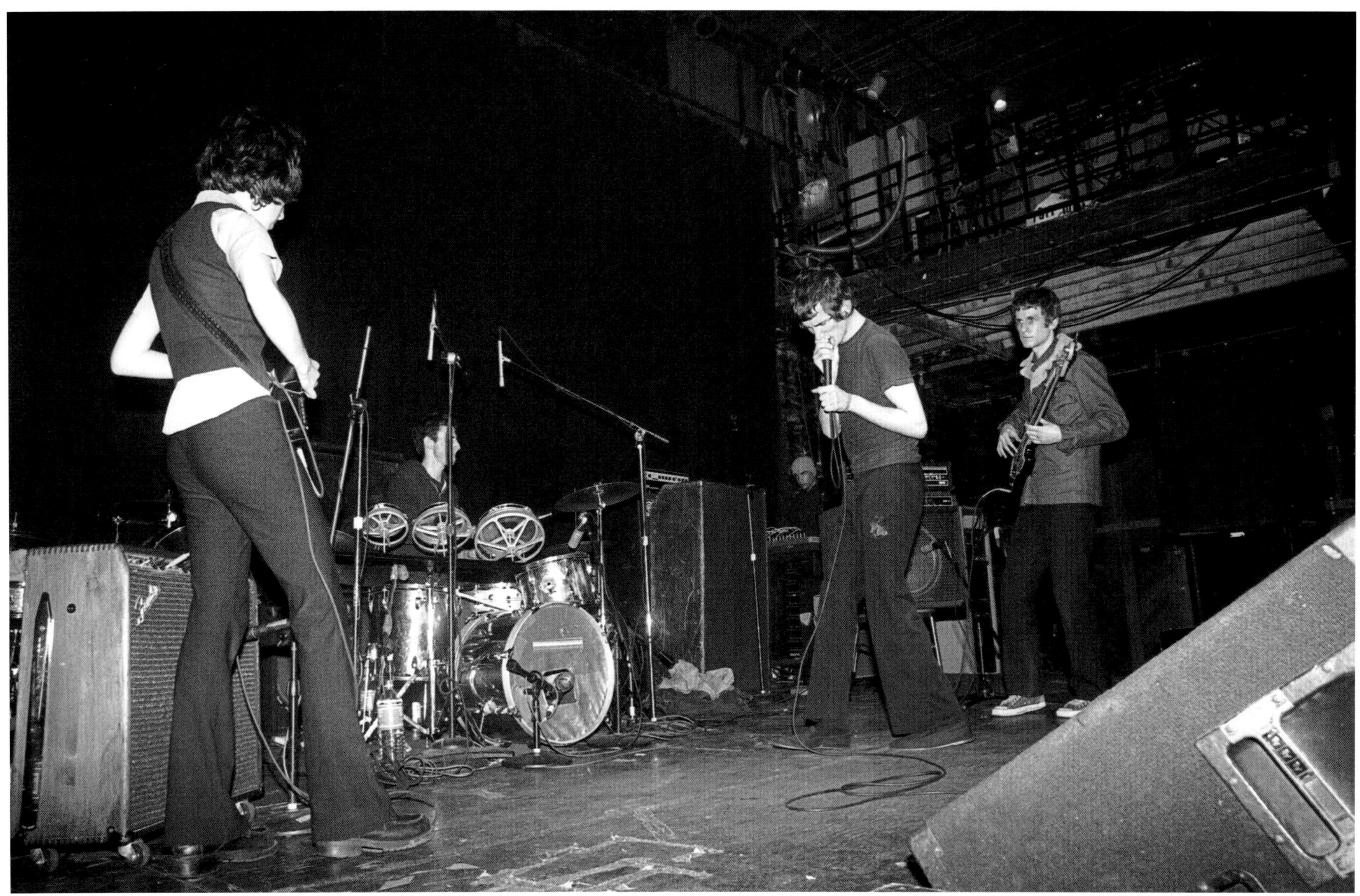

The Crainium, Flood Zone / Richmond, VA, 1998

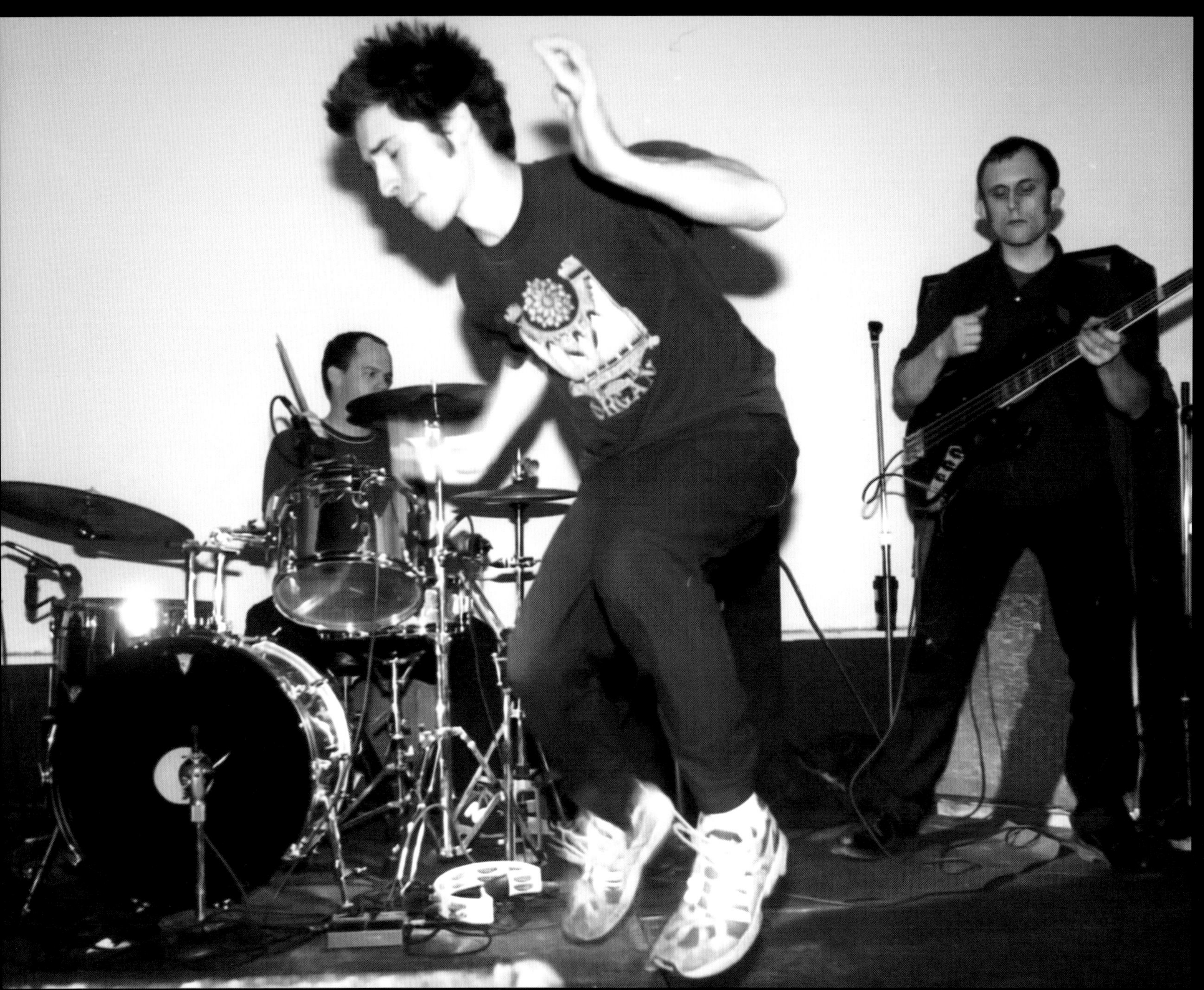

All Scars, Wilson Center / WDC, 1999

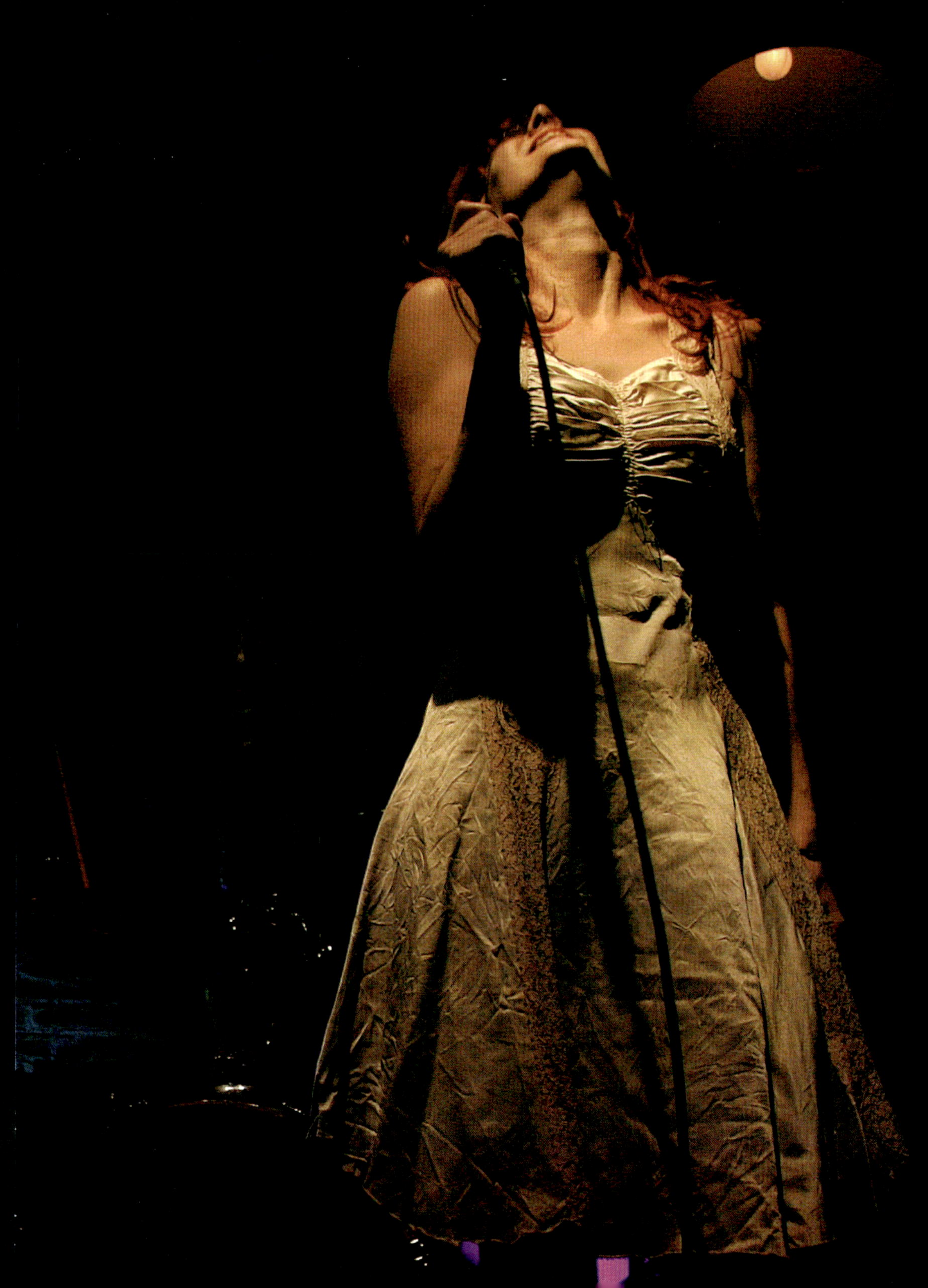

ALLISON WOLFE

My family moved to Olympia, Washington, in 1981 so my mom could start the first women's health clinic in town. My twin sister Cindy and I were in fifth grade and had to make all new friends. My teacher invited us to be in an after-school student singing group he was starting called the MusiKids. Complete with jazz hands and matching T-shirts, we performed choreographed covers of Neil Diamond and Jimmy Buffet songs at service clubs and community centers.

As we hit middle school and puberty, we grew out of the MusiKids scene and joined the school band. I played clarinet, then switched to bass clarinet when my first-chair status got challenged. Regardless, the clarinet quartet I played in with my challengers won the state competition three years in a row. I ended up quitting the school band in high school because my boyfriend who was also in band physically threatened me when I broke up with him. Also, band class didn't seem very new wave or punk, which was the direction I went as a rebellion against the ex-boyfriend incident.

Most musicians are fans first and foremost. The first concert I went to was Big Country on my thirteenth birthday, and my second was Duran Duran. I soon moved on, getting into Bow Wow Wow, Missing Persons, Joan Jett, the B-52s, and the Go-Go's. Though those bands provided awesome female role models in music, they didn't necessarily make me feel like I could start a band too. It usually takes something more local and accessible.

In high school and beyond, I was going to punk shows that were well attended by women, but the stage was mostly a boys' club with a pit too violent for the likes of me. The grunge scene loomed large early on in the Pacific Northwest, and it often seemed like just a long-haired, flannel dress-up of the same old sexist, shock-value punk.

By the summer of 1989, the local K Records do-it-yourself, minimalist approach to creating music made an impression on me, as did seeing performances by strong women in the local scene like Kathleen Hanna, Tobi Vail, Donna Dresch, and Calamity Jane.

That fall, I went away to school at the University of Oregon, where I met my partner in crime, Molly Neuman. We had no idea what we were doing, but knew we had something to say and wanted to create a vehicle for saying it. With encouragement from the newly formed Bikini Kill and from K Records–related people, we started a fanzine, a band, and eventually a punk feminist network. The goal of Girl Germs, Bratmobile, and riot grrrl was to make our punk scene more feminist and to make academic feminism more punk.

A lifer, I went on to sing and dance in Dig Yr. Grave, Cold Cold Hearts, Deep Lust, Bratmobile reboot, Partyline, Cool Moms, and Sex Stains. It's important to maintain a creative outlet and a platform for cultural activism. I'll stay in the game as long as I have something to say and as long as women remain stifled and underrepresented in music. We are responsible for creating and actively participating in the culture and community we want to see.

BRATMOBILE • DIG YR. GRAVE • COLD COLD HEARTS • DEEP LUST • BRATMOBILE REBOOT • PARTYLINE • COOL MOMS • SEX STAINS • EX STAINS

Allison Wolfe, Comet Ping Pong / WDC, 2016

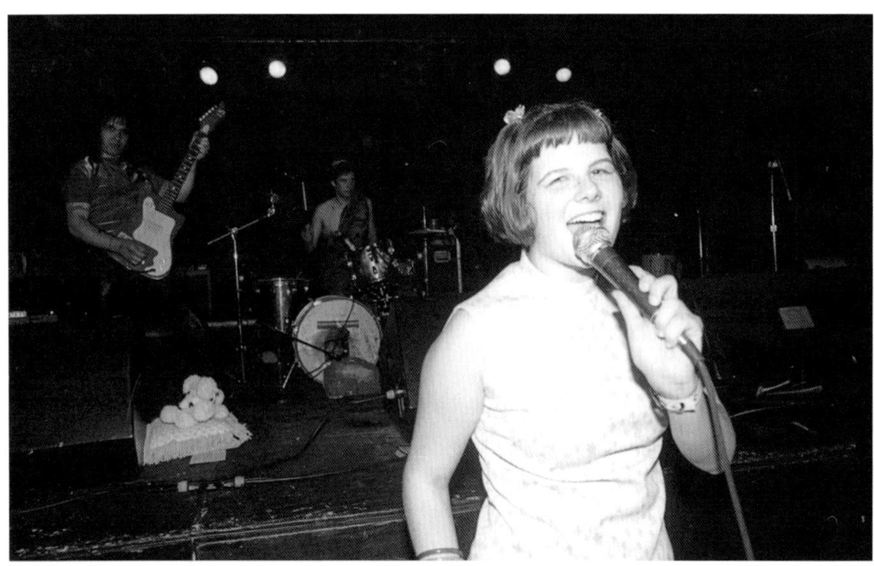

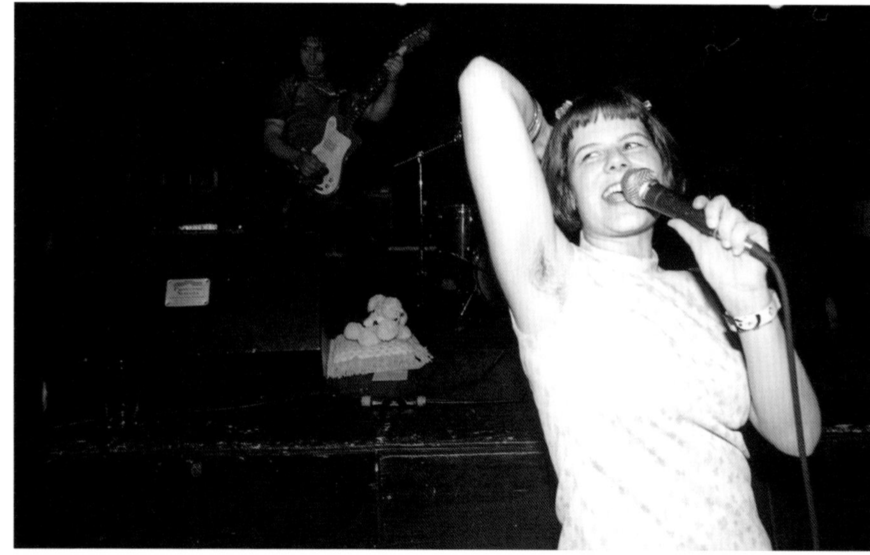

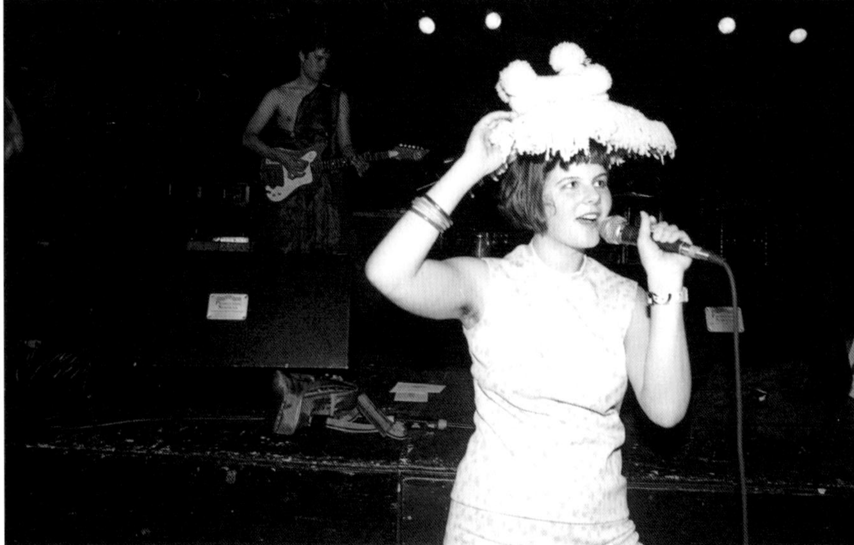

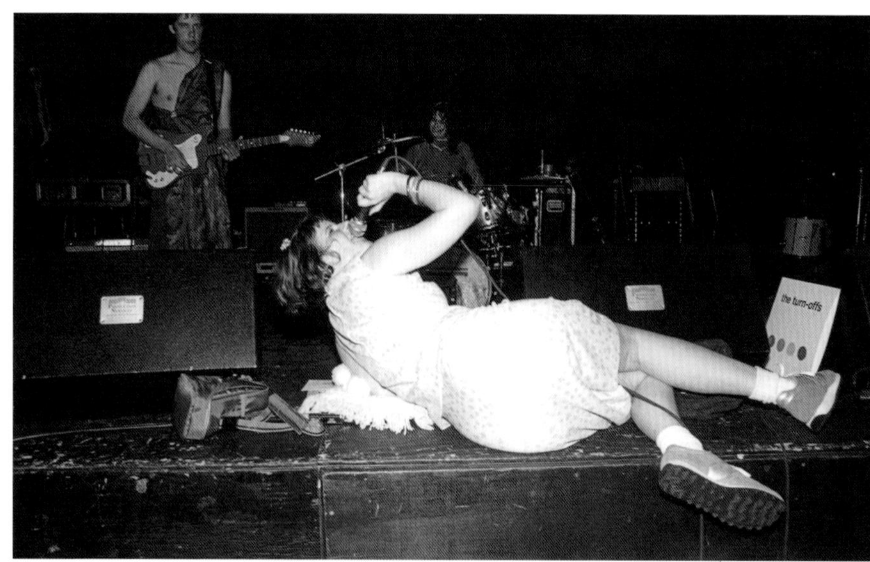

Deep Lust, Black Cat / WDC, 1999
Opposite: Spirit Caravan, CBGB / NYC, 1999

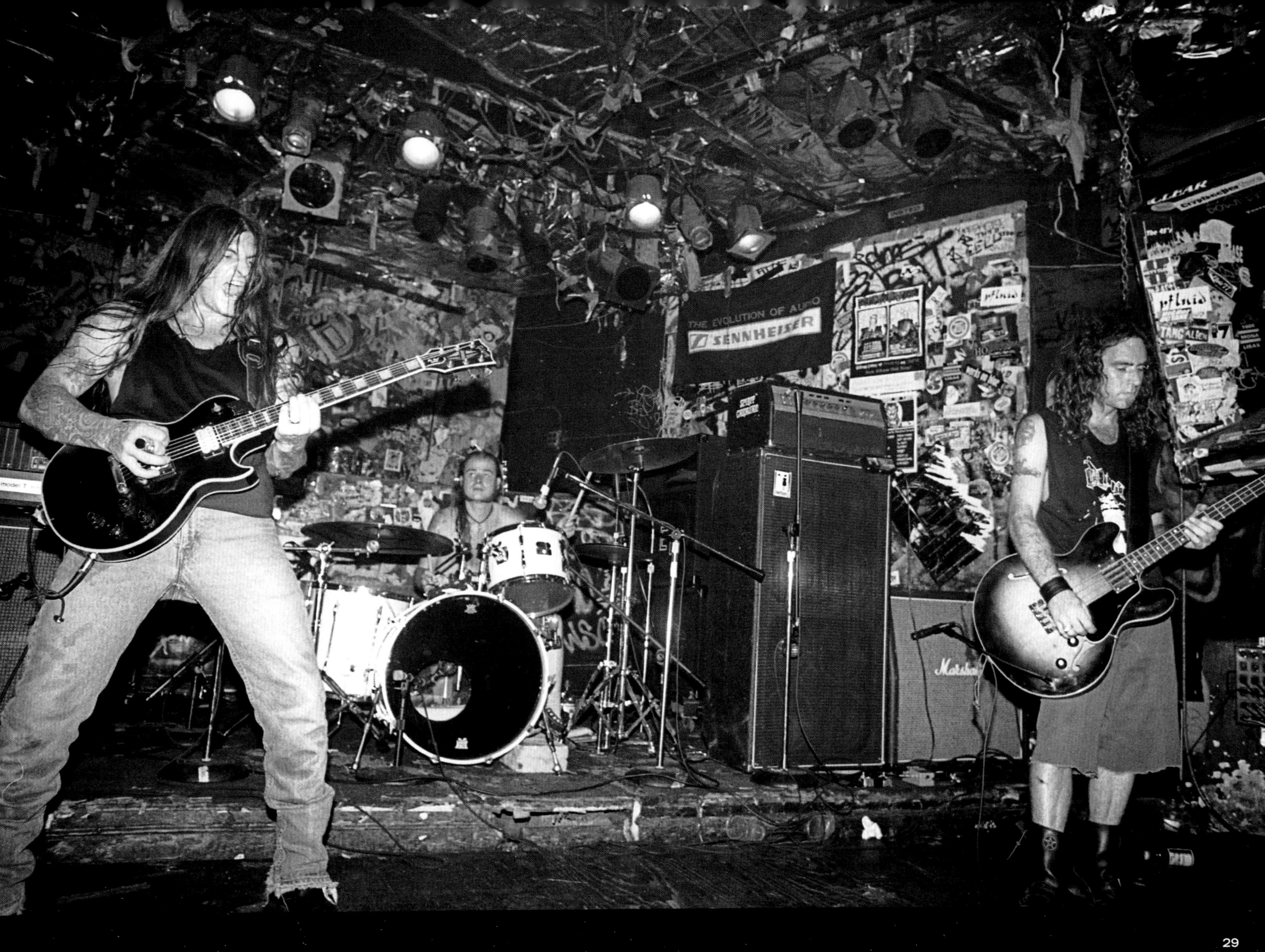
SENNHEISER

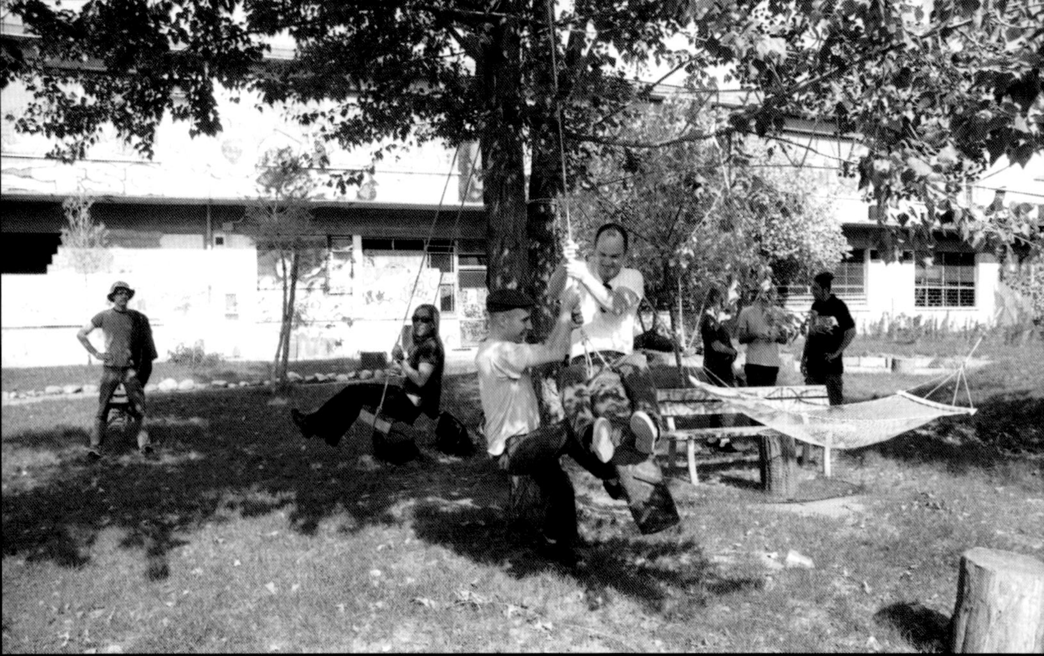

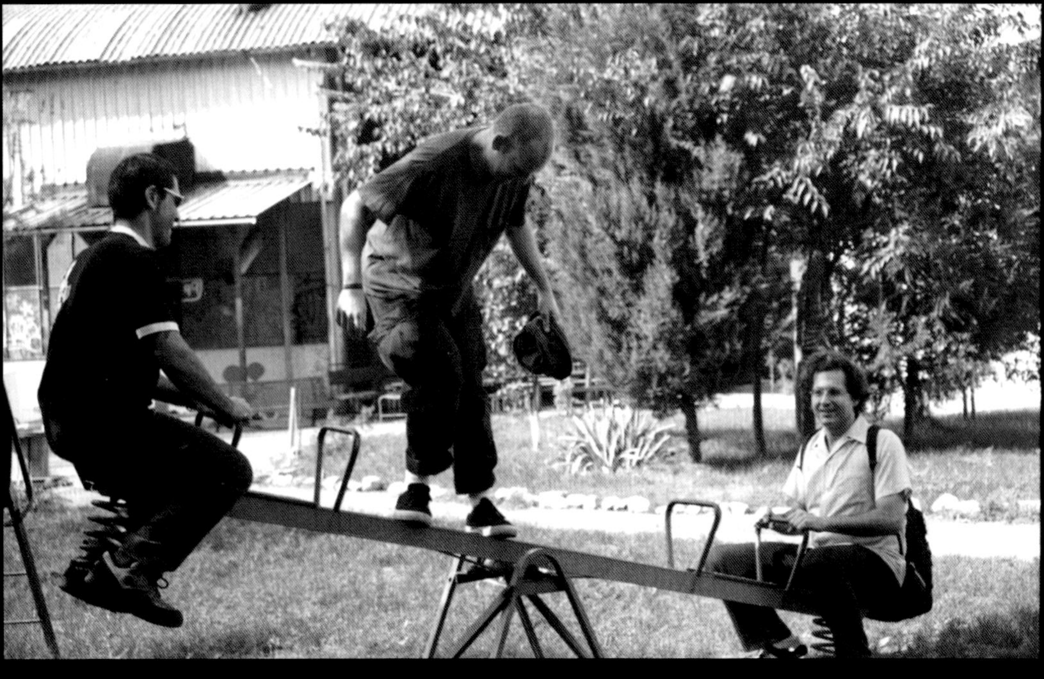

Fugazi and crew, playground / Florence, Italy, 1999

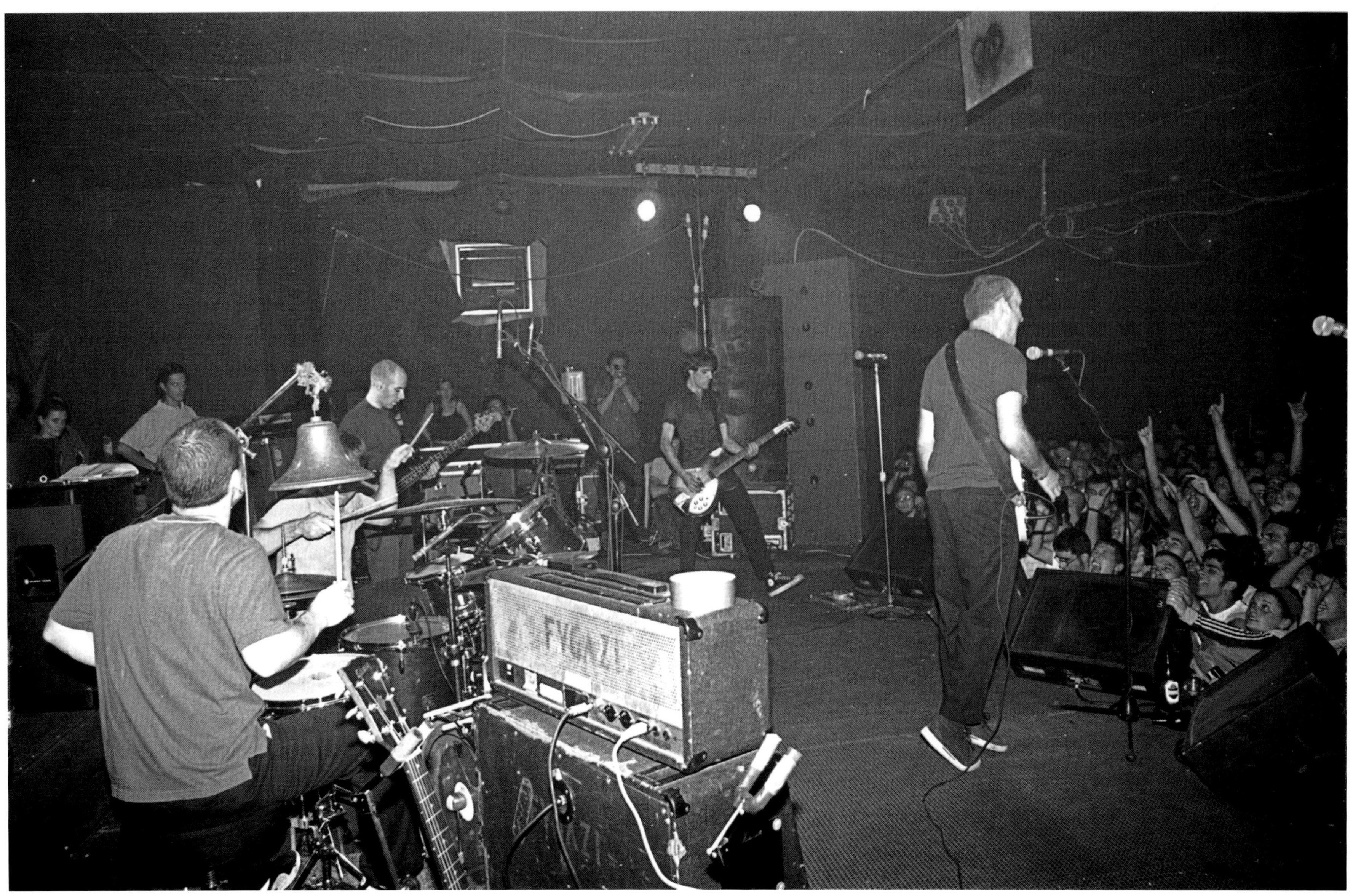

Fugazi, CPA / Florence, Italy, 1999

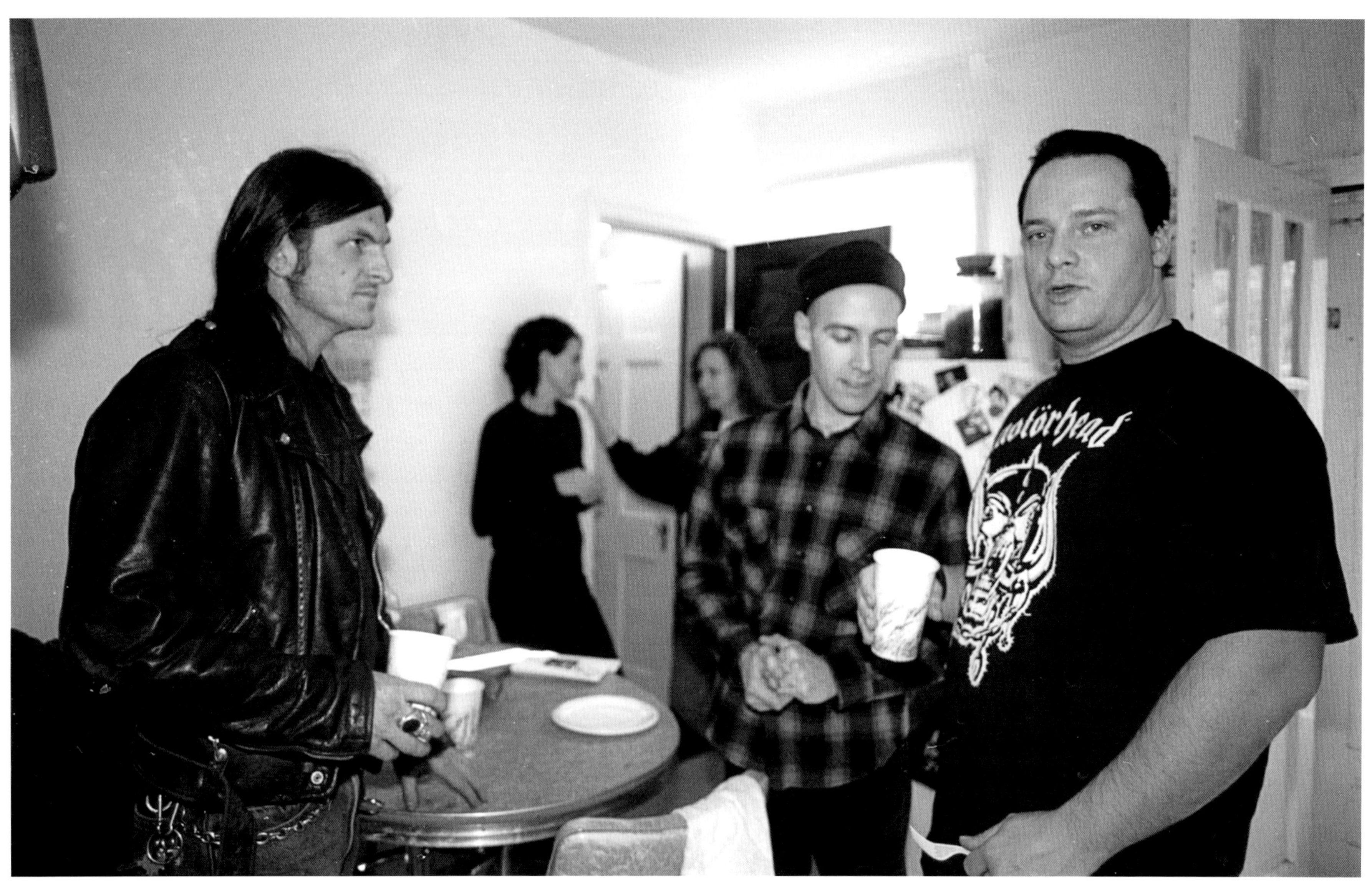

Birthday party: Scott, Lely, Katie, Joe, and Dave / WDC, 1999

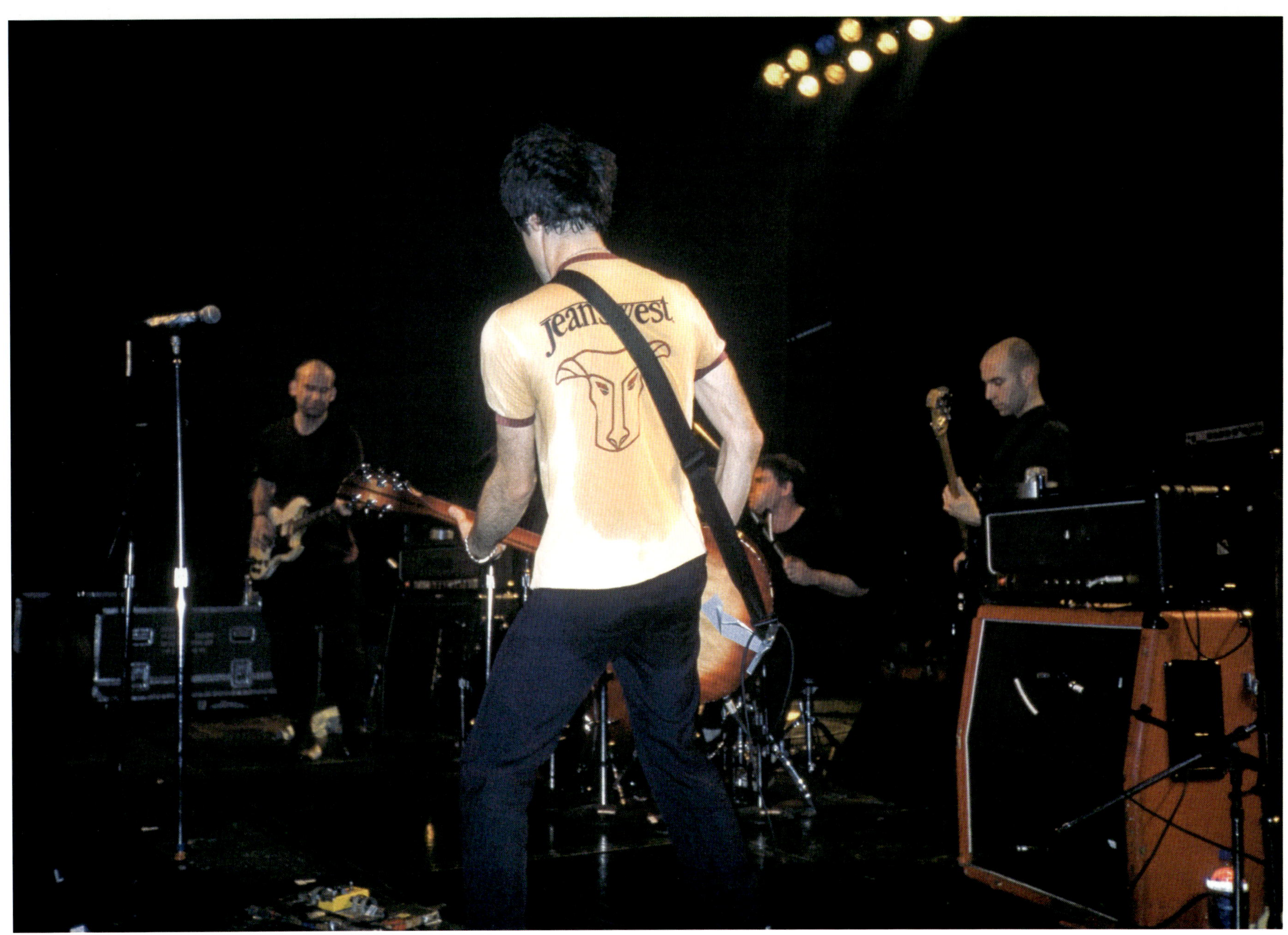

Fugazi, Electric Factory / Philadelphia, PA, 1999

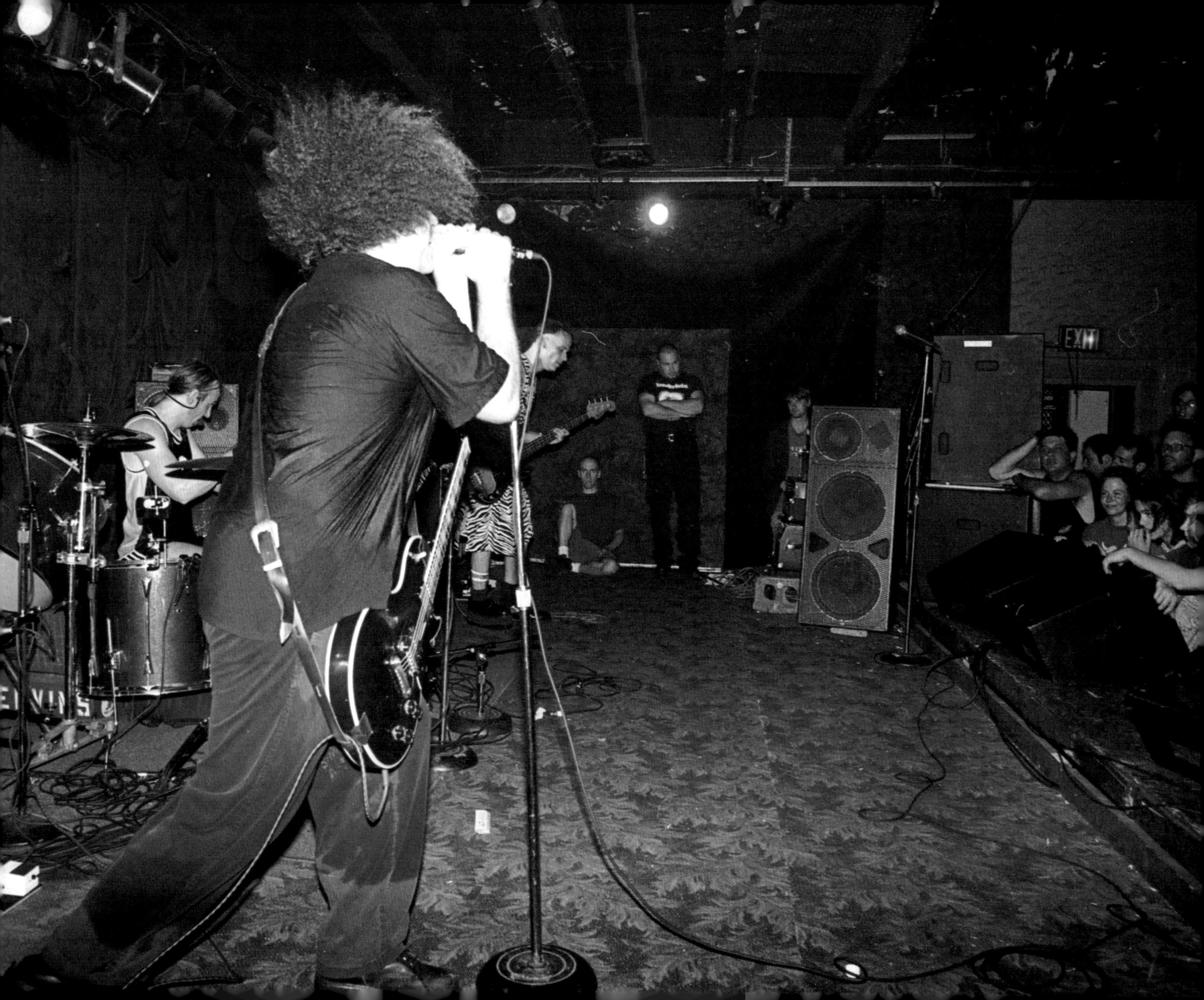
EXIT

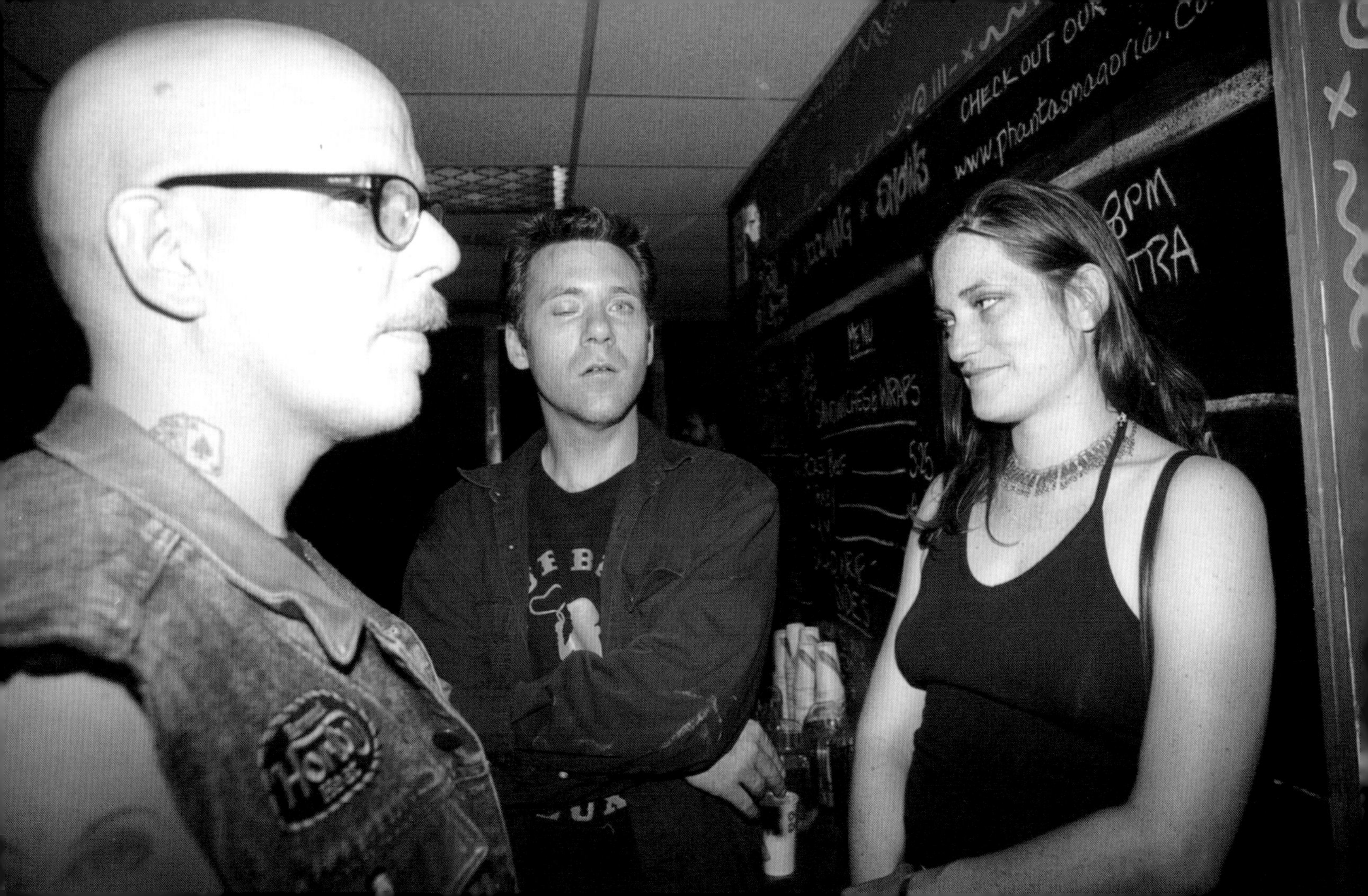
CHECK OUT OUR
www.phantasmagoria.Co
8PM
MENU

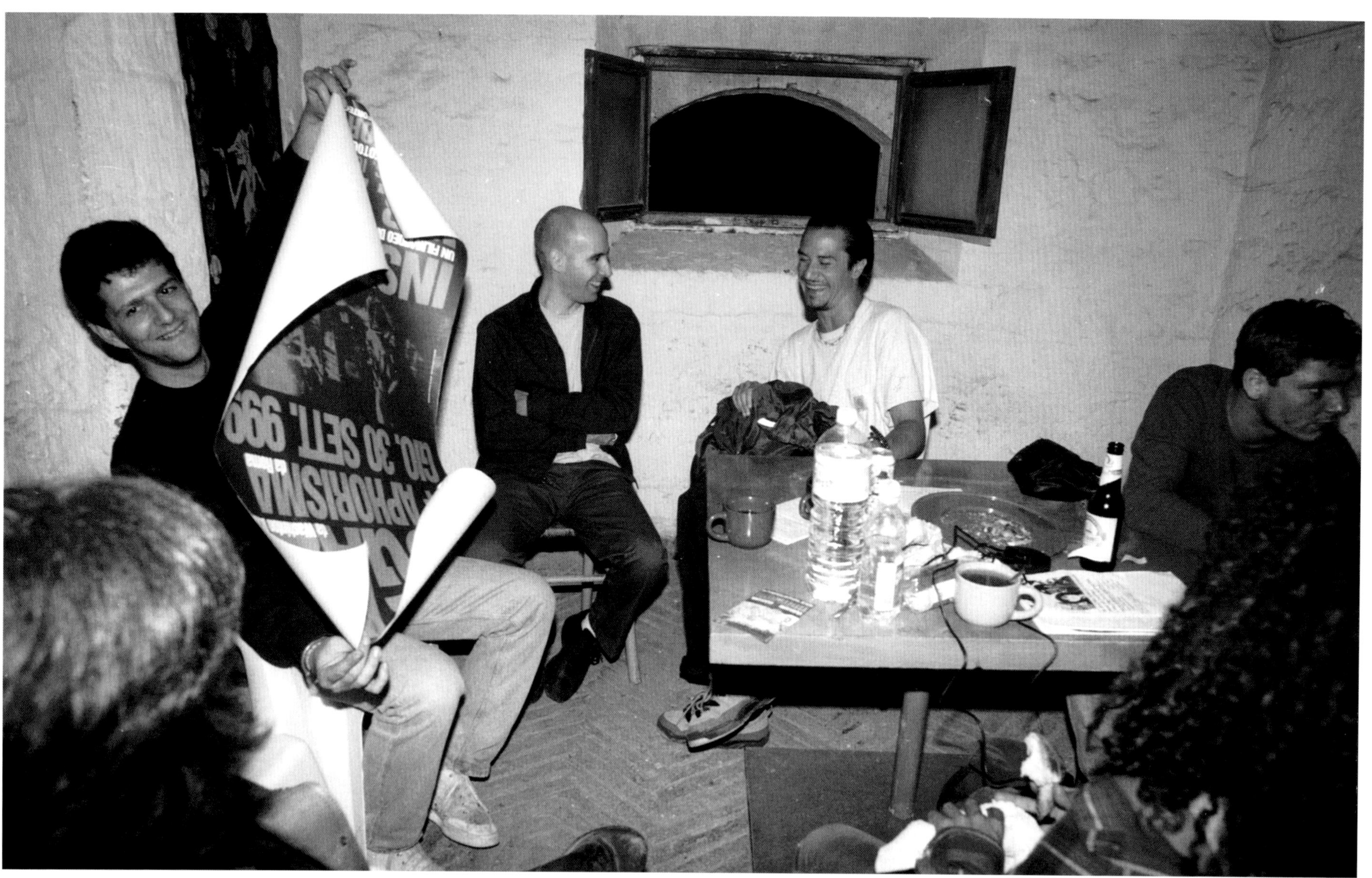

Joe Lally and Mike Patton, Forte Prenestino / Rome, Italy, 1999

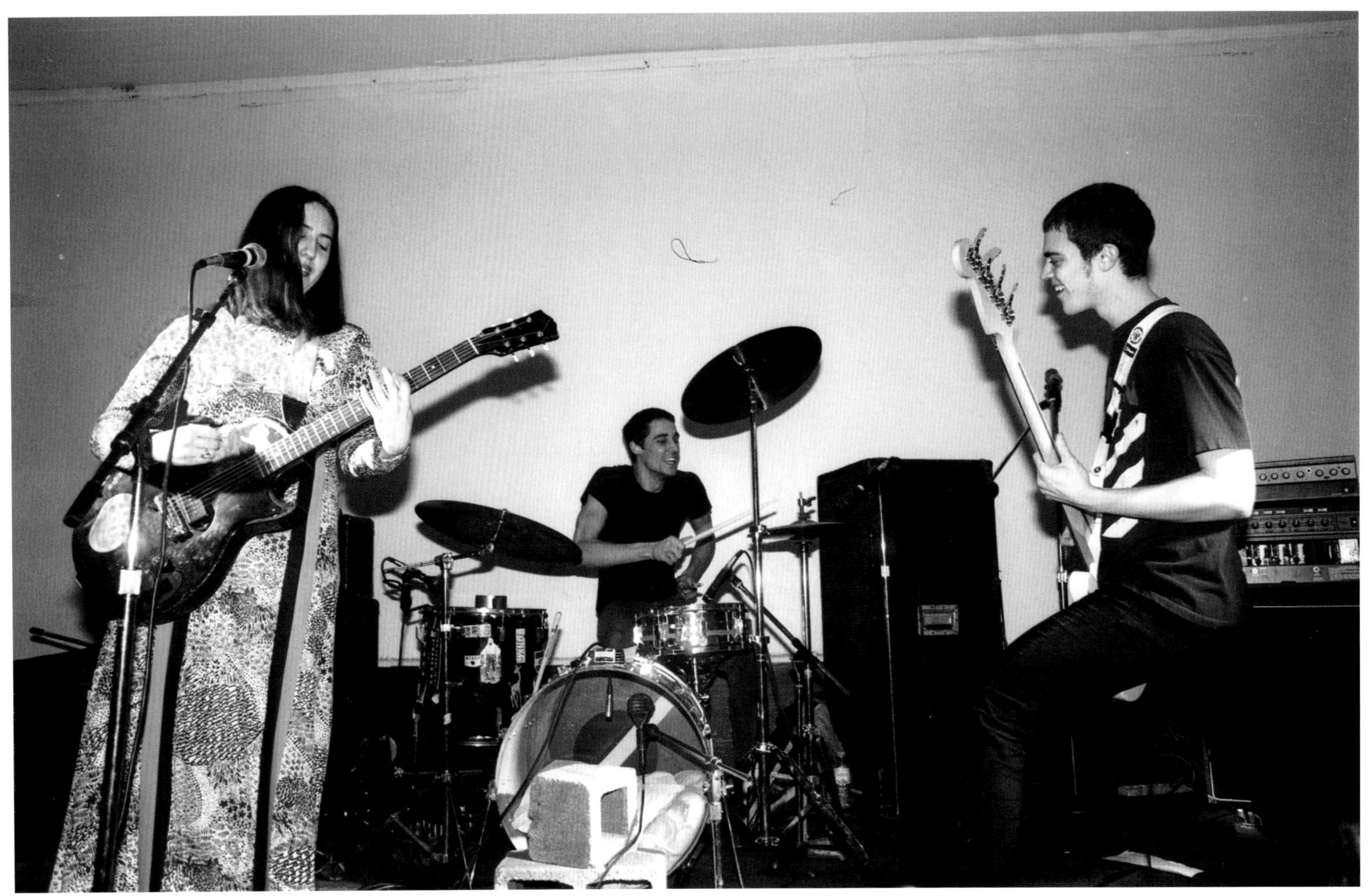

Savage Boys and Girls Club, Wilson Center / WDC, 1999

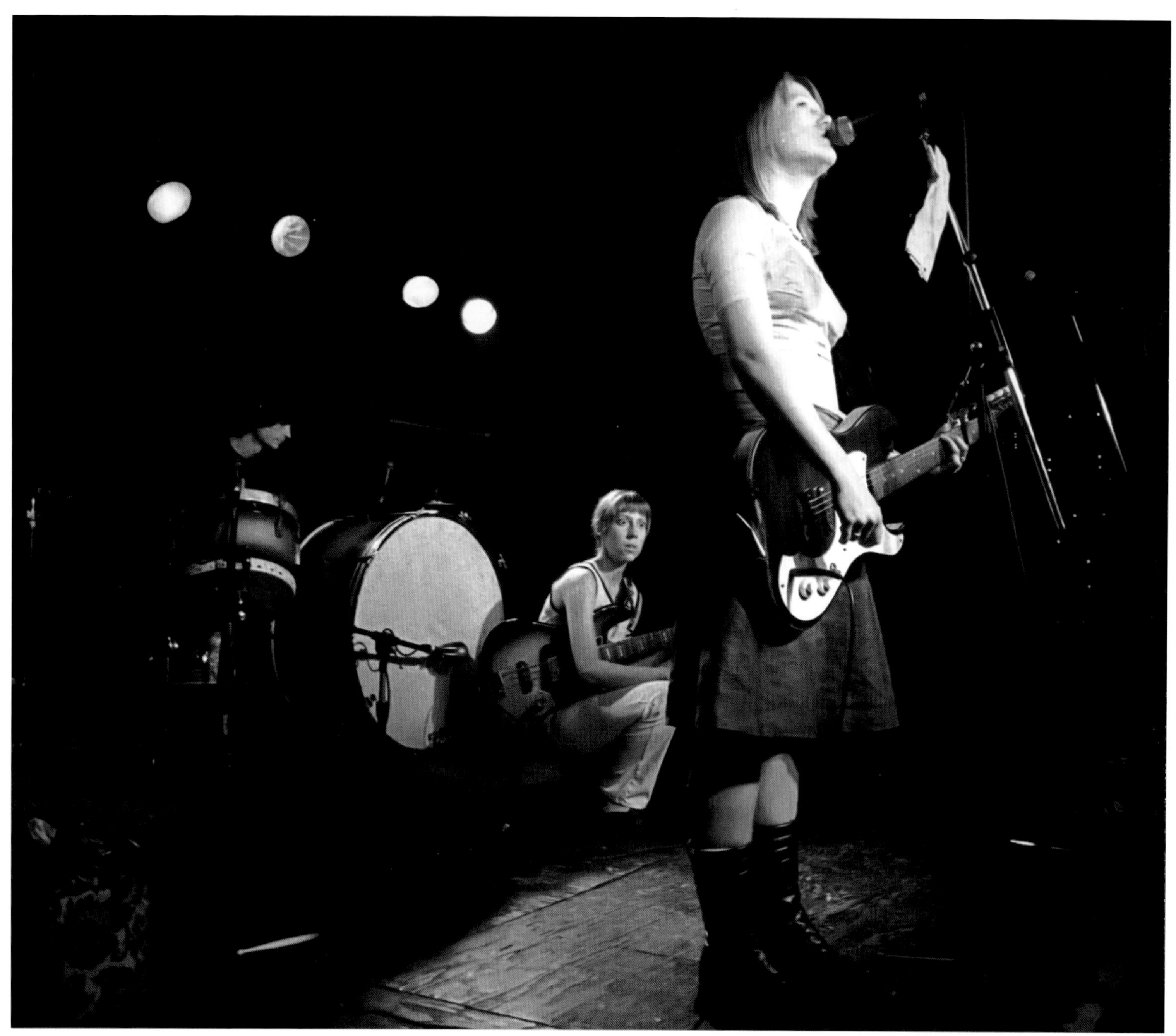

Quix*o*tic, Black Cat / WDC, 1999

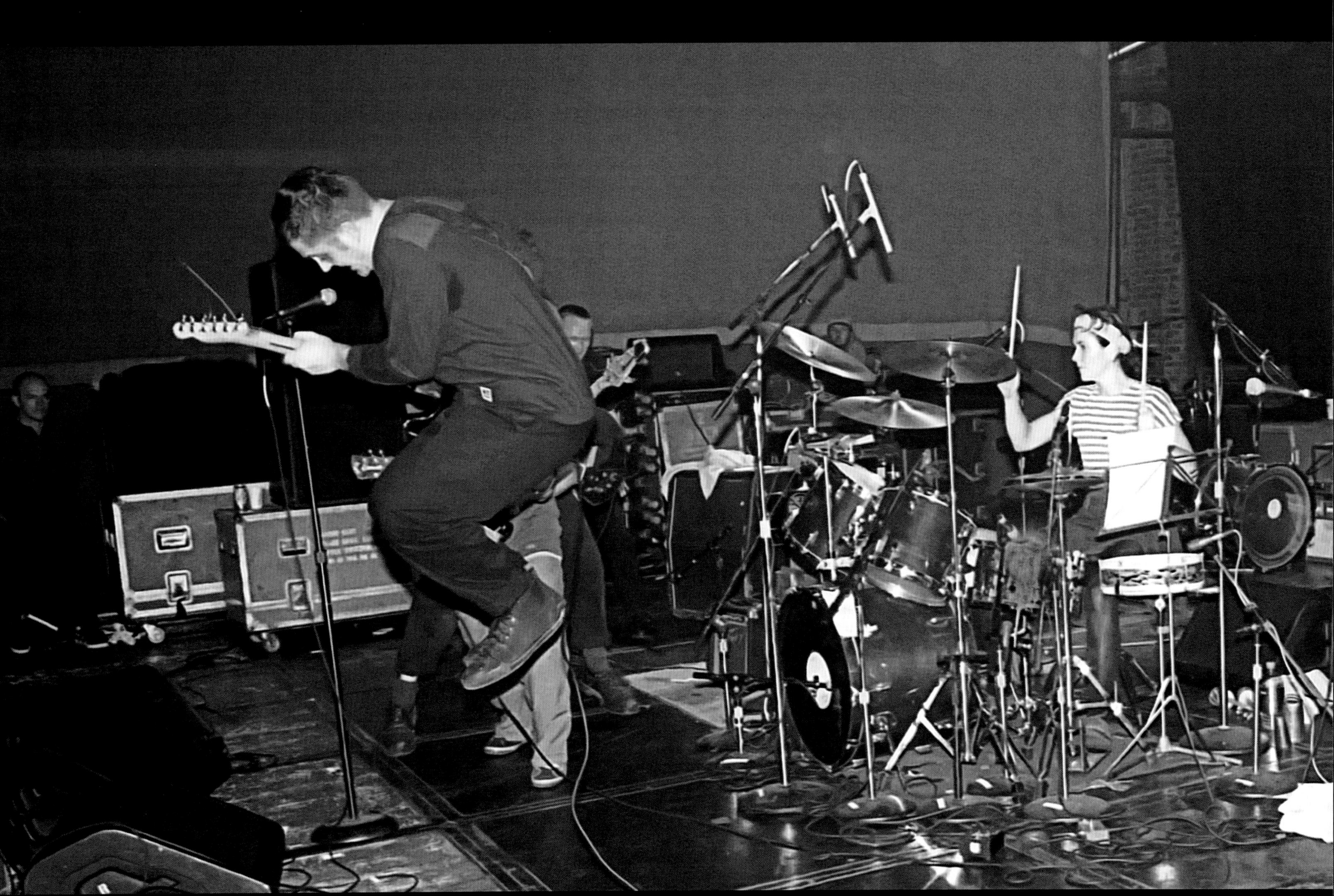

The Ex, Electric Factory / Philadelphia, PA, 1999

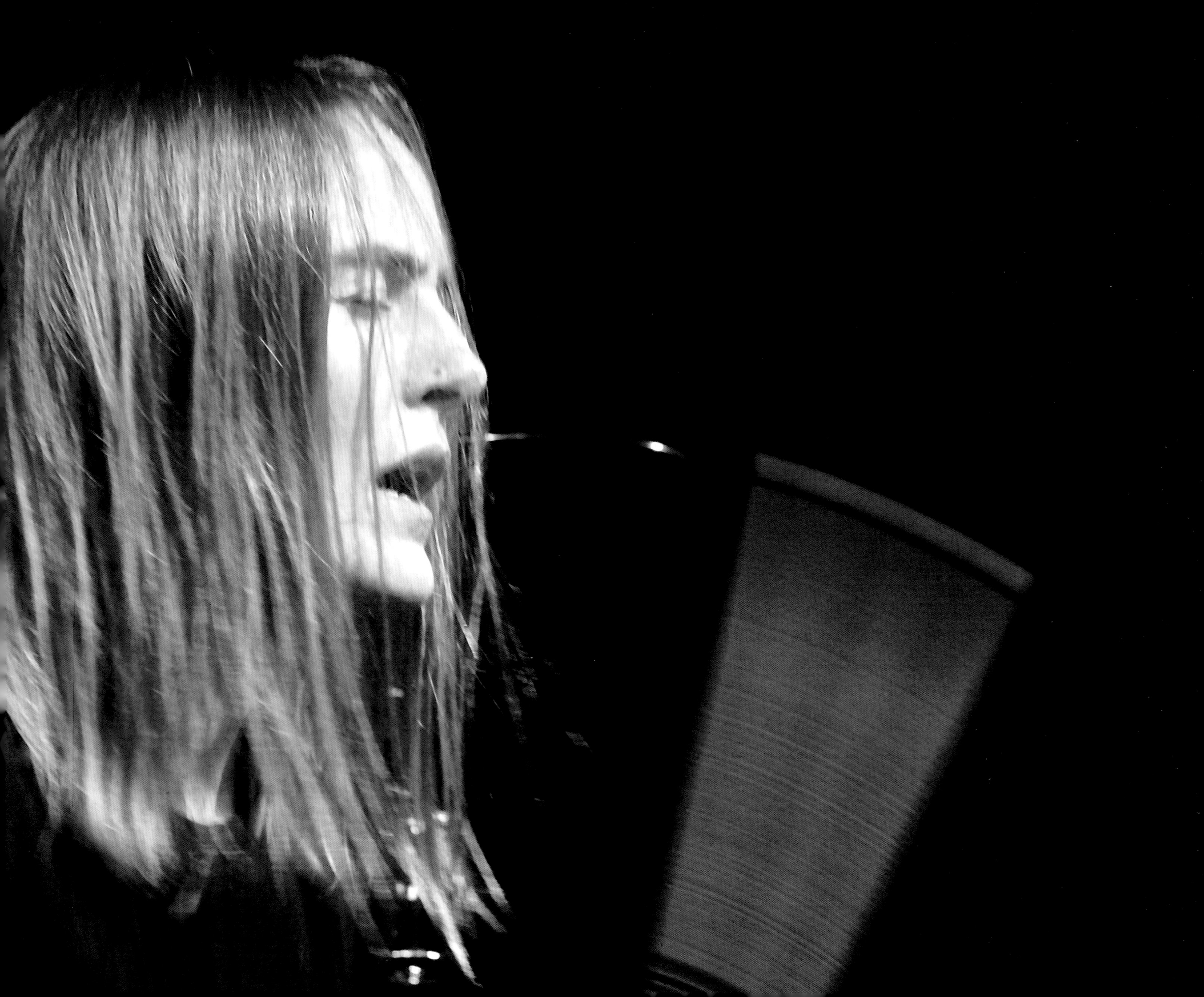

AMANDA HURON

In 1997 in Washington, DC, I started a band with Natalie Avery and Cristina Calle called the Stigmatics. We were a group of people who wrote songs and played shows, but we were also interested in communicating in ways beyond our music. So together with our friend Andrea Blatchford we started a zine called *Brickthrower*. The zine was named in honor of a guy who'd been fired from his job at a Burger King in Miami, and then came back later to throw bricks at the restaurant, and then was confronted by cops, who were being trailed by the TV show *Cops*. The cops, grimacing at the pathetic nature of the guy's crime, then arrested him on-camera for throwing the bricks. Natalie happened to see the episode, and something about the injustice of it all stuck.

We had the idea to make each issue of *Brickthrower* for a particular show we had coming up, and we would pass out that issue at the show. This was in a time before cell phones, and sometimes it was awkward for people, standing around by themselves at shows, or sometimes they got bored. So we figured they could stand around and read our zine in between bands.

We made just five issues: the first for a show we played at Fort Reno with the Most Secret Method in the summer of 1997; the second for a show we played with Fugazi at their tenth-anniversary concert at the Wilson Center, then home to the Latin American Youth Center, where I was working that fall; the third I lost and have no memory of; the fourth we made for our tour of the upper Midwest in late winter 1998; and a final one that we made for a tour of the South in the summer of 1998.

We wrote about lots of things in these zines, including public space, and instructions for getting a permit to throw a block party in DC; homelessness and the politics of pissing in public; gentrification; the nightmare of Bill Clinton's welfare "reform"; the changing landscape of corporate telecommunications; the destruction of our public university's jazz radio station, and new prospects for community radio; student organizing and walkouts at the public high school in our neighborhood; our experiences protesting war and militarism in Dupont Circle, and tutoring kids at our neighborhood elementary school; an interview we did with El Vez, "the Mexican Elvis," about his politics and performance. Mostly we wanted to voice our opposition to capitalism's expression in our neighborhood and our city, and our feeling that collectively, creatively, we could do something about it.

The zine and the band and the shows we played where the zine was passed out were all part of the same thing. And the *thing* was a punk community that was formed through a mystical alchemy of collective noise and spirit. The spirit develops because people are coming together to experience the words, the music, the being together, all together, against atomization, against the society that creates the person throwing bricks, alone. Twenty years, six bands, and many shows later, I'm even more convinced that this spirit is magic, and real.

PUFF PIECES (present) • WEED TREE (present) • MIRACLES • CAUTION CURVES • VERTEBRATES • SCARAMOUCHE • STIGMATICS • DIVISIONARIES • IMPETUS INTER • PERIOD

Amanda Huron, Puff Pieces, Black Cat / WDC, 2015

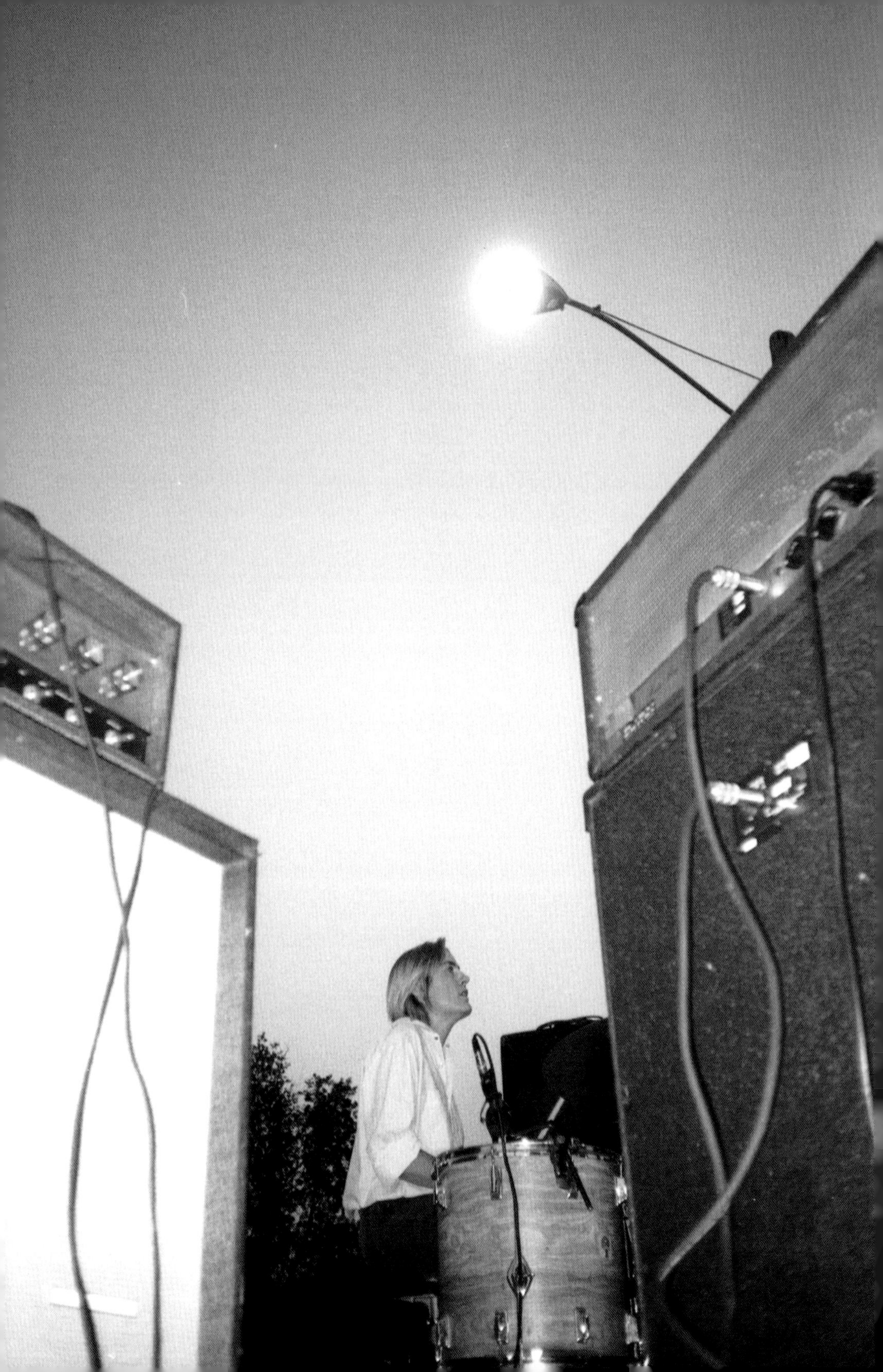

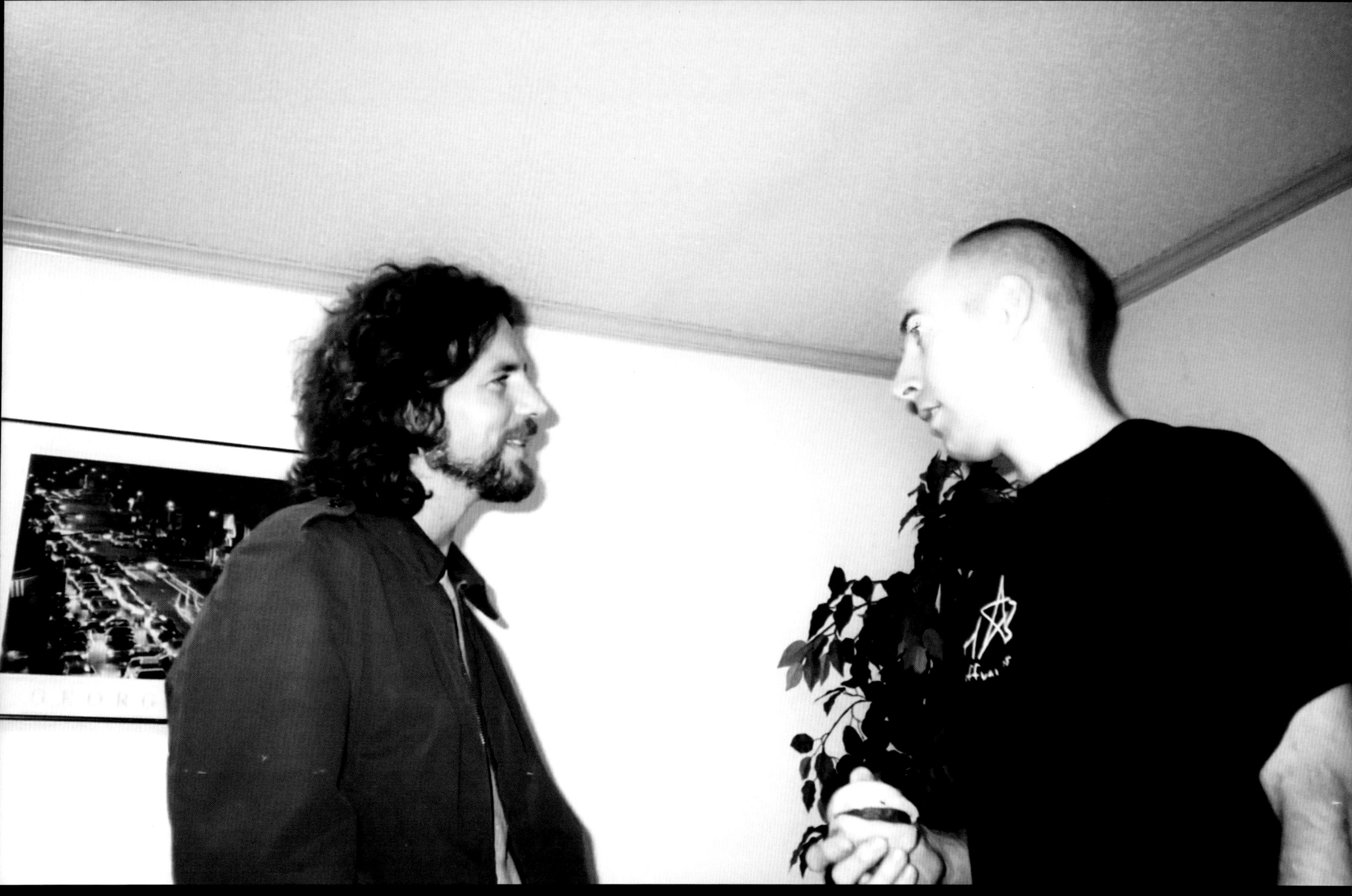

Eddie Vedder and Joe Lally, Merriweather Post Pavilion / Columbia, MD, 2000
Opposite: Amanda Huron, Fort Reno / WDC, 2000

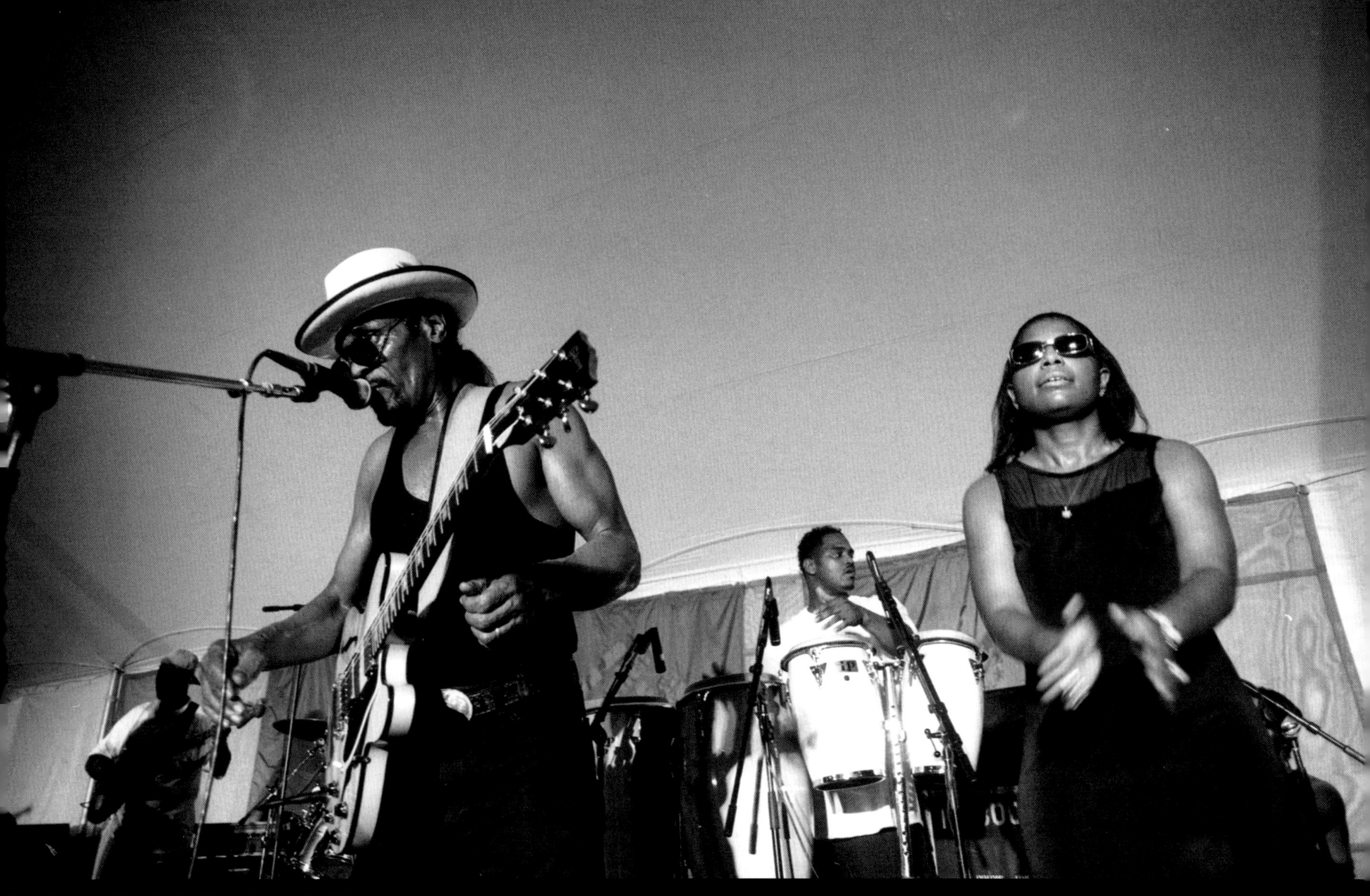

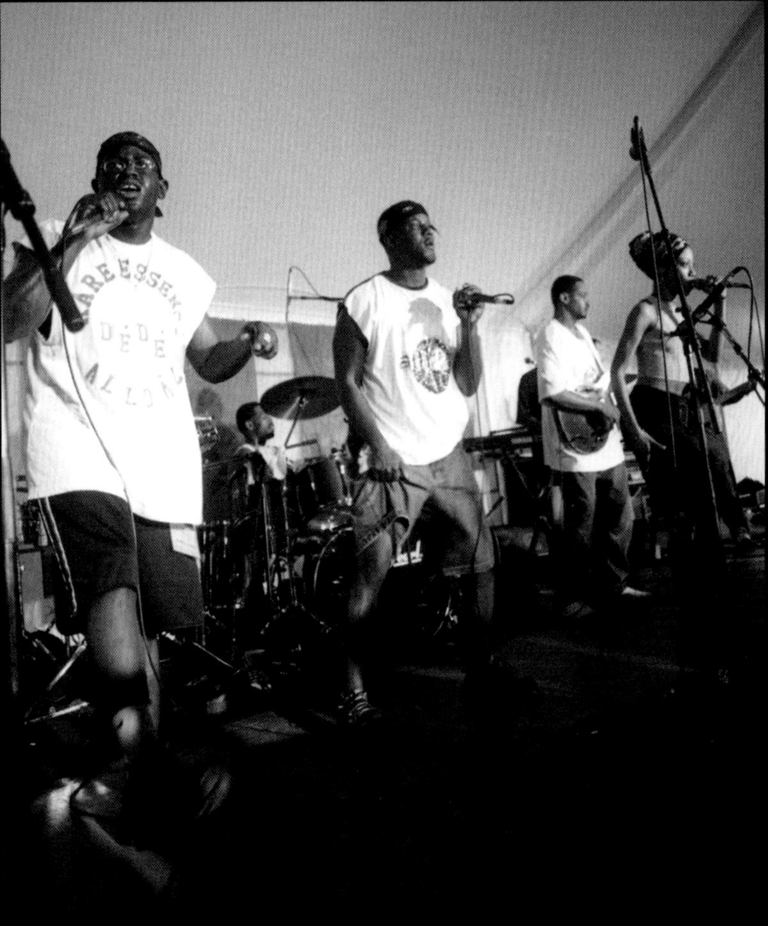

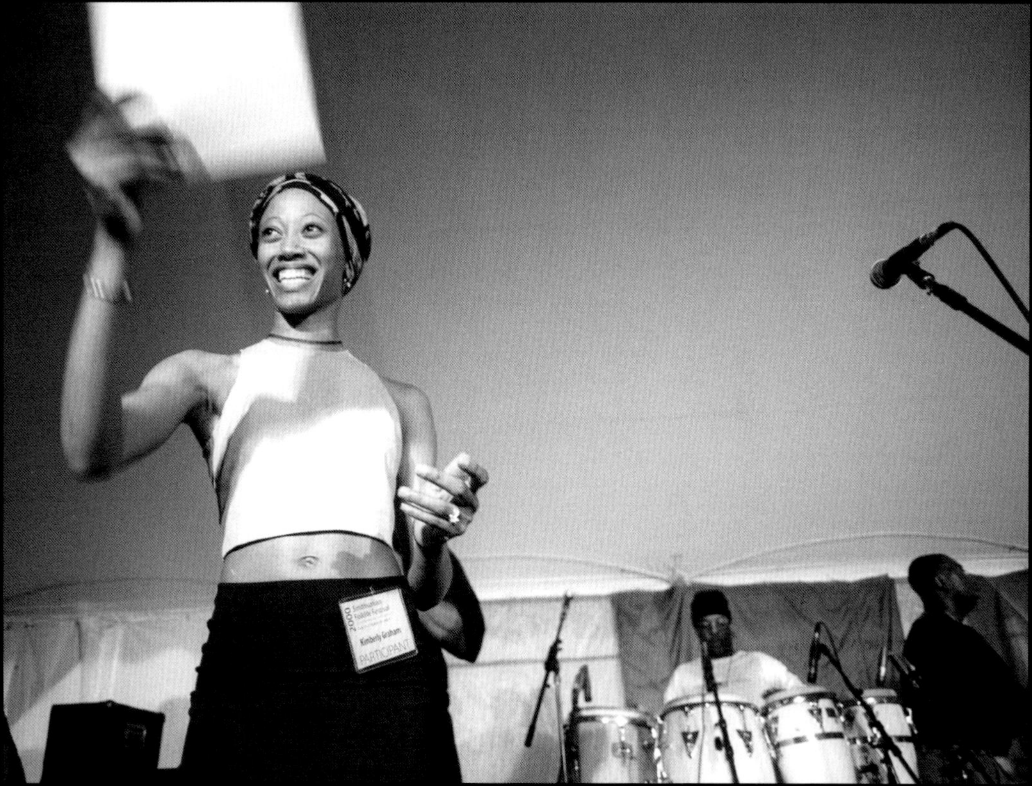

Rare Essence, Smithsonian Folklife Festival / WDC, 2000

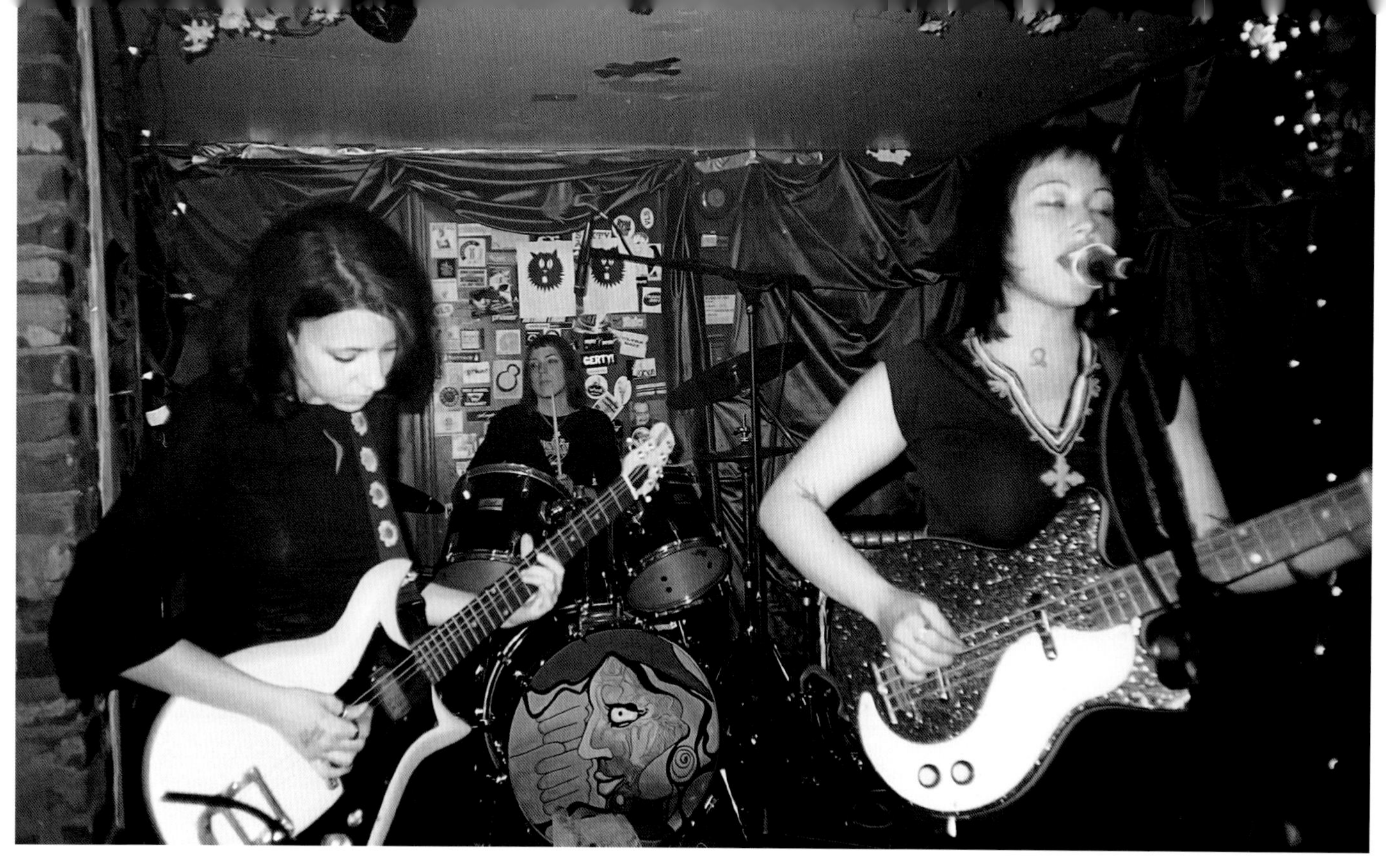

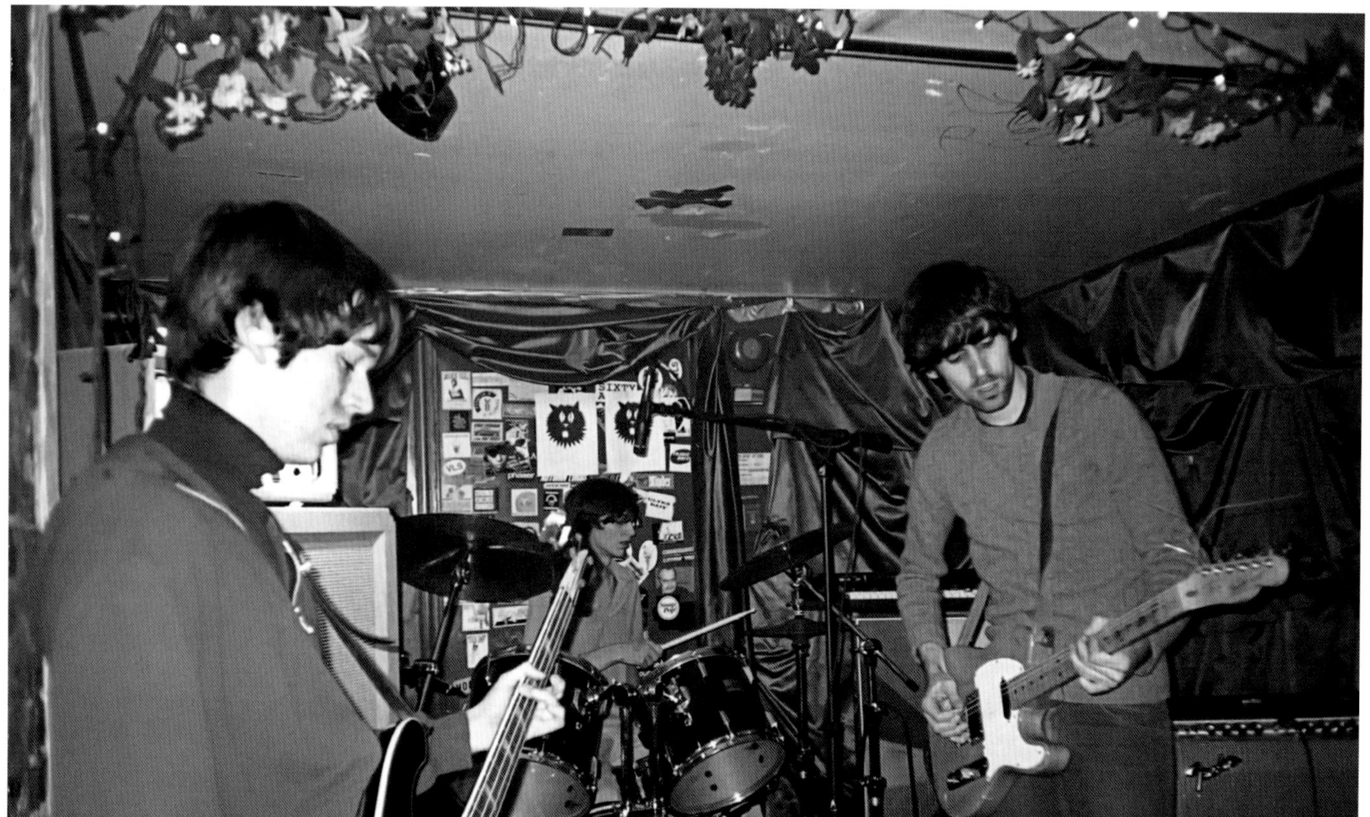

From top:
Dame Fate and Dead Meadow, Velvet Lounge / WDC, 2000

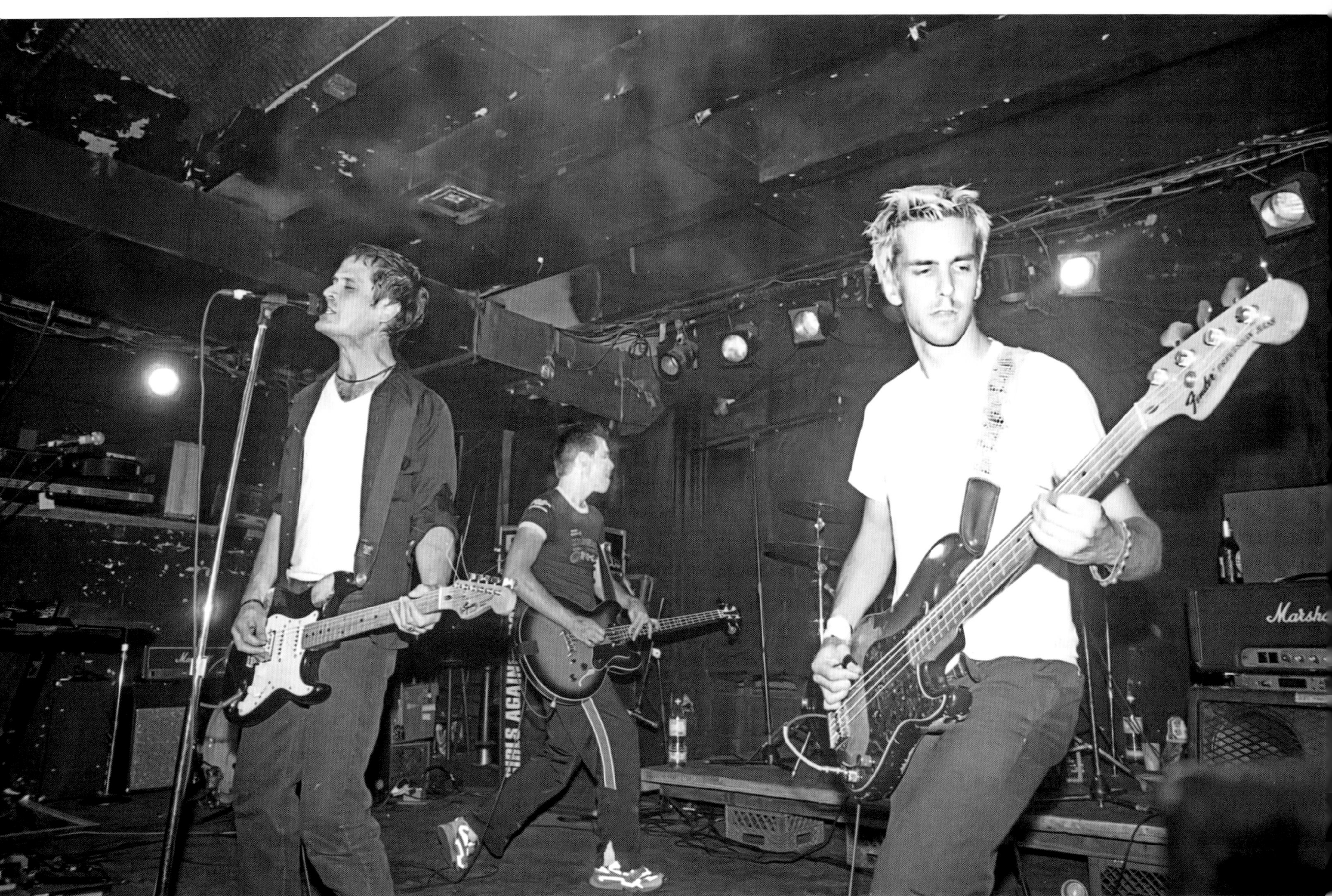

Girls Against Boys, Black Cat / WDC, 2000

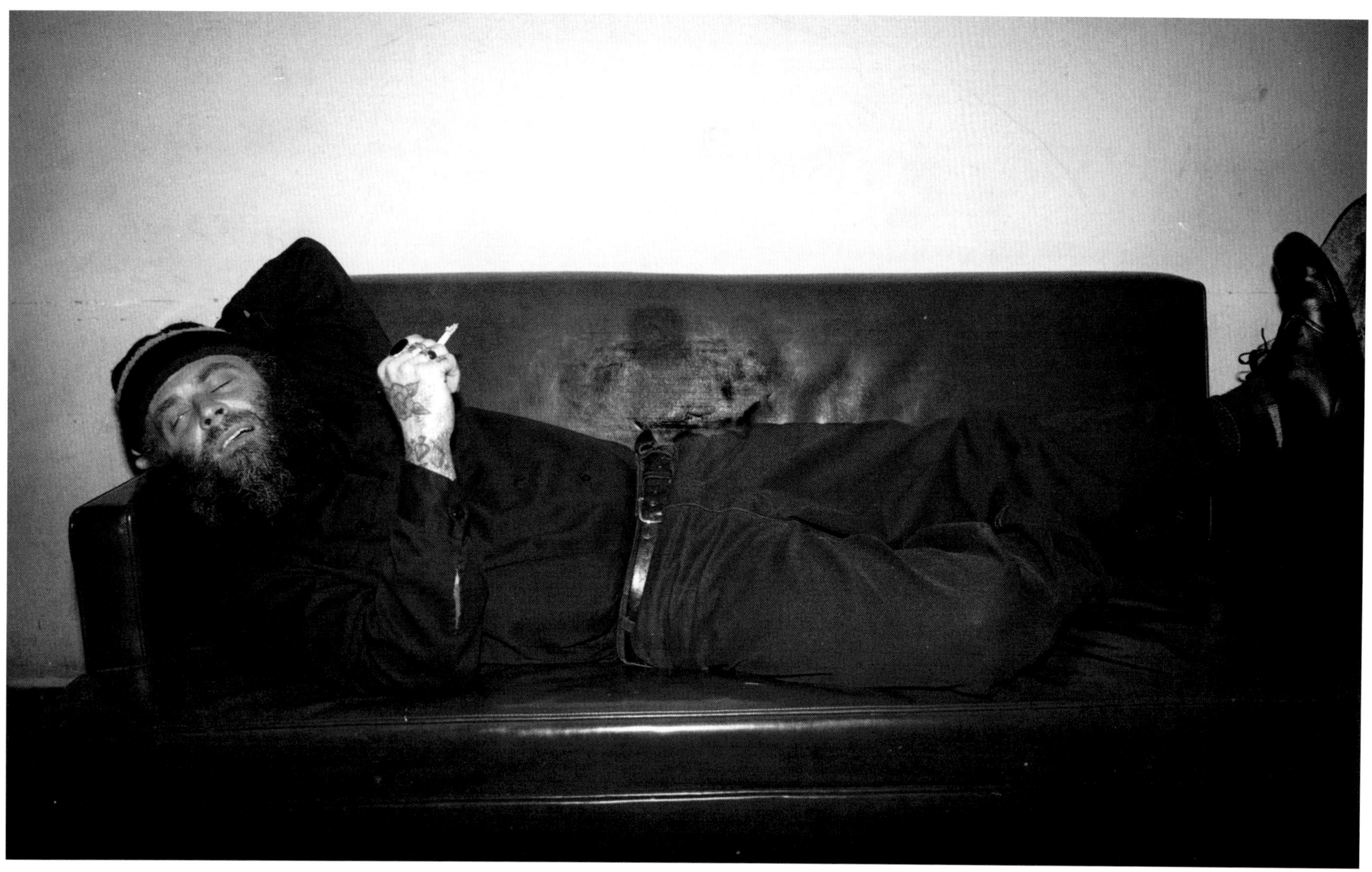

Daniel Higgs, 2000

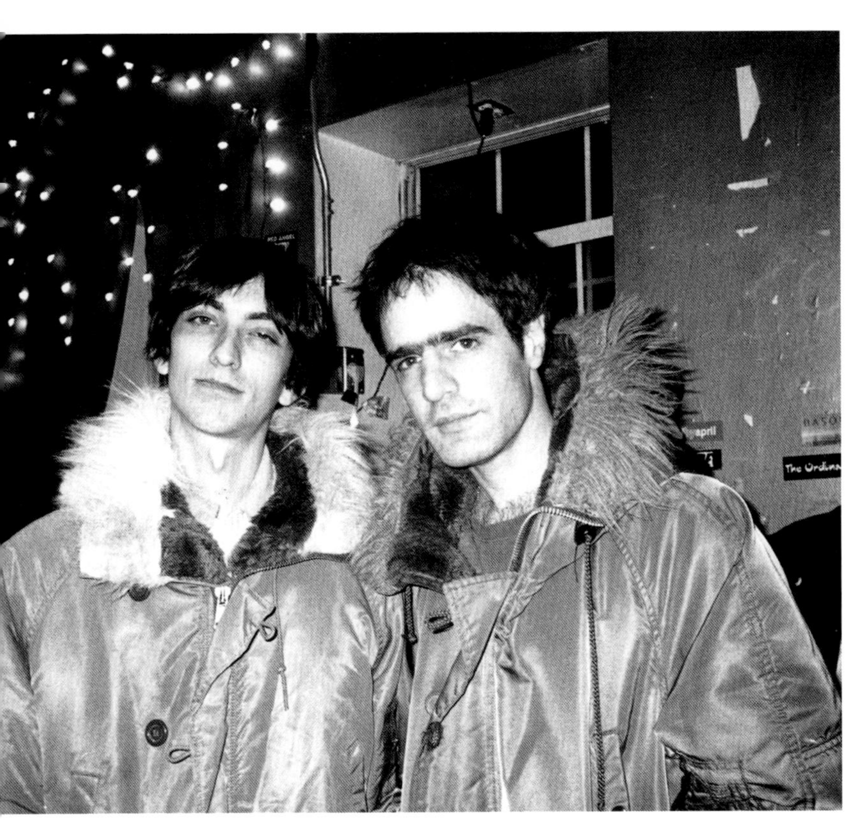

Marc Laughlin and Guy Picciotto, Velvet Lounge / WDC, 2000

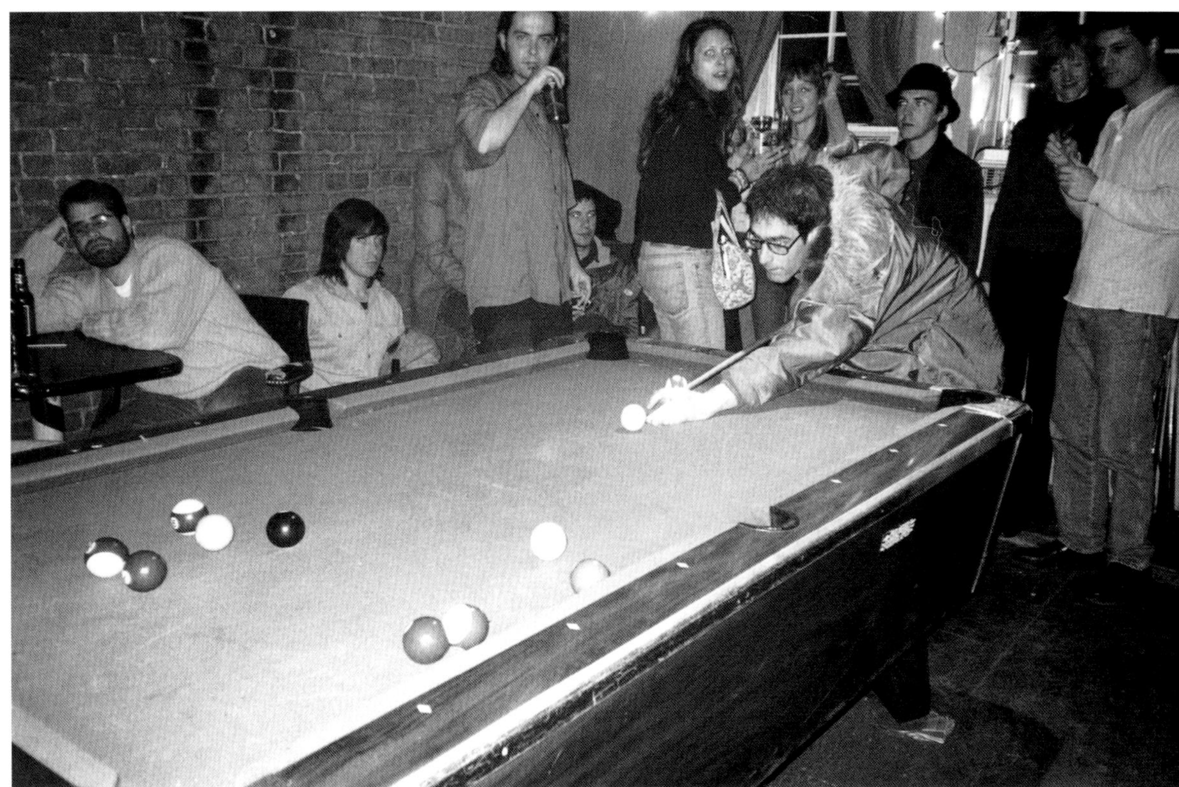

Guy Picciotto, Velvet Lounge / WDC, 2000

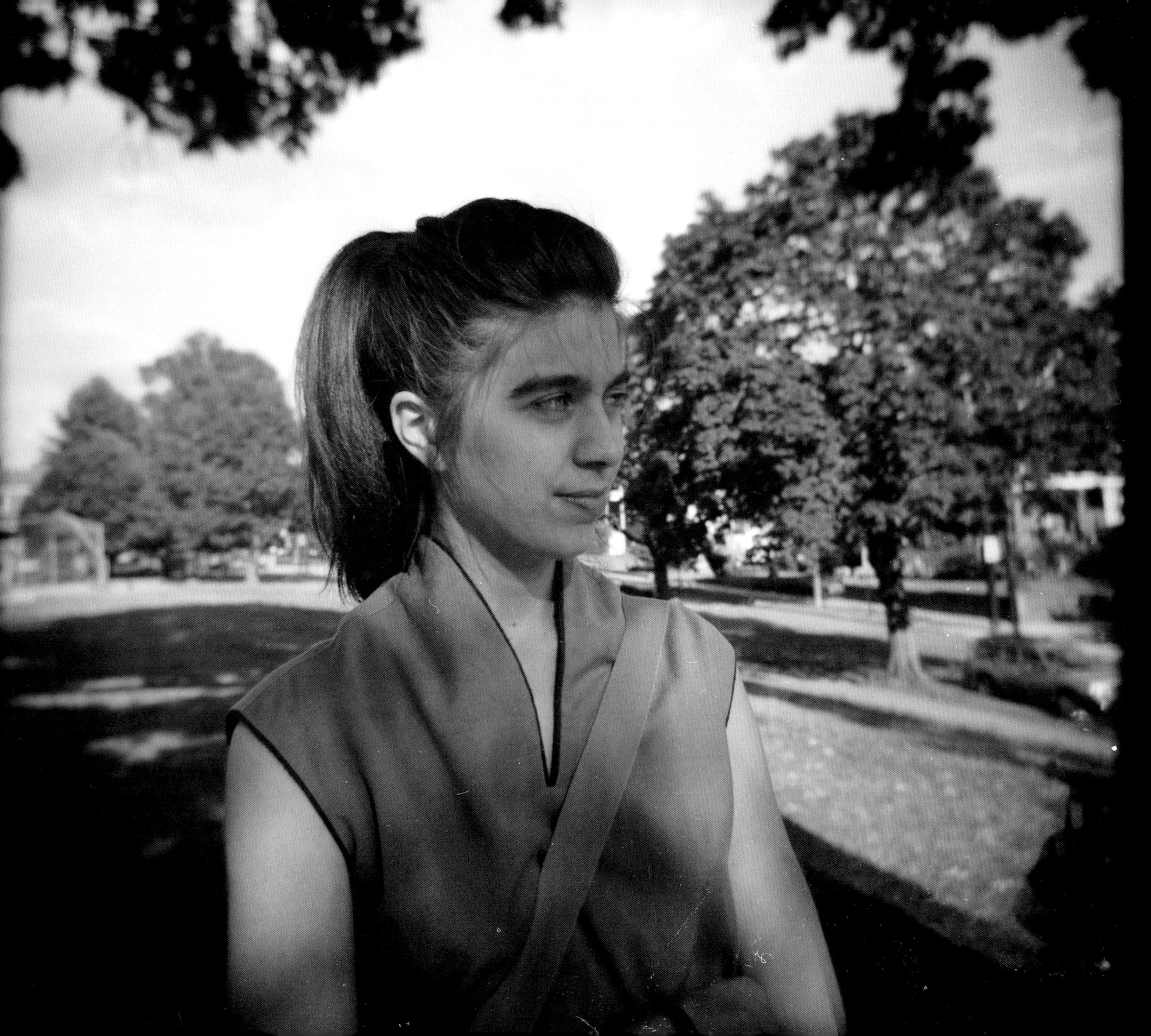

AMY FARINA

Communicating is so complicated. The ceaseless requirement to arrange words together to express oneself and elicit meaning is hard to do, and it's a task that's never really done. I admire and envy those who are masters of written and spoken language. Largely, words just confuse me, and it can be humiliating to be ineloquent, or to misunderstand. It always seemed to me that words, exempting some forms of experimental prose or poetry, needed to be concrete. I assumed that what one said would be equal to what that same person meant, but of course this isn't always the case, and things are often left to implication or interpretation, with no guarantee of understanding. I've gotten a handle on this now, but as a kid it was very disorienting. When the grown-ups were talking, I never knew what words to believe, and I definitely didn't know how to state my own truths. It's also hard to communicate with words when you think in scent, or texture, or temperature.

Thankfully, my world opened up to art and music, all ready to be seen, heard, felt, and made. Like magic, it made sense and was not dependent on words to do so. While a word typically has to mean something agreed upon, a sound or a shape is not bound by representing any one thing in particular. Music and art begin as ambiguous—just nebulous raw material, bouncing around. Eventually, through gentle guidance, compulsion, or something in between, that raw material finds a way to fit together. It doesn't have to follow form or order to work, or even to be wildly successful. Though, when it does work, it creates profound understanding, and often shared understanding, in ways that you probably can't even articulate with words.

This method of communication serves very well for the world, and for me. It is universal language right here for all of us. It fills the many tiny and massive spaces where words are too big or too small to fit. I guess if I were able to paint a picture here, it might illustrate my idea more clearly . . . Thank goodness for all the photographs.

MR. CANDY EATER • MOATS DEFINITELY • LOIS • THE WARMERS • TED LEO AND THE PHARMACISTS • THE EVENS

Amy Farina, Stoddert Recreation Center / WDC, 2007

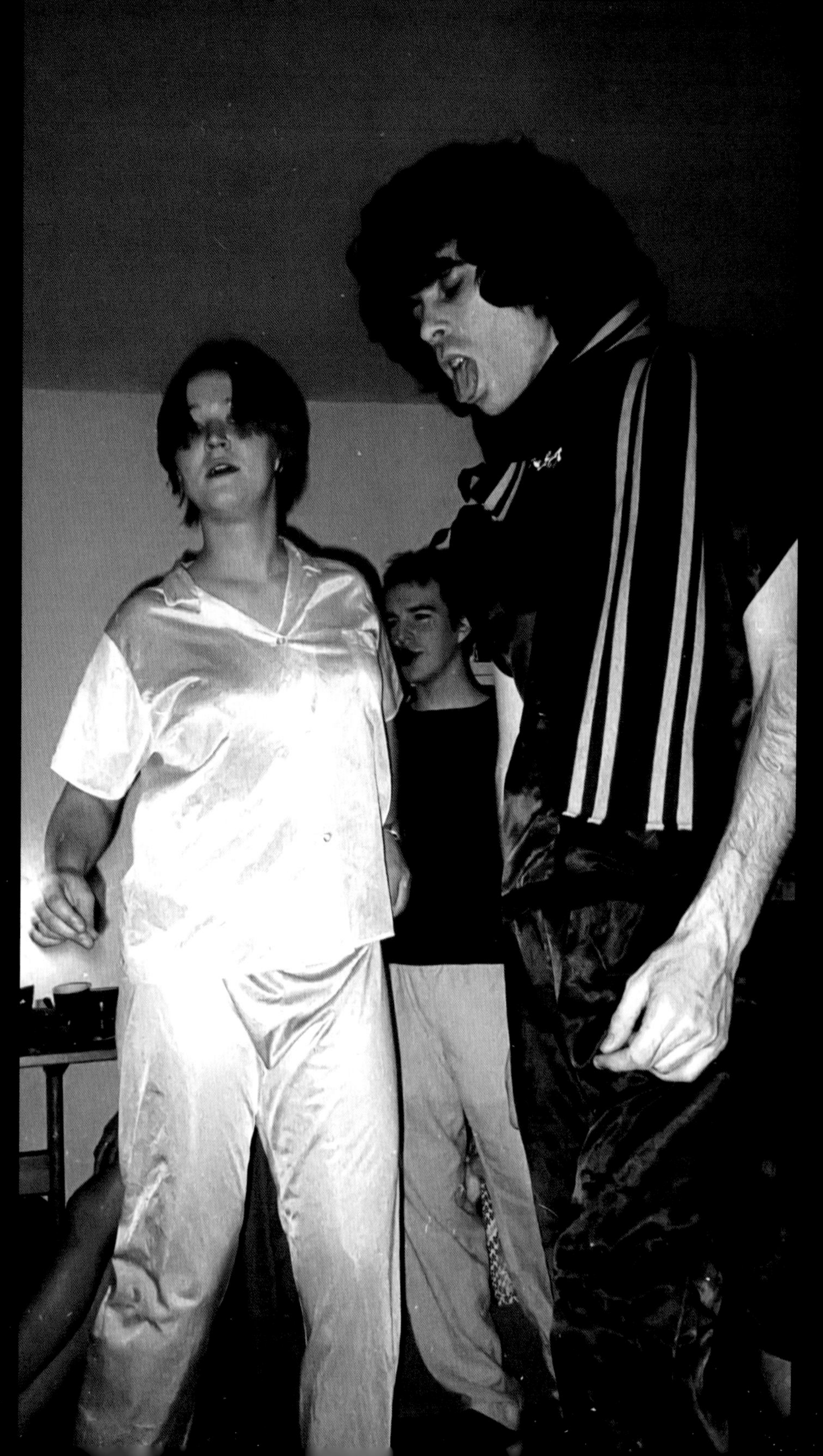

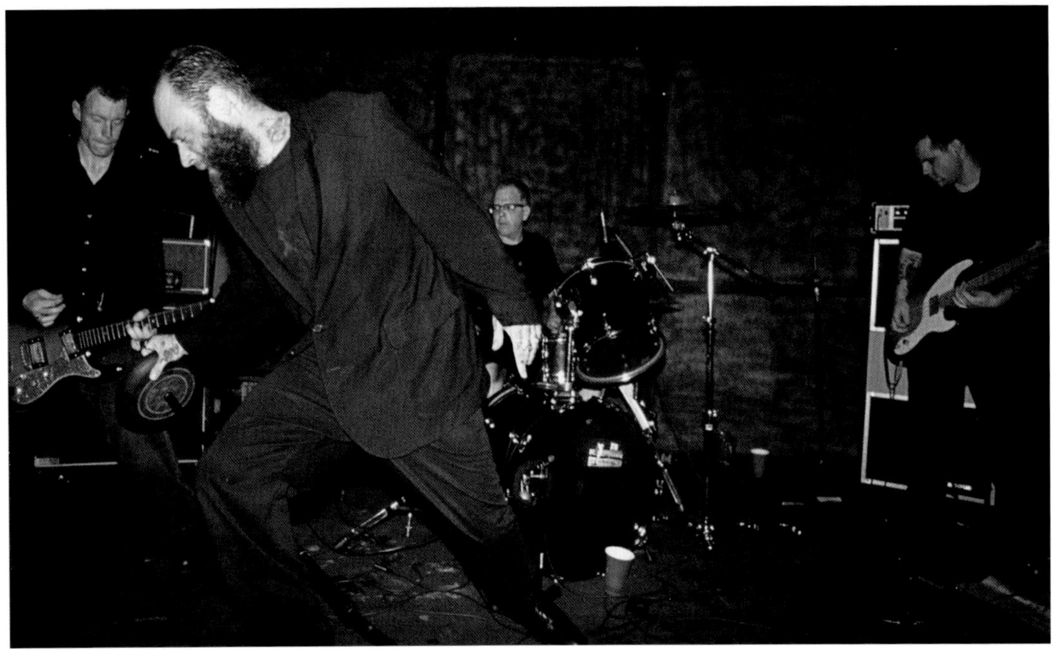

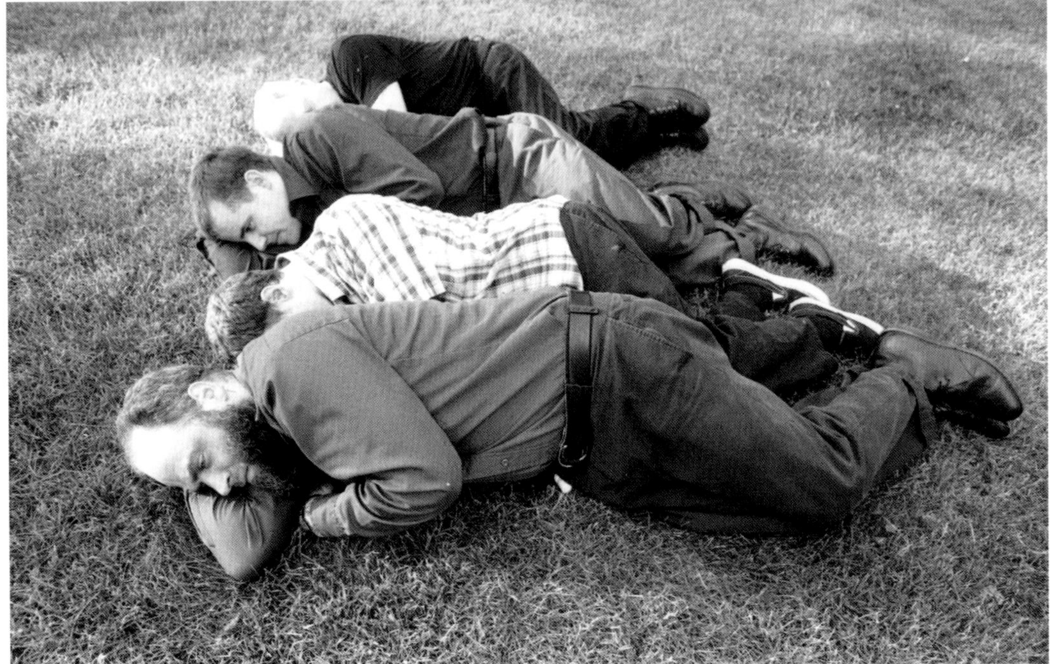

From top: Lungfish / Asbury Park, NJ, 2000; Lungfish / Baltimore, MD, 2000
Opposite: pajama party / WDC, 2000

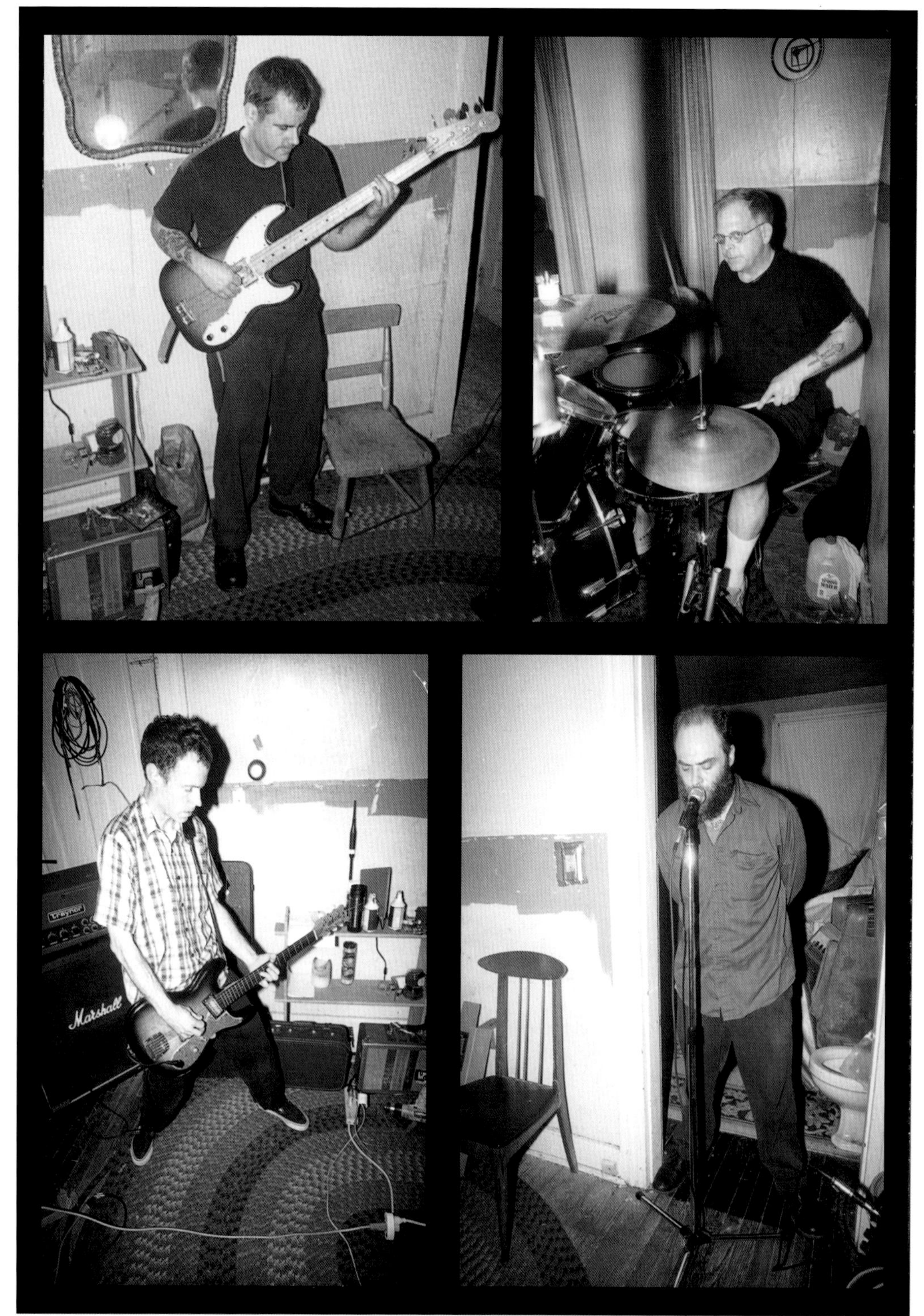

Lungfish, rehearsal space /
Baltimore, MD, 2000

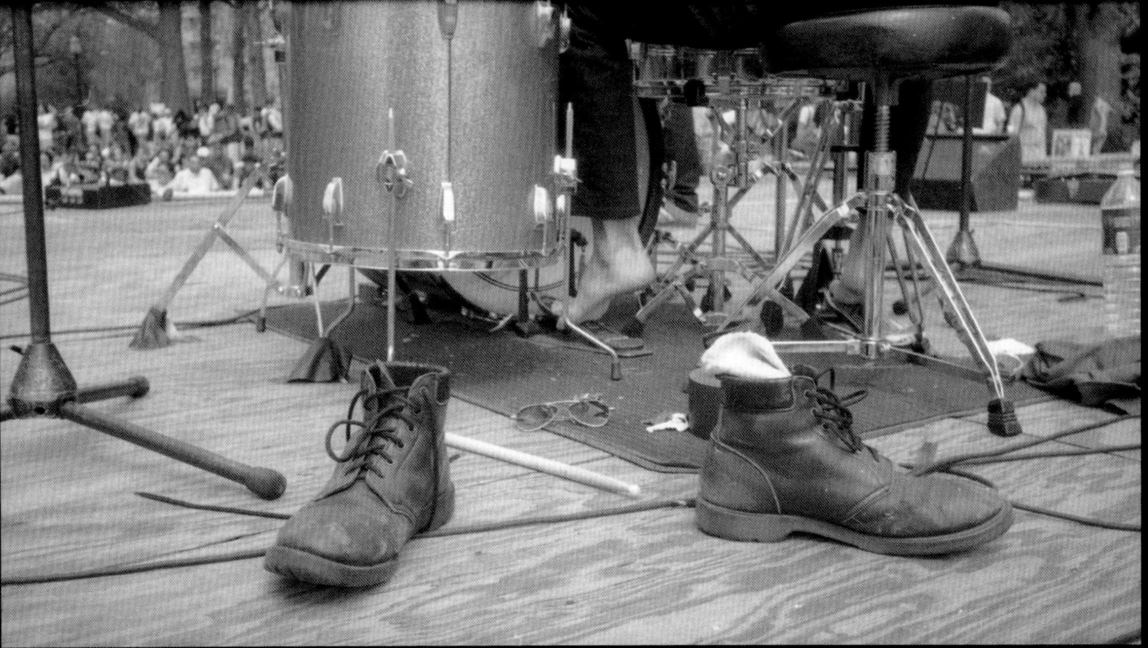

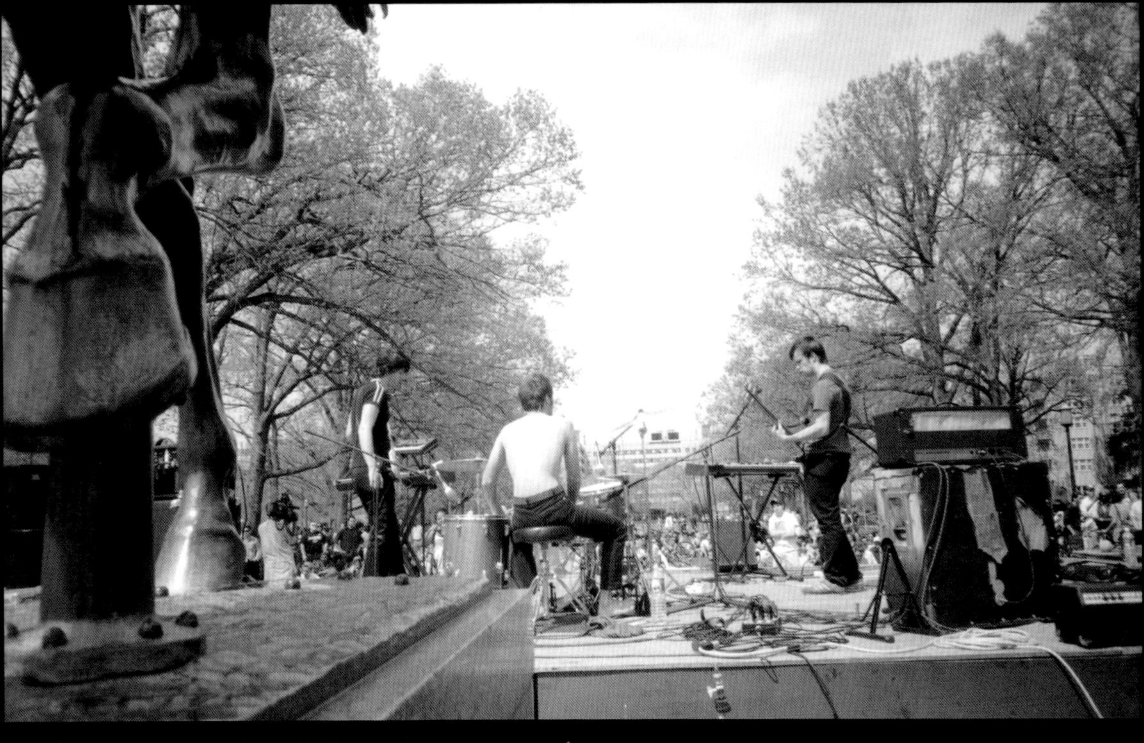

Trans Am, Malcolm X Park / WDC, 2000

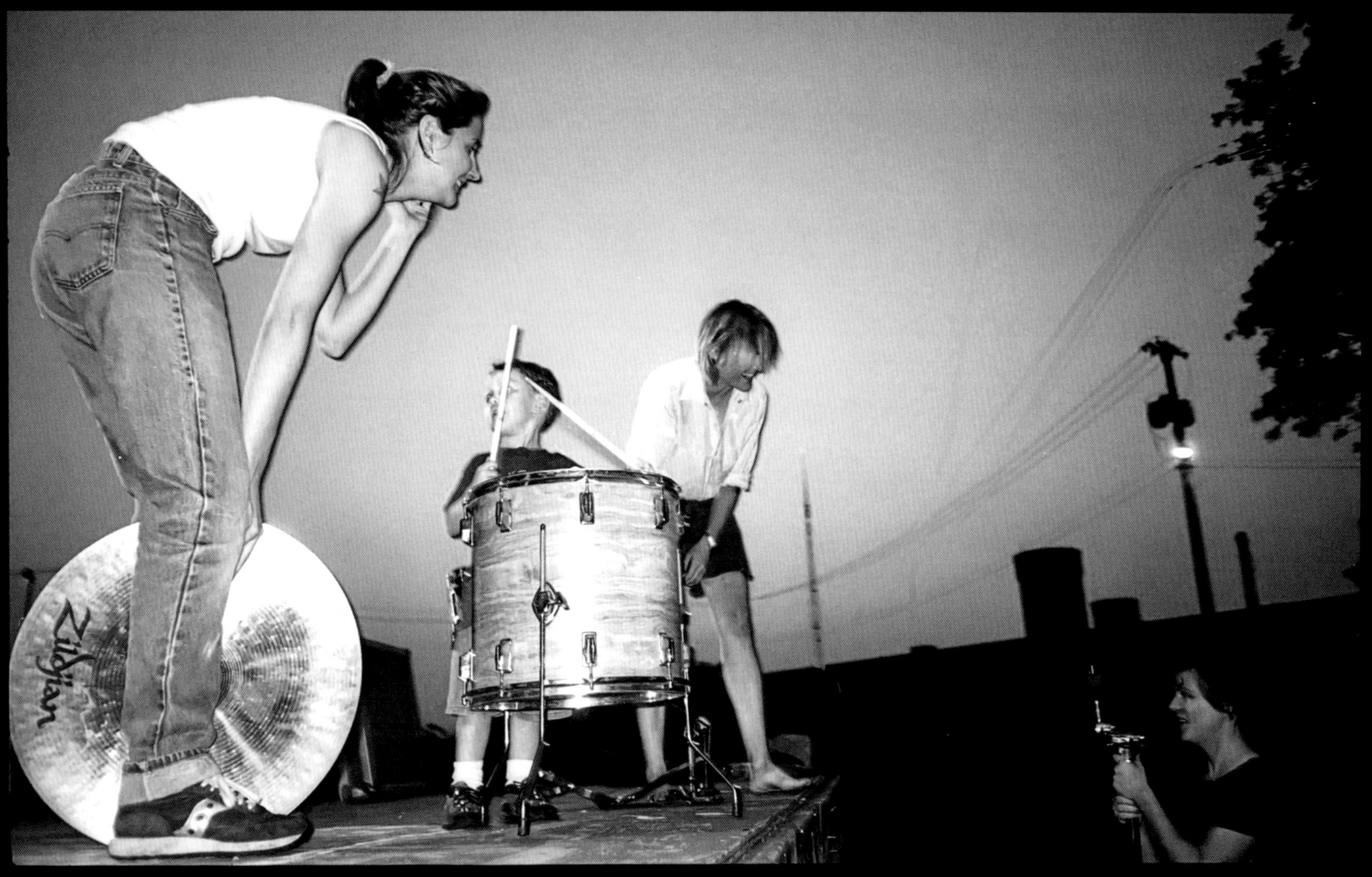

Scaramouche, Fort Reno / WDC, 2000

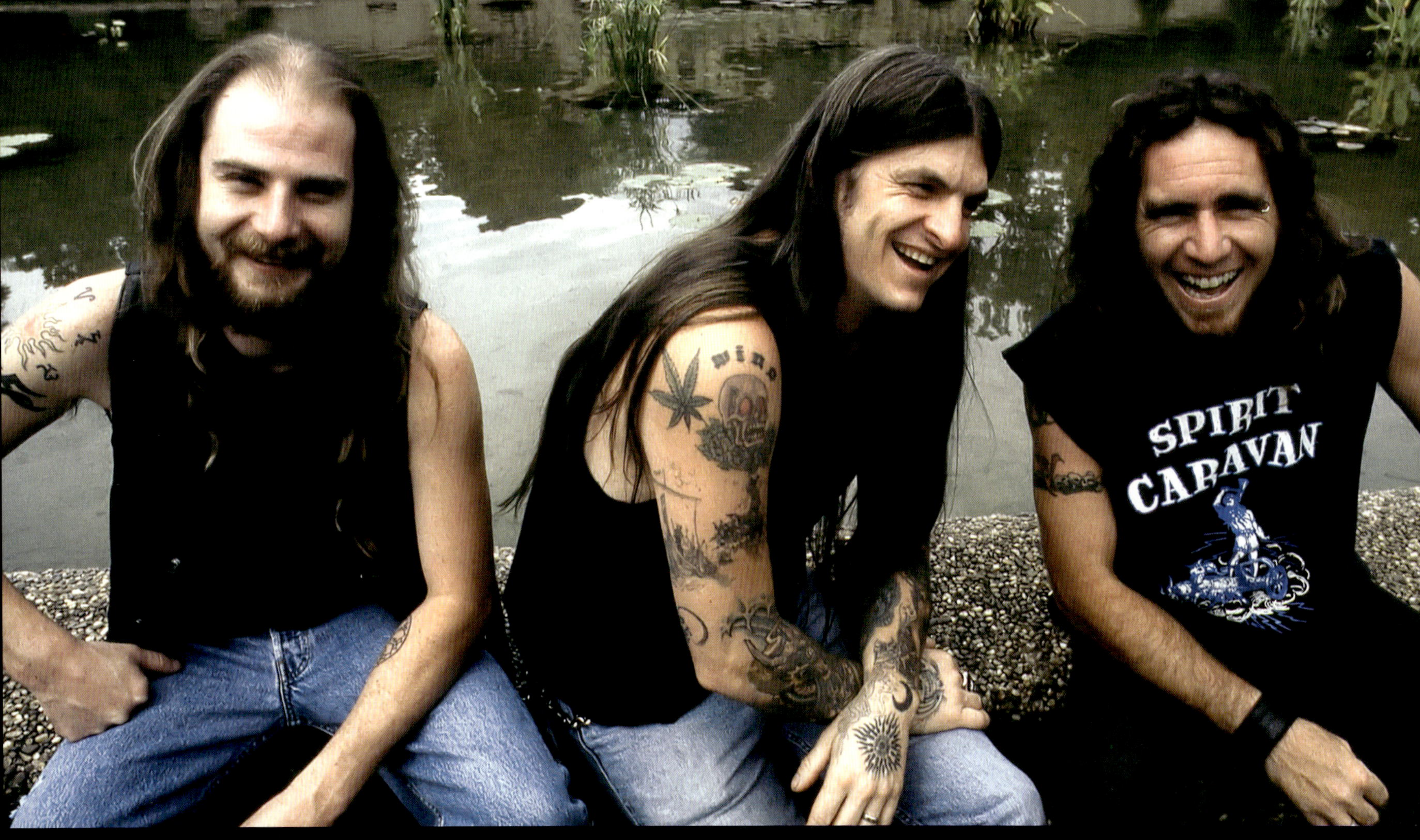

Spirit Caravan, Malcolm X Park / WDC, 2000

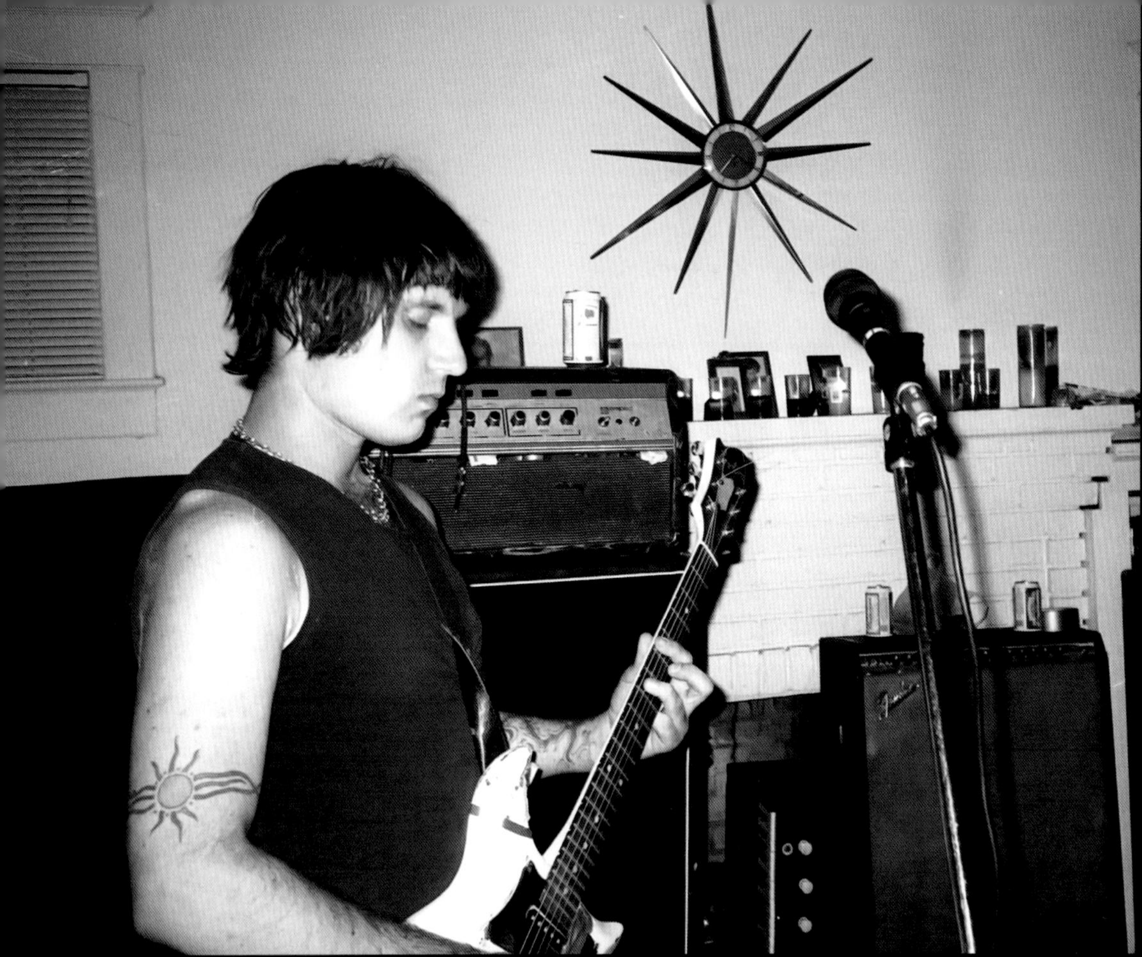

ommy Orr, The Pigs, Kansas House / Arlington, VA, 2000

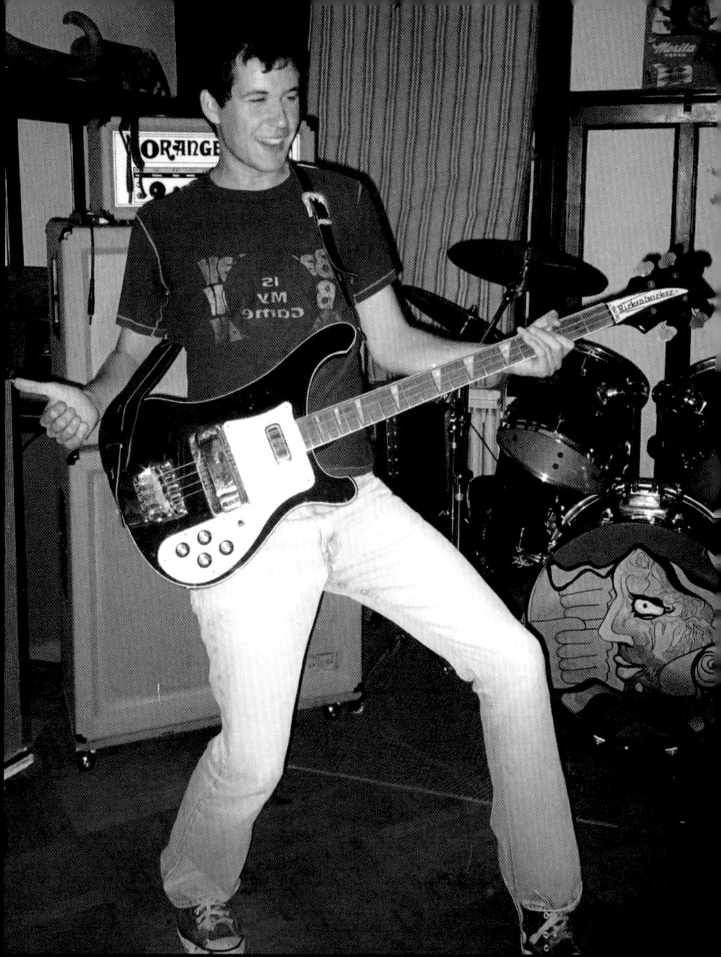

Steve Dore, The Pigs, Kansas House / Arlington, VA, 2000

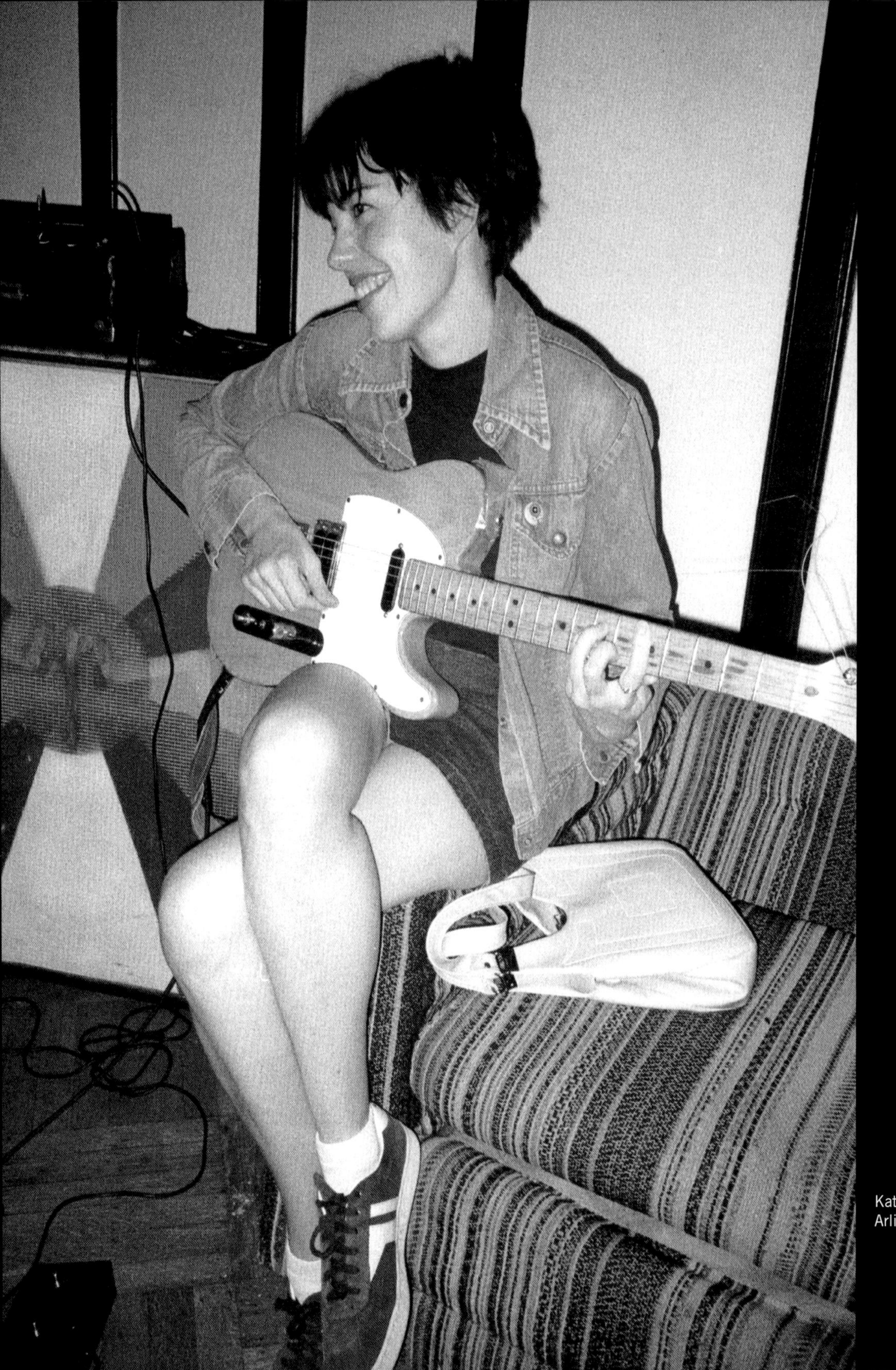

Kathi Wilcox, Kansas House
Arlington, VA, 2000

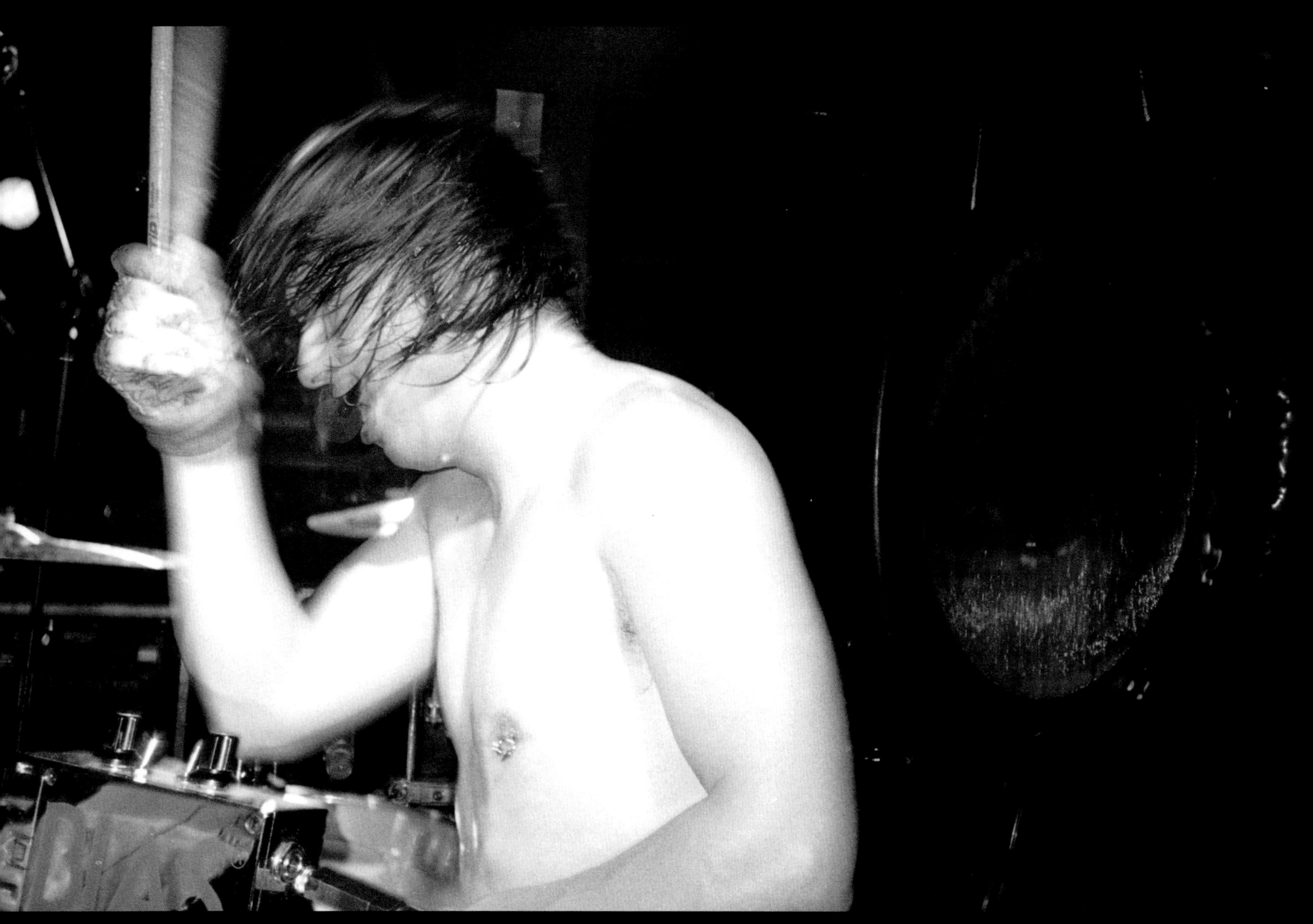

Dale Crover, Melvins, Black Cat / WDC, 2000

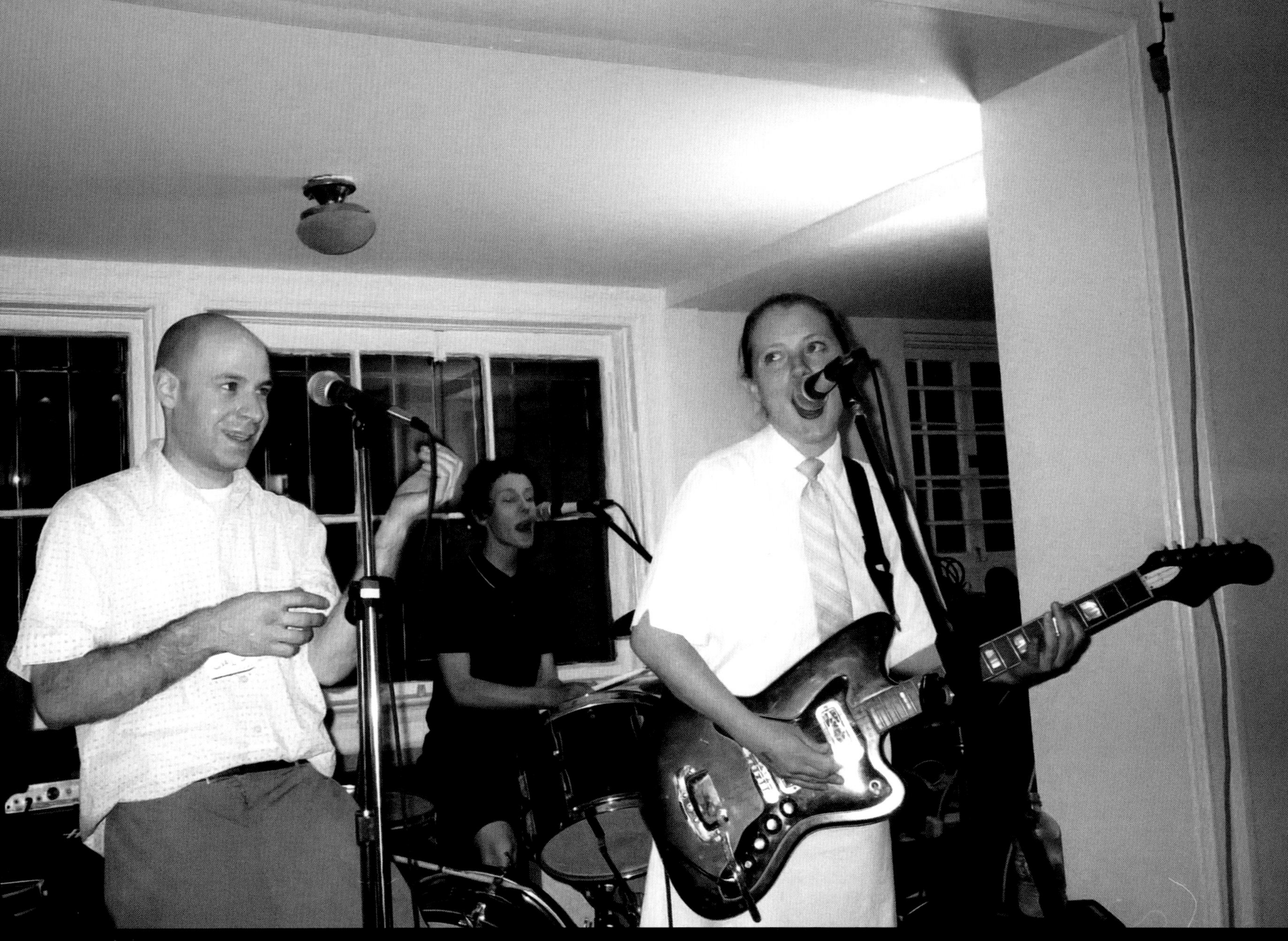

The Quails, La Casa / WDC, 2000

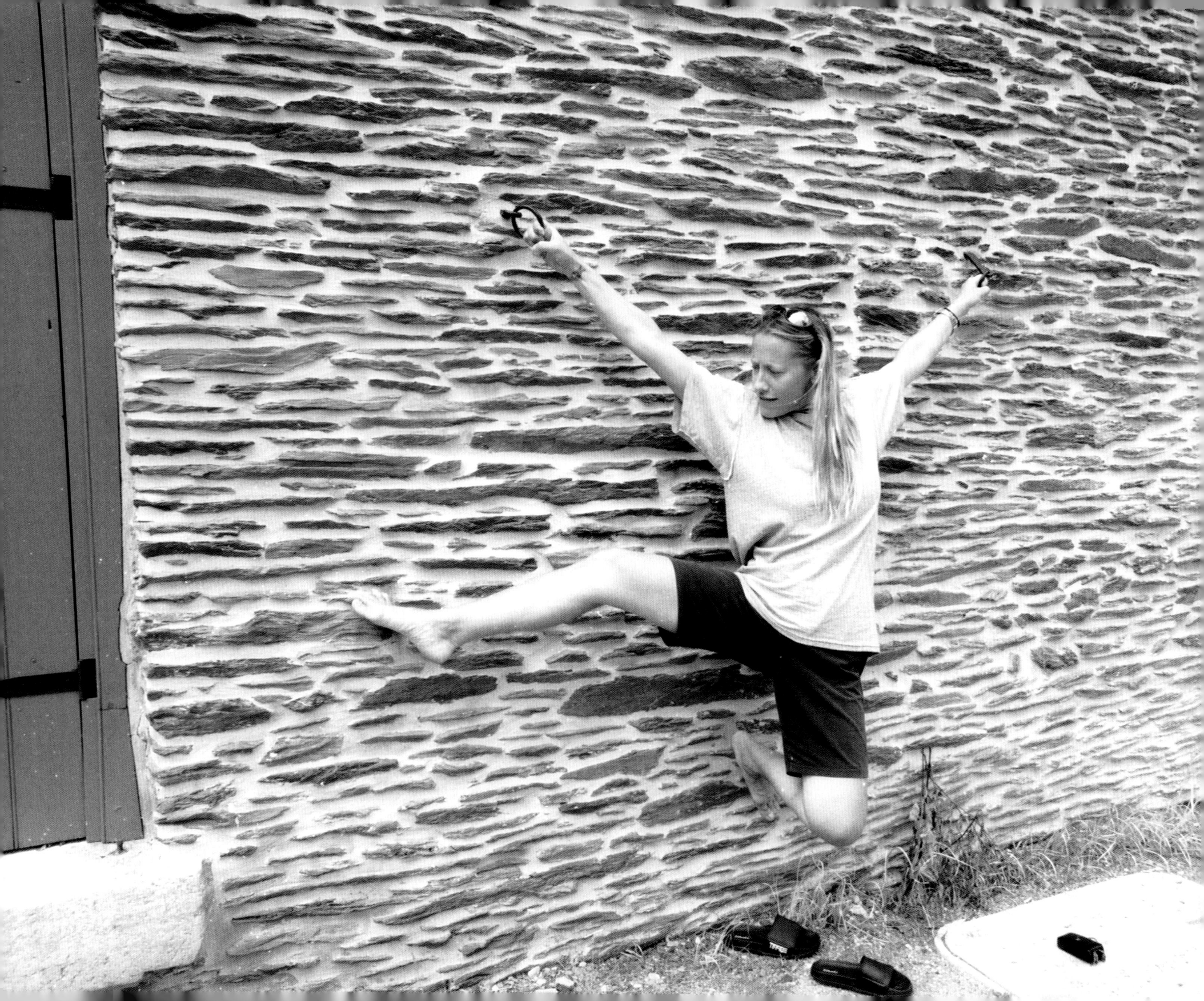

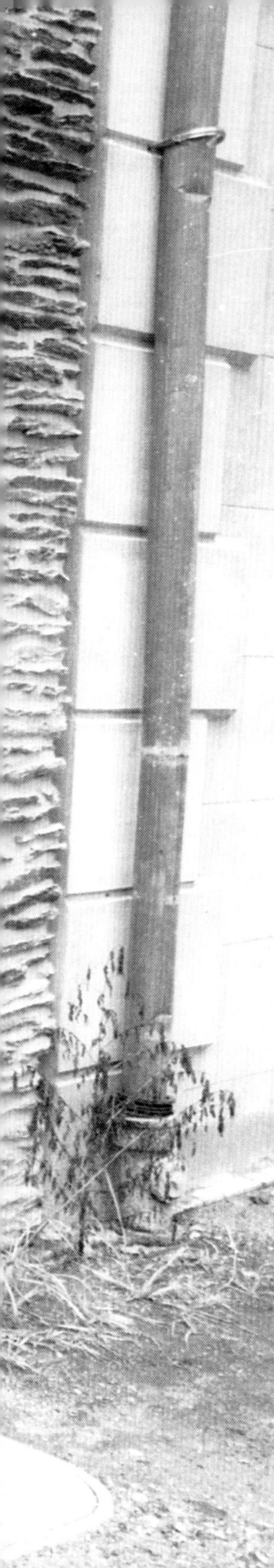

AMY PICKERING

I never dreamed of being in a rock band, I dreamed of singing with an orchestra. When I was a kid my mom forced me to take singing lessons, which I mostly hated except for the sensation of fully making use of "the instrument," a full-body activity. Then there was suffering through church services (again with my mother), where the only thing that I looked forward to was the postlude; after the service, I was allowed to go up into the apse, where the largest organ pipes were housed, and sit in front of the swell shades. When the organist turned up the volume for a particular passage of some massive Bach fugue, those swell shades flew open and the air and sound blasted over me. It was LOUD and it vibrated me to my core. It was the power of the music at such volume that I loved, so when I discovered punk bands my life shifted.

I continued to sing classical choral music (two hundred people loud), and I loved watching live music and singing along in the crowd, but the idea of being in a band eluded me. Performance anxiety? I dunno, but after being around bands and musicians in DC, and friends' repeated suggestions that I join a band, I allowed room for the idea of being part of the performing side of our world. I sang backups with some bands, which was fun, but not self-propelled. Truly, it was only the joining up with Natalie Avery, Nicky Thomas, and Kate Samworth that made a band feel like a possibility, and become a reality.

In the eighties, when I met people, I felt okay making assumptions about the way they thought, what they supported, what they didn't support—totally naive, but perhaps at the time I was mostly meeting people from our community, who I felt were very like-minded. Later, that feeling faded somewhat but I still felt that we understood the same power, that of music.

Performing is the most exciting thing about music for me, that closure of separation from the crowd—having them join us in what we were doing. The hardest thing about performing is when the audience isn't moved, and the best part is moving them.

The whole experience of touring Europe was incredible. The Dutch punk label De Konkurrent set up the tour and we were playing with one of my favorite bands of all time: Scream. The networks that were in place—shows, housing, food, everything—were eye-openers for me. The squat connection was fully happening and there was a deep sense of community at the places we played. The US didn't have this same feeling; there were pockets of community but often it felt much more disjointed, so this was amazing. The crowds were energetic and open-minded overall, and despite being a relatively unknown band, we were able to connect with people. The DC scene was a pretty politically minded group, but in Europe the communities seemed to me to be many times more active than we were. To this day, our touring in Europe informs my ideas about protest and community.

FIRE PARTY

Amy Pickering / Virginia, 1999

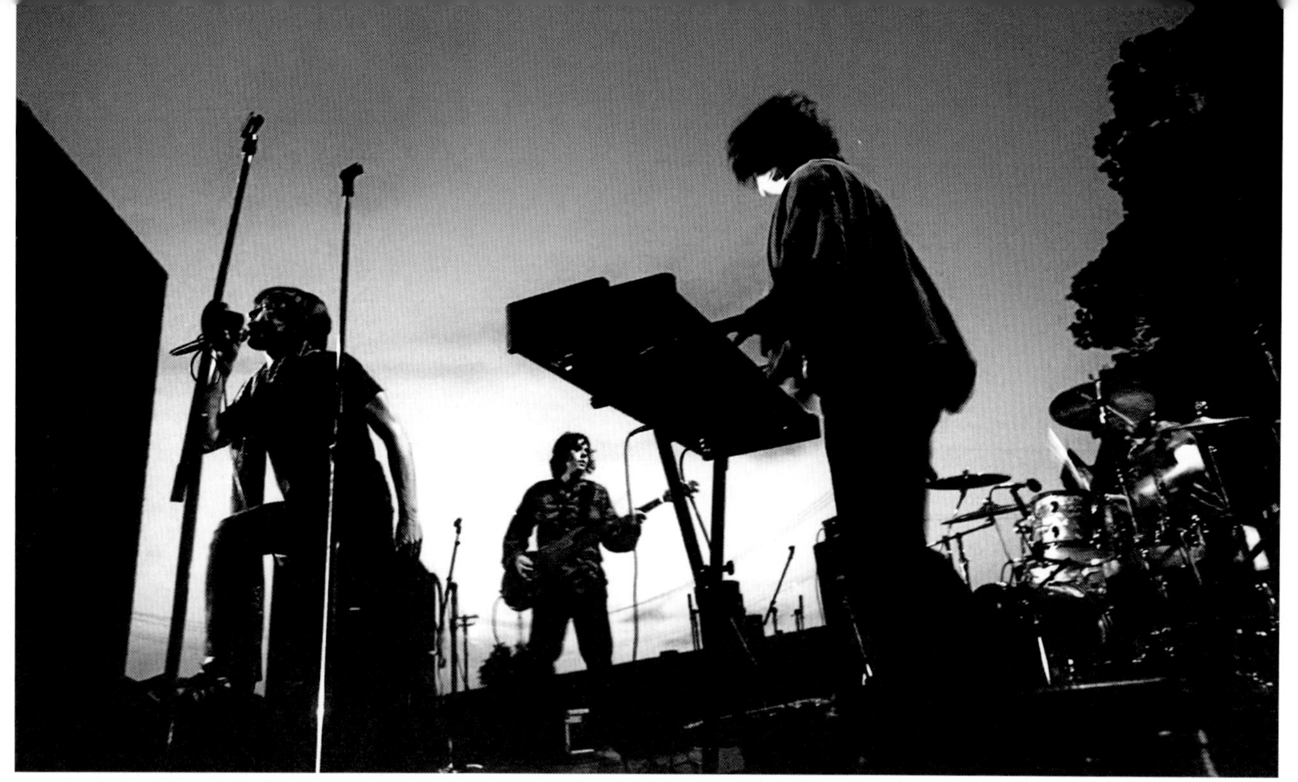

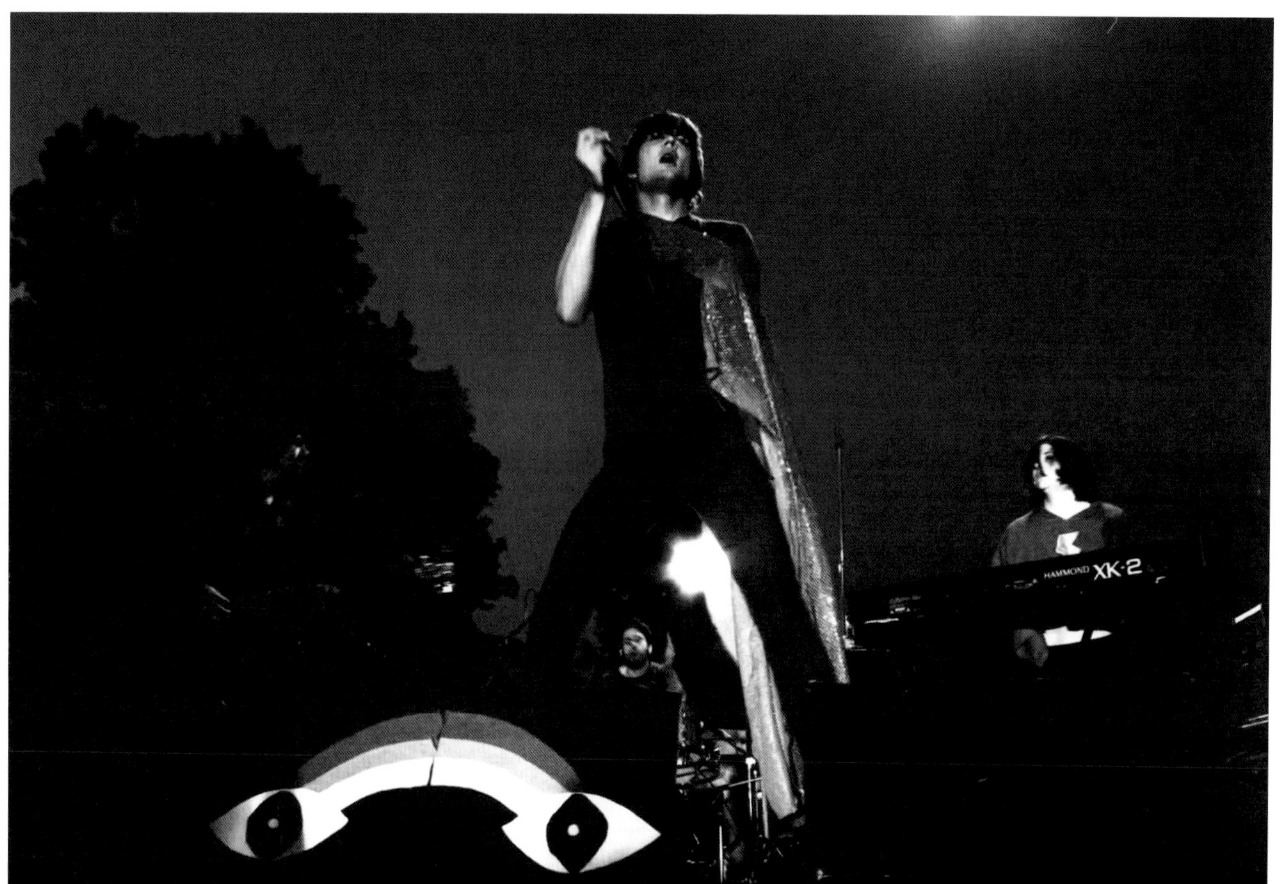

The Apes, Fort Reno / WDC, 2001
Opposite: Scott "Wino" Weinrich
with family / Maryland, 2001

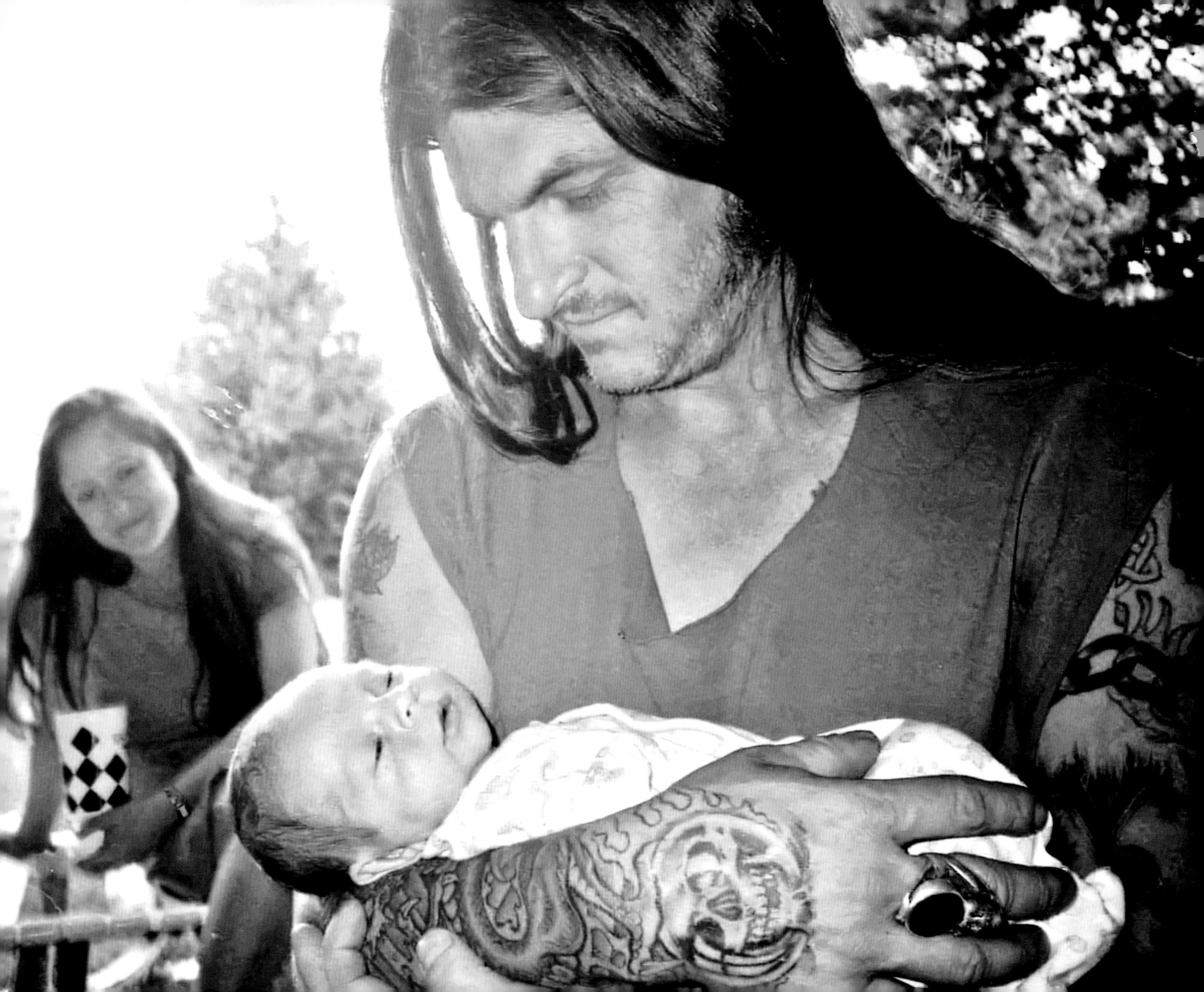

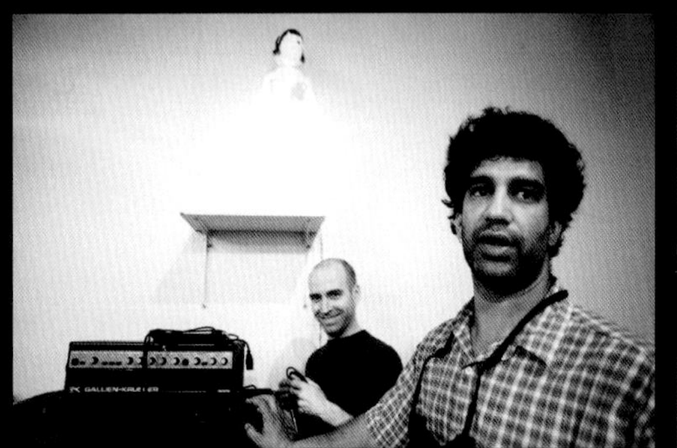
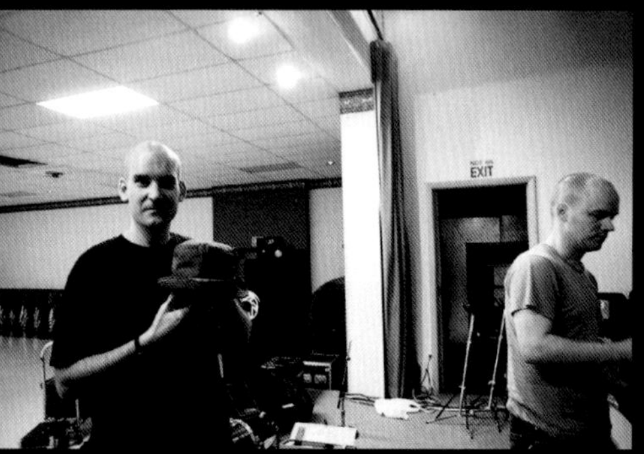

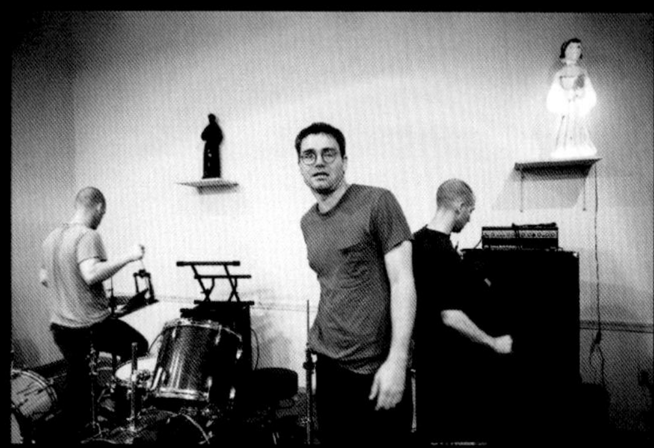
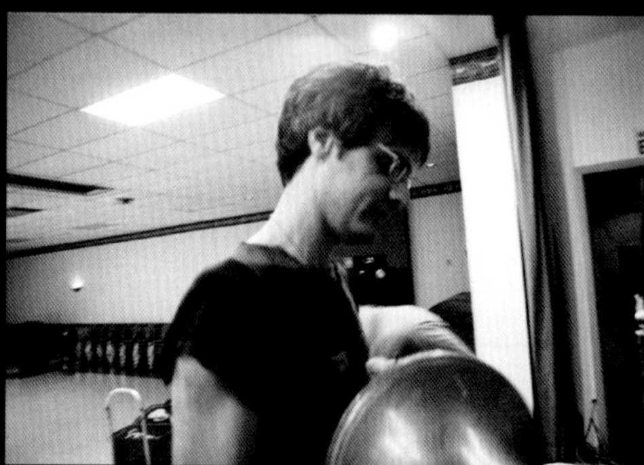

Fugazi and crew, Columbian Center / Severna Park, MD, 2001
Opposite: Lightning Bolt, Black Cat / WDC, 2001

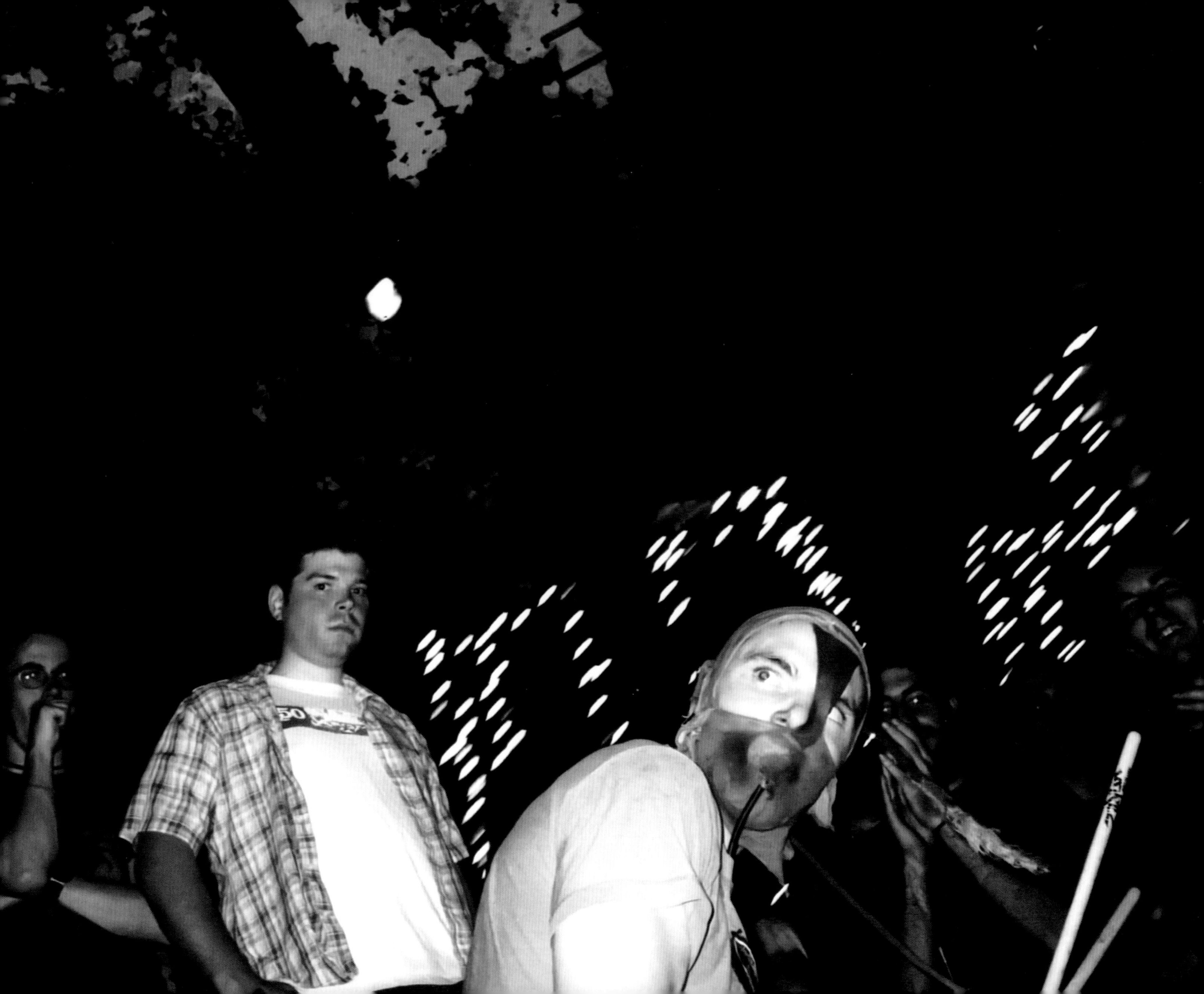

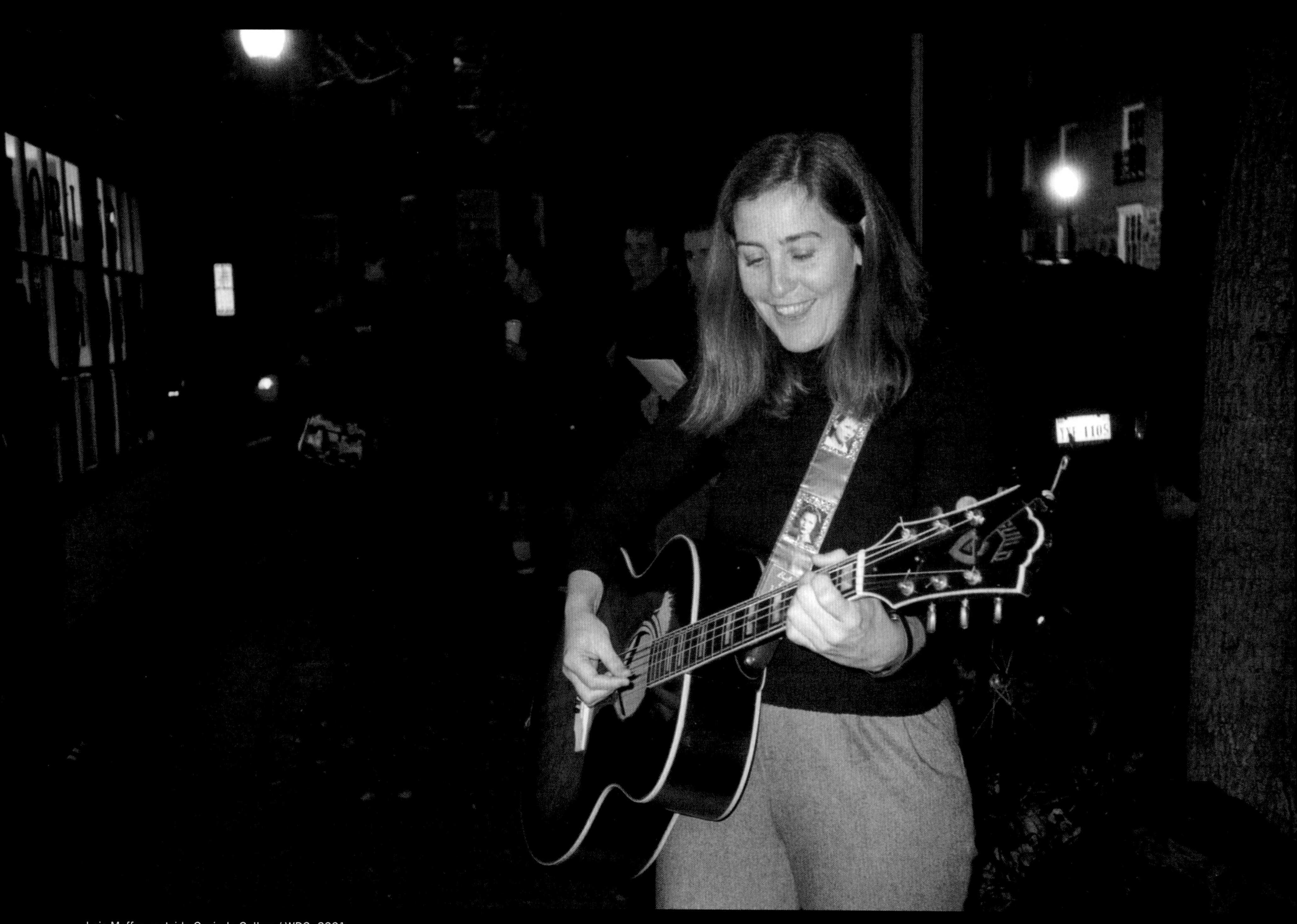

Lois Maffeo, outside Govinda Gallery / WDC, 2001

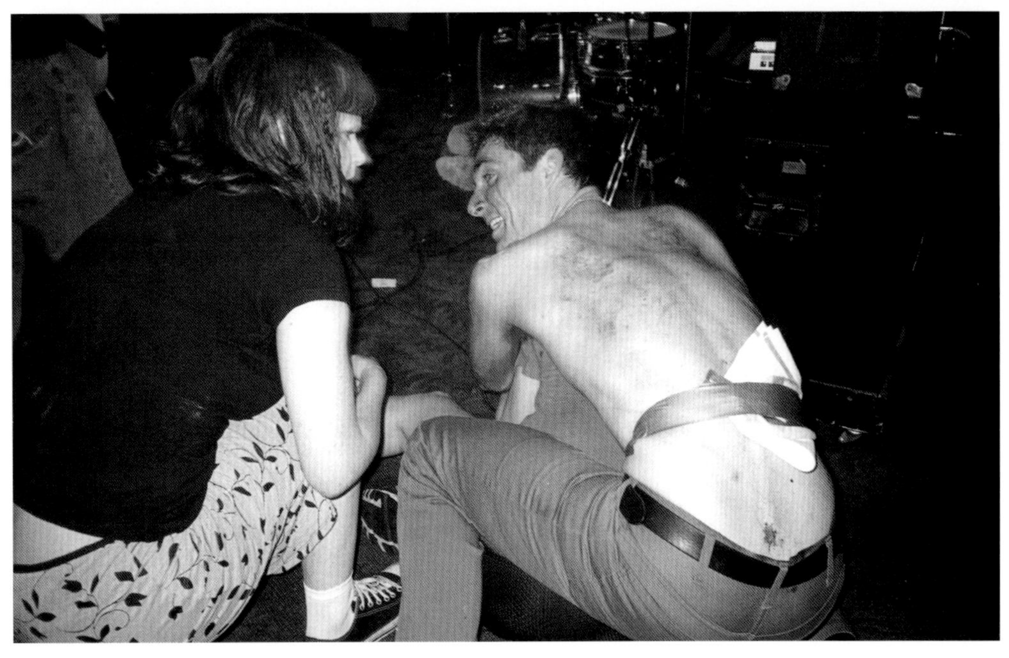

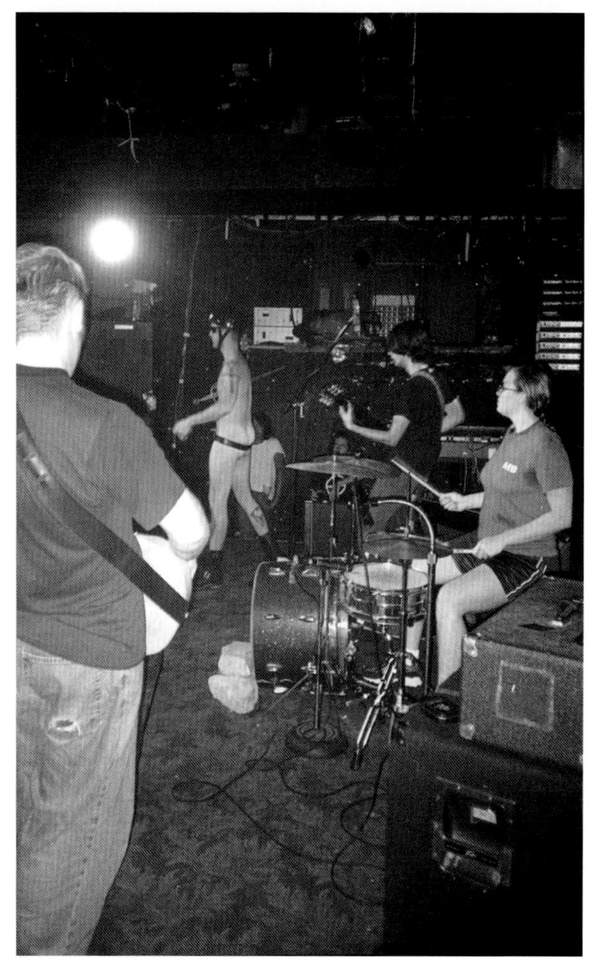

Clark Sabine, Motorcycle Wars, Black Cat / WDC, 2001

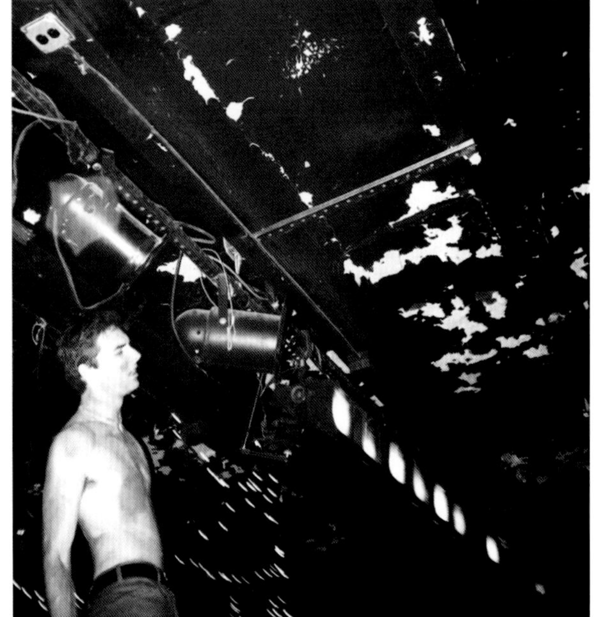

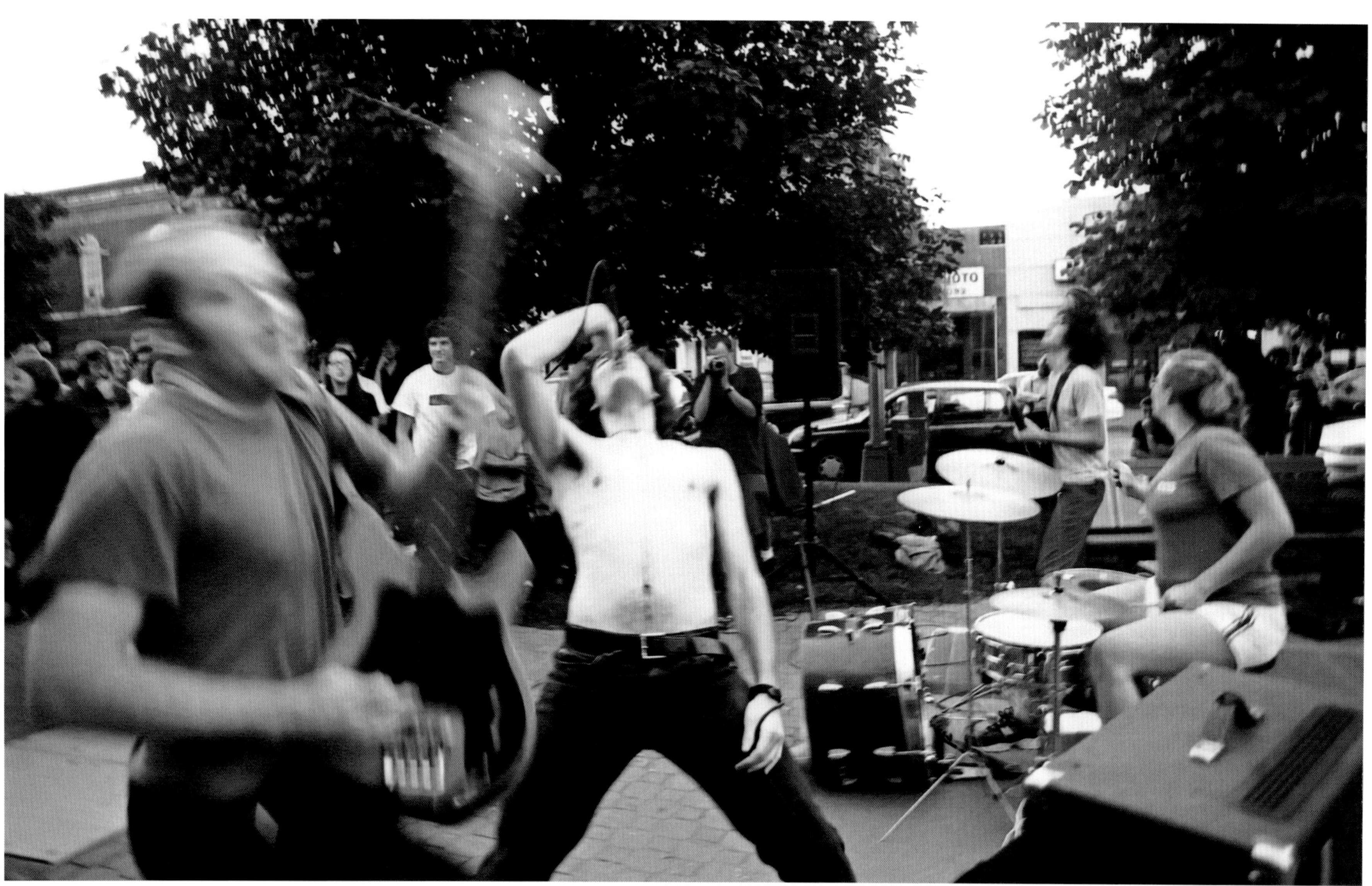

Motorcycle Wars, Clarendon Park / Arlington, VA, 2001

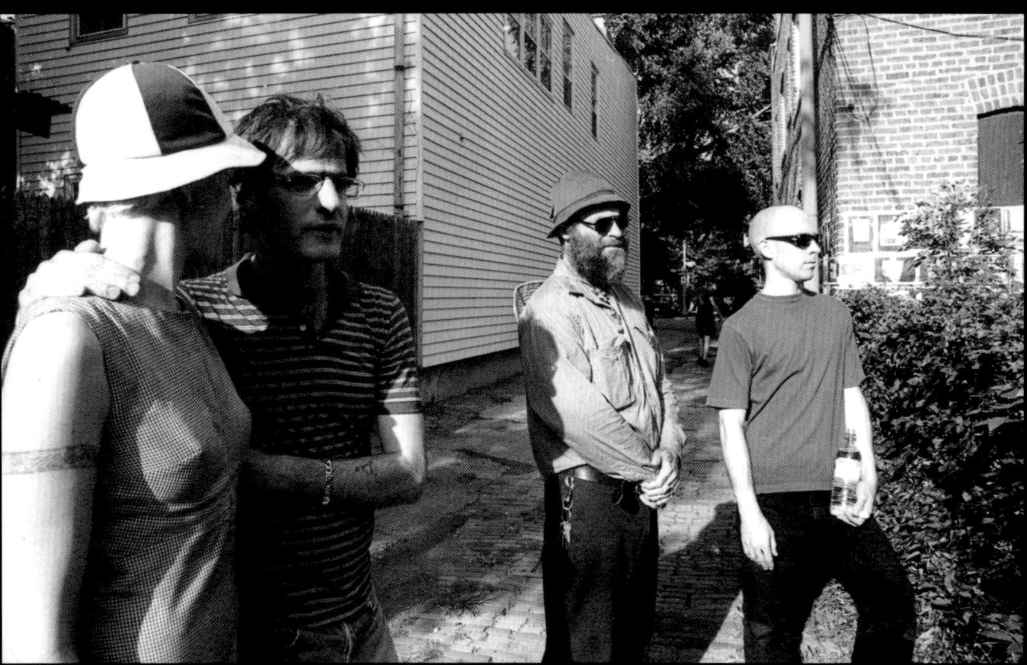

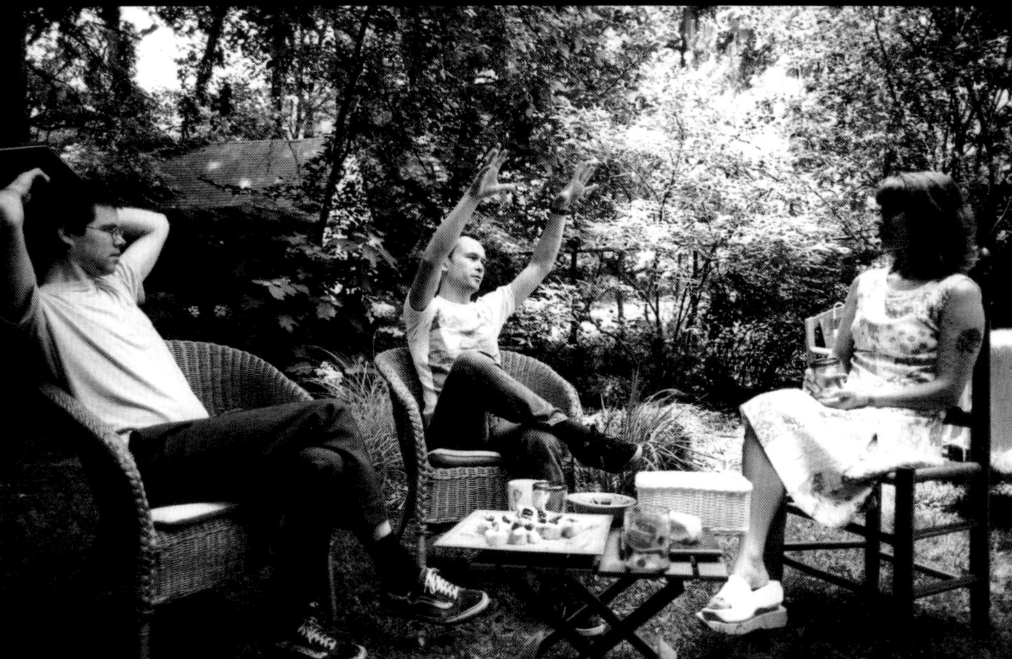

From top: Kathi, Guy, Daniel, and Joe, 2001; birthday party: Eddie, Alec, and Allison / WDC, 2001

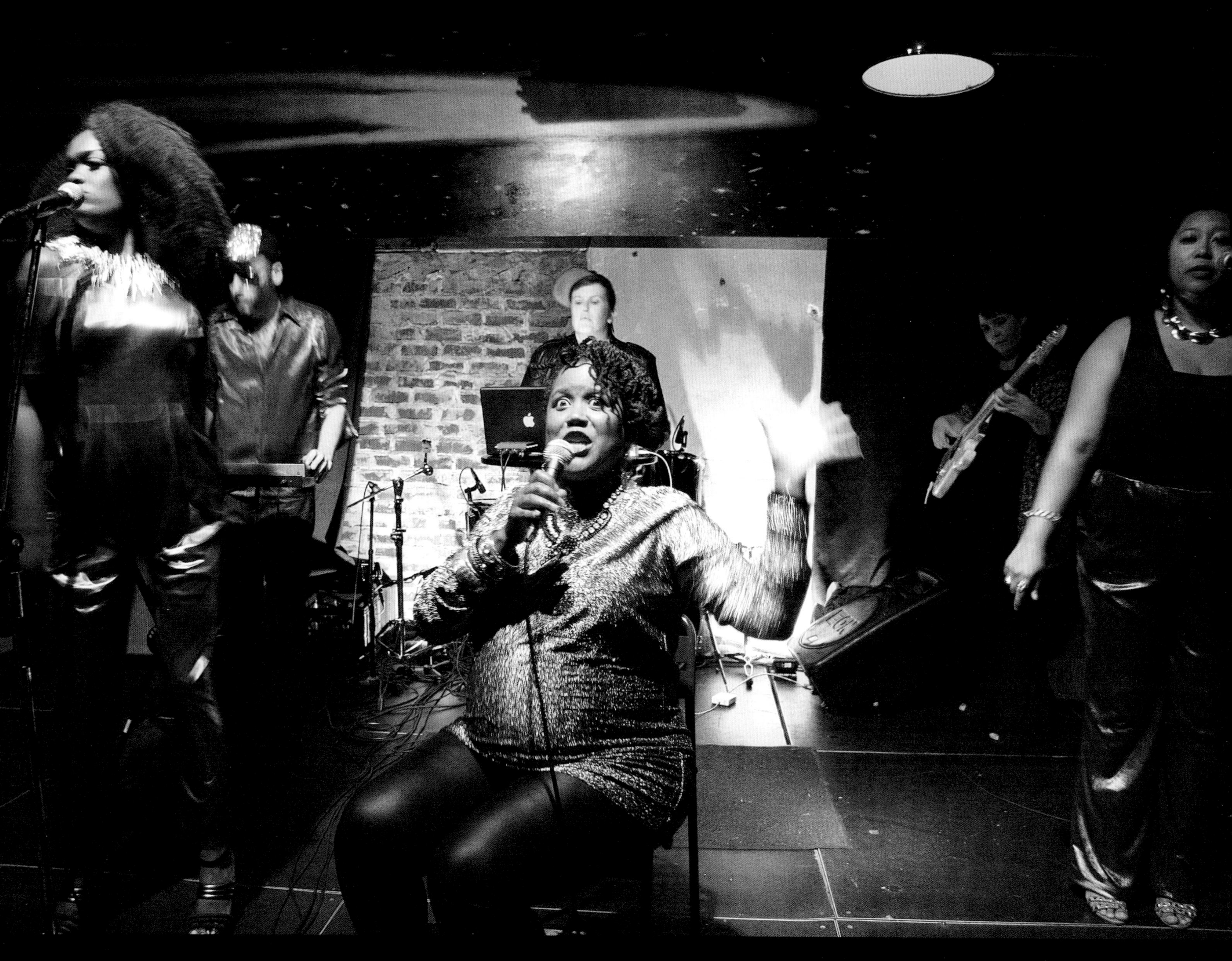

KRISTINA SAUVAGE

We started making music together because voices like ours seldom get heard. Representation matters and so much of our music is about reflecting and celebrating who we are, what we love, and where we come from. We got tired of straight white dudes taking up so much space, not just in music but everywhere. And since we didn't see spaces for people like us, we made our own.

Forming Coup Sauvage has been a way to center the experiences of folks who are on the margins. Making music allows us to not only reflect our world but also imagine the world we want to see—one that's way more brown, way more feminist, way more queer, and way more fierce. We're a band that doesn't really fit in anywhere. We know we don't necessarily look or sound like your typical punk or indie band. But we're equally as inspired by weird postpunk as we are the sweaty release of disco and sophistication of Motown girl groups. But that's also what makes us do what we do. We want to challenge assumptions about what a band is supposed to be like. Or how people like us are supposed to act.

For us, there's something transgressive about a group of mostly women screaming, dancing, and wilding out onstage. Especially when there are three black women in front wearing sequined gowns singing about things like gentrification and street harassment while doing choreographed dance moves. Making music is a way for us to be defiantly glamorous, radical, and irreverent, all at the same time. Things that women aren't always allowed to be or that we can't always be in our day-to-day lives. We're also driven by this notion of dance floors as sites of liberation and solidarity. We think there's power in bringing people together on the dance floor. We have a lot to get off our chest and the dance floor is where we can bring our outrage, our pain, our joy, everything. It's just this place of release, affirmation, and shared community.

Most of the band members come from activist and social justice backgrounds. So music is another way for us to get our message heard. And writing songs is a far more danceable way for us to agitate and organize. People are far more willing to talk about issues like displacement and police brutality when they're set to bangin' club beats. We're not making policy here, we're making people move their asses. But we've seen over and over again how that can spark dialogue in some really interesting ways.

KRISTINA SAUVAGE:
FIRST LADIES DJ COLLECTIVE • COUP SAUVAGE

MAEGAN SAUVAGE:
FIRST LADIES DJ COLLECTIVE • SHE-REX • COUP SAUVAGE

CRYSTAL SAUVAGE:
DOWNBEAT:BEATDOWN • COUP SAUVAGE

JASON SAUVAGE:
HOTT BEAT • TROLL TAX • GAUCHE • FLAMERS • COOL PEOPLE • COUP SAUVAGE

ELIZABETH SAUVAGE:
MESS UP THE MESS • TROLL TAX • COUP SAUVAGE

RAIN SAUVAGE:
COUP SAUVAGE

Coup Sauvage and the Snips, Comet Ping Pong / WDC, 2016

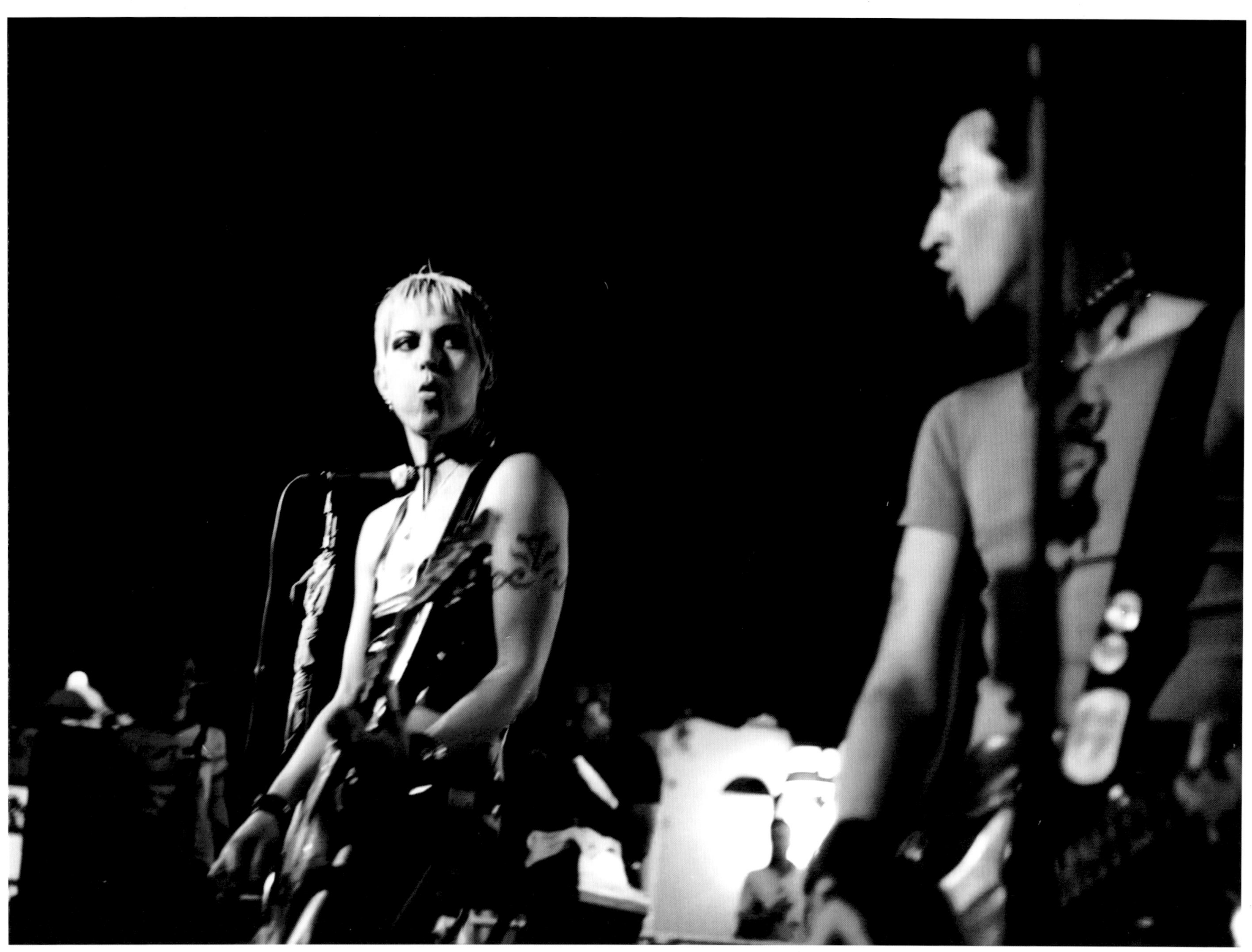

Joan Jett / WDC, 2002
Opposite: Bratmobile, Black Cat / WDC, 2002

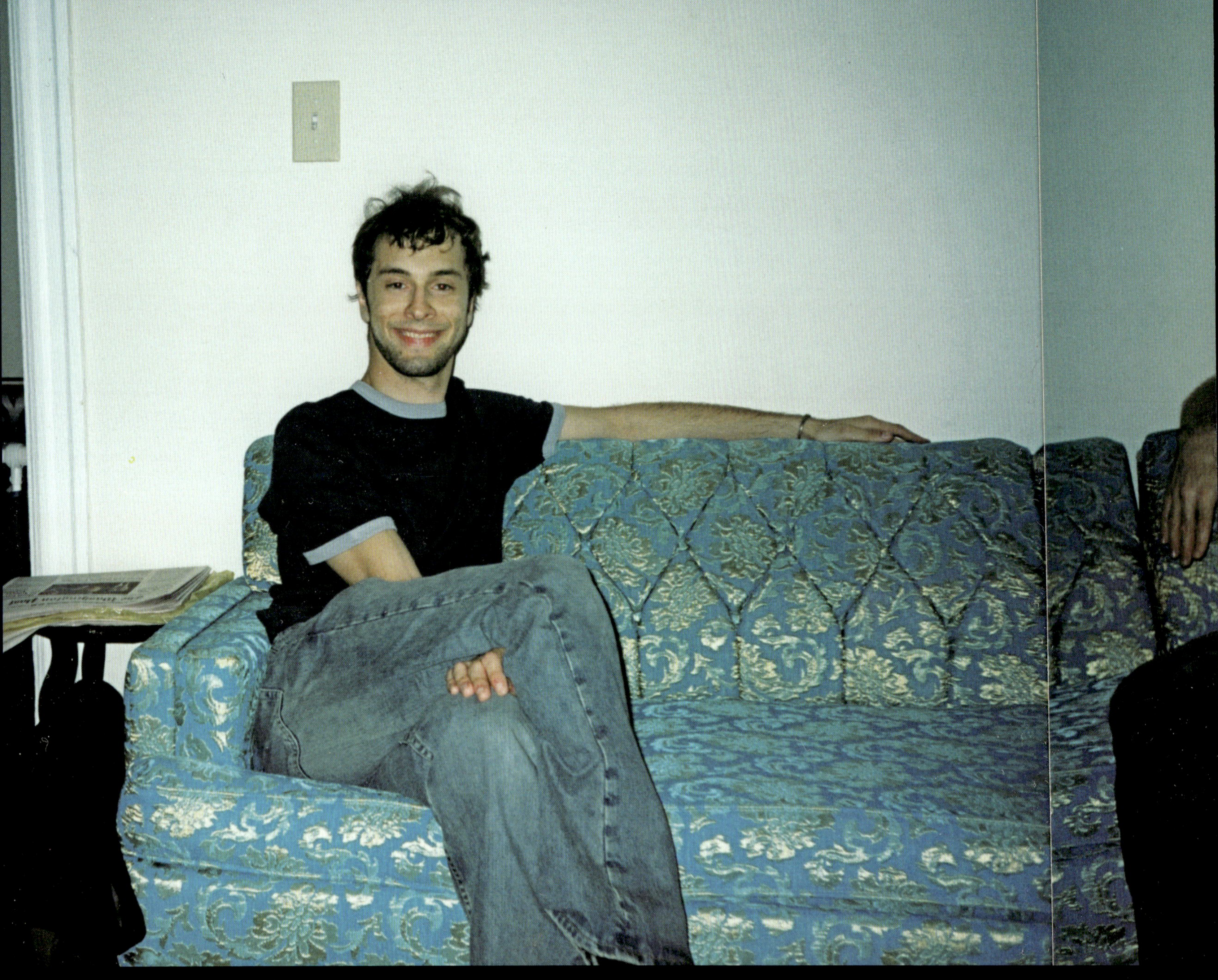

The Black Sea, Holmead Place NW / WDC, 2002

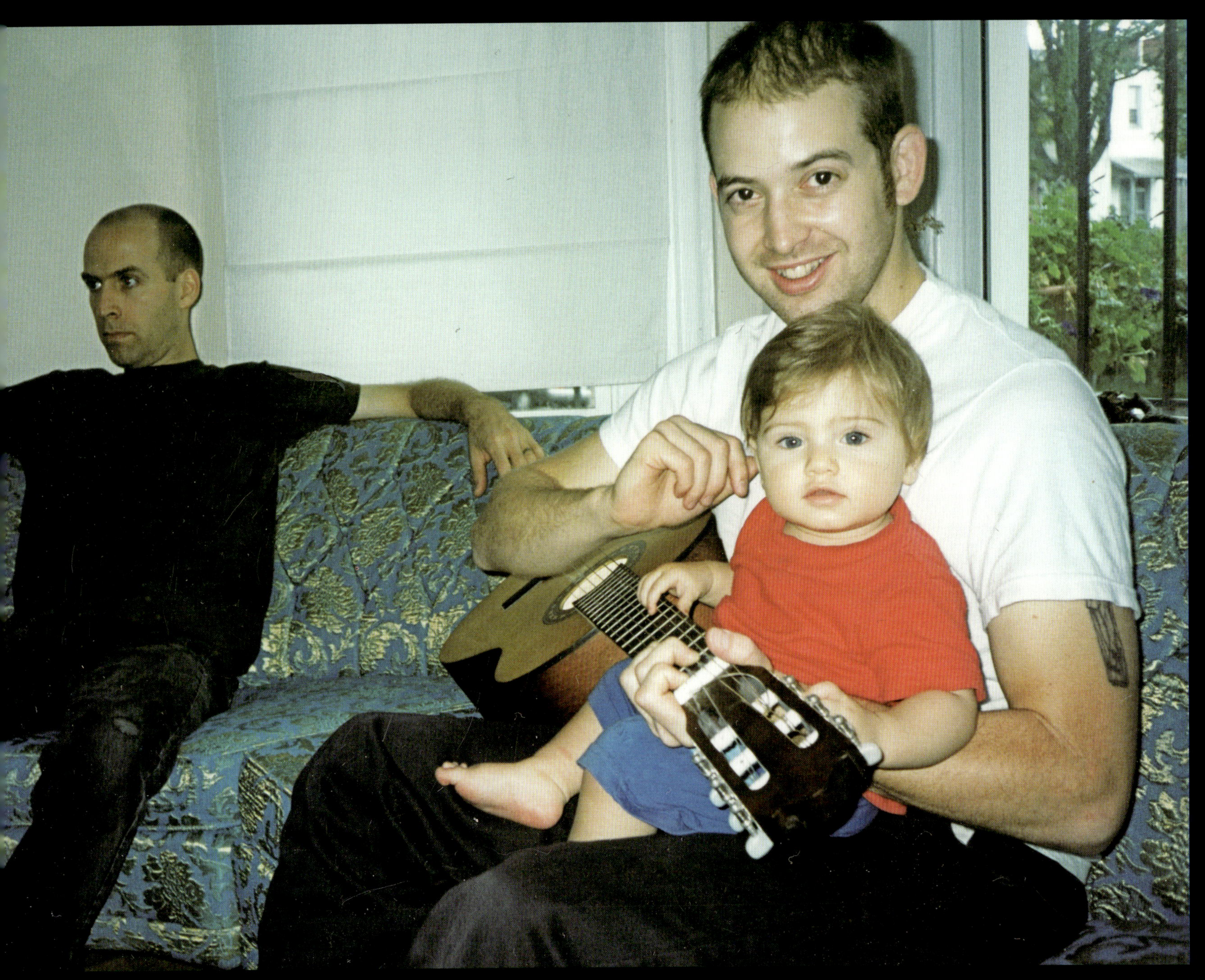

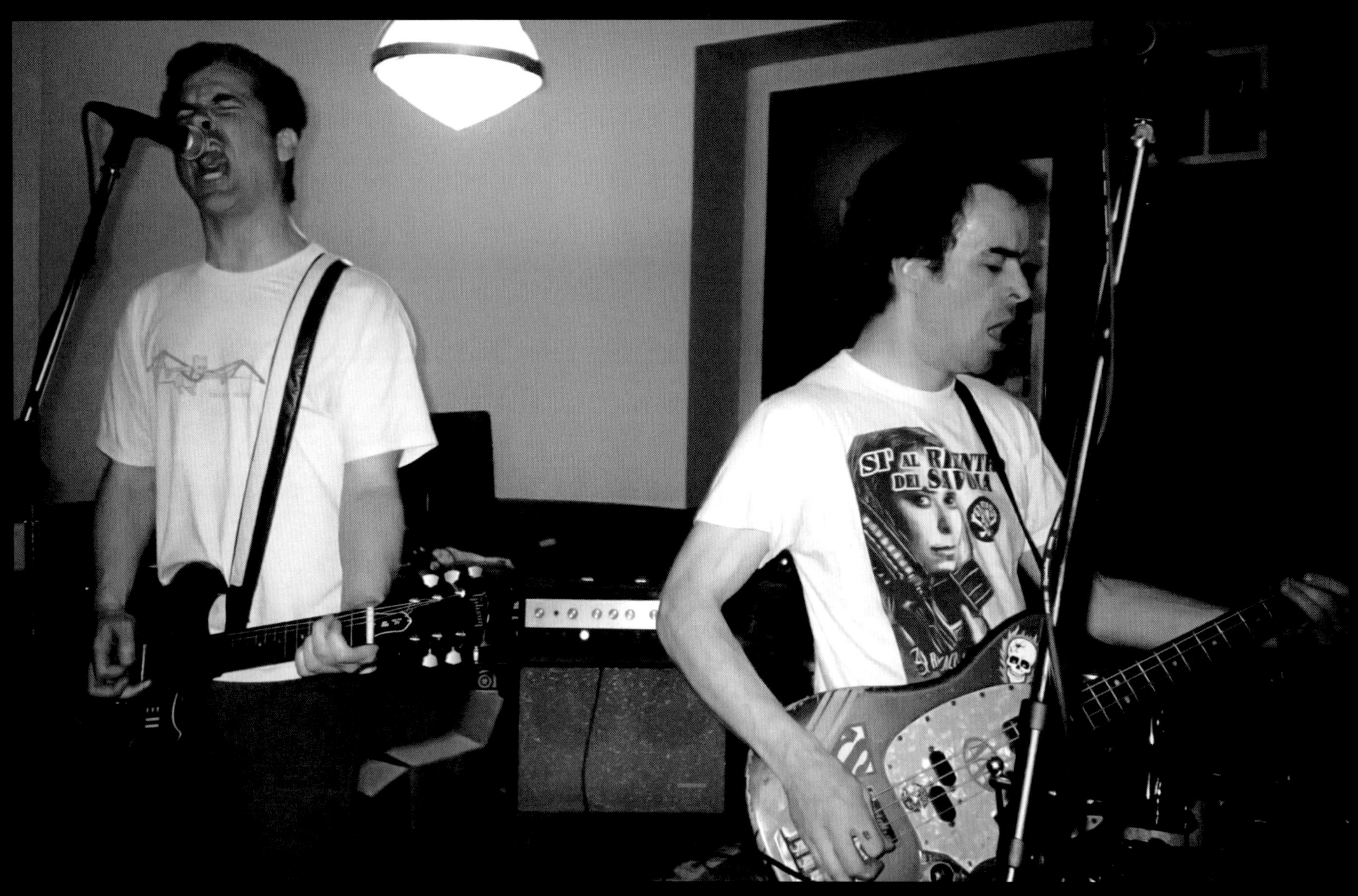

Capitol City Dusters, Firehook Bakery / WDC, 2003

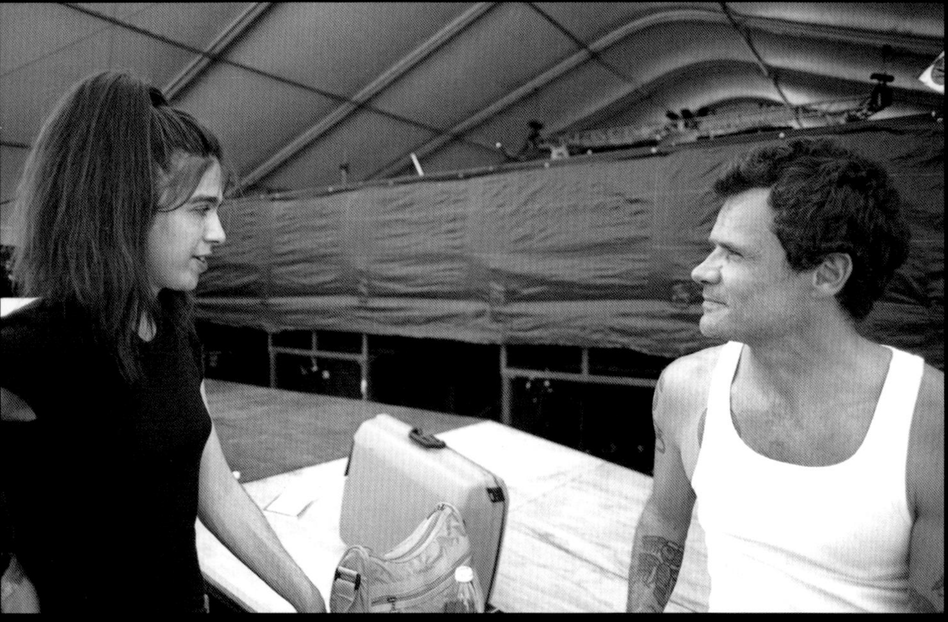

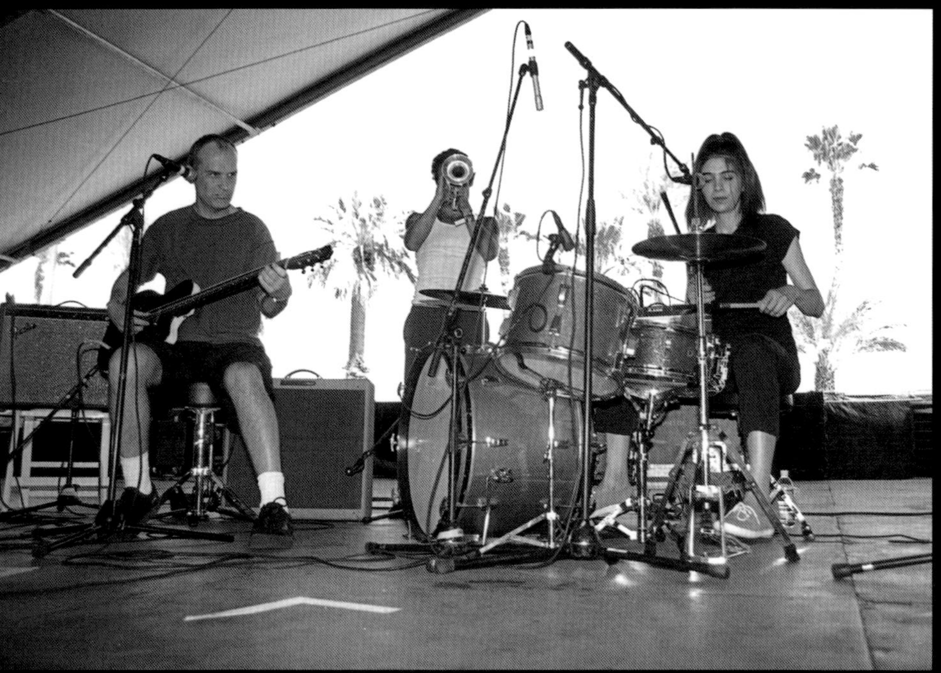

From top, Amy Farina and Flea, Coachella / Indio, CA, 2003; The Evens with Flea, Coachella / Indio, CA, 2003

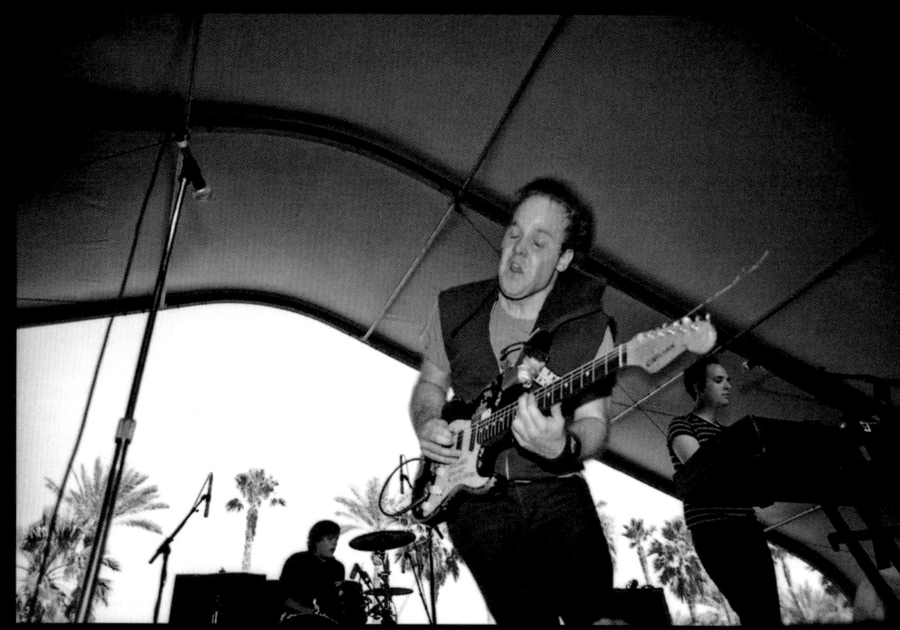

Q and Not U, Coachella / Indio, CA, 2003

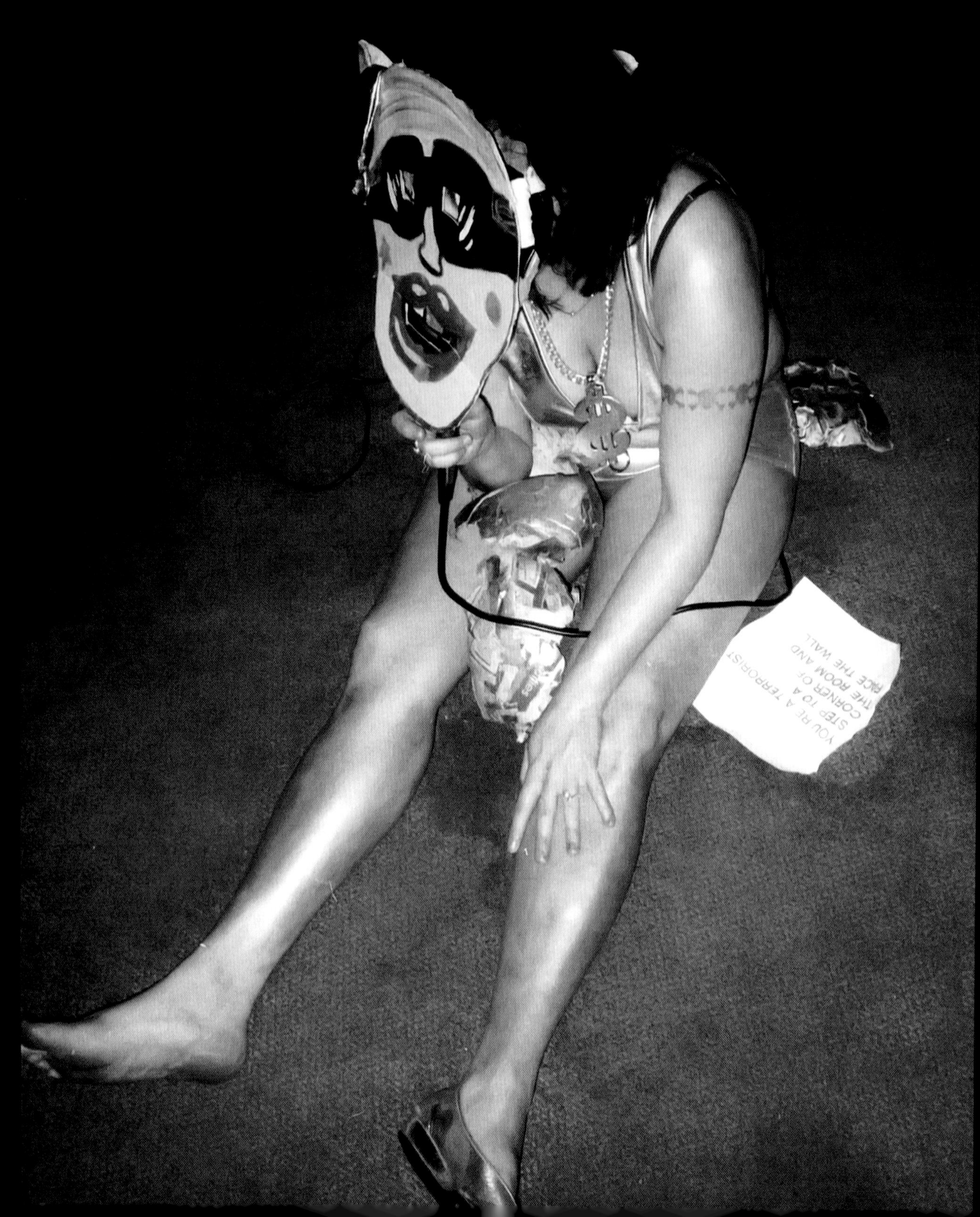
YOU'RE A TERRORIST
STEP TO A
CORNER OF
THE ROOM AND
FACE THE WALL

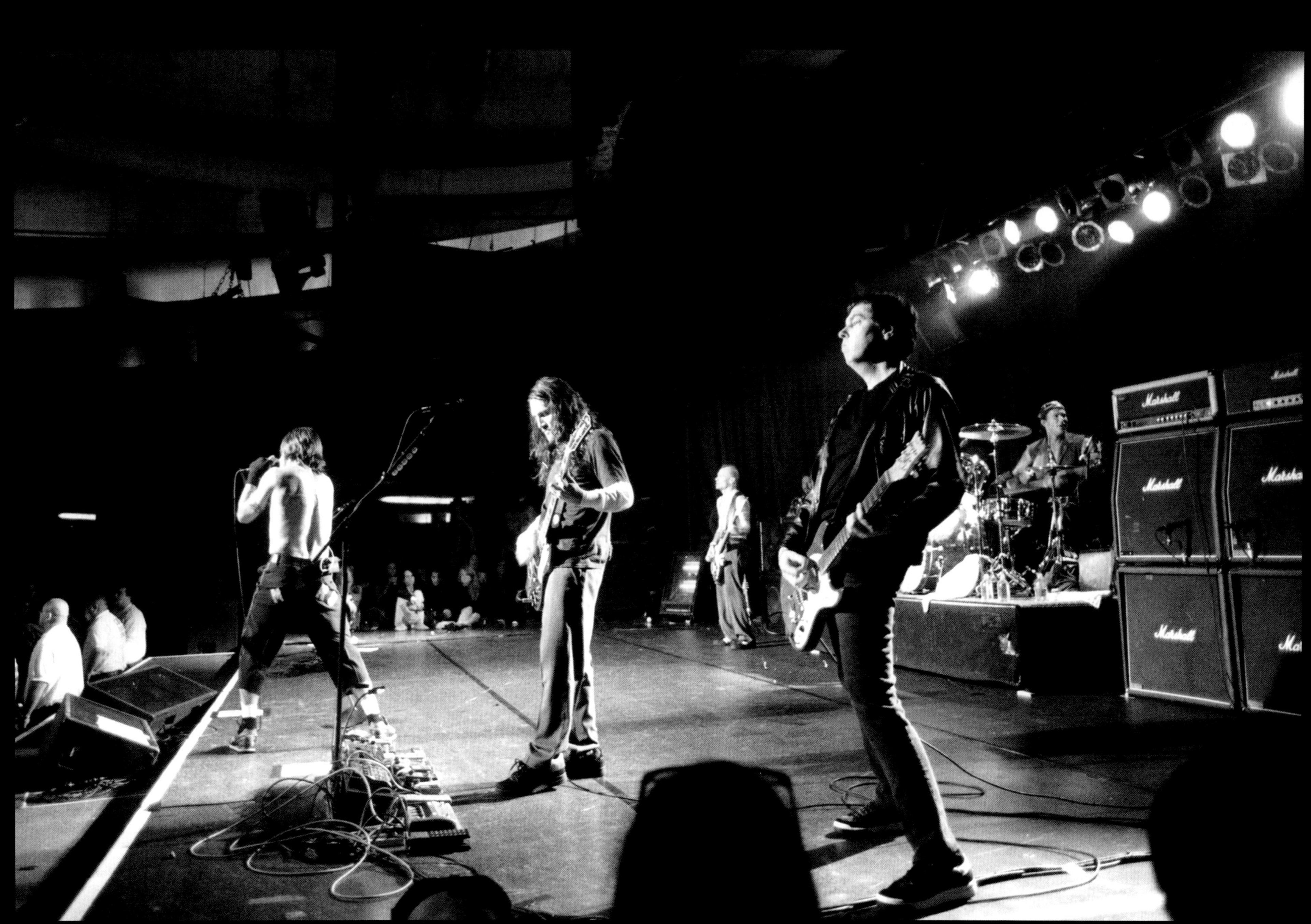

Red Hot Chili Peppers with Johnny Ramone, Hollywood Palladium / Hollywood, CA, 2003
Opposite: Angela Melkisethian, Hott Beat, La Casa / WDC, 2003

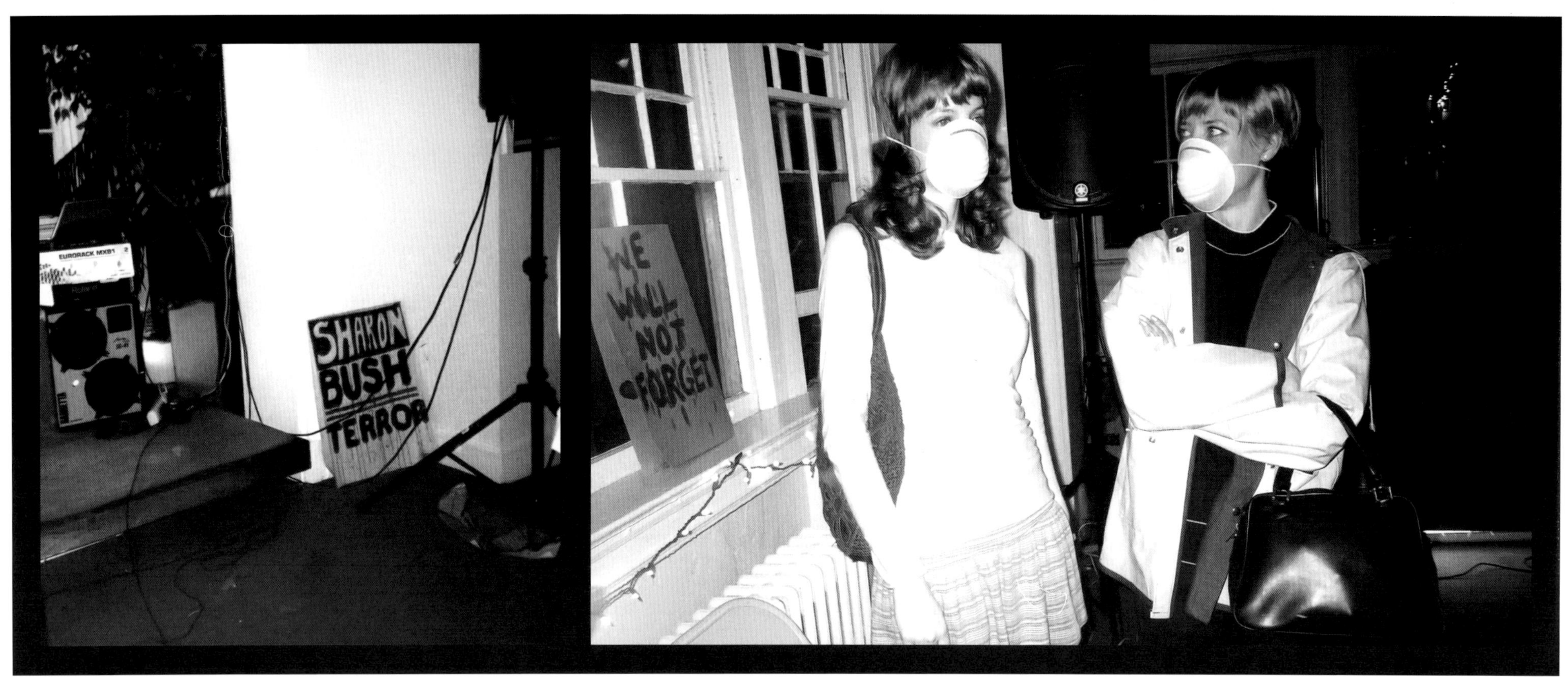

From left: La Casa / WDC, 2003; Garnett Soles and Christina Billotte, La Casa / WDC, 2003
Opposite: The Routineers, Black Cat / WDC, 2003

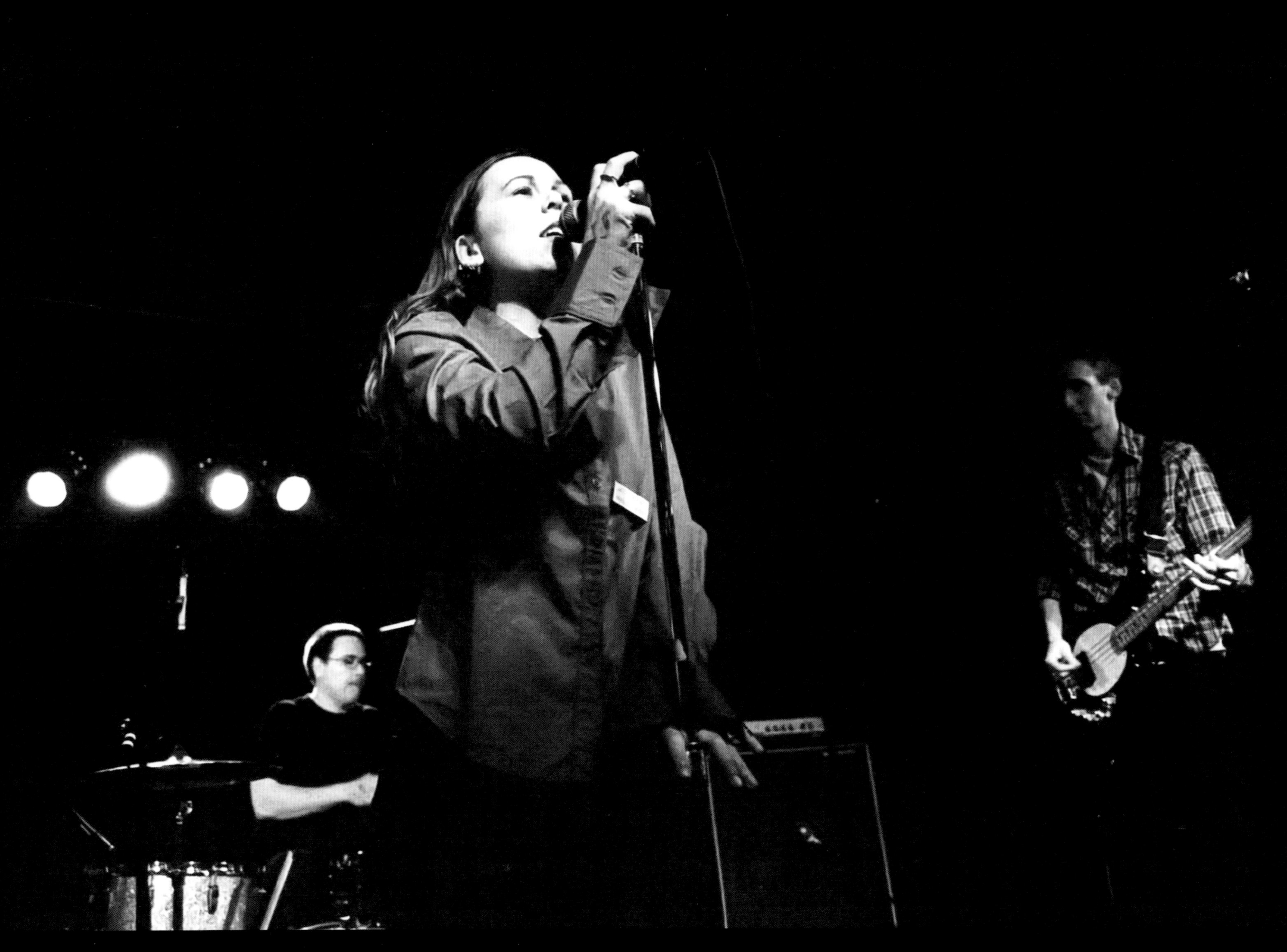

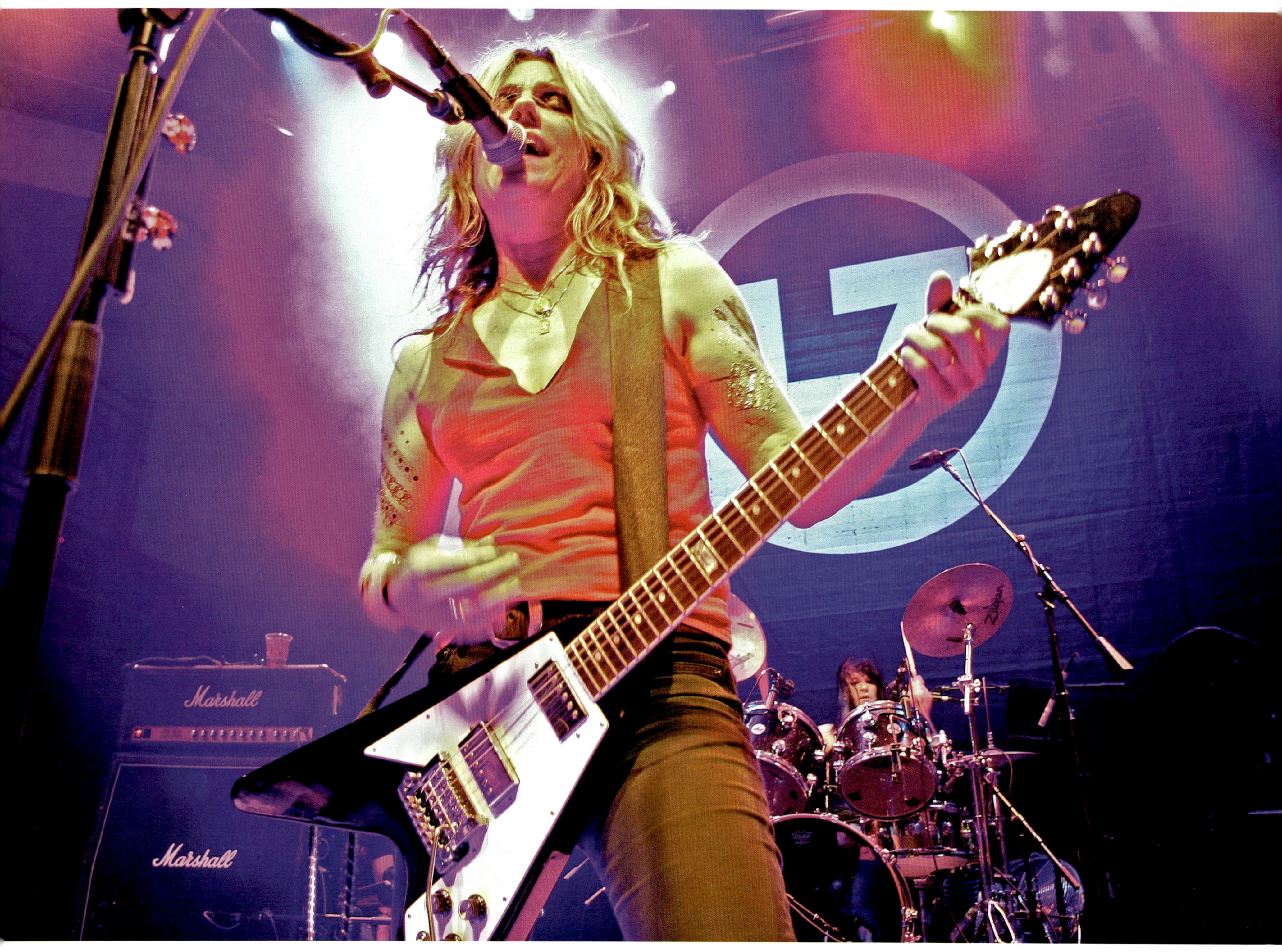
Marshall
Marshall

DONITA SPARKS

Music has always been my fantasy tool, my transporter to other places, other lives. It has served as my Dream Machine, a time traveler, a shapeshifter. As early as I can remember I've loved Hollywood musicals, Girl Scout camp songs, school choir, and dance lessons. I'd listen to the radio late into the night spinning the dial from end to end. Because I have older siblings, rock and roll and soul were always in the house as well, along with my parents' jazz and Broadway cast albums.

My sister went away to college and came back with punk records and an electric guitar. I'd watch her practice rudimentary scales. The movement of her fingers fascinated me. I took a few guitar lessons on my own, but once I learned how to make a barre chord and play a couple of Ramones songs, I quit the lessons. That's all I felt I needed. I actually haven't progressed that much in my technical playing since then.

I'm not in love with playing guitar especially. I am not what they call a "musician's musician" and I find conversing about gear insufferably boring. What gets me off is a good melody, vibe, and groove. I'm more of a right-brain musician. I play by ear and have my own shortcuts to get me where I need to go. My limitations give me my own style. That's the thing about punk rock which is so liberating: you don't have to be a great technical player to have a cool, unique thing going on with your sound.

In fact, it always strikes me as ironic when some dude who happens to see me sound checking or something inevitably asks me in that smiling, passive-aggressive way, "Why do you play that chord like that?" or, "You know, you should play that like this." In the moment it might make me feel insecure, even though I know in my heart that they are just a bit jealous and trying to put me down. See, when you have something going for you that's unique, that is way more elusive to obtain than technical chops. You can be the best player in the world, yet cannot come up with a catchy riff if your life depended on it. Some musicians (usually non–punk rockers) get very pissed off about this. To them it's all about the amount of noodles, not the taste of the sauce.

That said, I have A LOT of respect for people who can play really well, so I hope that I don't sound disrespectful or cavalier about the craft. I'm just speaking for myself.

Art is not fair. Some people spend many years working toward something to get nowhere, and some can write a classic song in thirty seconds. It's just the way it is.

But the discipline that it takes to be a proficient player is super cool in itself. I'm blown away by people who are great players, but I'm also blown away by bands with energy that sound like they're about to fly off the rails.

When Suzi Gardner and I started L7, we wanted to do something cool, something creative, something fun just for the hell of it. Our goals were very small when we started, but our dream was to be a really good band. Being a BIG band didn't even come into our heads. It was about having the "band" experience and expressing ourselves.

Along with the music, of course, is performance, and for me at least, the physicality of showmanship is a high. I love walking off a stage exhausted and drenched in sweat, hopefully with the feeling that I gave it all I've got. I think everyone at a rock show wants to experience some kind of transcendent out-of-body moment, either as an audience member or performer. It's a cool, powerful thing. I have to remind myself to appreciate the experience, to have a good time, take it seriously, but not get overly precious about it.

That's my secret sauce. L7's power as a unit is more than the sum of its parts. Back to the elusive . . . we had chemistry. Any one of us on our own may not have amounted to much, but together, well, that's another story.

L7

Donita Sparks, 9:30 Club / WDC, 2016

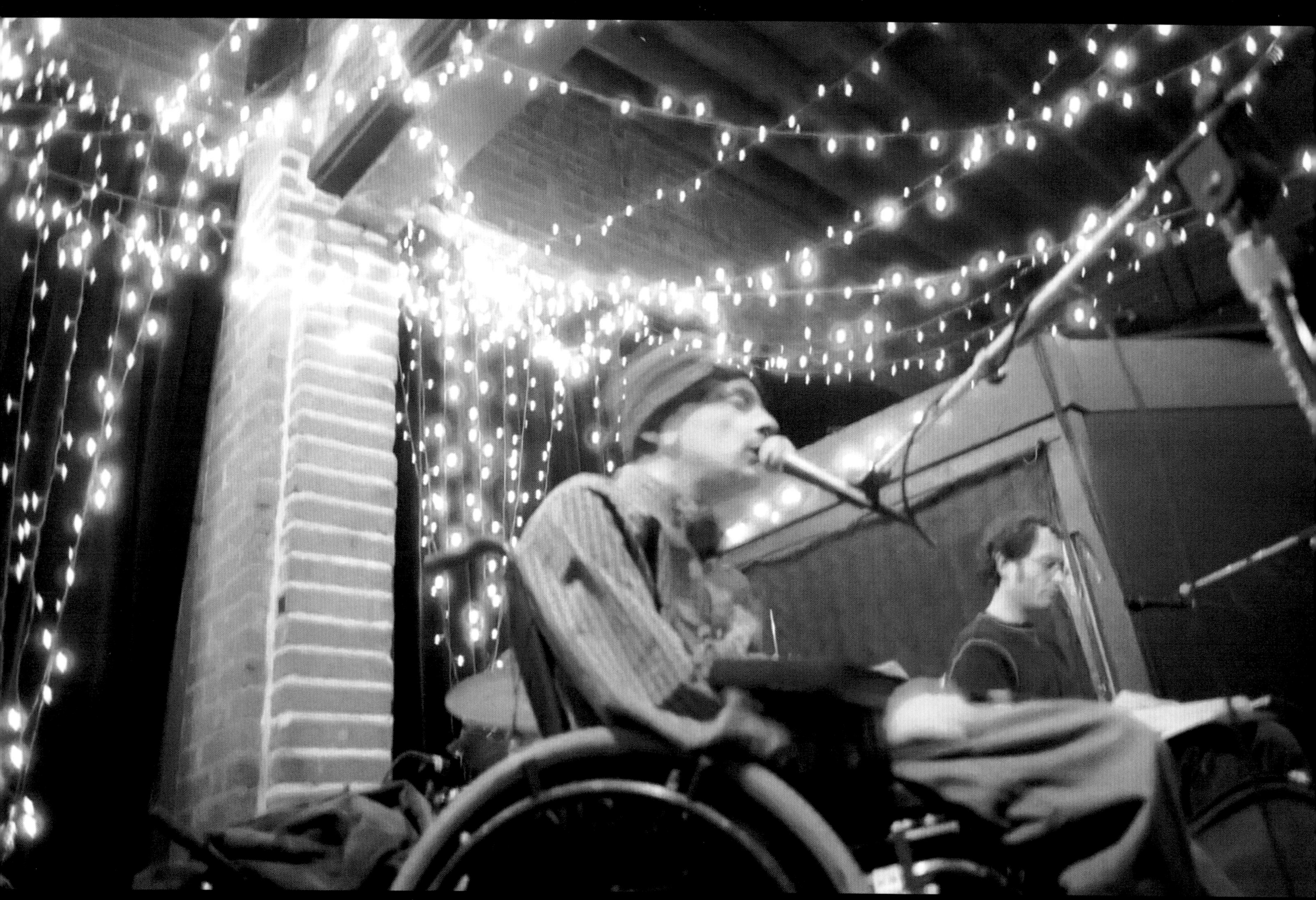
Vic Chesnutt, Iota Club / Arlington, VA, 2003

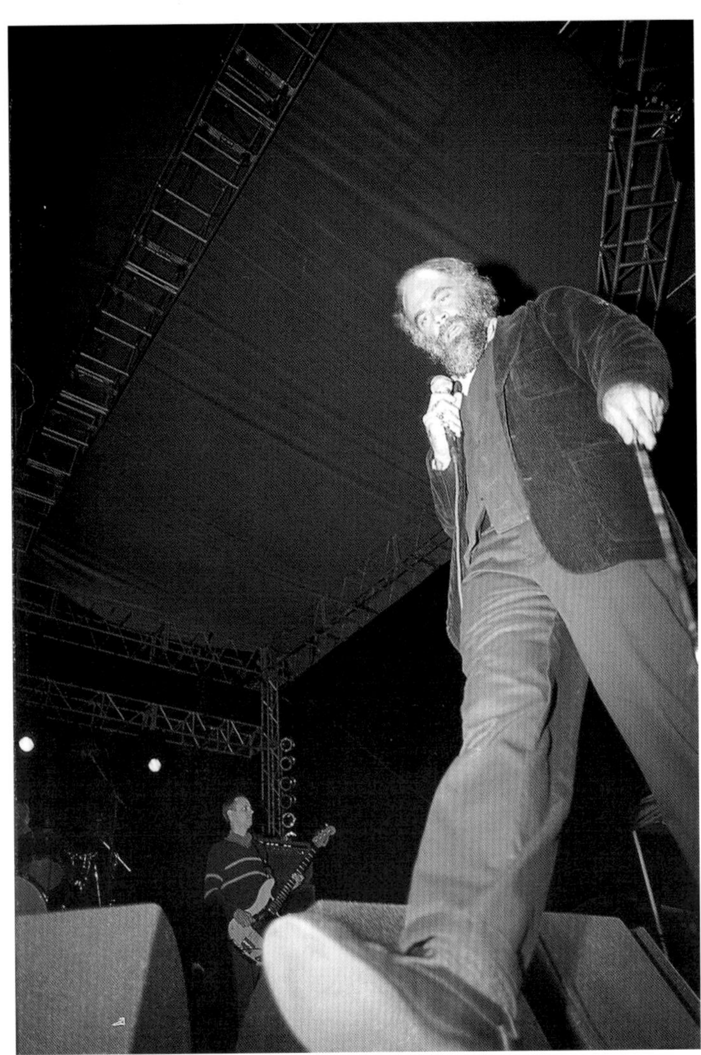

Lungfish, All Tomorrow's Parties / Long Beach, CA, 2004

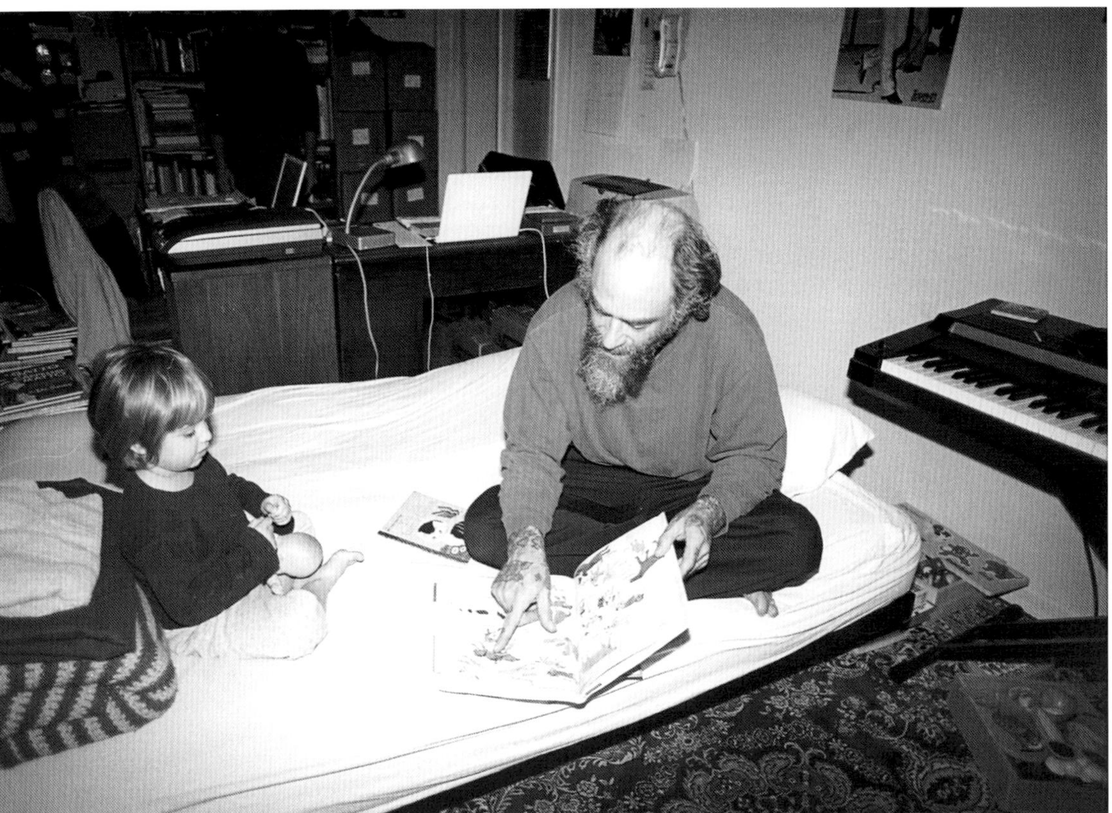

Daniel Higgs / Los Angeles, CA, 2004

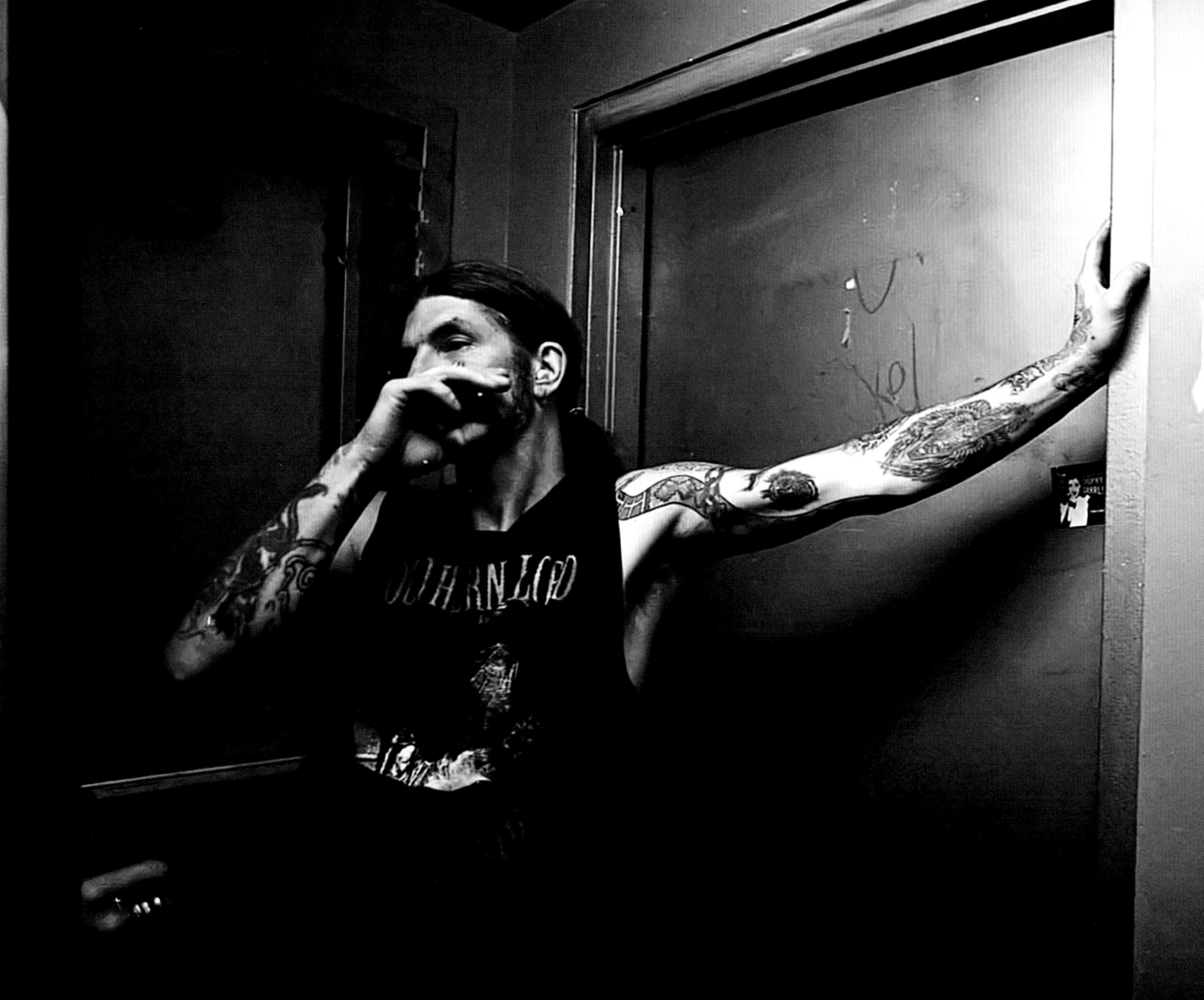

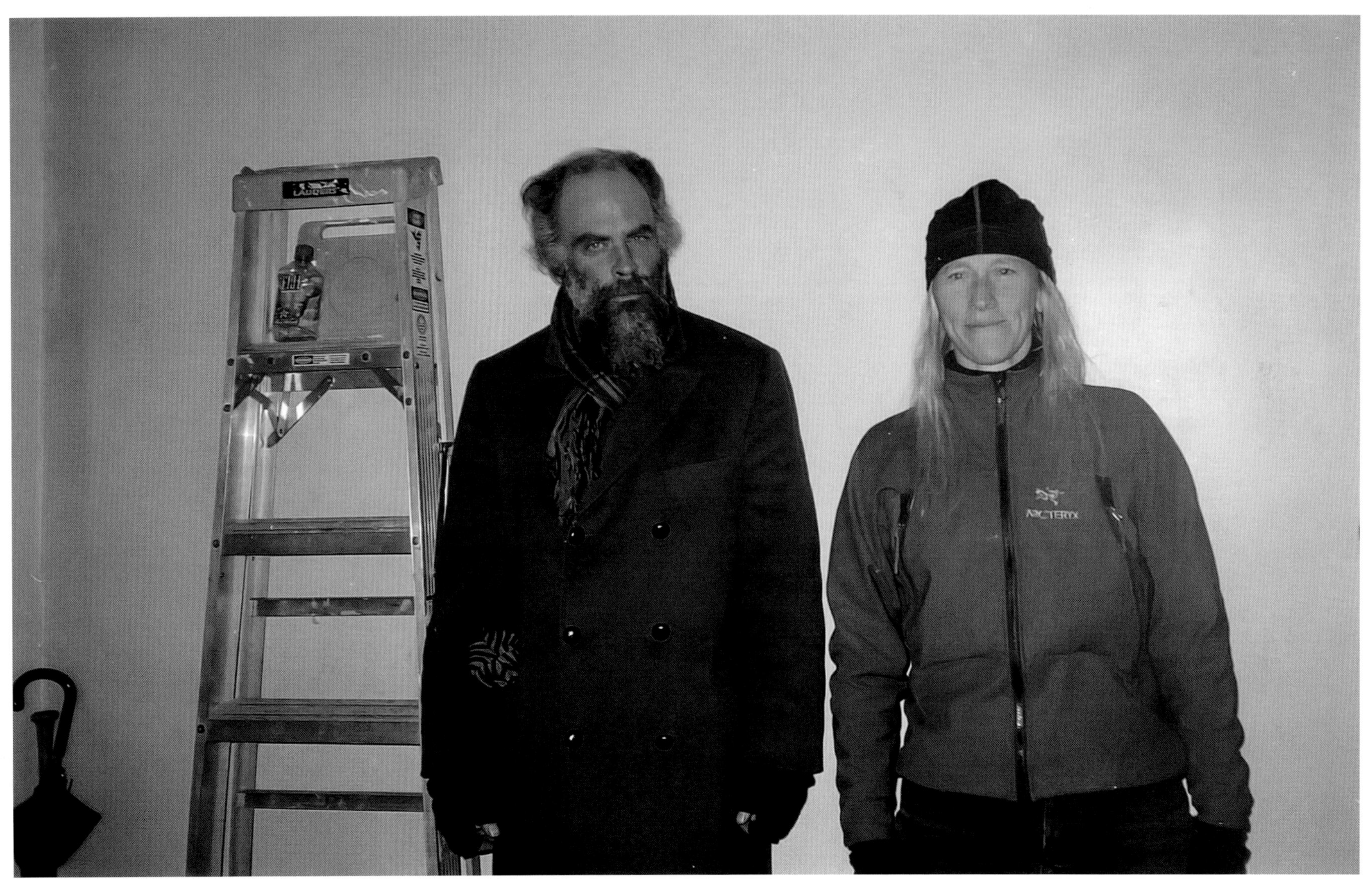

Daniel Higgs and Amy Pickering / WDC, 2005
Opposite: Scott "Wino" Weinrich, The Hidden Hand, Knitting Factory / Los Angeles, CA, 2004

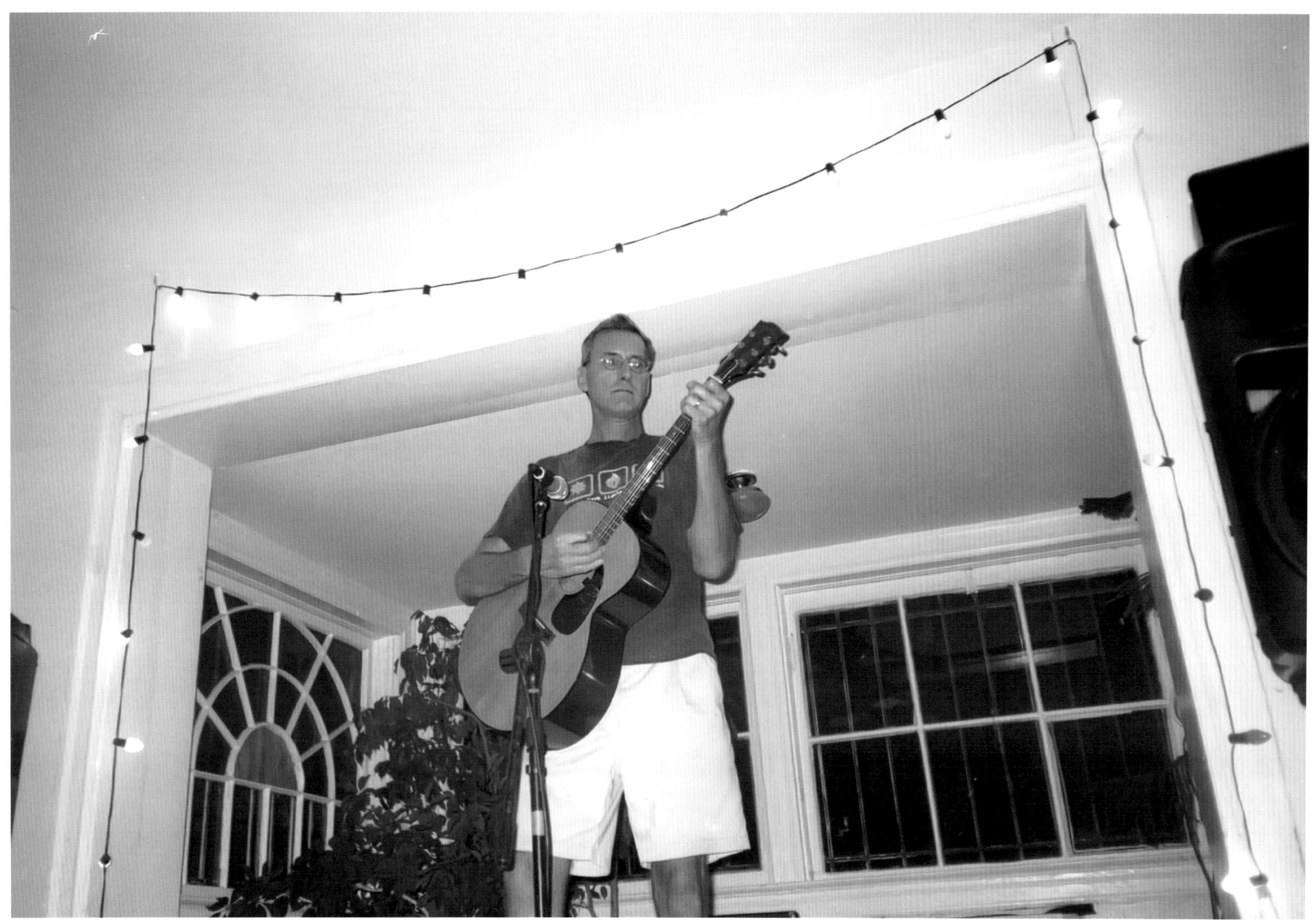

Don Zientara, La Casa / WDC, 2005

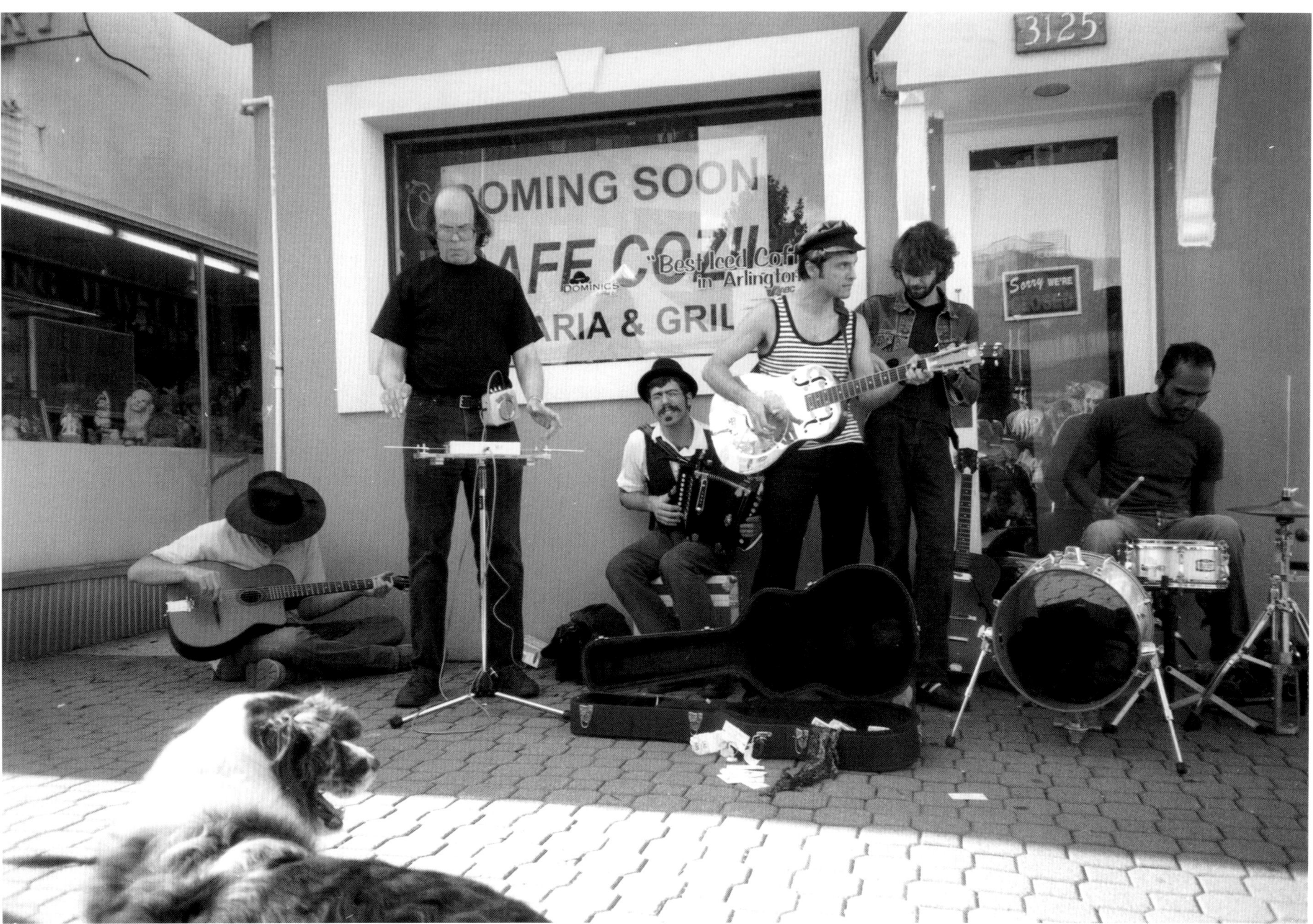

The Cassettes, Clarendon Park / Arlington, VA, 2005

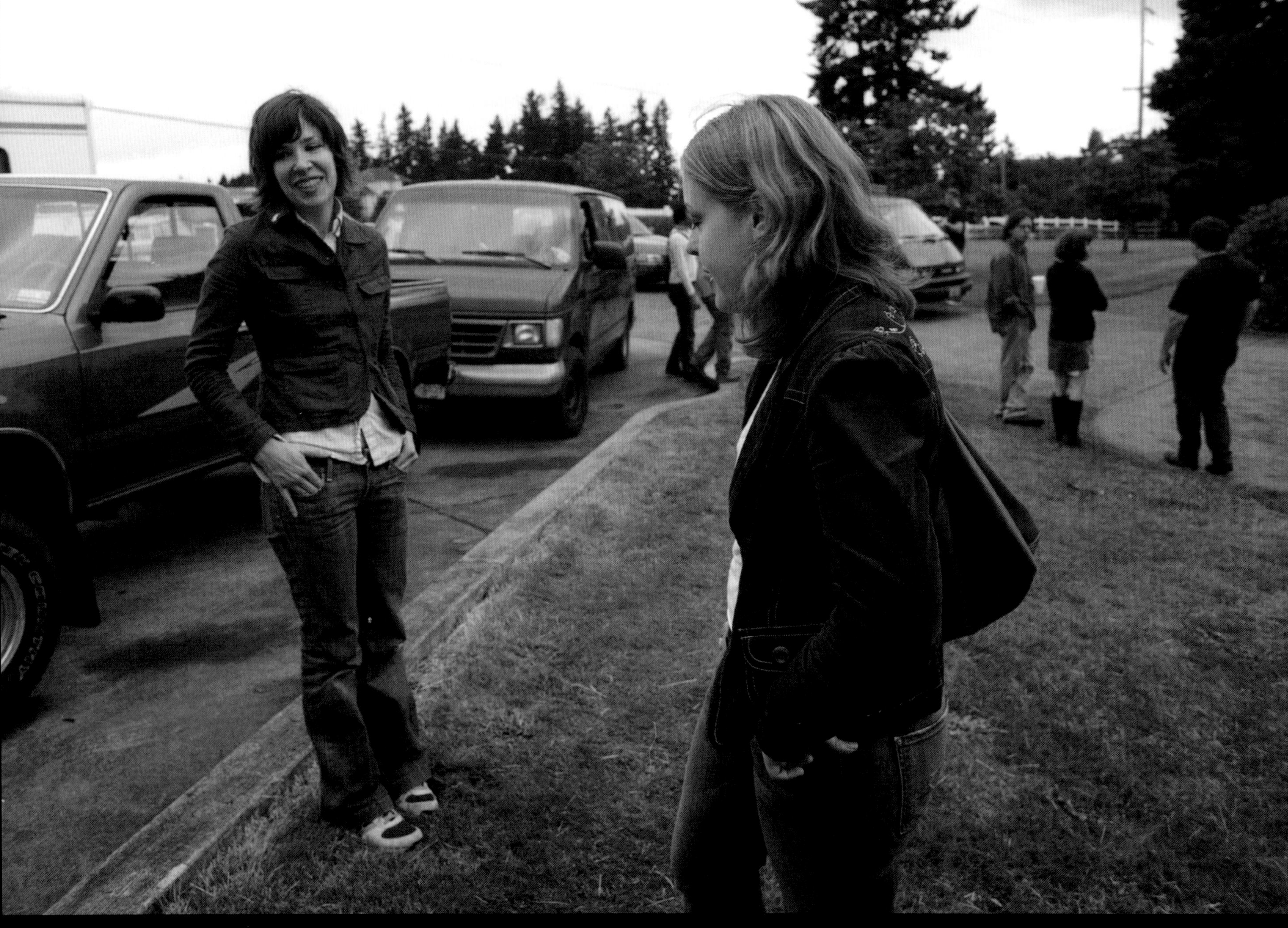

Sleater-Kinney, Burn to Shine / Portland, OR, 2005

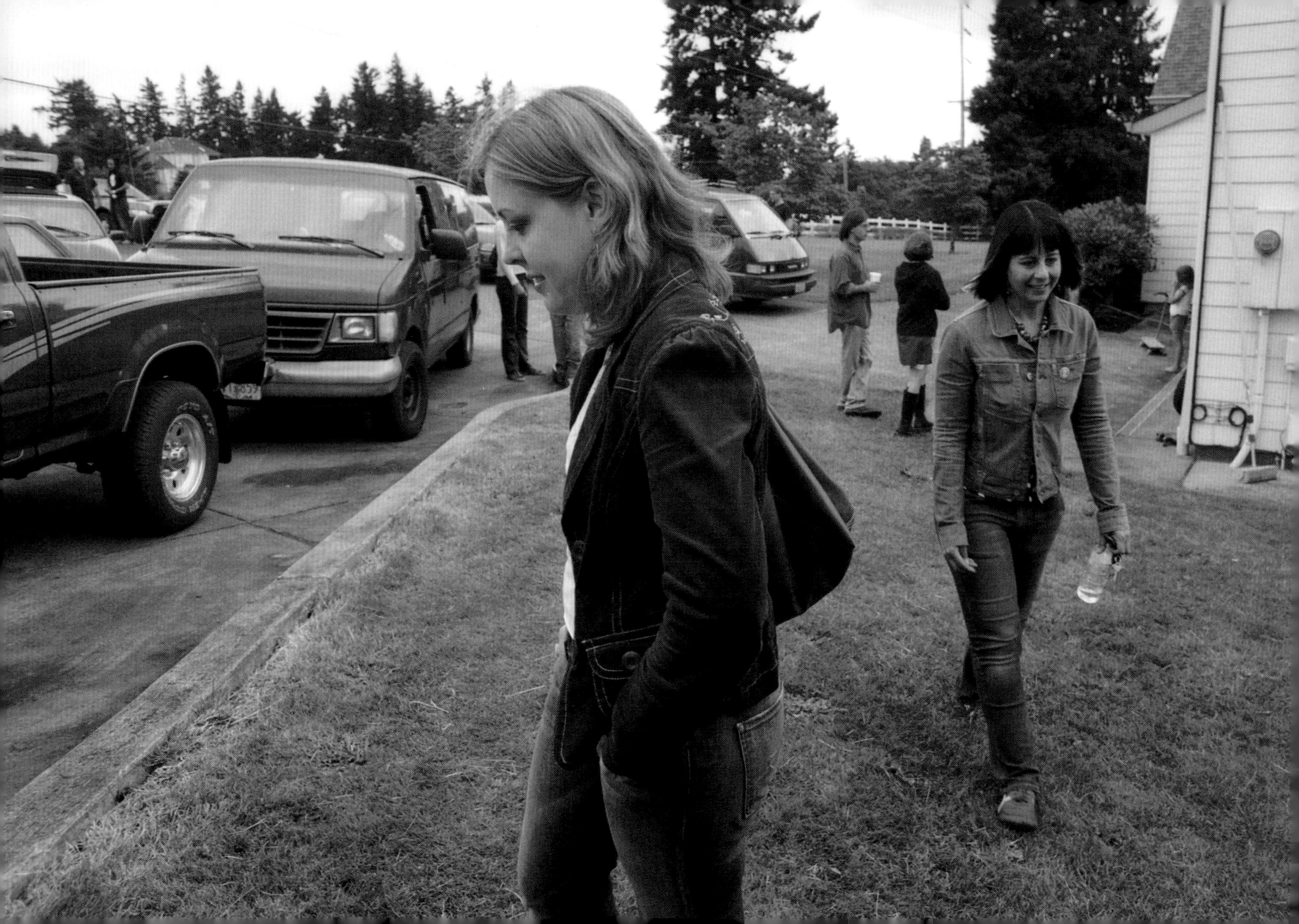

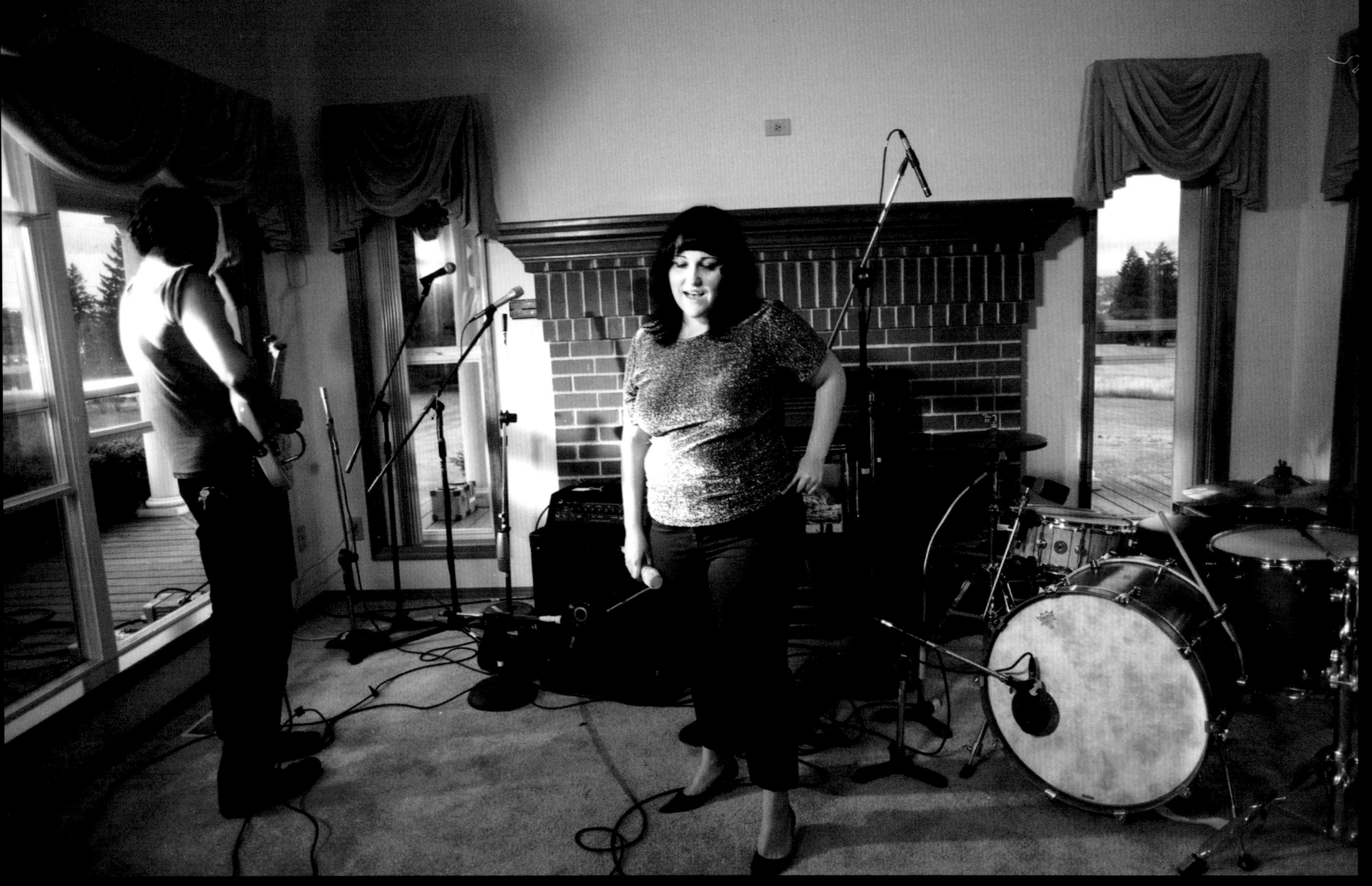

The Gossip, Burn to Shine / Portland, OR, 2005
Opposite: The Routineers, Fort Reno / WDC, 2005

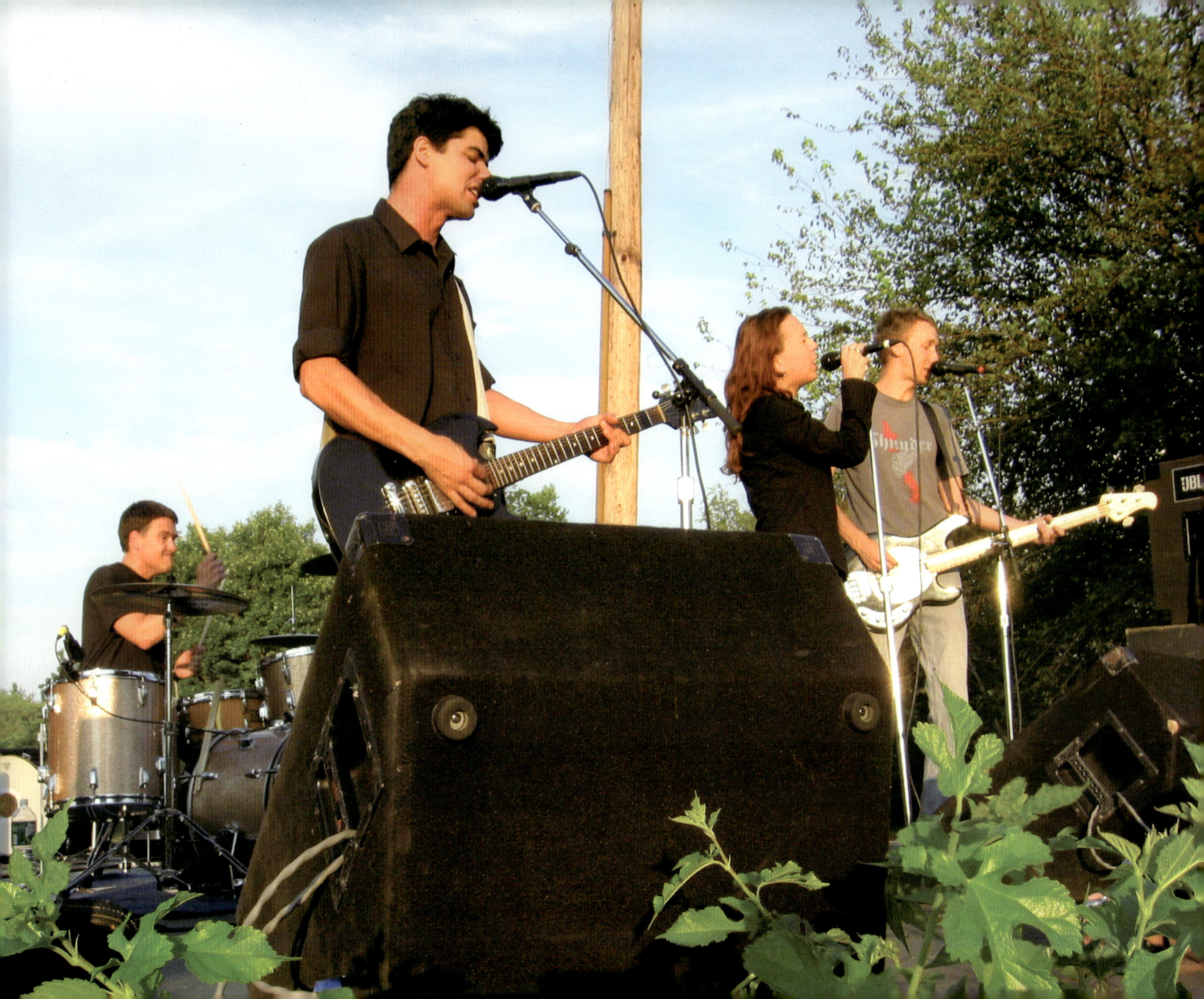

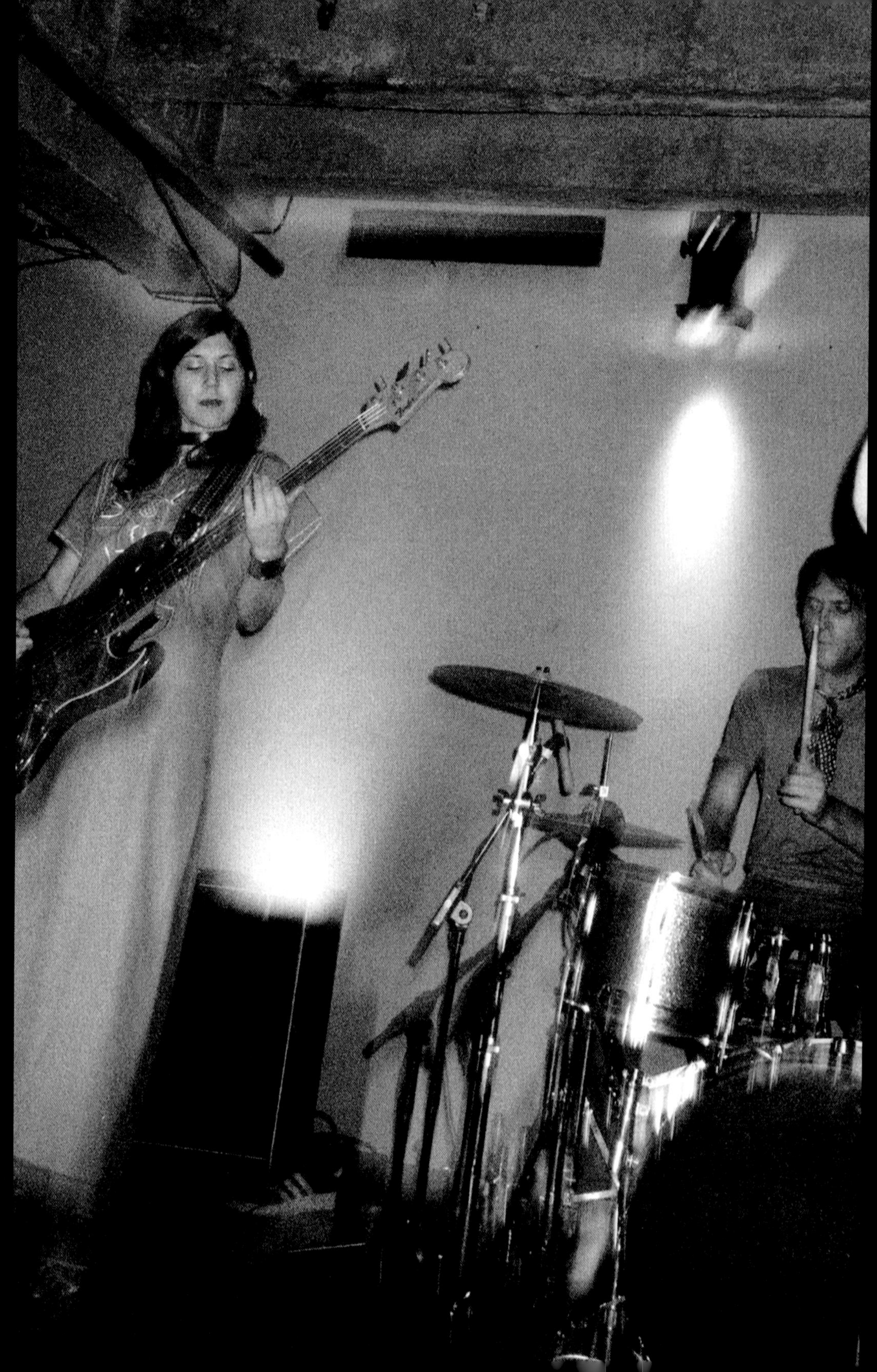

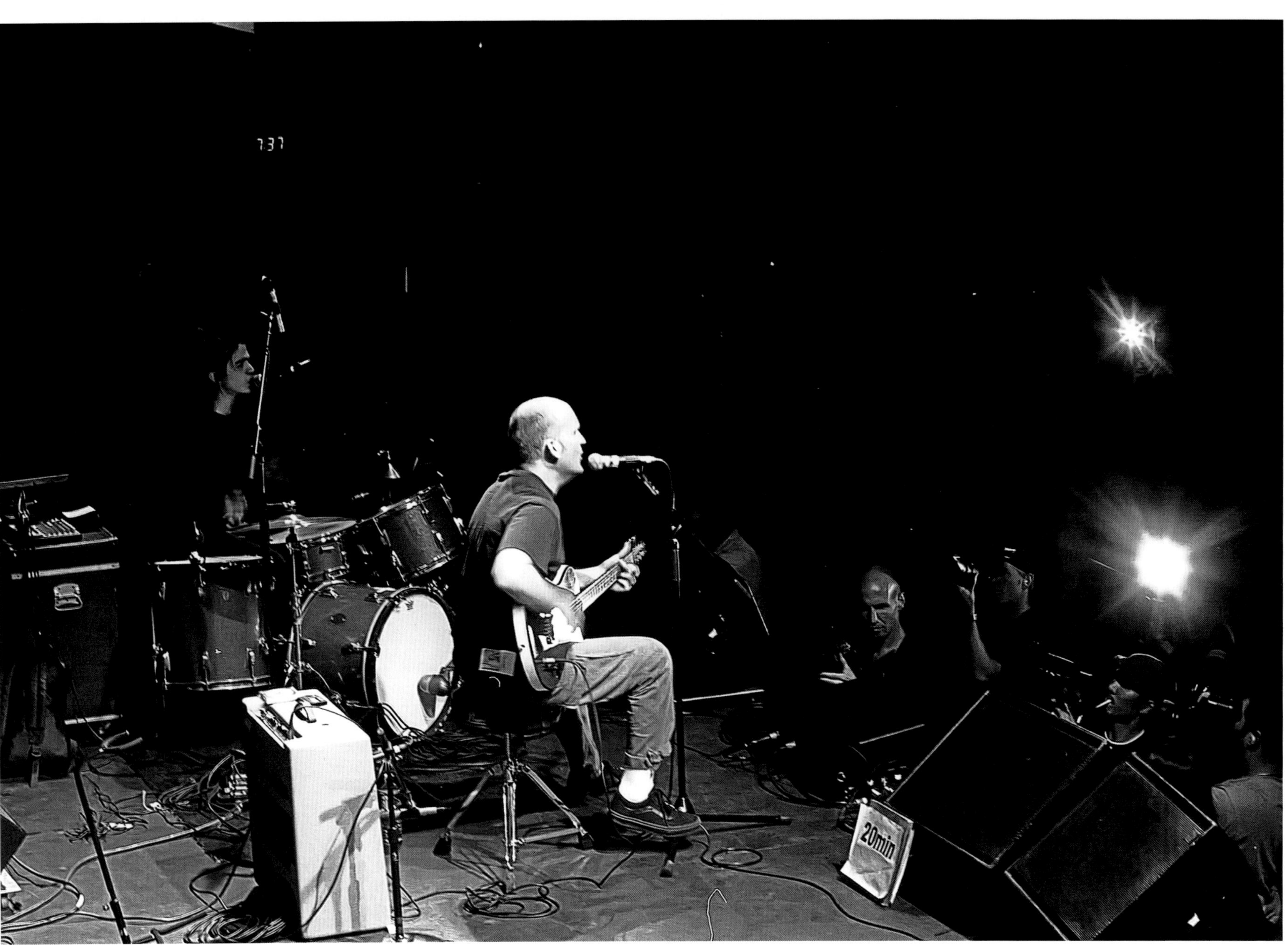

The Evens, Operation Ceasefire, Washington Monument / WDC, 2005
Opposite: Weird War / Portland, OR, 2005

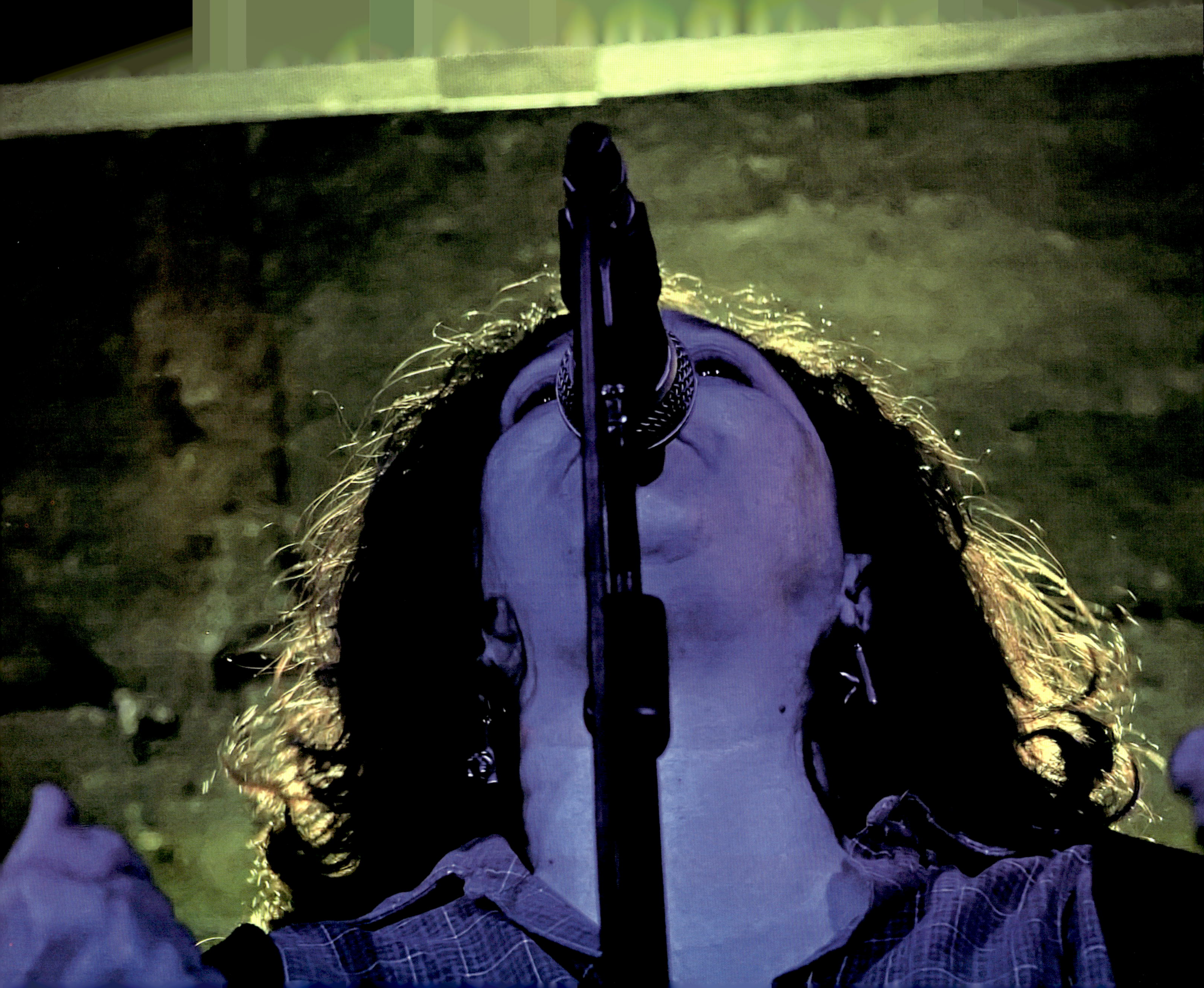

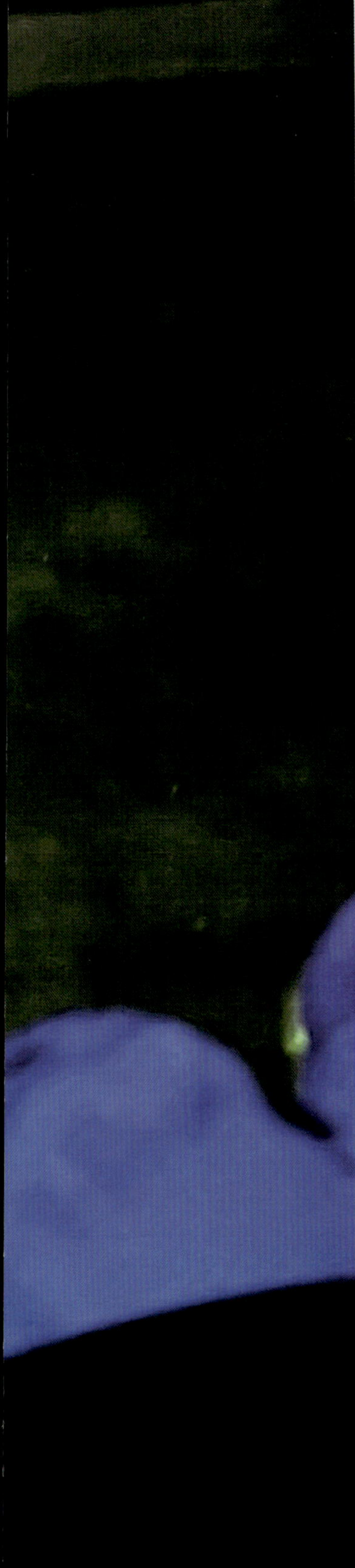

GIOVANNA CACCIOLA

When I joined a band for the first time, I wasn't a teenager. I was twenty-six, and I had a husband and a five-year-old son. My hometown was a chaotic, crazy, and Mafia-dominated city in the deep south of Italy. Living in a place like that, growing up in a place like that, wasn't easy at all, especially for young people. The only thing you could do without being told "you can't do that" or "there's no way to do that" or "that's impossible" was dreaming and playing music. Even fighting felt wrong, as we knew that the enemy was usually invisible, untouchable, and still too big to fight against. My personal situation was far different from many friends my own age, and I felt like a stranger, in music and out of music, walking with a different rhythm, in a different direction.

Going to a rehearsal room every evening, after having worked and lived through so many frustrations, was like being in a different dimension and getting in touch with an unknown side of human relationships—it was easier and made me stronger. In a land where even just stating an opinion could be dangerous, where you felt like your future would be enormously influenced by the political situation and corruptions, by a newborn invisible criminal era, music gave me the opportunity to communicate through new channels running much deeper than I had ever expected.

Even if I was singing in a different language, I felt like the audience understood my feelings and my intentions. Discovering this new way of social participation, sharing precious time with other human beings—it was and it still is the main gift I've received from music, as it has allowed me to interact on a deeper emotional level, clean and clear. So I can raise my voice and call out to all the other souls.

BOILERS • UZEDA • BELLINI

Giovanna Cacciola, Uzeda, Init / Rome, Italy, 2012

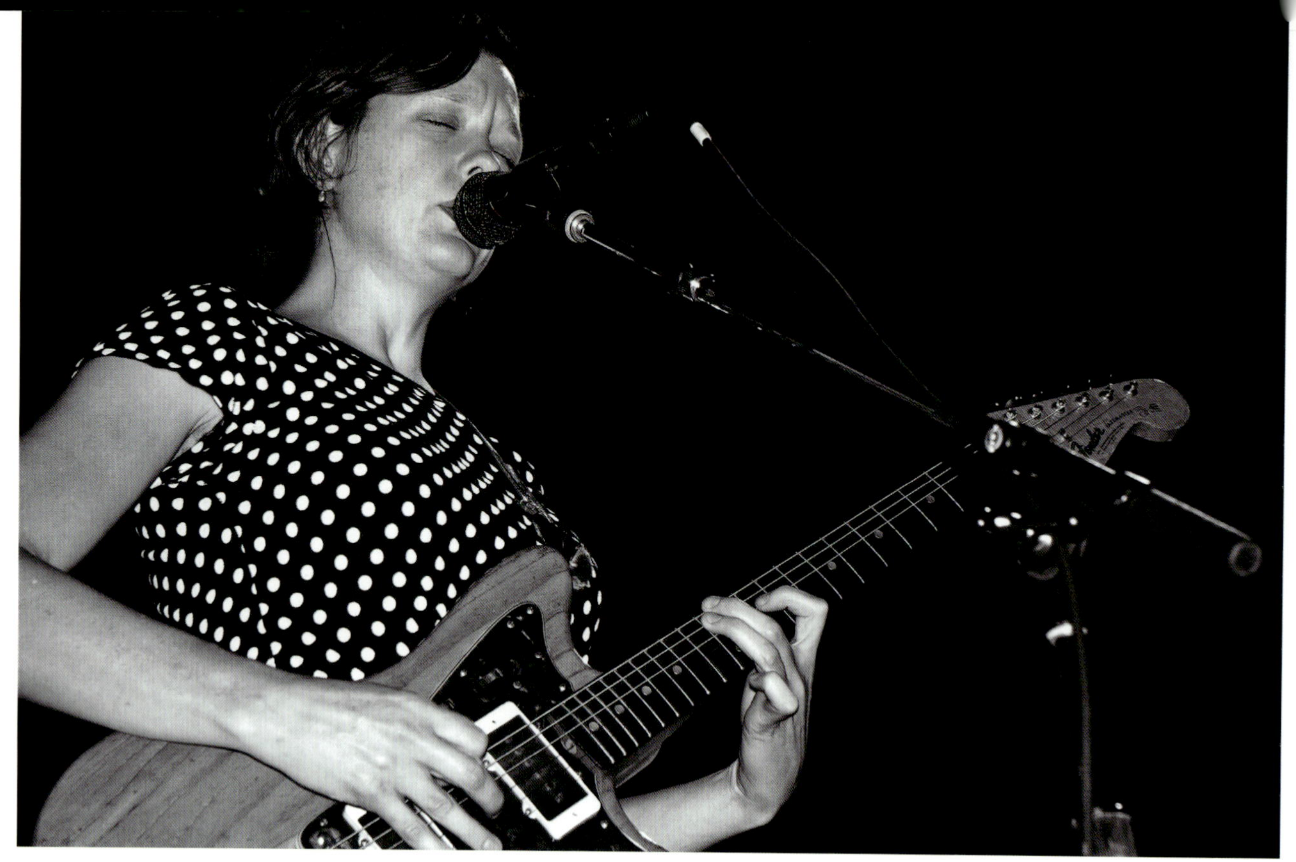

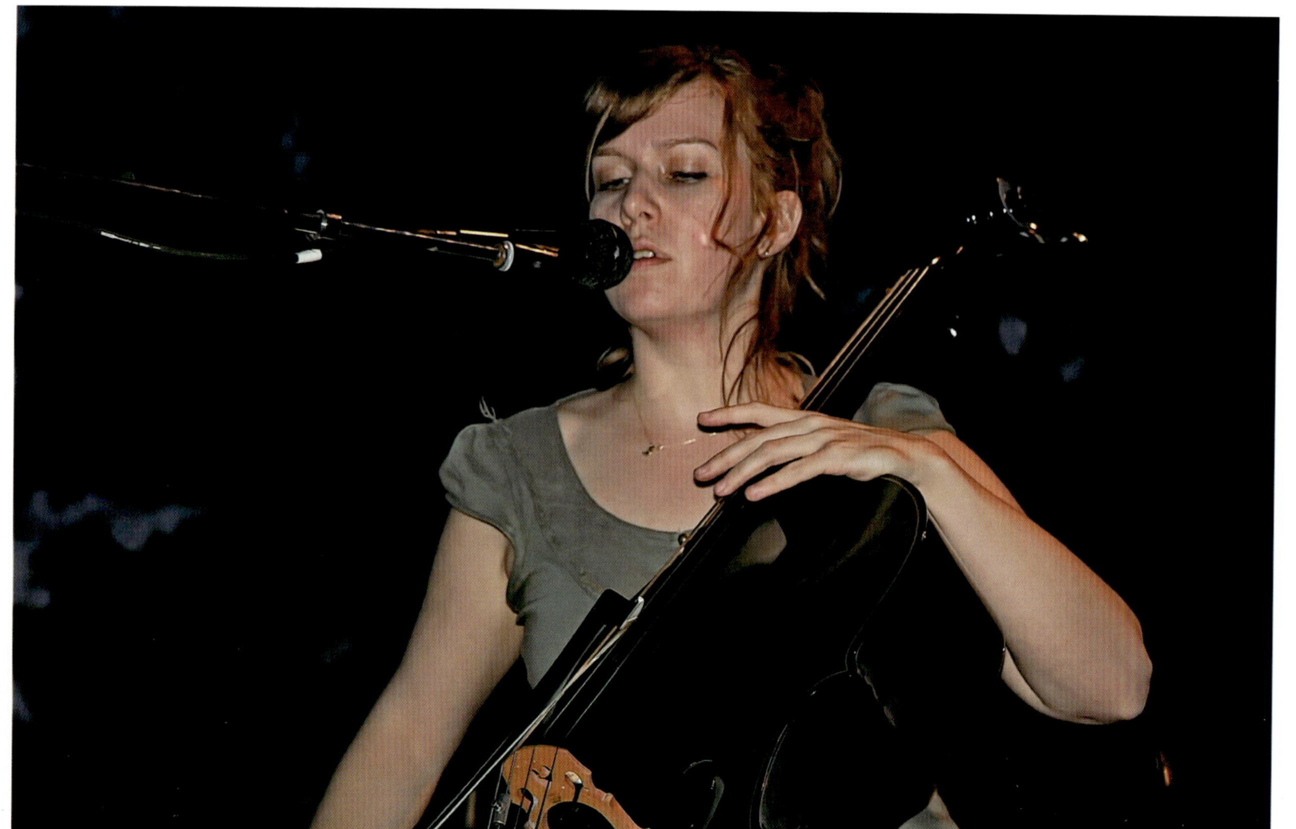

From top: Mary Timony,
Fort Reno / WDC, 2006;
Amy Domingues, Garland of Hours,
Fort Reno / WDC, 2006

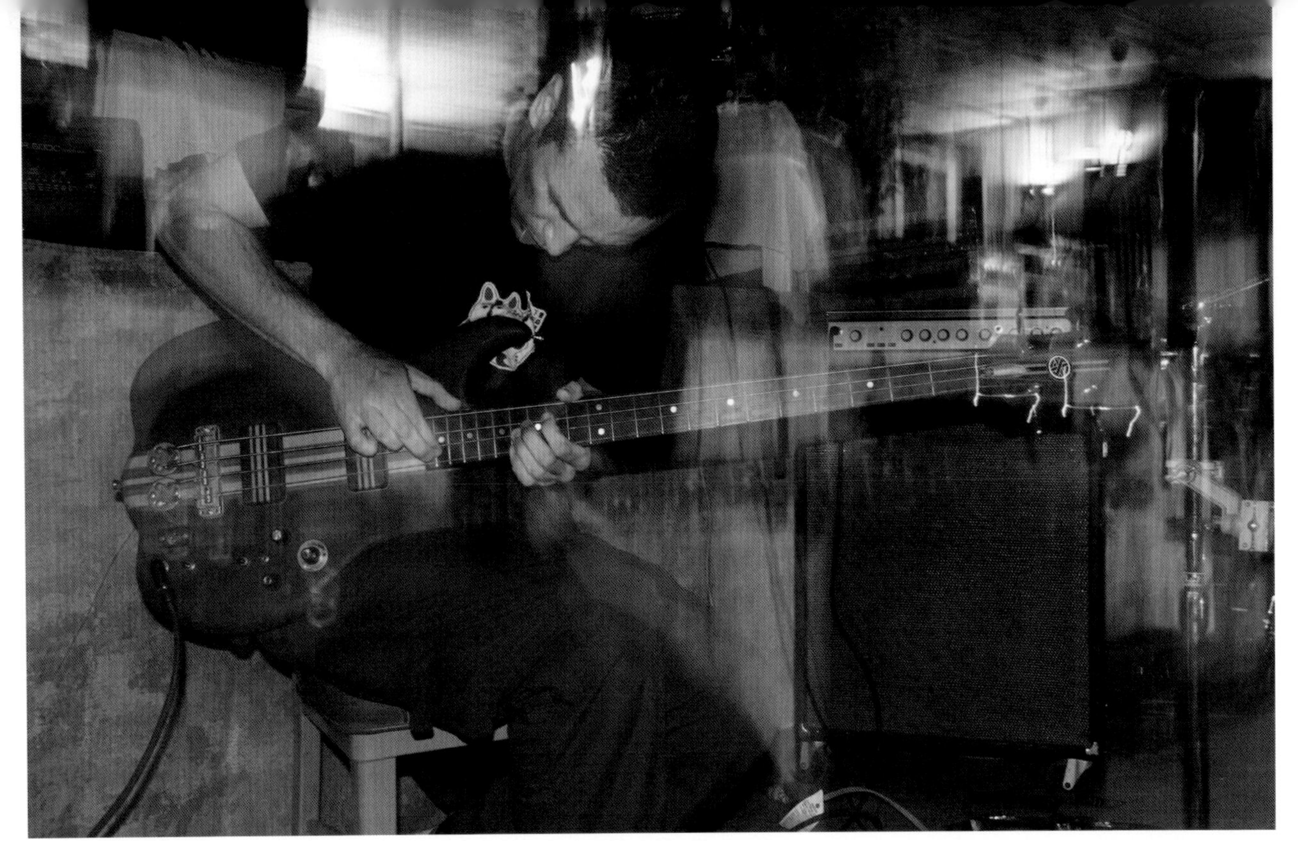

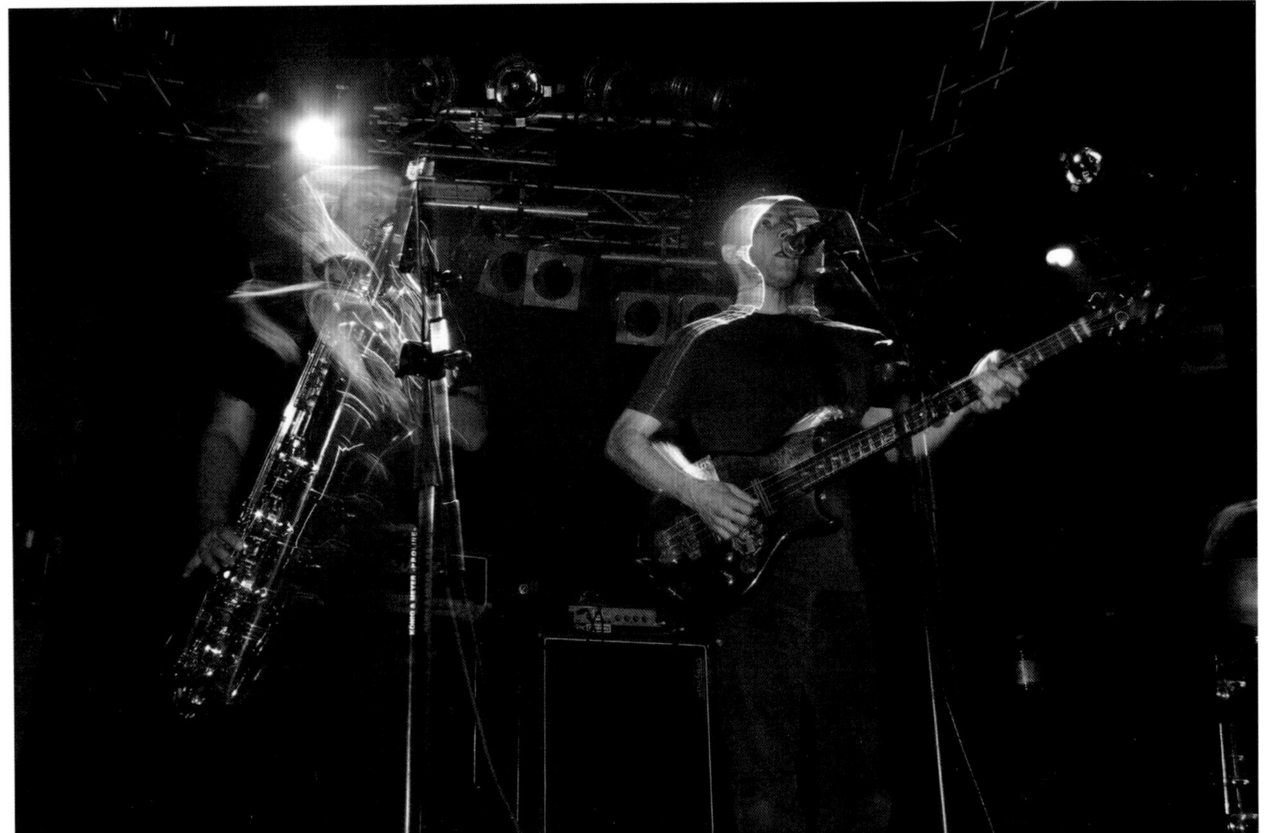

From top: Massimo Pupillo, Zu / WDC, 2006; Joe Lally with Zu, Circolo degli Artisti / Rome, Italy, 2007

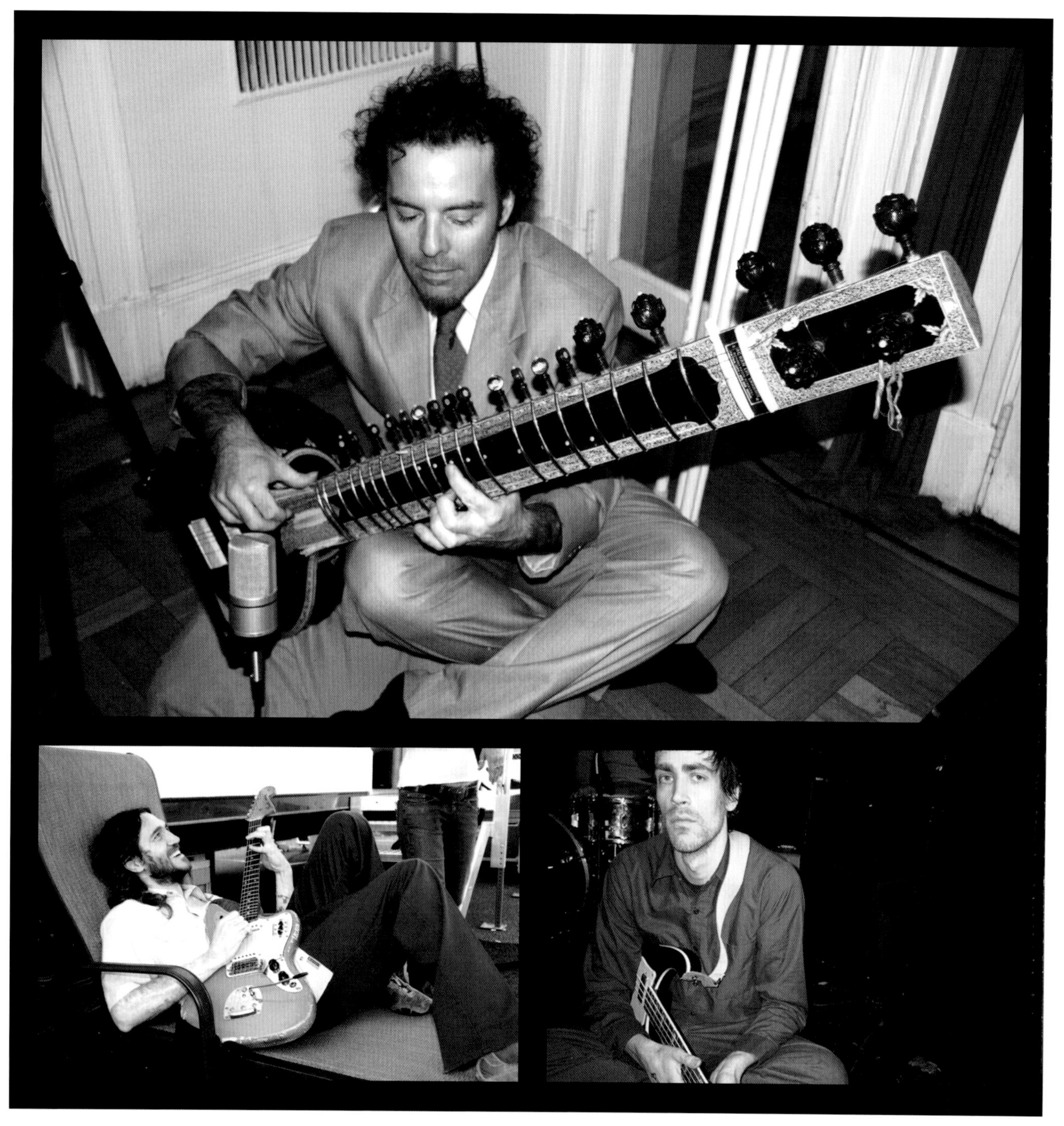

Clockwise from top: Rob Myers (Thievery Corporation, Fort Knox Five), Josephine Butler Parks Center / WDC, 2006; Mike Andre, Antelope, Black Cat / WDC, 2006; John Frusciante (Red Hot Chili Peppers, Ataxia), Baltimore, MD, 2006

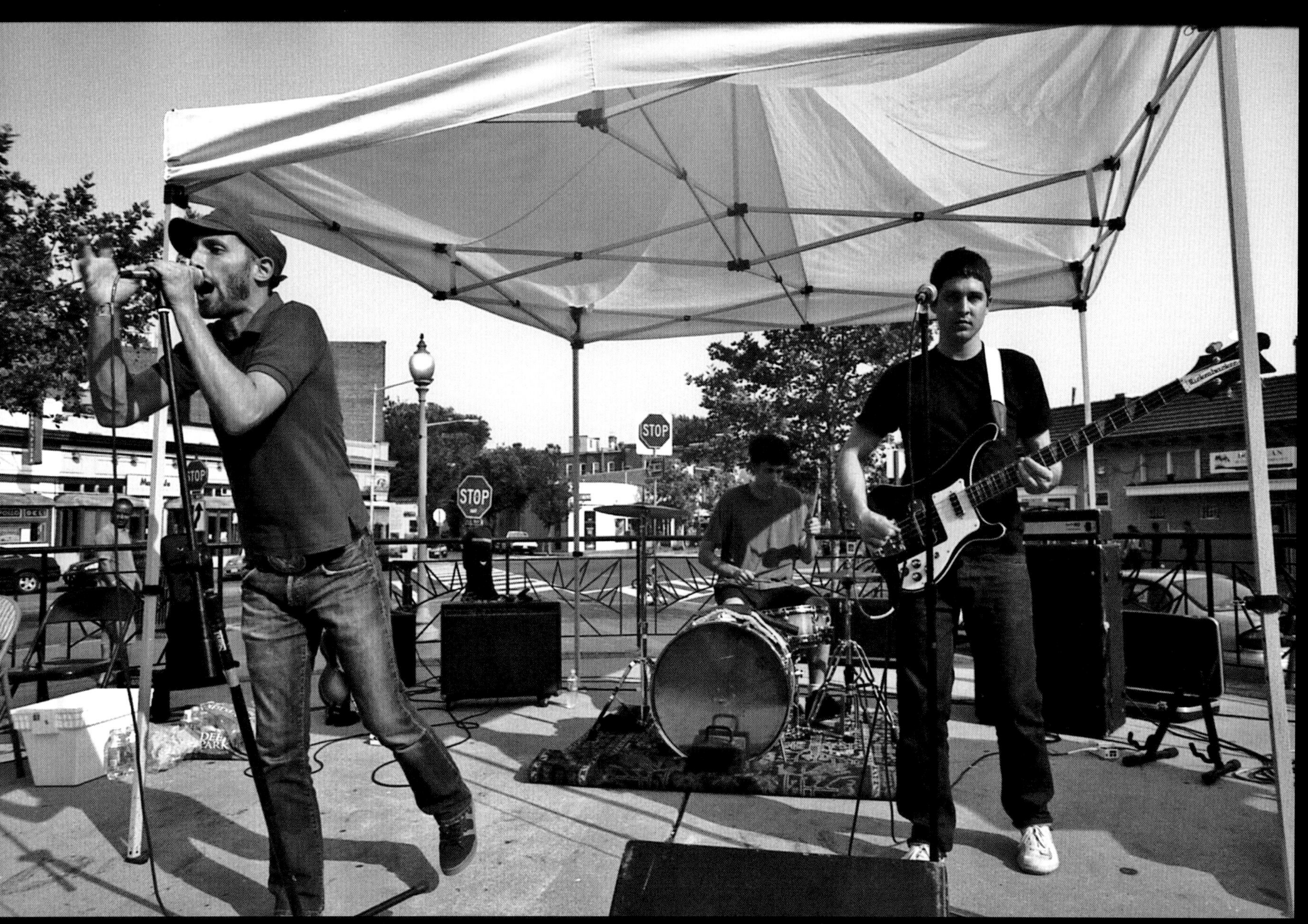

Antelope, Mount Pleasant / WDC, 2007

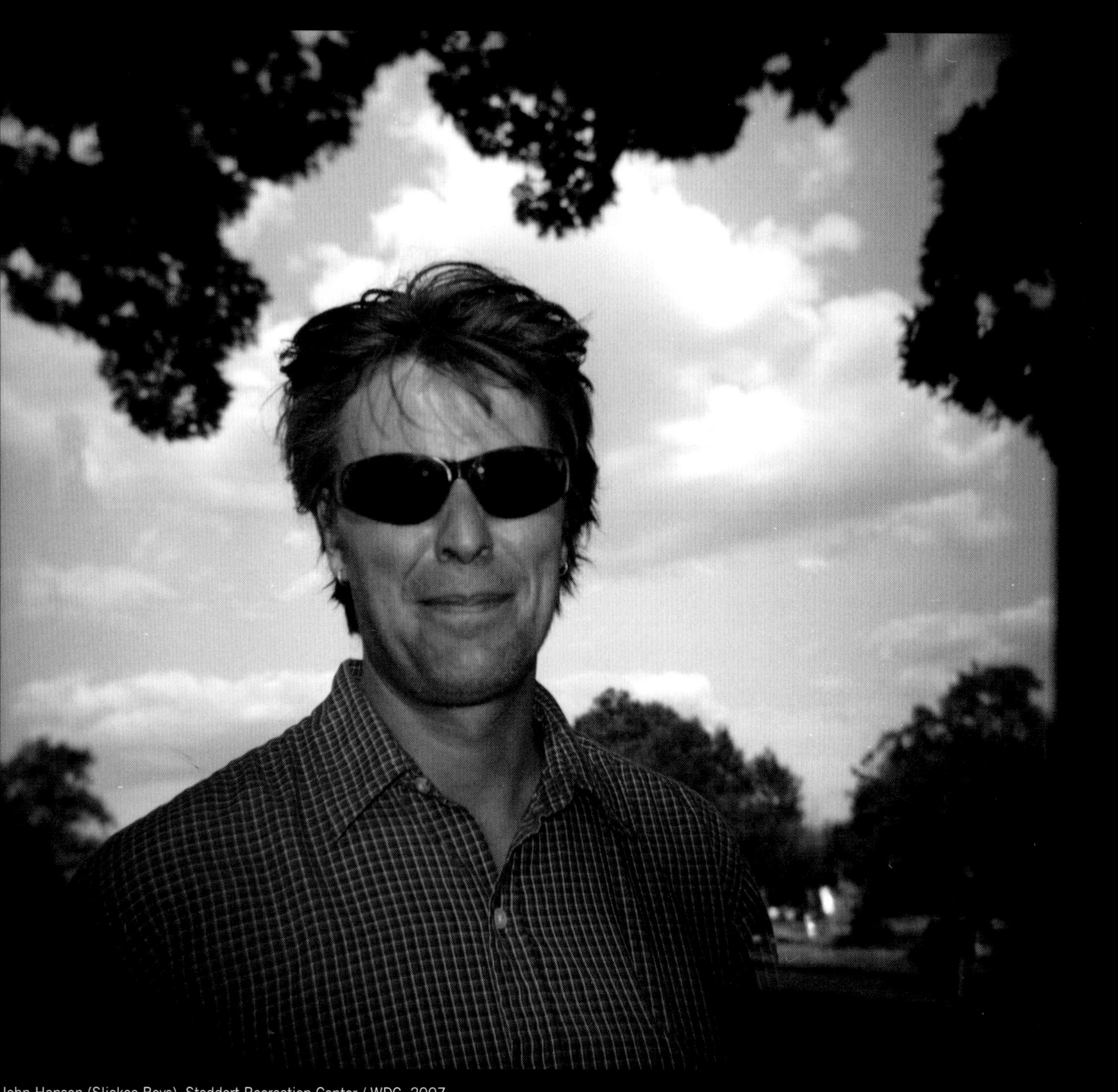

John Hansen (Slickee Boys), Stoddert Recreation Center / WDC, 2007

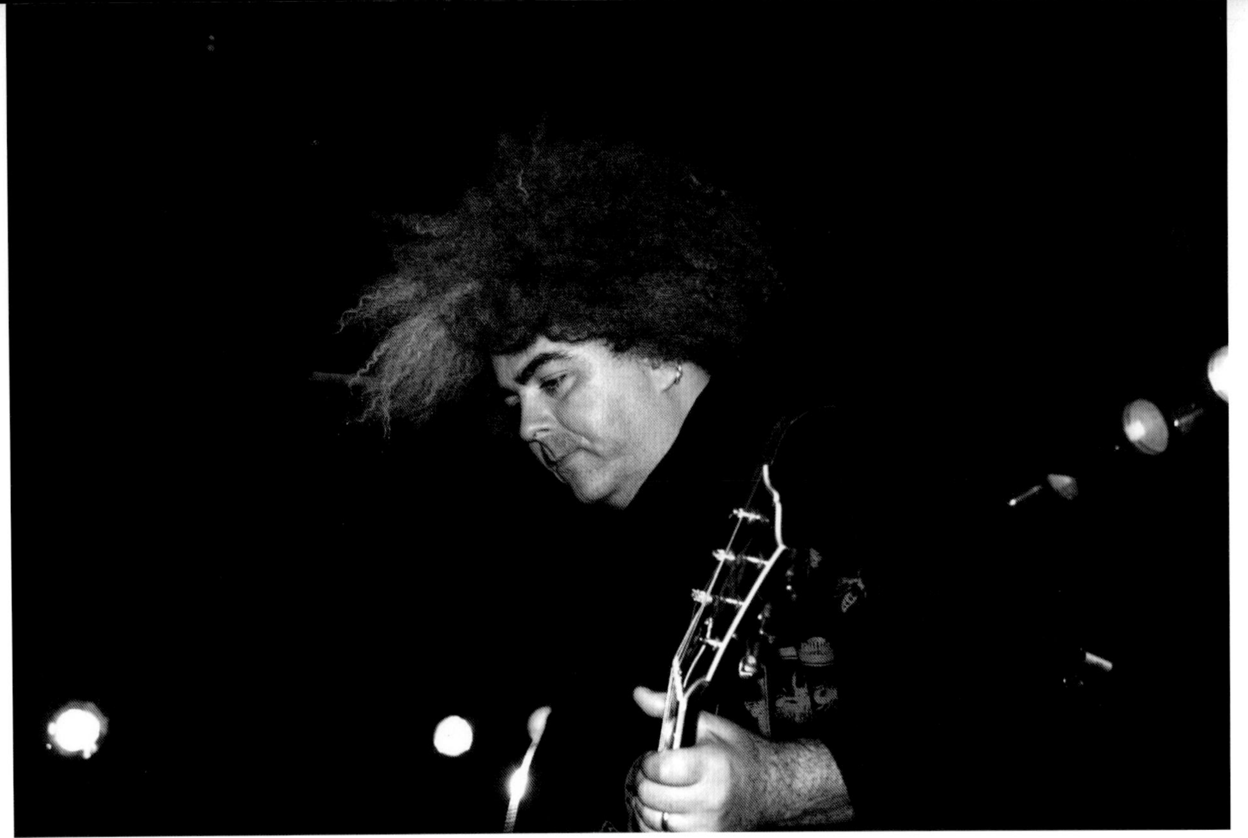

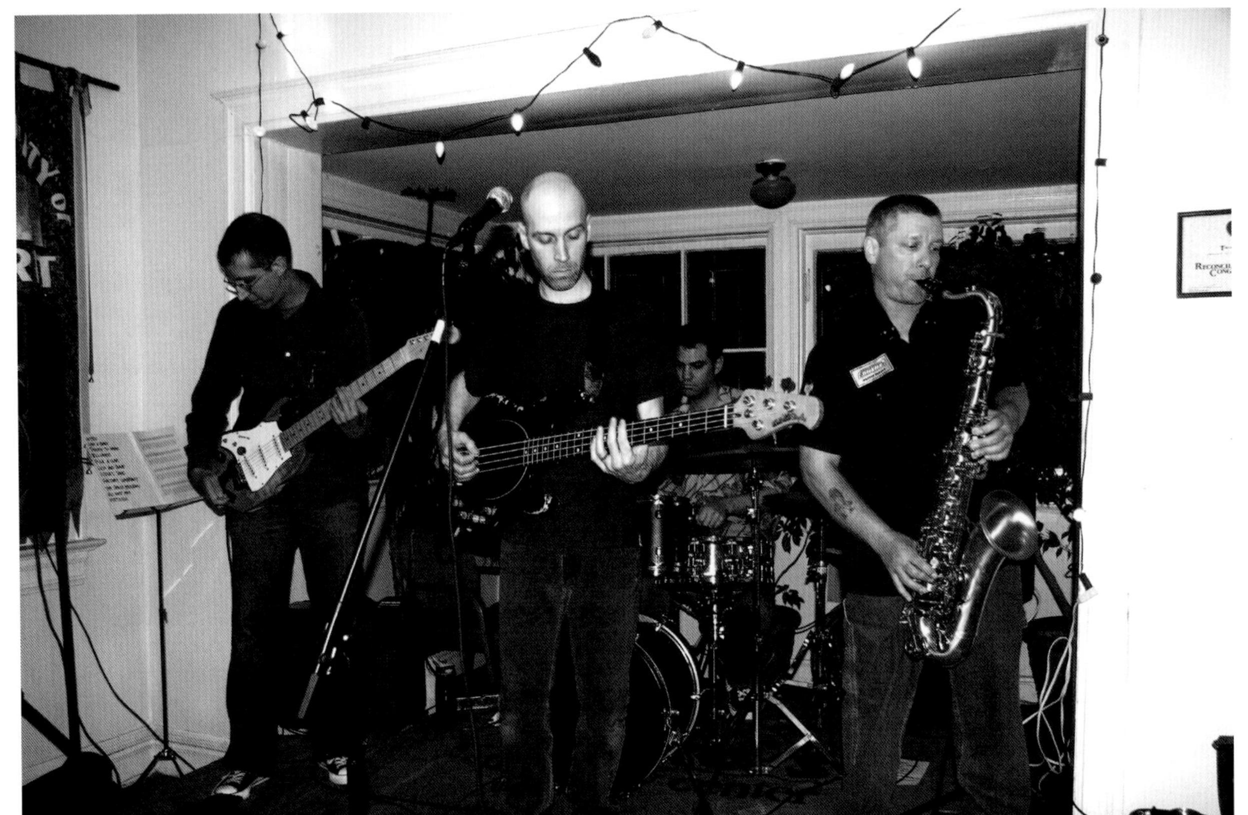

From top: Buzz, Melvins, Black Cat / WDC, 2006; DCAC, La Casa / WDC, 2007

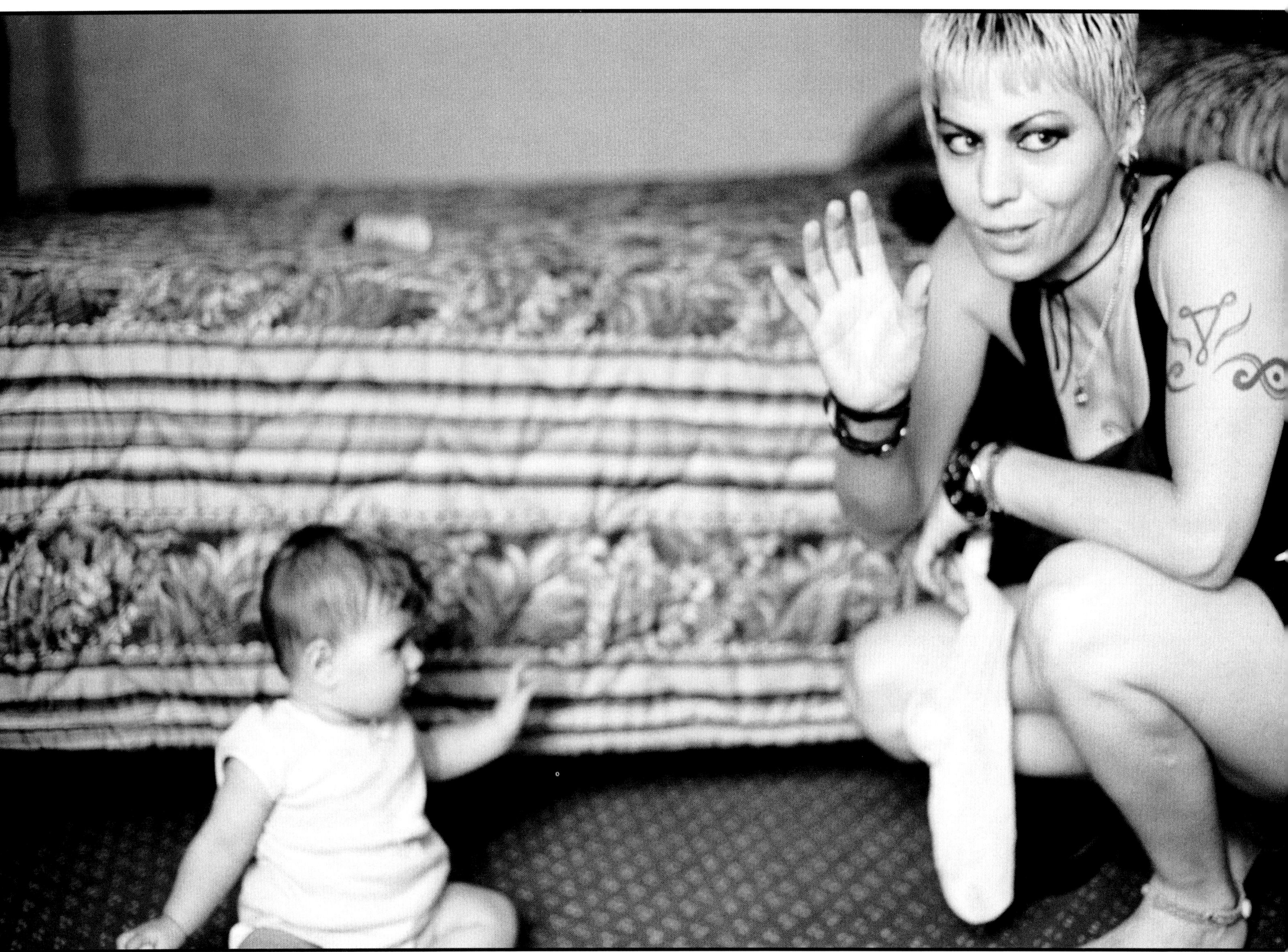

JOAN JETT

I guess it was around the time puberty hit that I recall music, the music I heard on the radio, starting to become more than catchy melodies to follow. I started to really notice the rock and roll songs, the guitars, and I wanted to make those sounds. Specifically, "All Right Now" by the Free was the song that really hit me in the gut and crotch, though I didn't make that connection then. It was the slightly out-of-tune guitars, combined with the simple riff, and I wanted to make those sounds! When I was thirteen, I asked my parents for a guitar for Christmas. An ELECTRIC guitar, and they got one for me. A Sears Silvertone.

I wanted to learn to play it, and went to a guitar teacher, who told me girls don't play electric guitar, and tried to teach me "On Top of Ol' Smokey." Needless to say, I didn't go back, and these experiences started to form my worldview on the bias I would face just for being "a girl," which also informed my songwriting later on, and still does.

When I was sixteen, I had learned to play a bit, my family had moved to Los Angeles a couple years earlier, and I started to think about forming a band of all girls. If I wanted to play rock and roll, there had to be other girls in LA who did too.

I was lucky enough to achieve my dream of playing guitar and singing in a couple bands, the Runaways, and the Blackhearts, my current band. The Runaways, my first, were and still are so important to me for so many reasons. Many women, girls, men, AND boys have written and told me in person how they've been inspired by me in some capacity, and that is really, for me, what it's all about at the root. It's connection, the connection, of music, of your life experiences that people recognize as their own too, that crosses all boundaries and touches people's hearts. And there you have the humble power to change things.

THE RUNAWAYS • JOAN JETT AND THE BLACKHEARTS

Joan Jett and Lidia Lally, hotel room / WDC, 2002

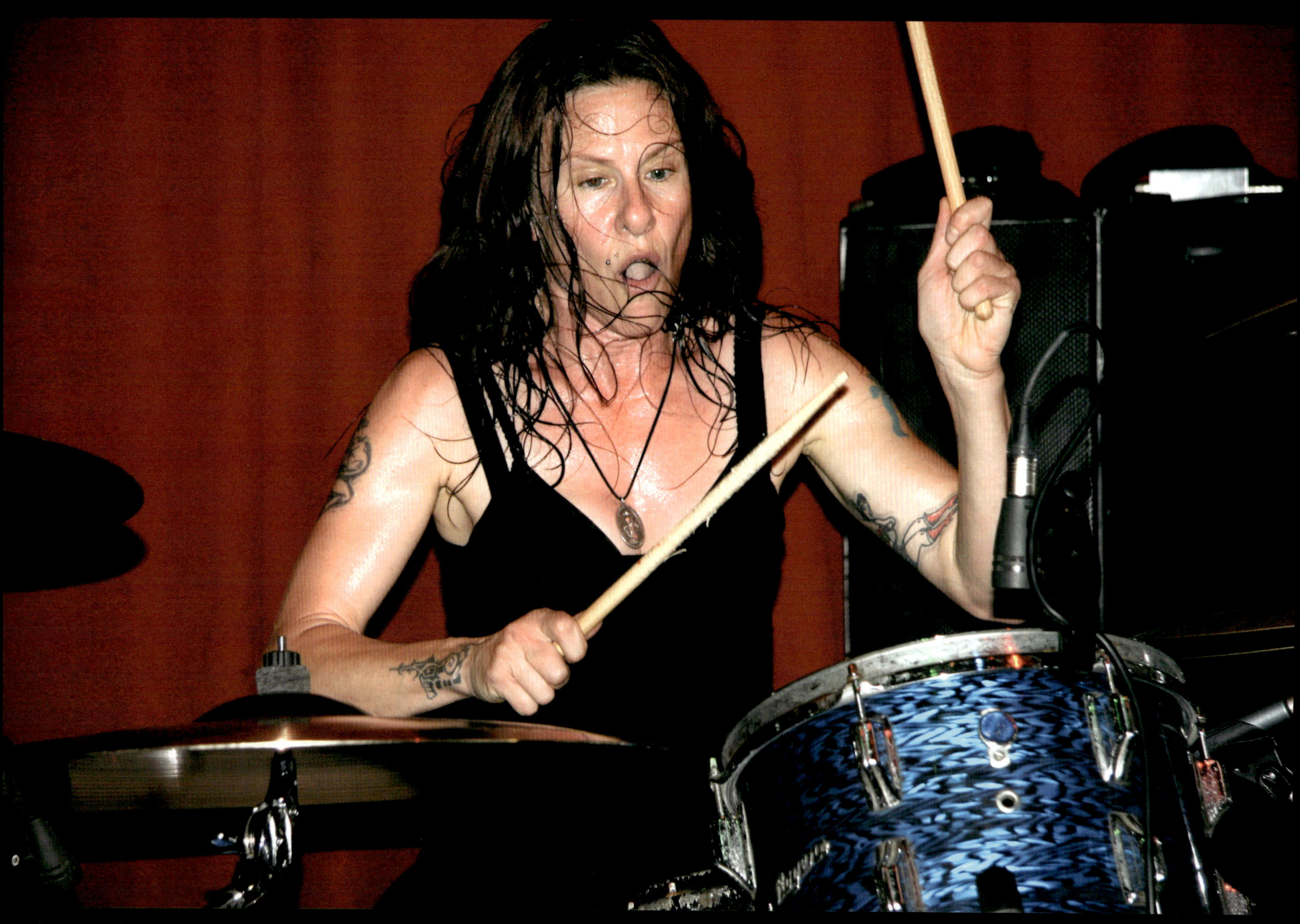

Cheshire Agusta, Stinking Lizaveta / Philadelphia, PA, 2009

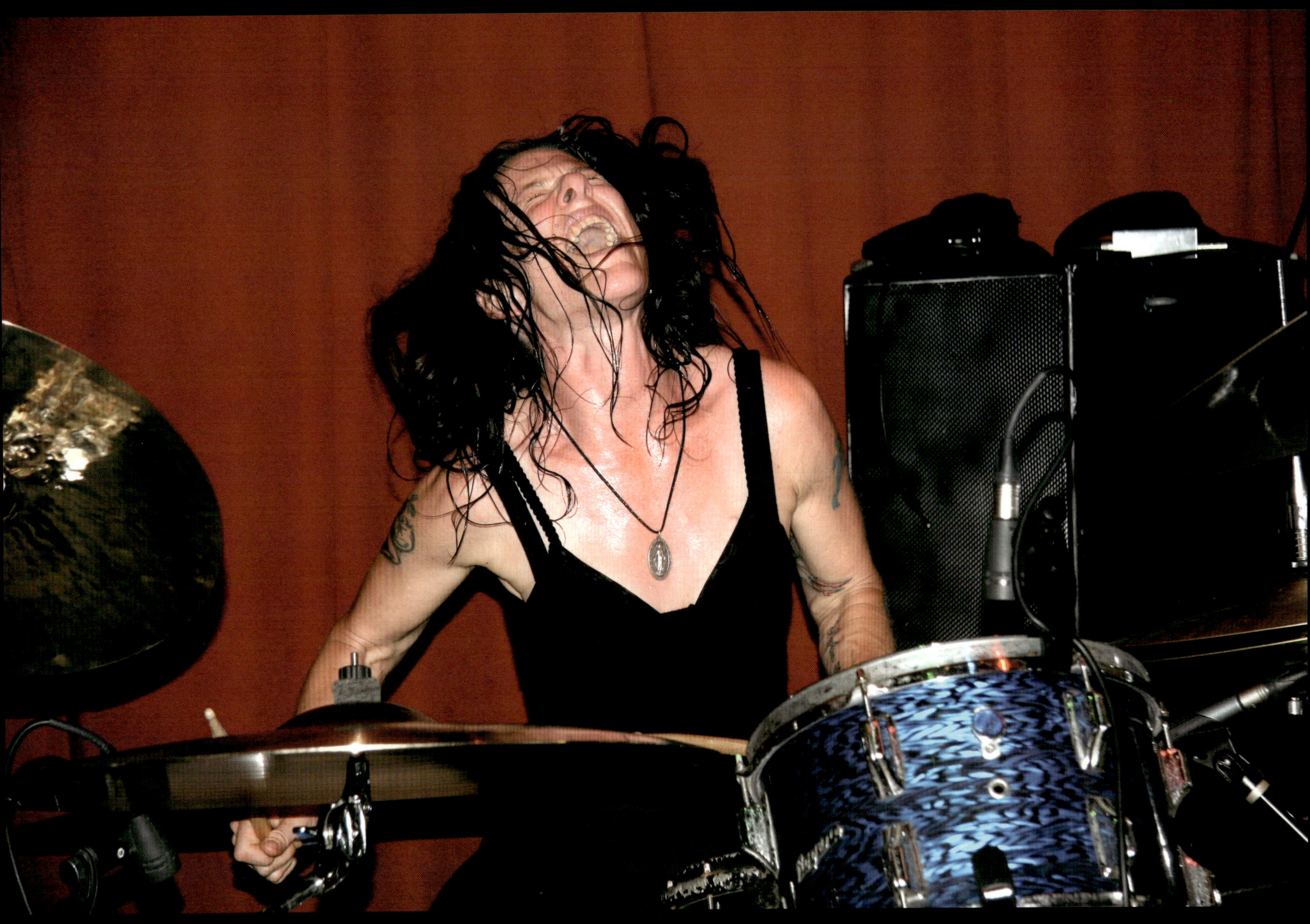

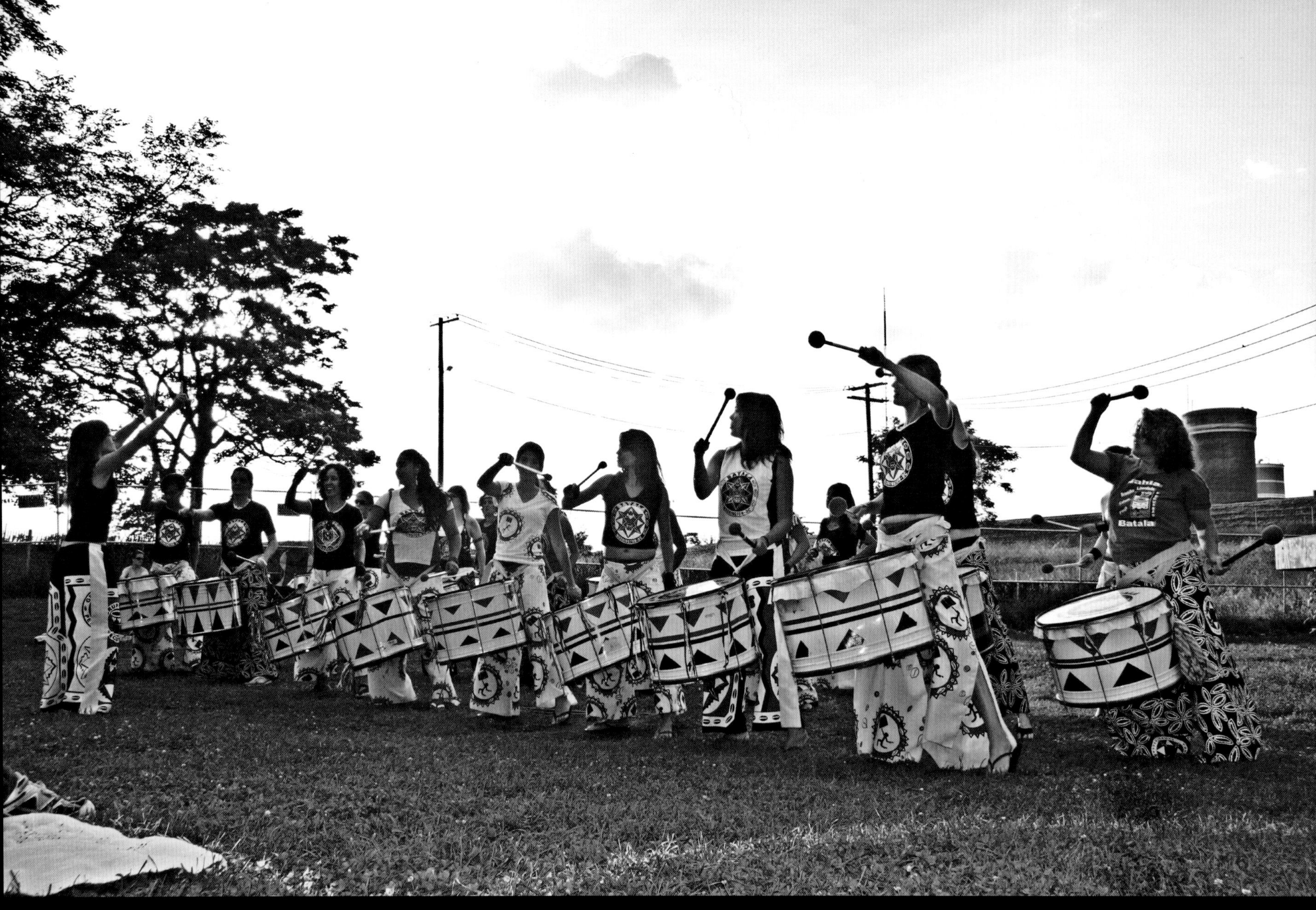

Batalá Washington, Fort Reno / WDC, 2009

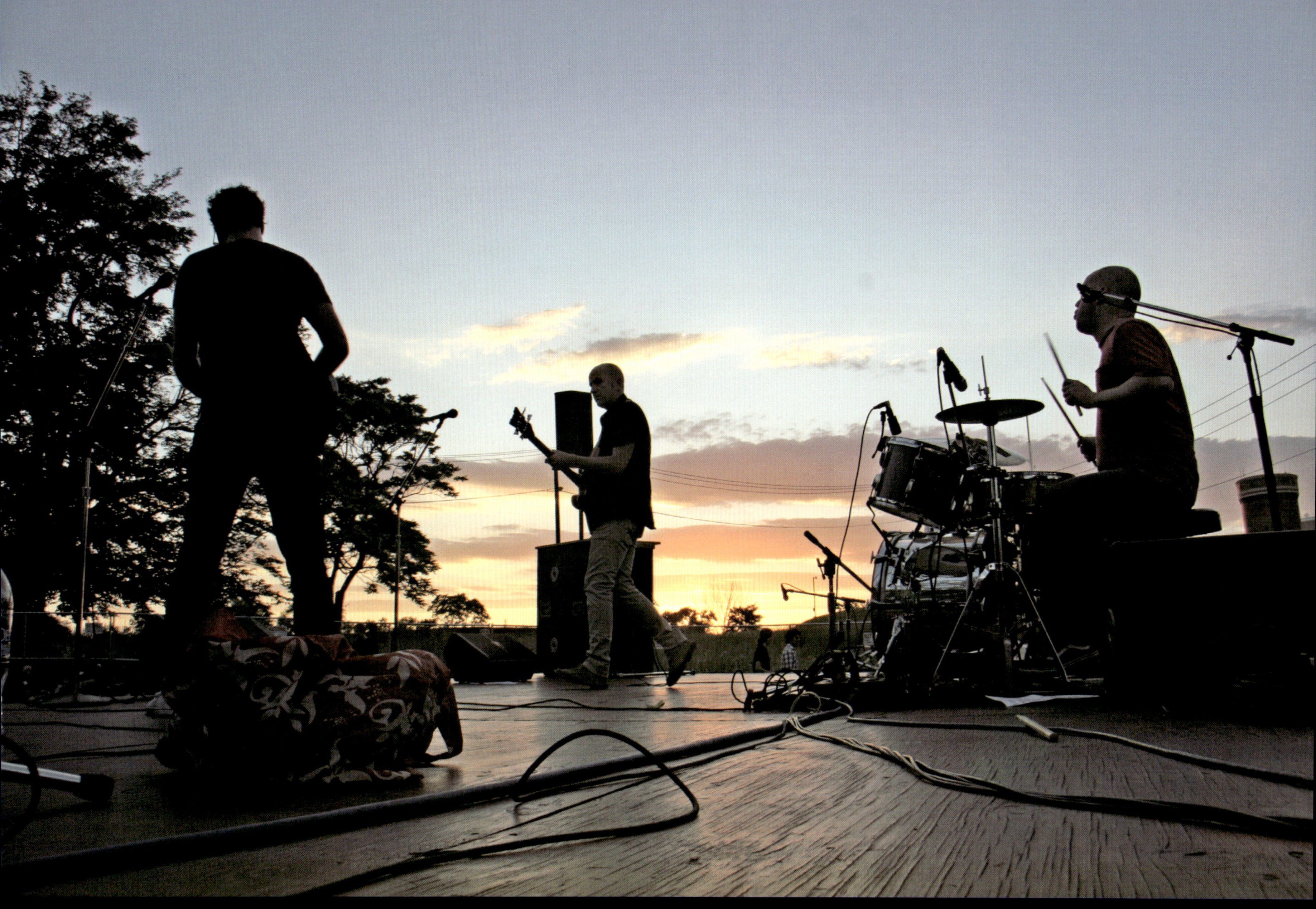

Small Doses, Fort Reno / WDC, 2009

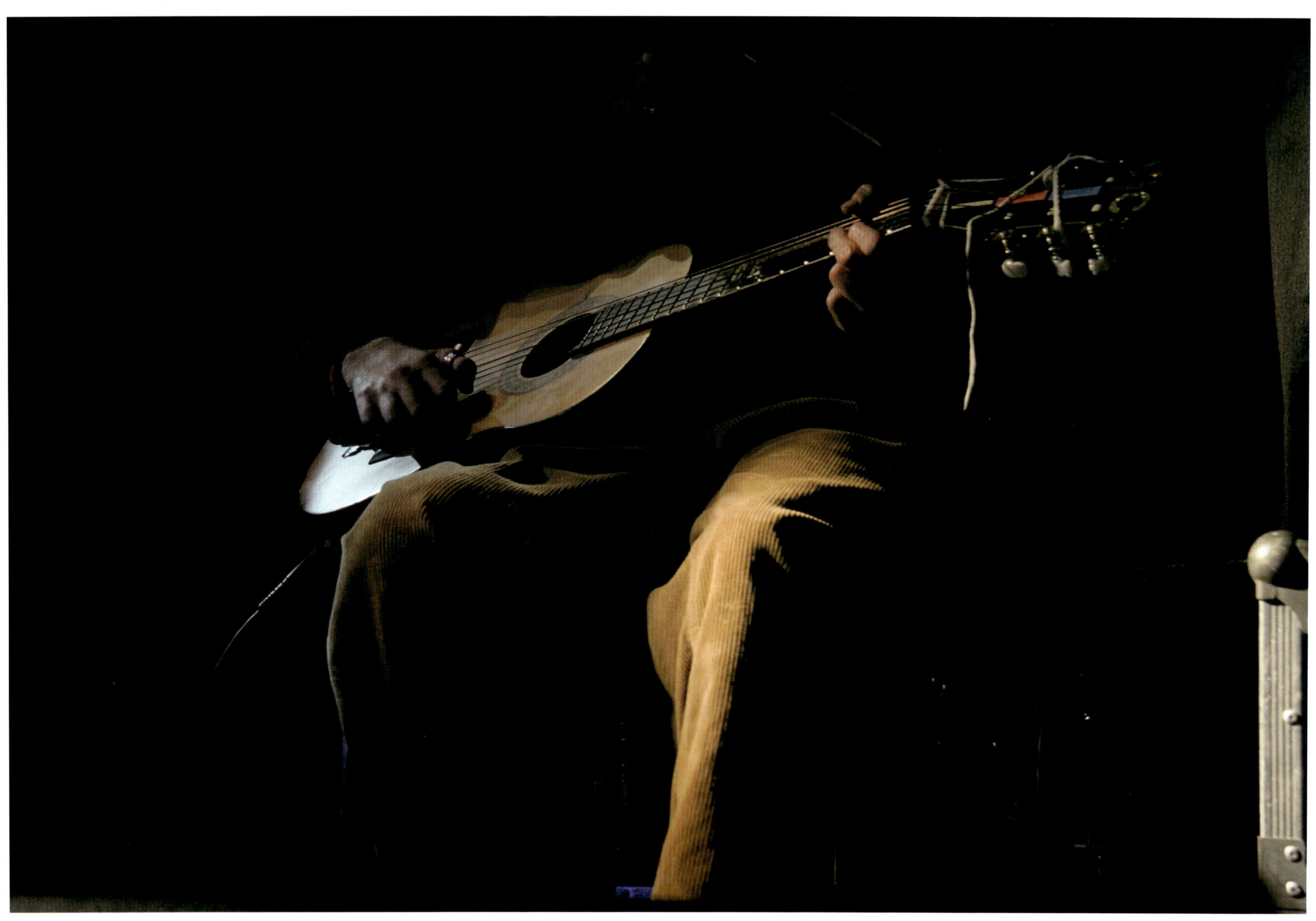

Vic Chesnutt, Circolo degli Artisti / Rome, Italy, 2009

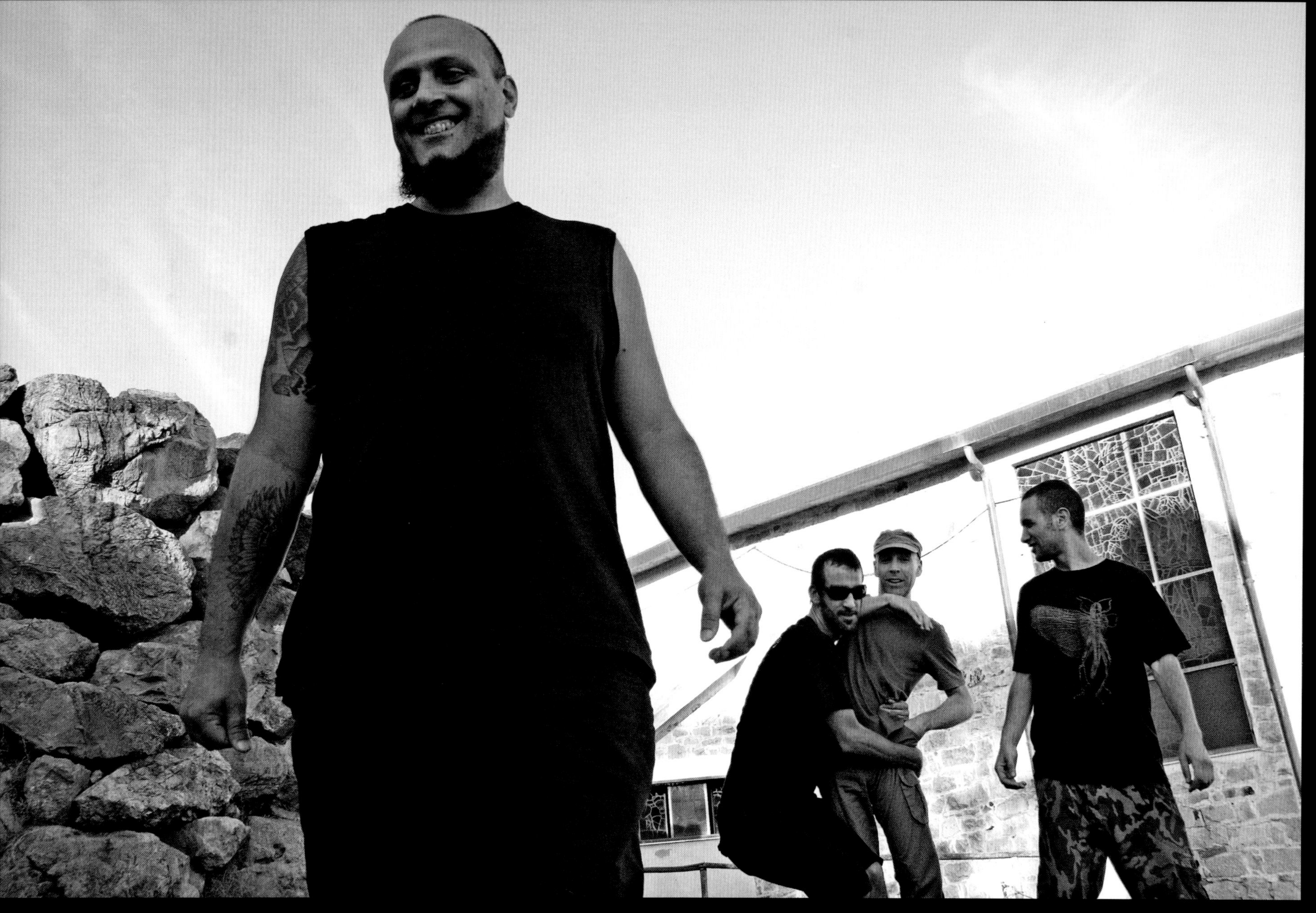

Zu with Joe Lally / Sardinia, Italy, 2010

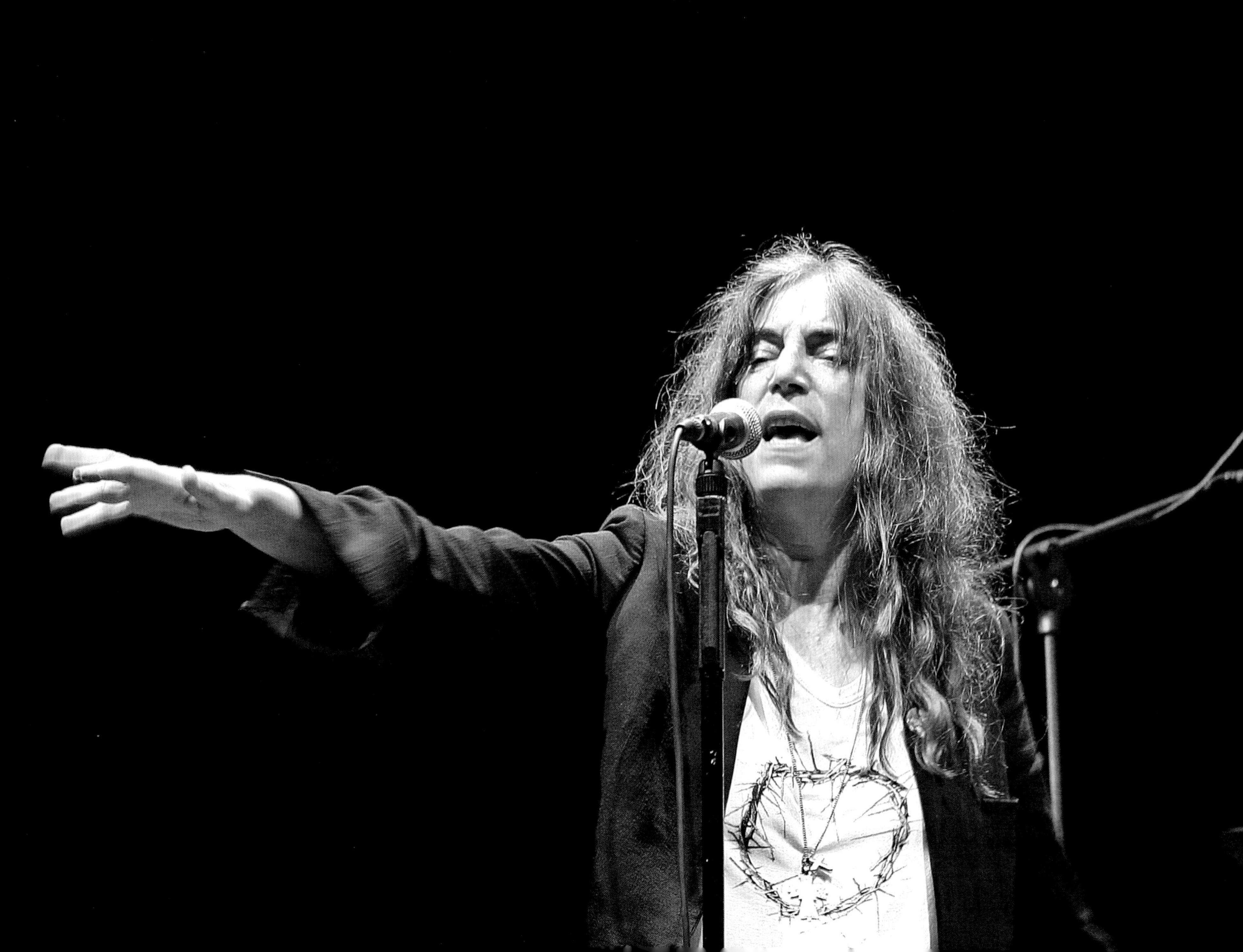

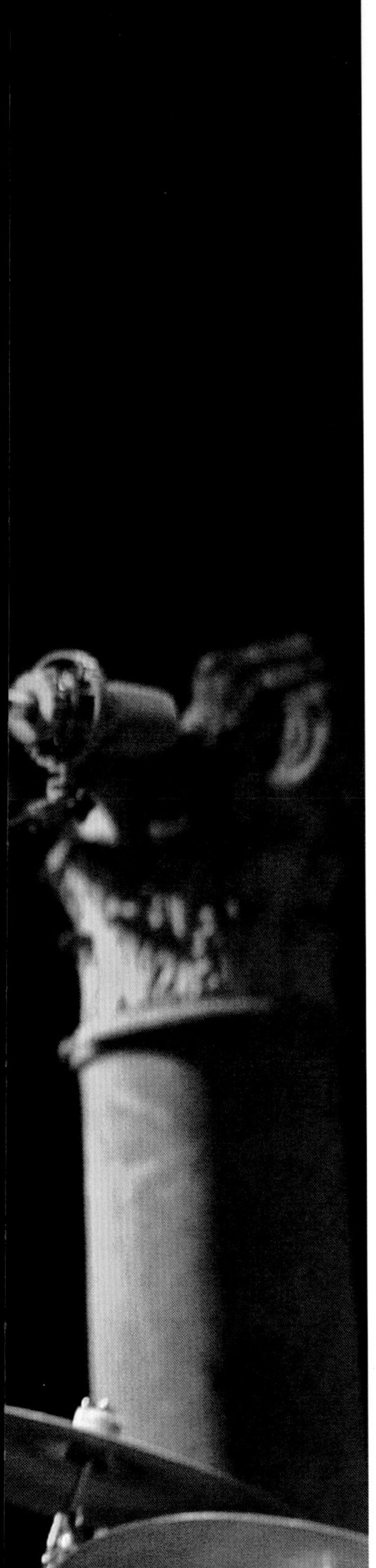

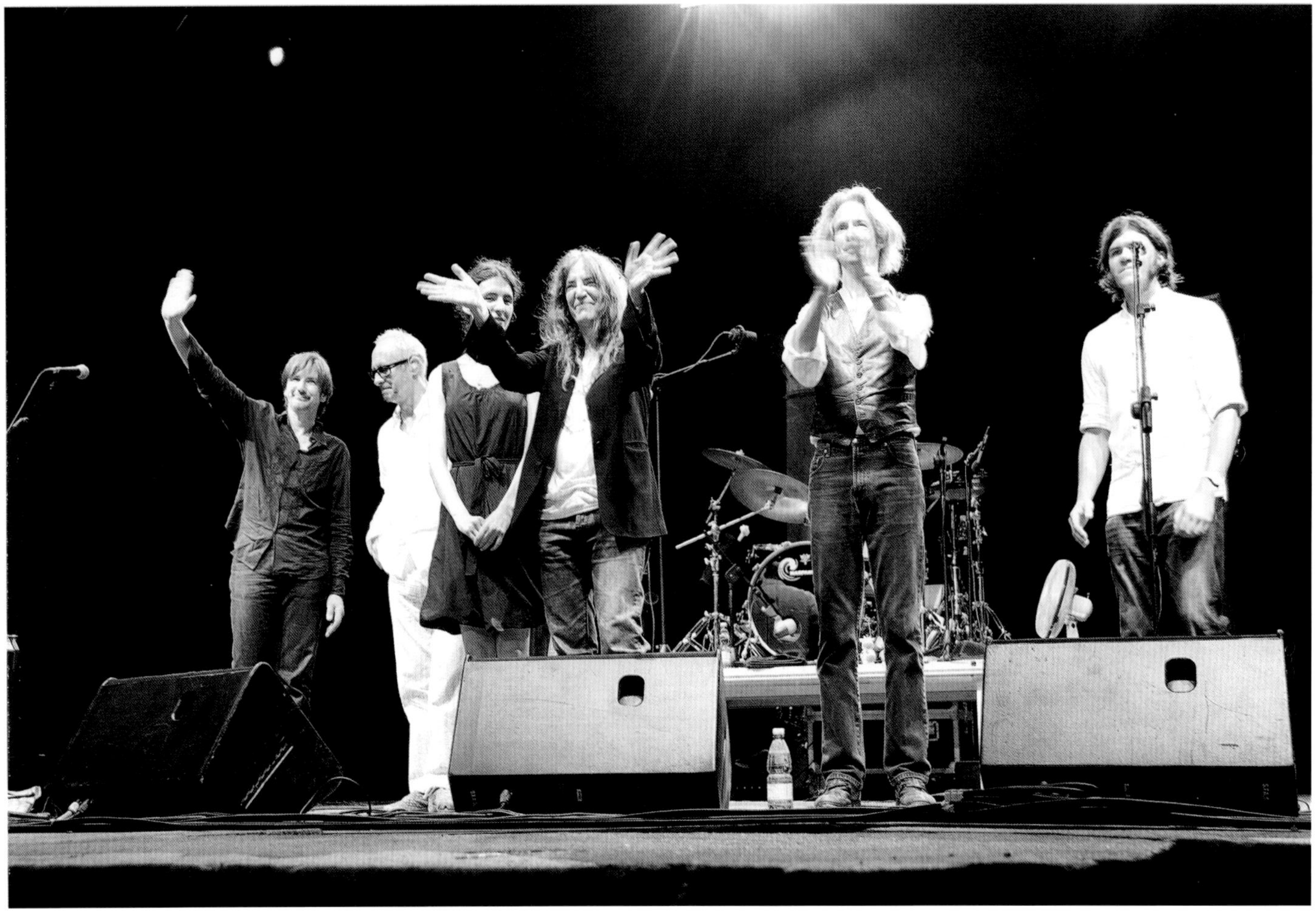

Patti Smith, Ostia Antica / Rome, Italy, 2011

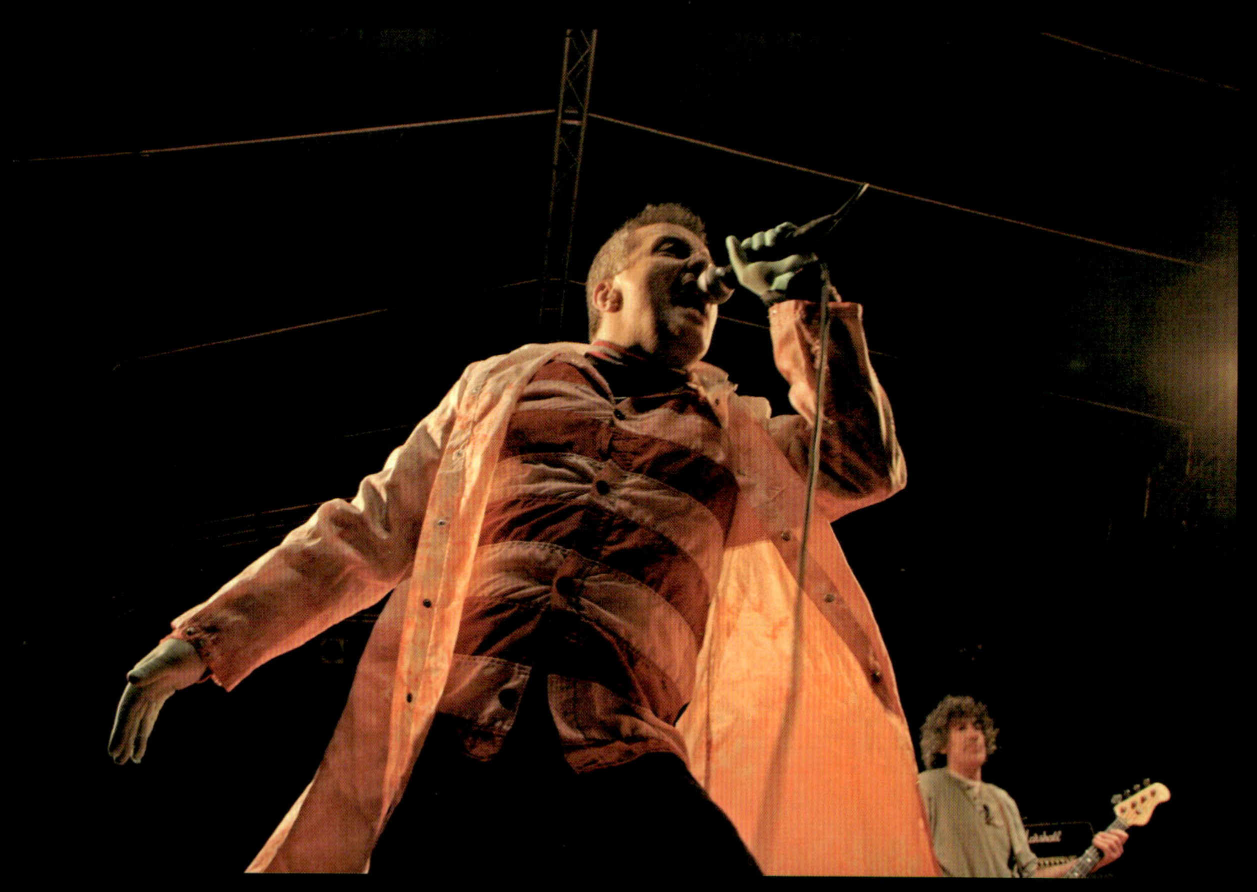

Jello Biafra, Forte Prenestino / Rome, Italy, 2011
Opposite: Scream, Forte Prenestino / Rome, Italy, 2012

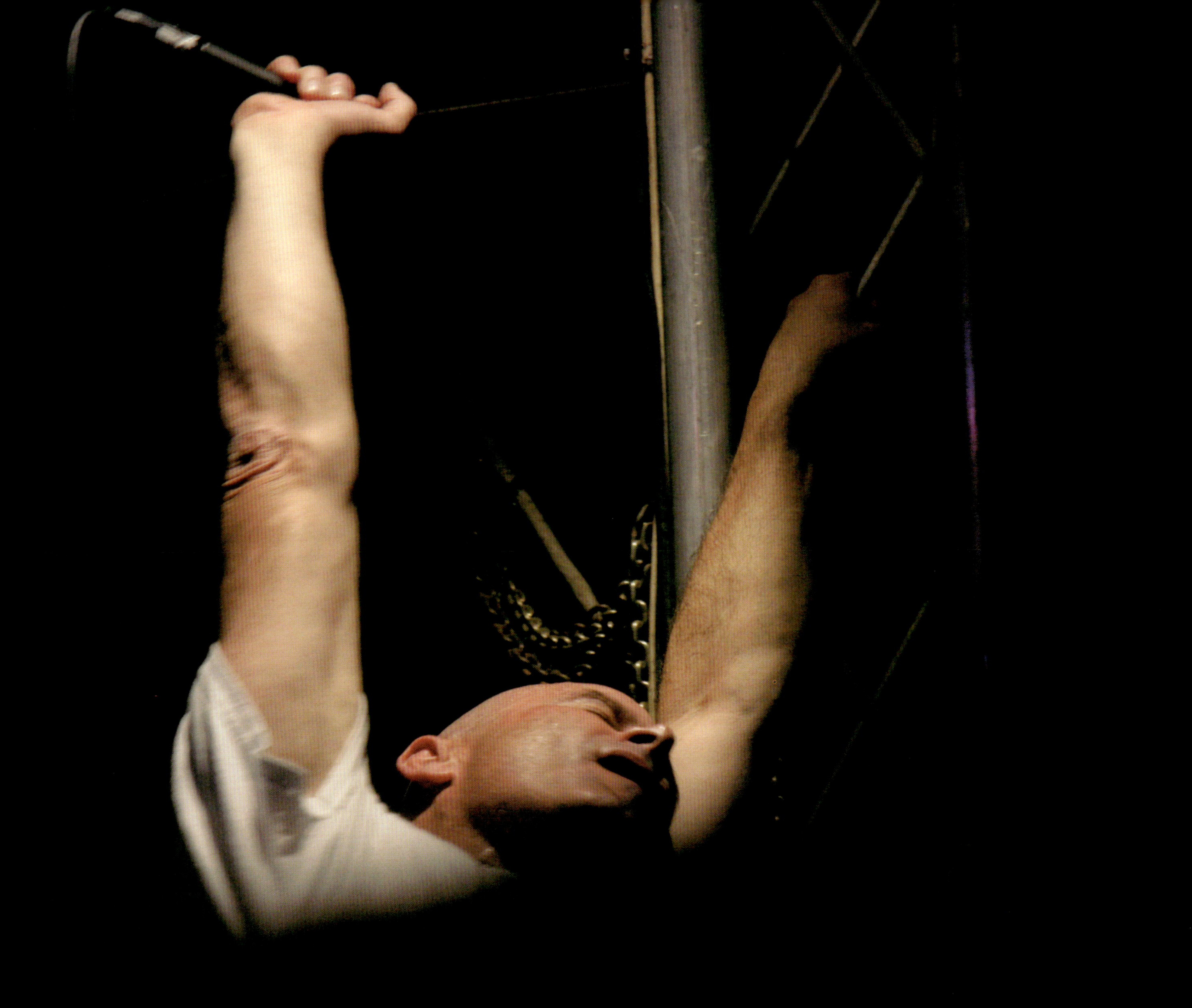

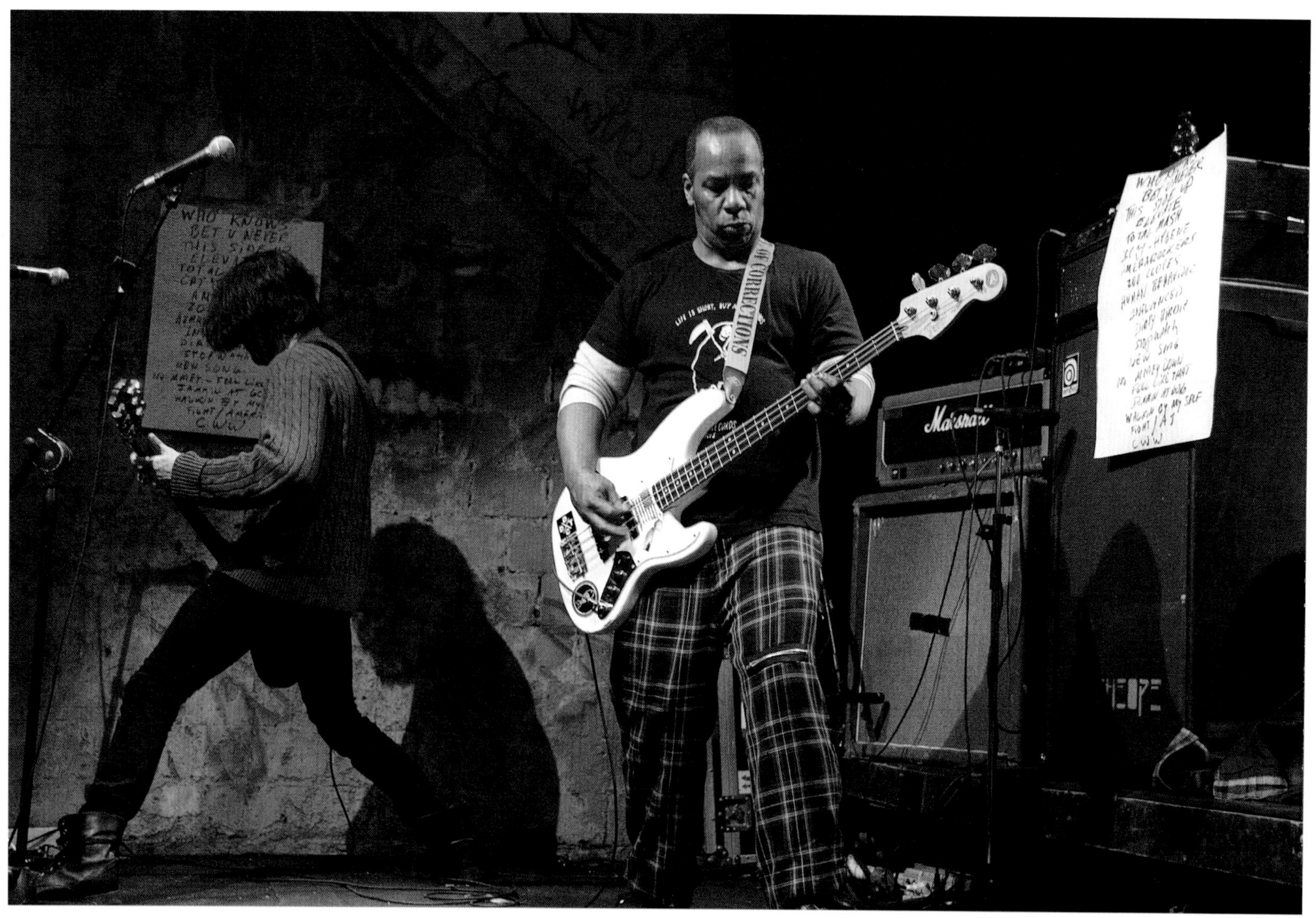

Scream, Forte Prenestino / Rome, Italy, 2012

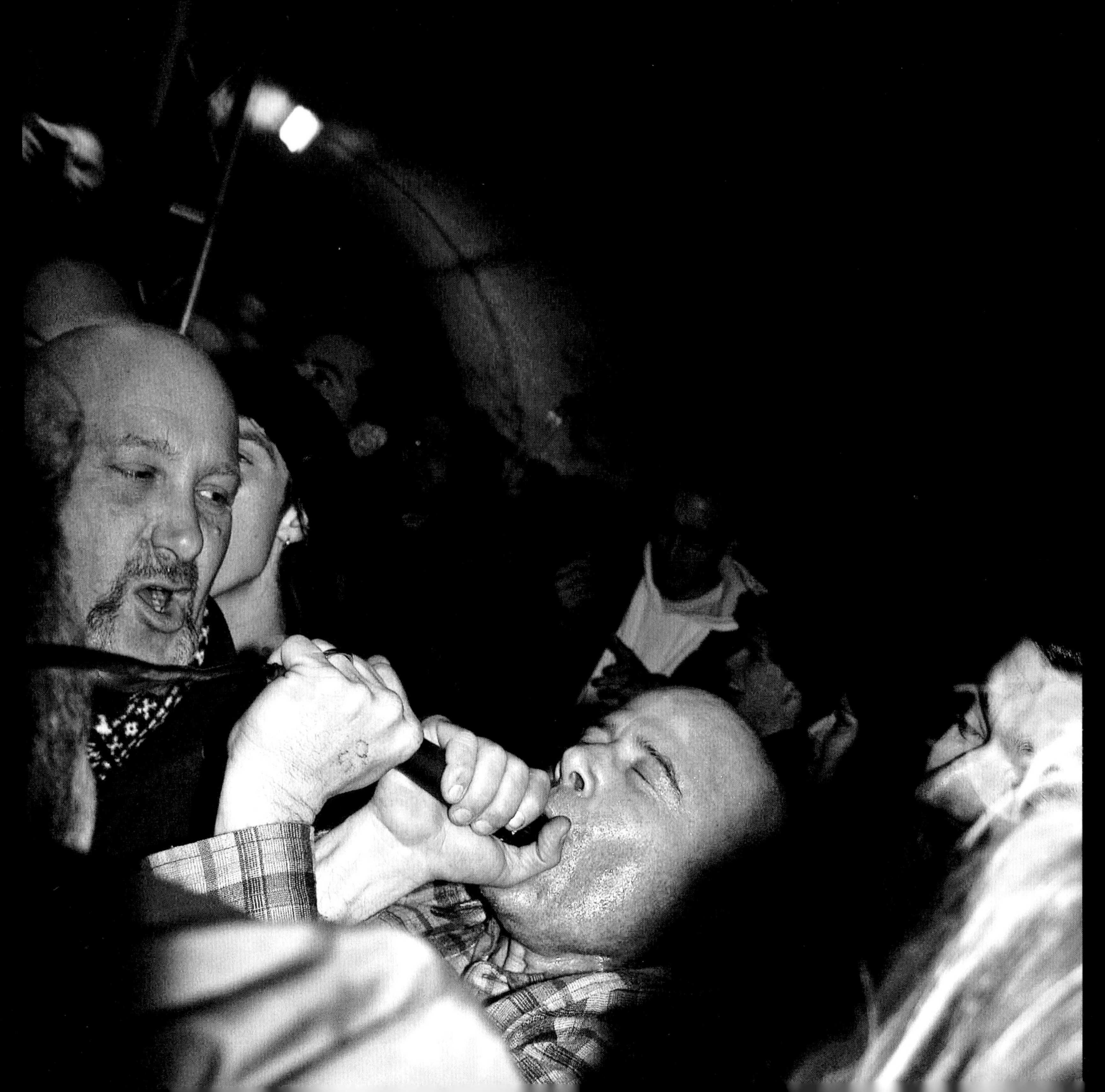

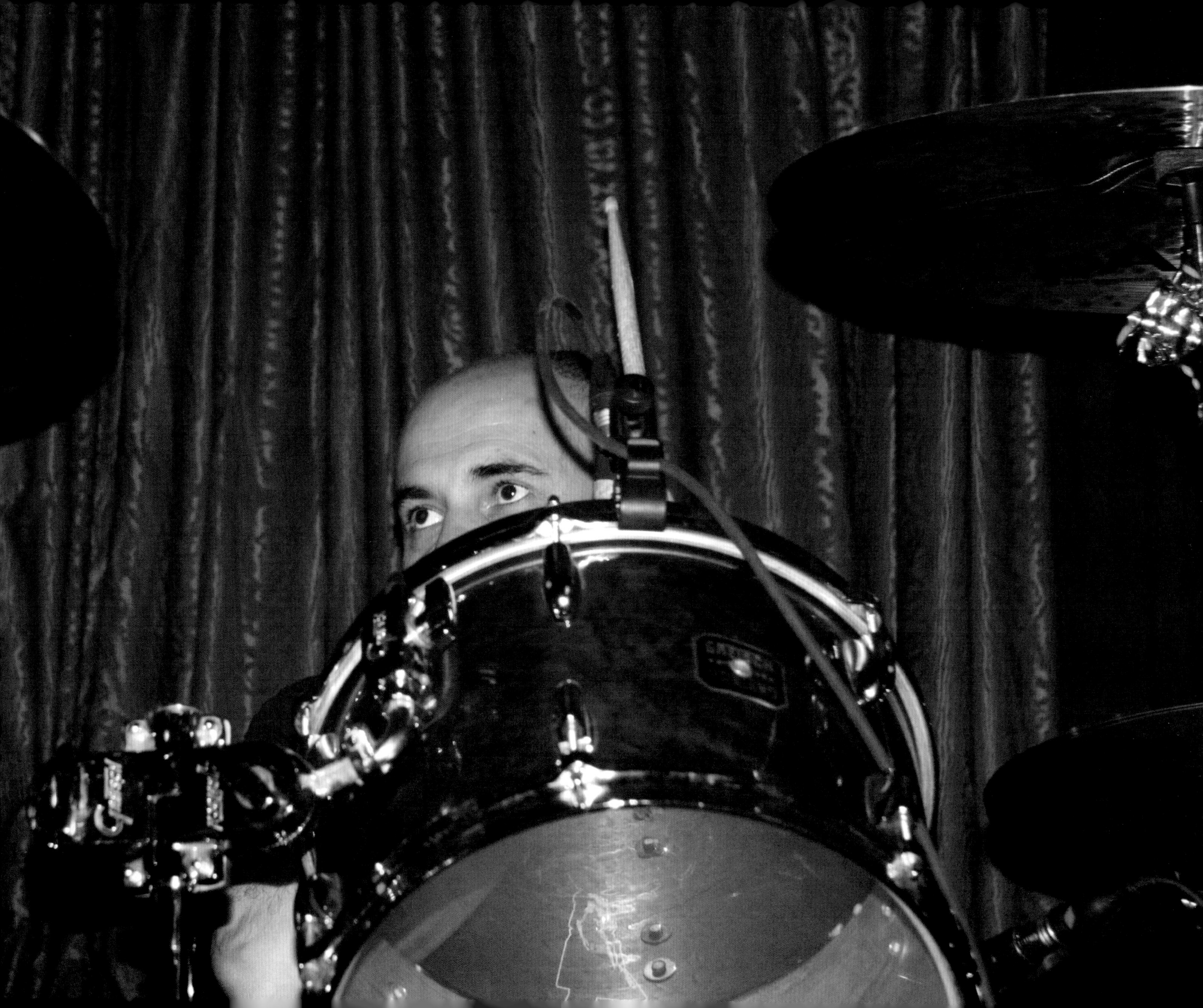

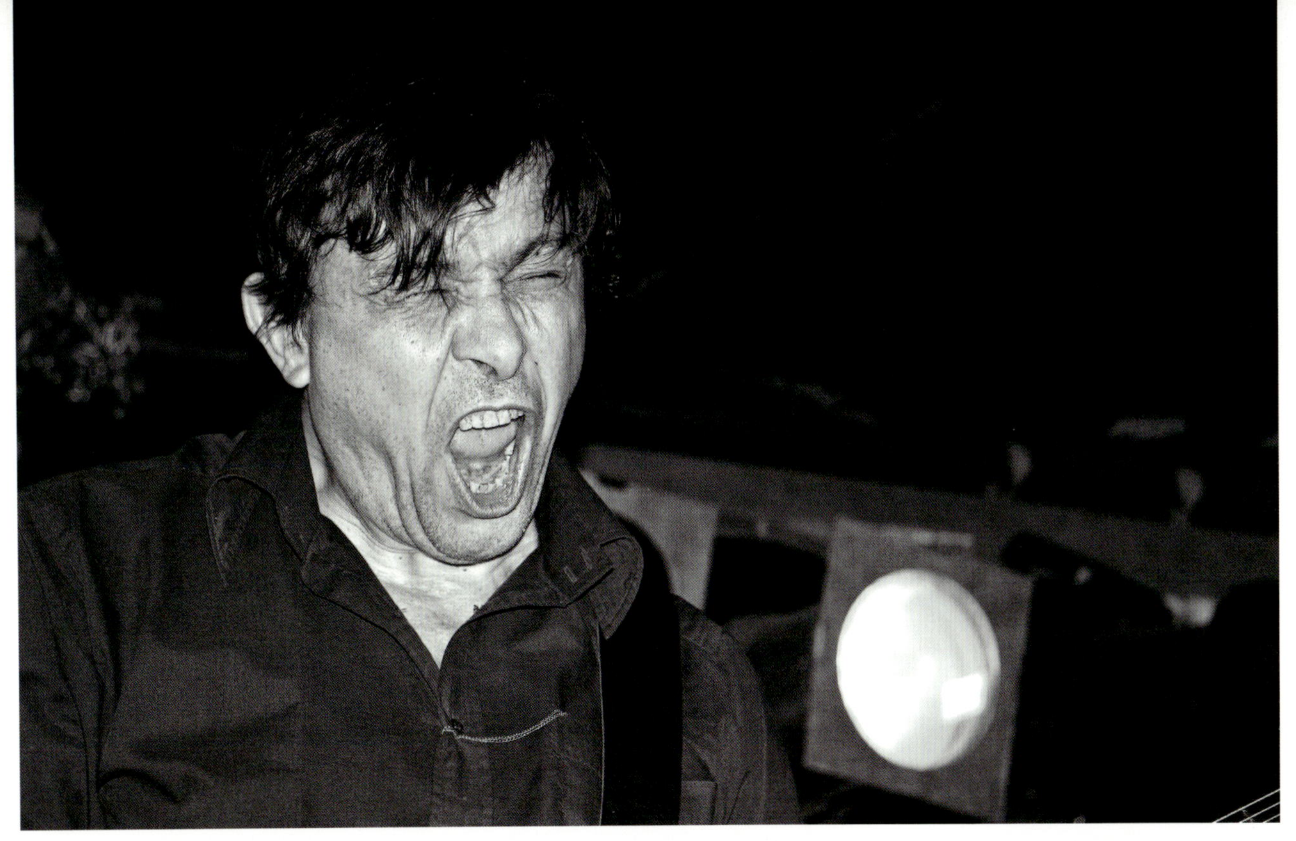

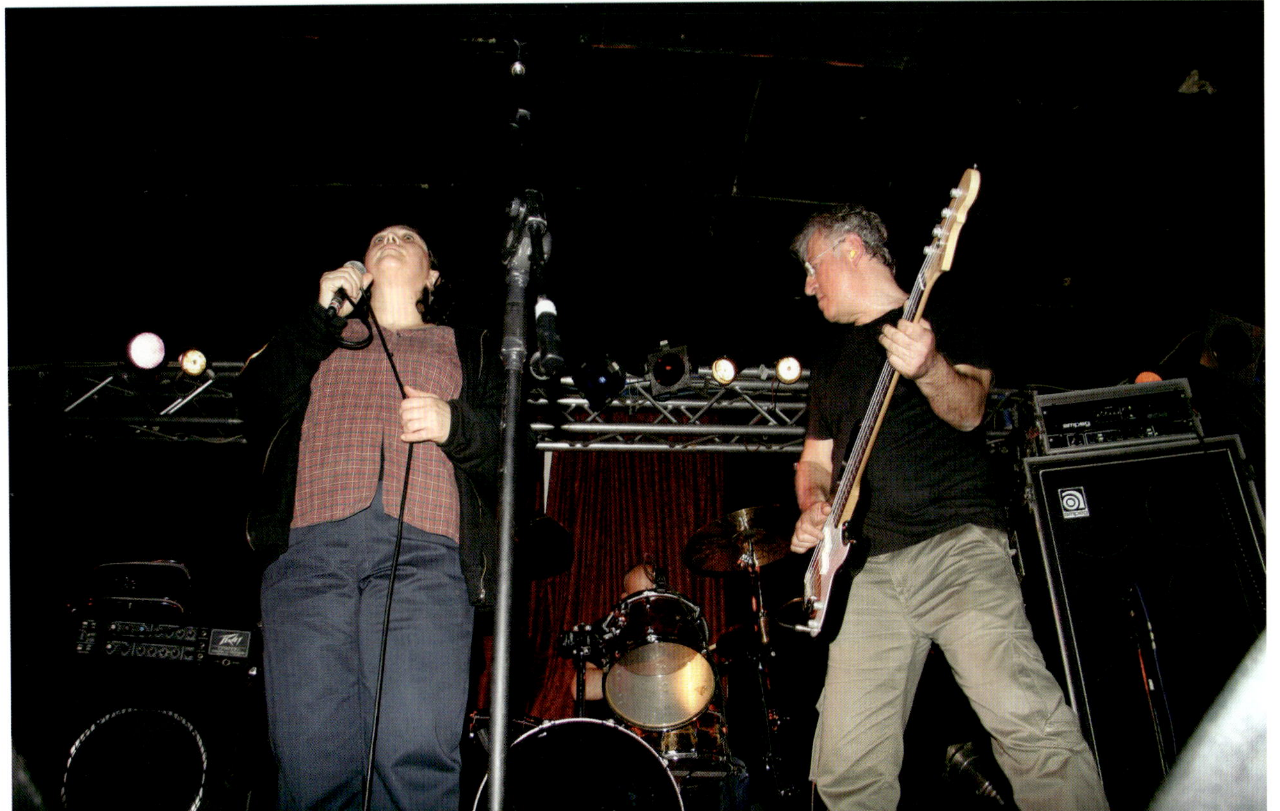

From top: Agostino Tilotta, Uzeda; and Uzeda, Init / Rome, Italy, 2012
Opposite: Davide Oliveri, Uzeda, Init / Rome, Italy, 2012

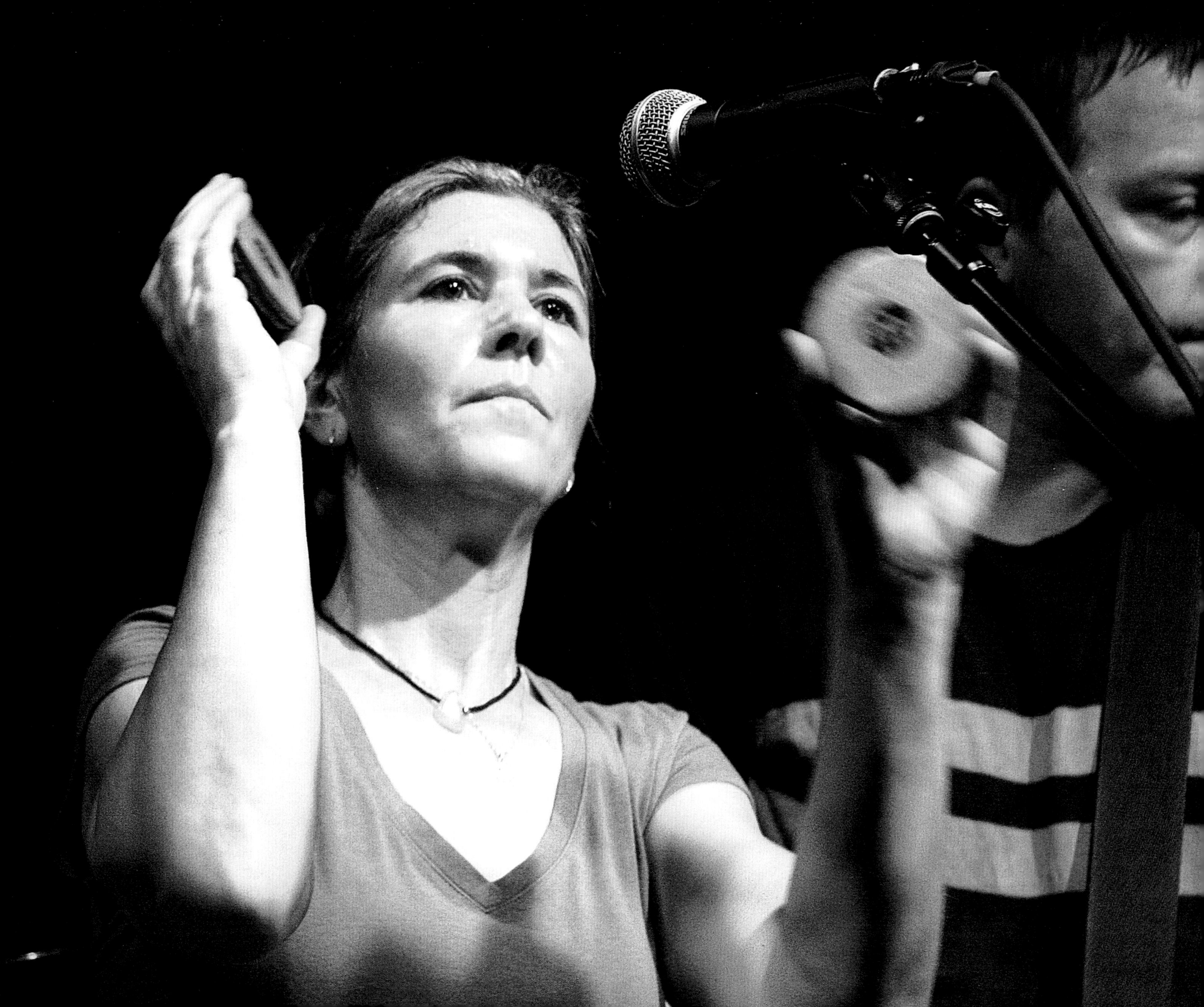

KATHERINA RIJCKEN-BORNEFELD

I've been a musician my whole life. My first experience with an instrument was with a piano, and I also discovered that I love to sing. My dad played piano and organ for his work in a church, so we had a piano at home. He taught me how to play piano and I went to many concerts in the church as a child and sometimes my dad let me play on the organ. My mother sang in the choir and she played violin. I got inspired to invent my own songs on the piano, also singing along, and I played my own little concerts to myself and nobody was allowed to listen then!

When I was about twelve years old I started to learn acoustic guitar, and later on I bought an electric guitar with a little amplifier. When I was about nineteen years old back in 1980, I was asked by a girlfriend if I would like to join their band and I said: "Yes, sure, I can play guitar and sing." But she told me that their drummer had left and asked if I would like to drum, and so I started to play the drums. A friend of mine loaned me his drums and showed me some basic rhythms, and from that starting point I developed my own playing and style. I liked to drum from the very start and I was lucky to play in bands right away.

It was a great opportunity when I was invited to play in the Ex at the end of 1984—that really pushed me forward. As a band, we still work the same way we have since the beginning. It's all about being independent and free in what we want to create. We make all the decisions about the music we write, the schedule of our shows, the releases of the CDs, records, and DVDs, the people we play with, the agents we deal with, the money we earn. I've learned over all these years that its best to let things happen in an honest and organic way.

It's enriching to play and work with other people. I enjoy and have enjoyed so many of our projects, including the Ex Orchestra, working with dancers, the Alex d'Electrique theater group, the Ethiopian alto saxophone player Getatchew Mekuria, the Ethiopian group Fendika, the Ex and Brass Unbound with horn players like Ken Vandermark, Mats Gustafsson, Wolter Wierbos, and Roy Paci, and many more. And I have loved collaborating and sharing stages with like-minded bands. It was always very helpful. You can achieve much more together than on your own. The collaborations have shaped me into a social, experienced, and happy musician.

Staying authentic is another important thing. It provides a good guideline and gives one the strength to survive in hard times. Touring together is a whole other chapter. You have to learn to stay in a good mood even when you feel tired or don't like the circumstances. It doesn't help to vent negativity, it only creates more negativity, and takes a lot of energy—and you probably won't play a good gig. It's better to go with the flow when you are on the road. At more quiet and less stressful moments you can sort things out. It's not always easy to keep in line with each other. Everybody has a different truth and their own worldview. As long as we respect each other and give each other space, it works.

It's always a challenge to play the best versions of the songs at every concert. It always demands a high level of concentration, physical fitness, playfulness, courage, commitment, and dedication. I love the moments when we are a real unit, when we are connecting with the audience, expressing our souls through music and lifting ourselves and the audience to magical levels. Then something happens that you can't describe, but it makes you so intensely happy that you want to do everything you can to reach this point again. Music unites people. It's an inspiration and a tool for healing.

THE EX

Katerina Bornefeld, Black Cat / WDC, 2016

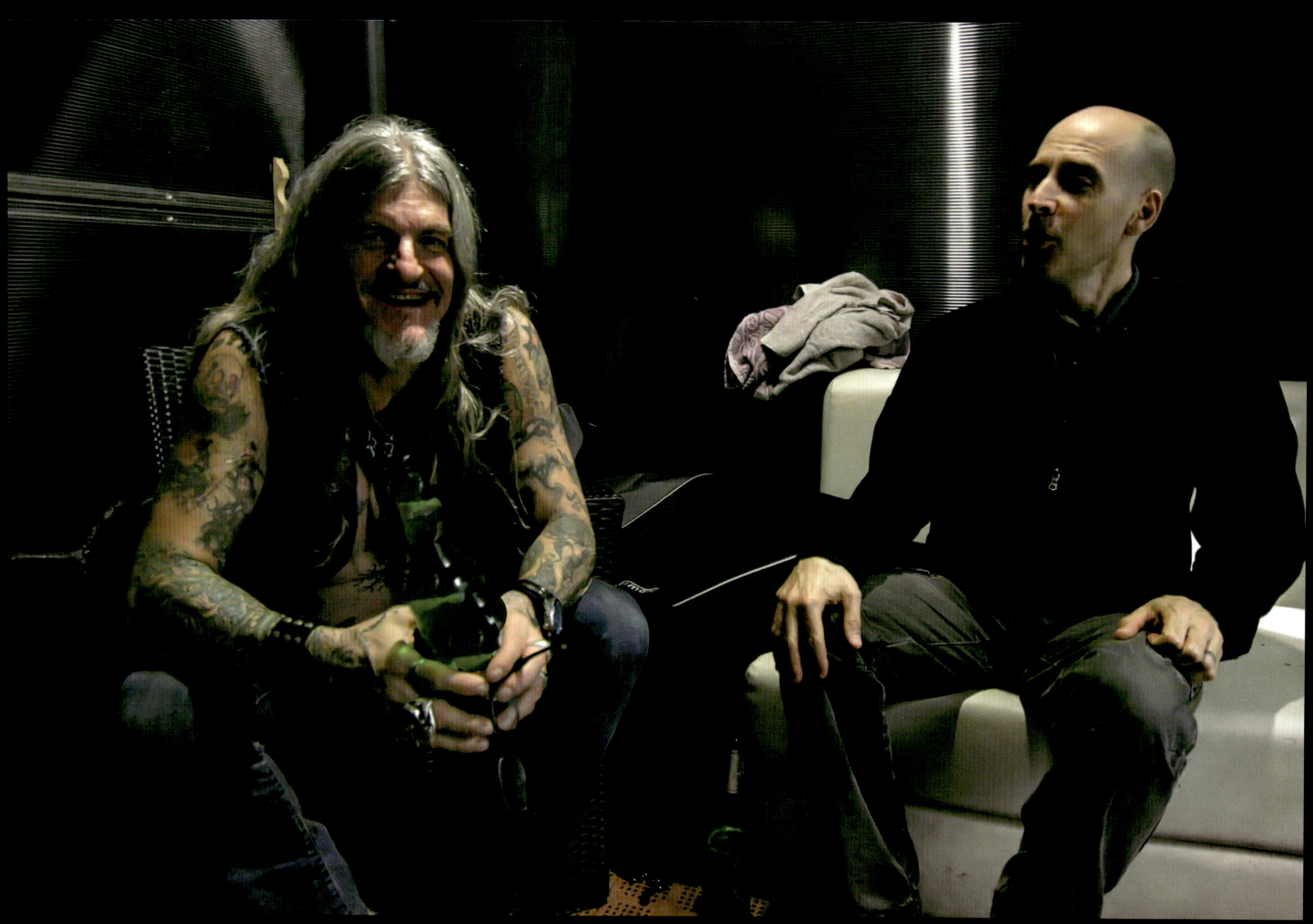

Scott "Wino" Weinrich and Joe Lally, Init dressing room / Rome, Italy, 2014
Opposite: Kat Bjelland, Babes in Toyland, Black Cat / WDC, 2015

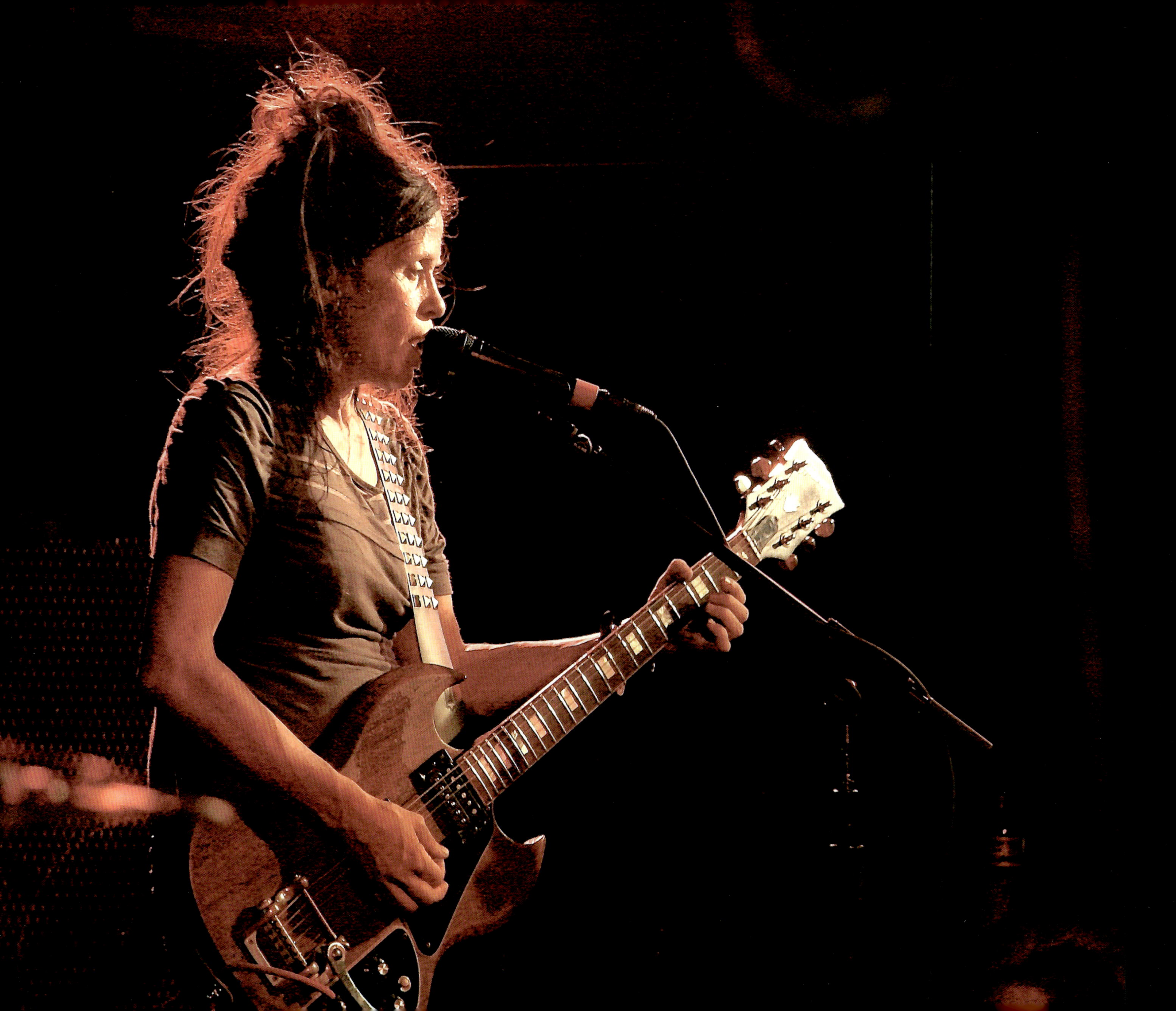

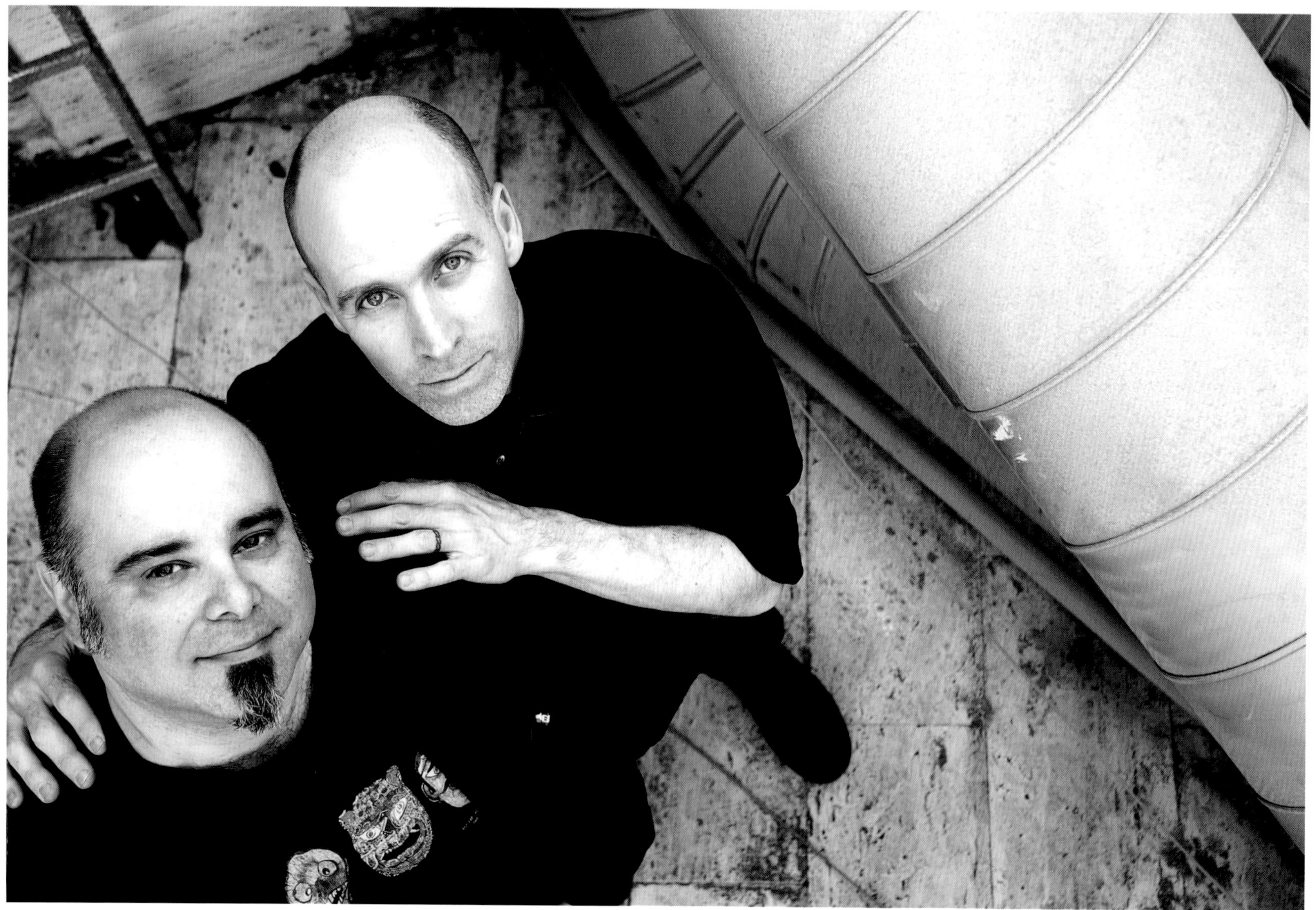

Teho Teardo (Meathead, Italian composer) and Joe Lally / Rome, Italy, 2015

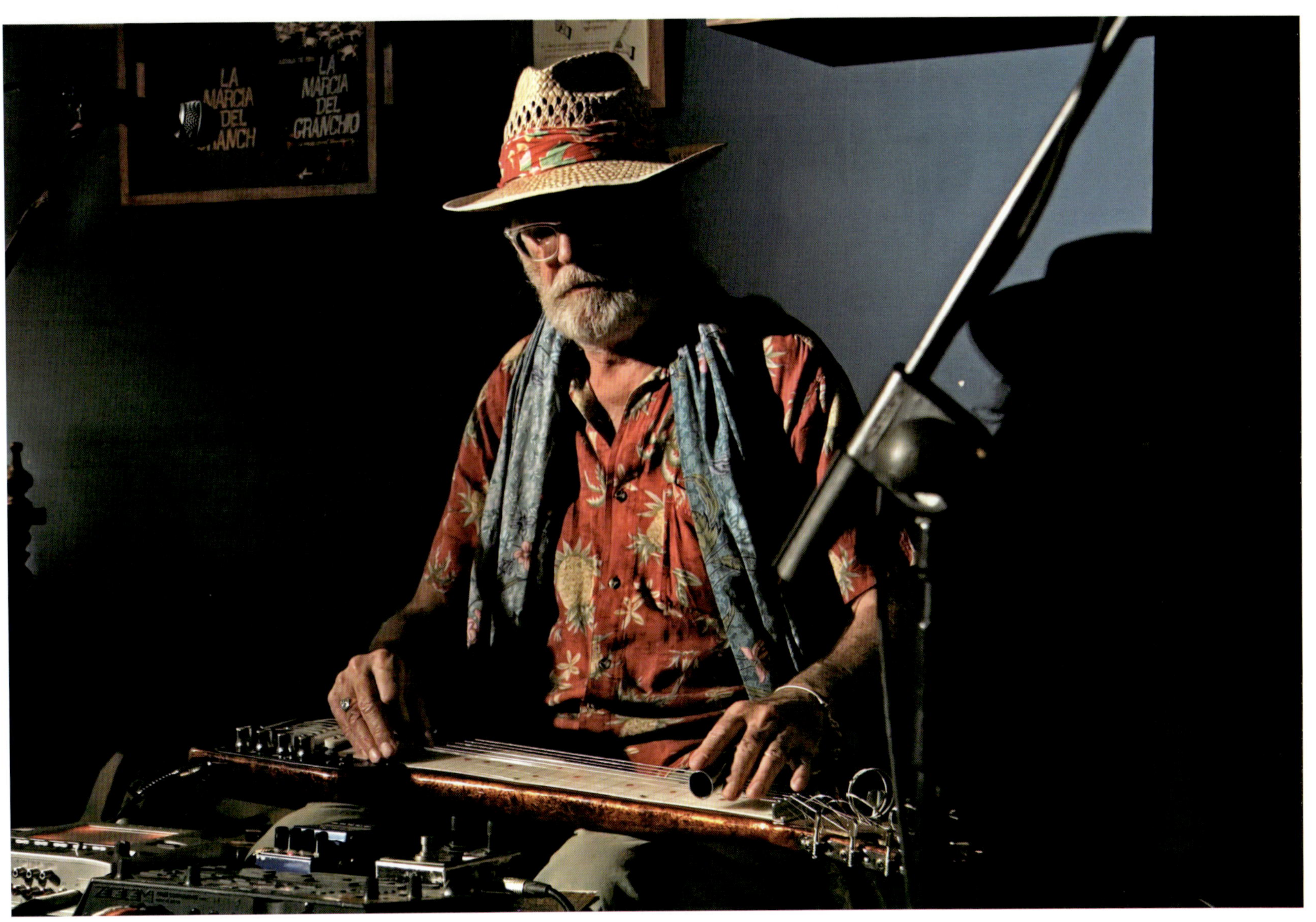

Mike Cooper, Grandma Bistrot / Rome, Italy, 2015

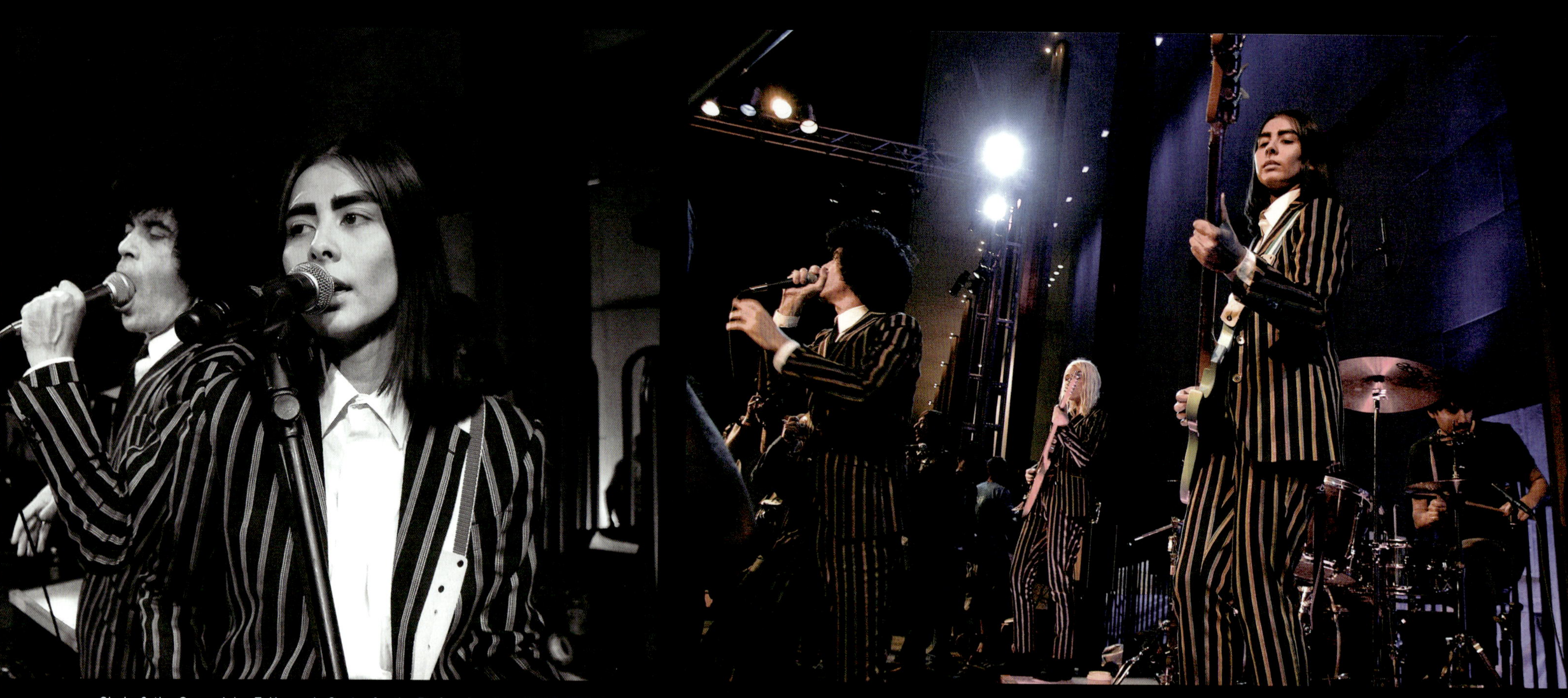

Chain & the Gang, John F. Kennedy Center for the Performing Arts / WDC, 2015
Opposite: Ex Hex, 9:30 Club / WDC, 2015

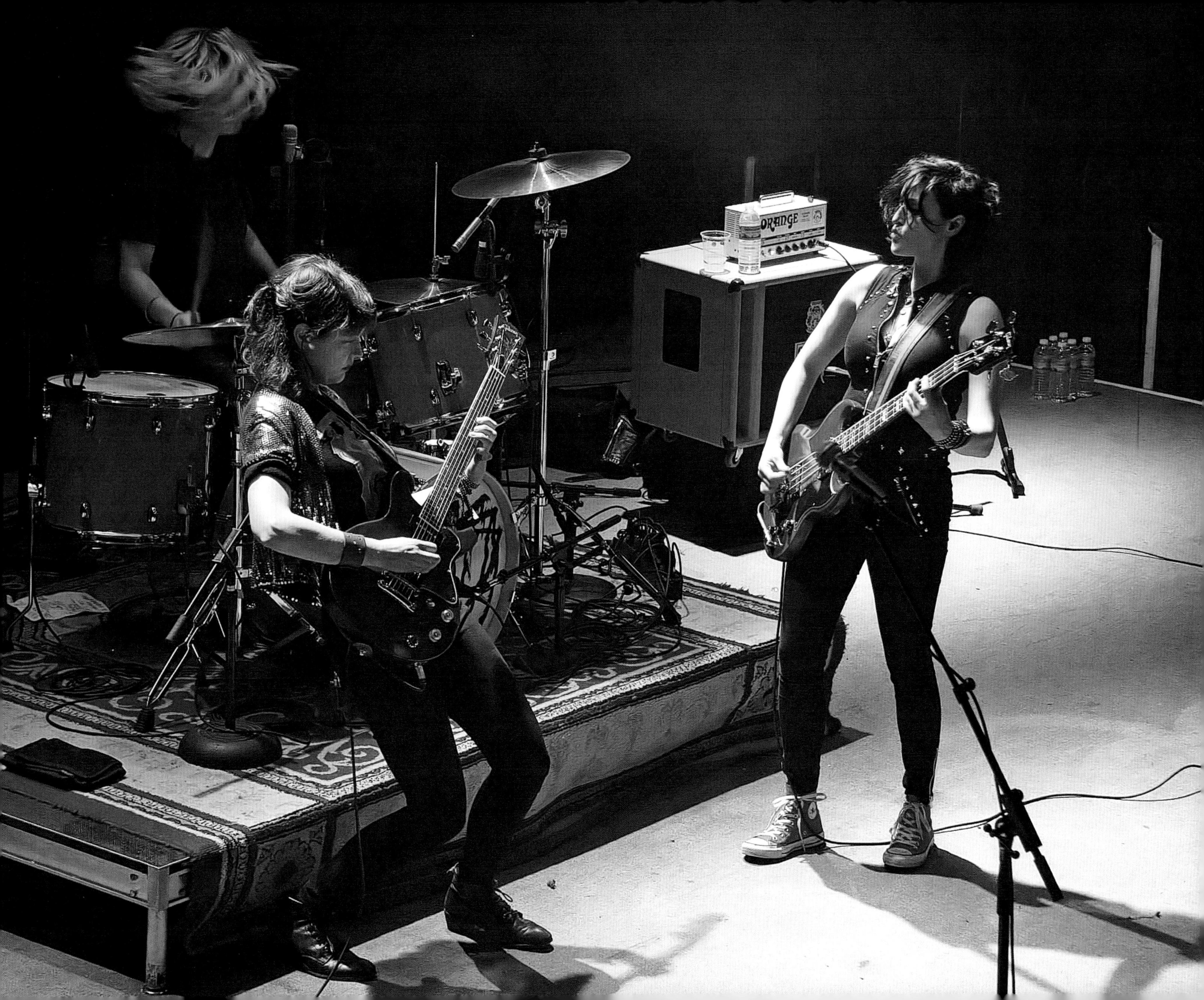
ORANGE

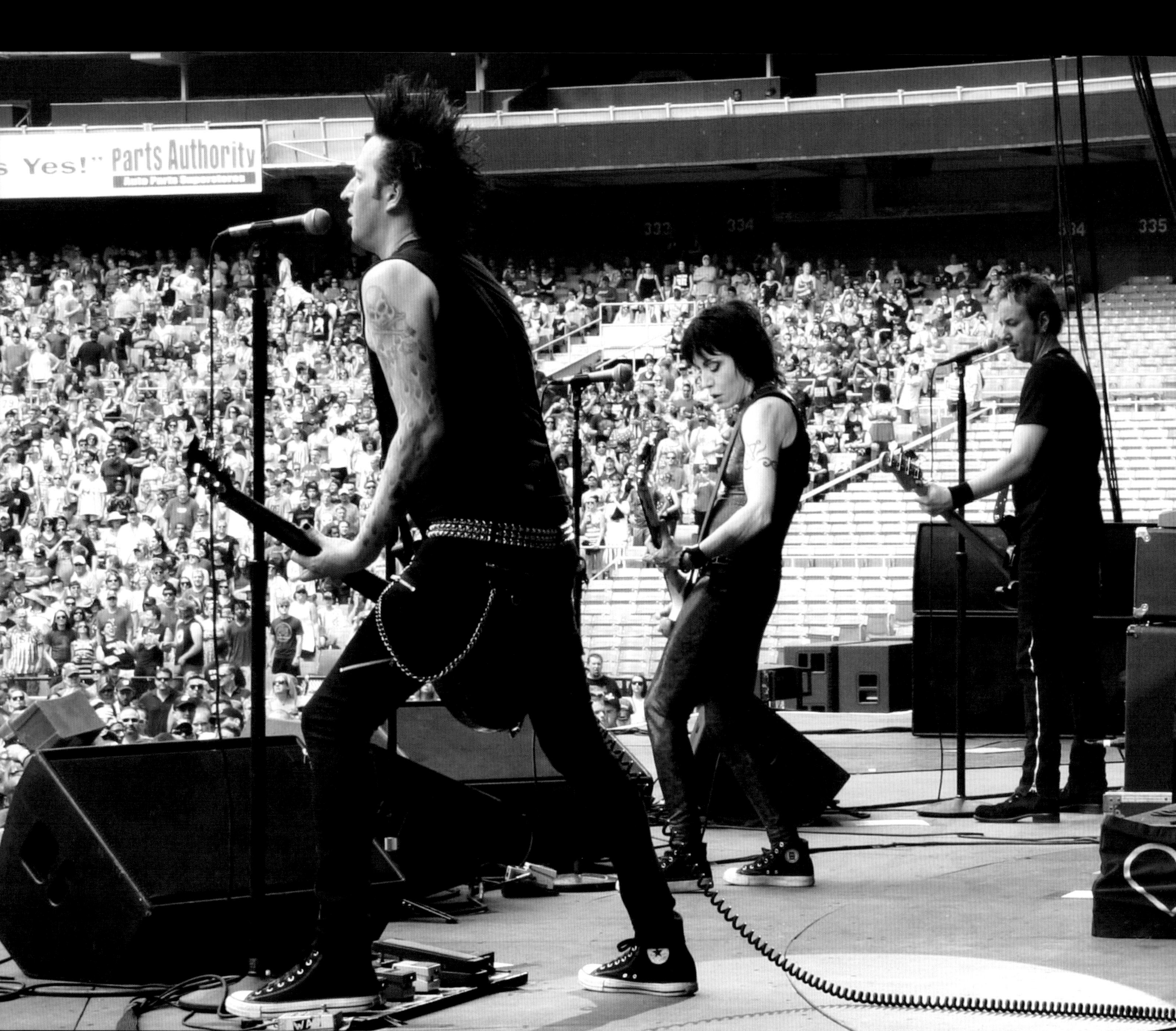
s Yes!" Parts Authority
333
334
335

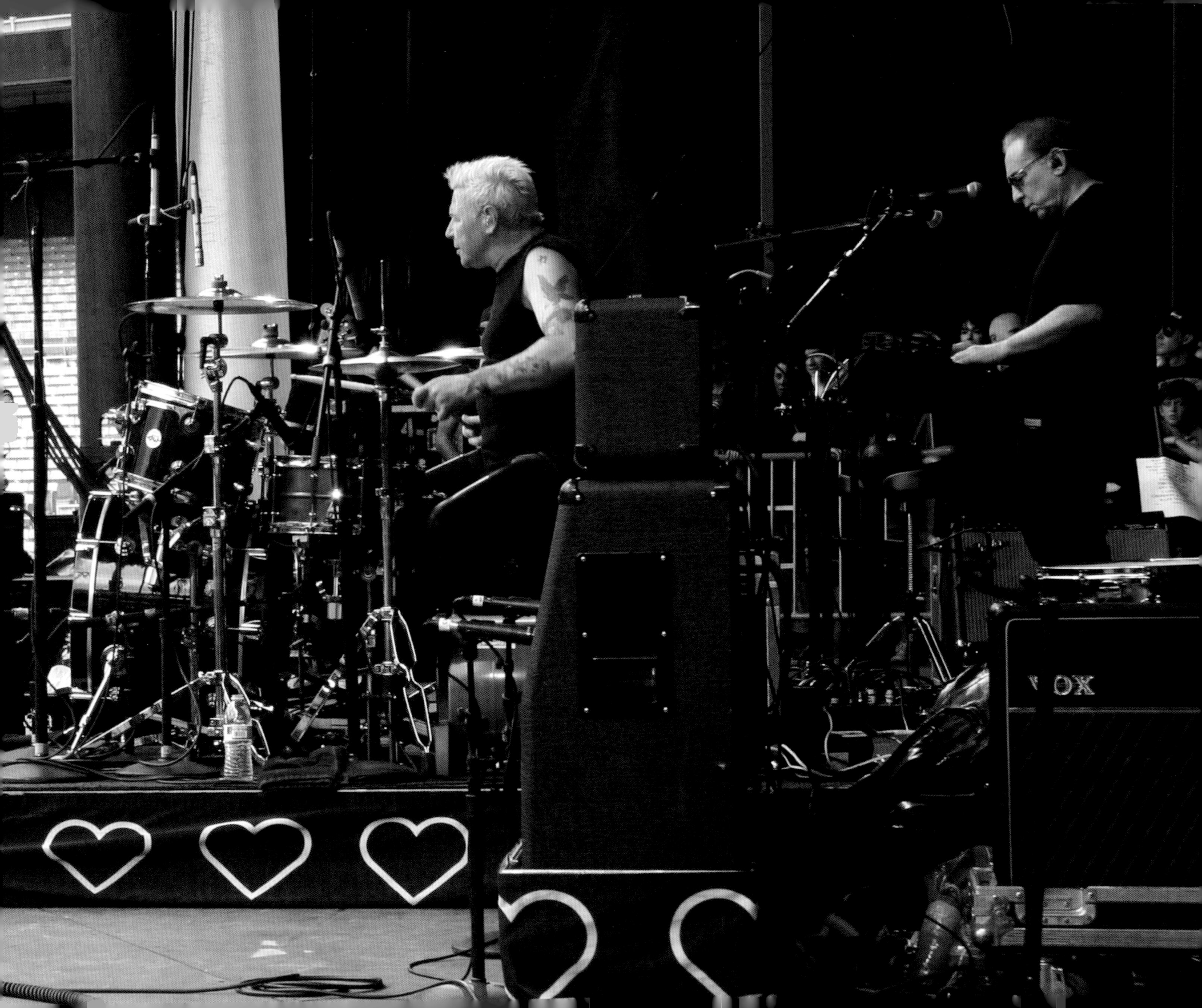
VOX

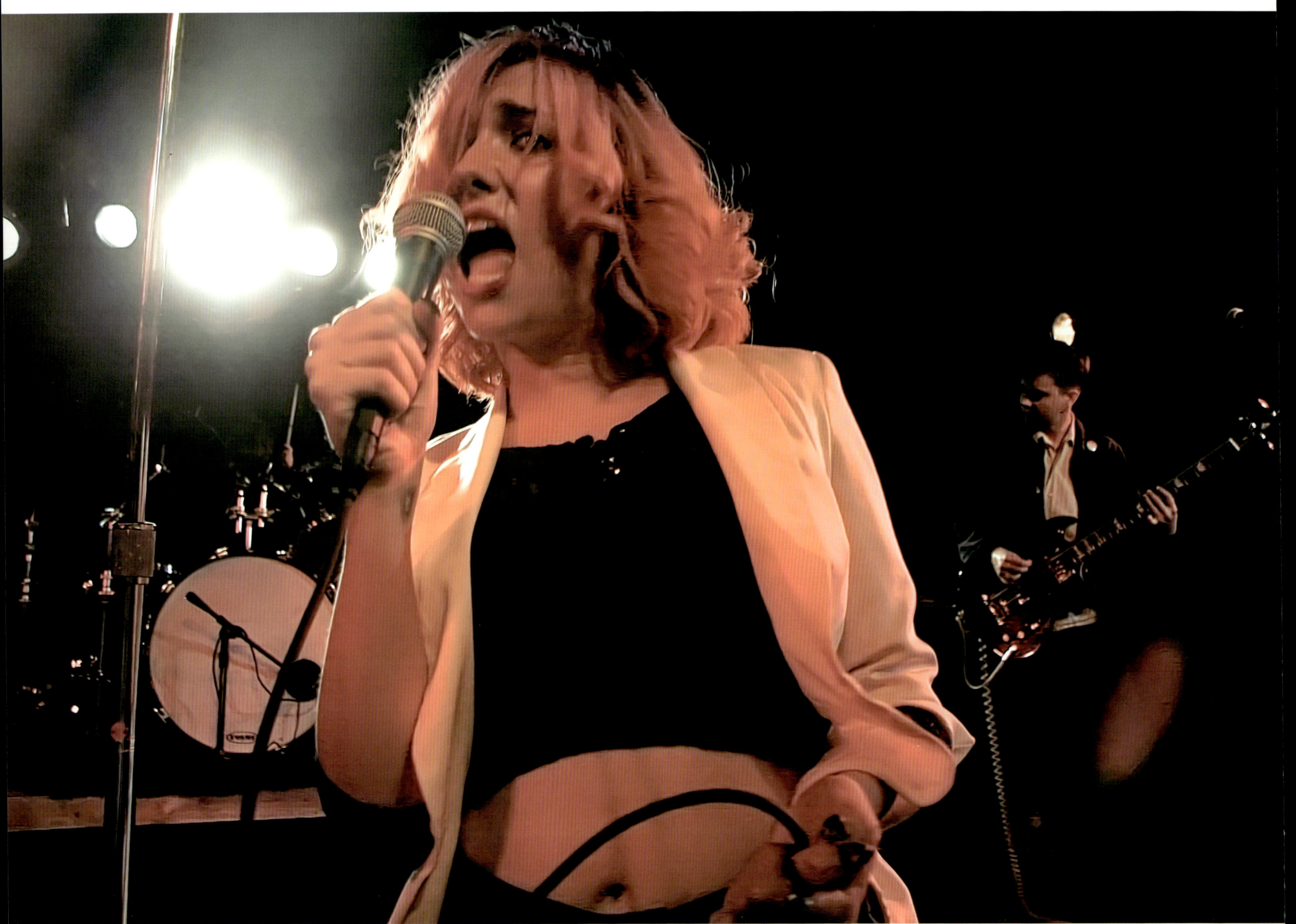

Priests, Black Cat / WDC, 2015; previous page: Joan Jett and the Blackhearts, RFK Stadium / WDC, 2015

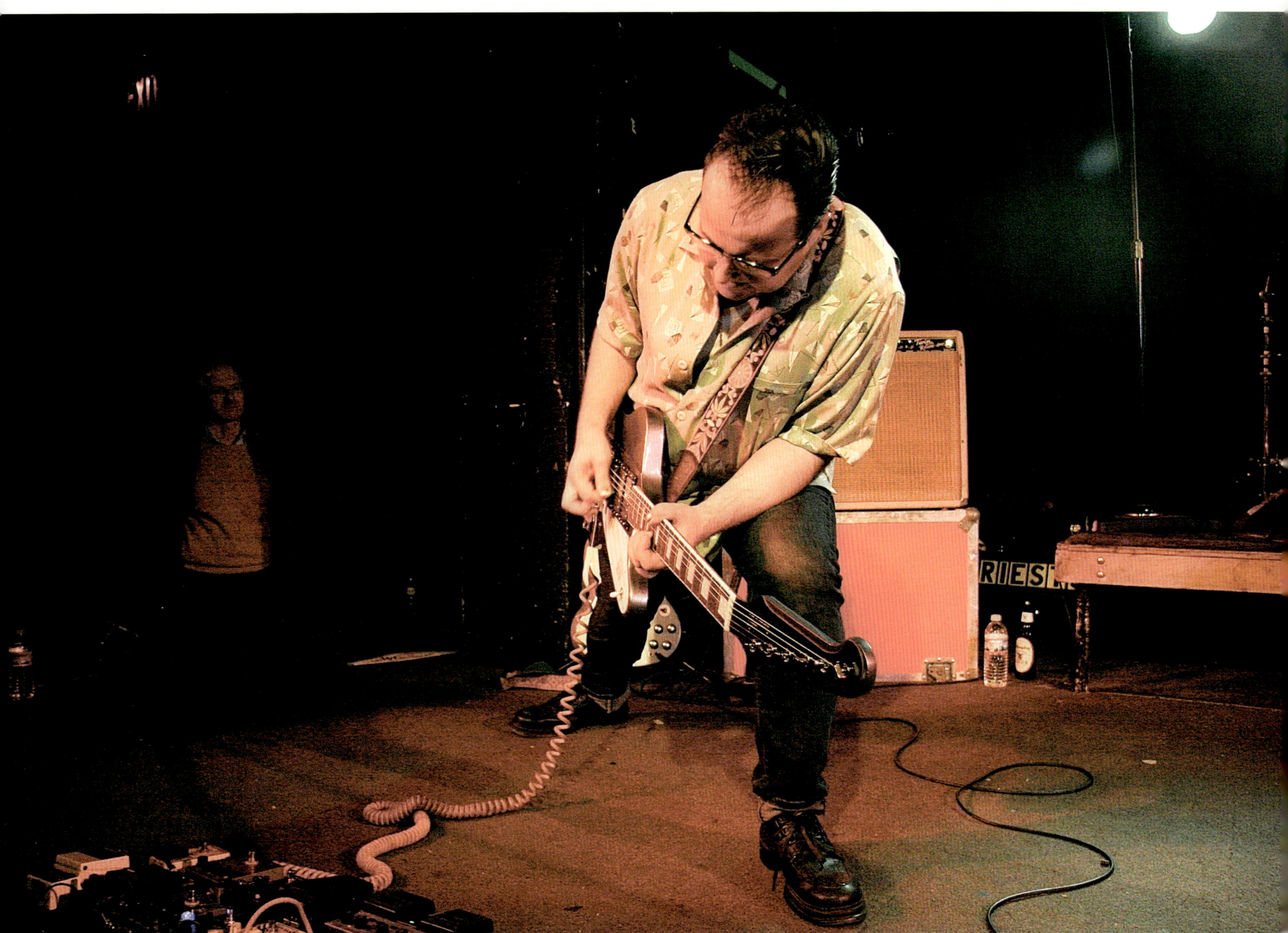

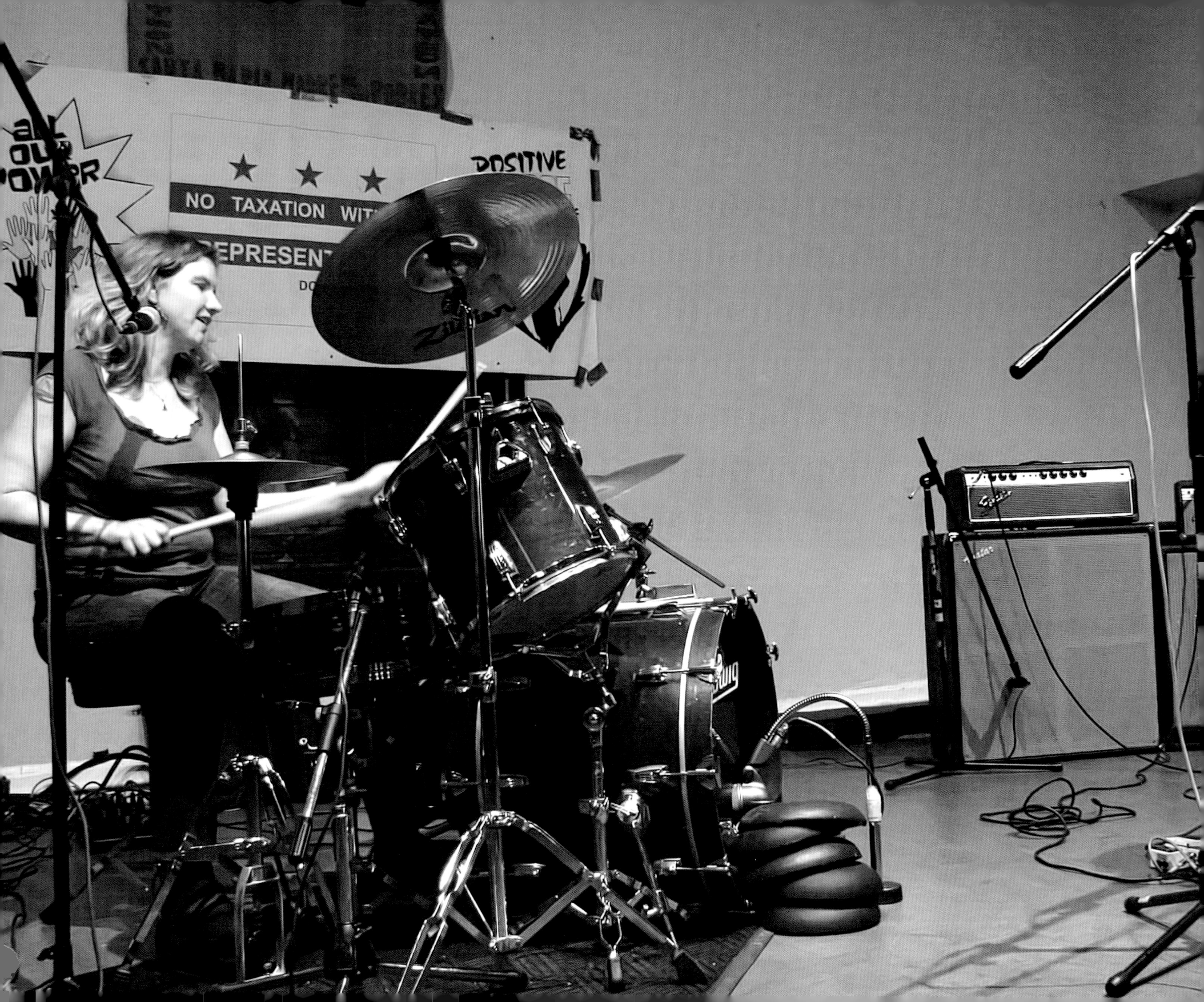

NO TAXATION WIT
REPRESENT
POSITIVE

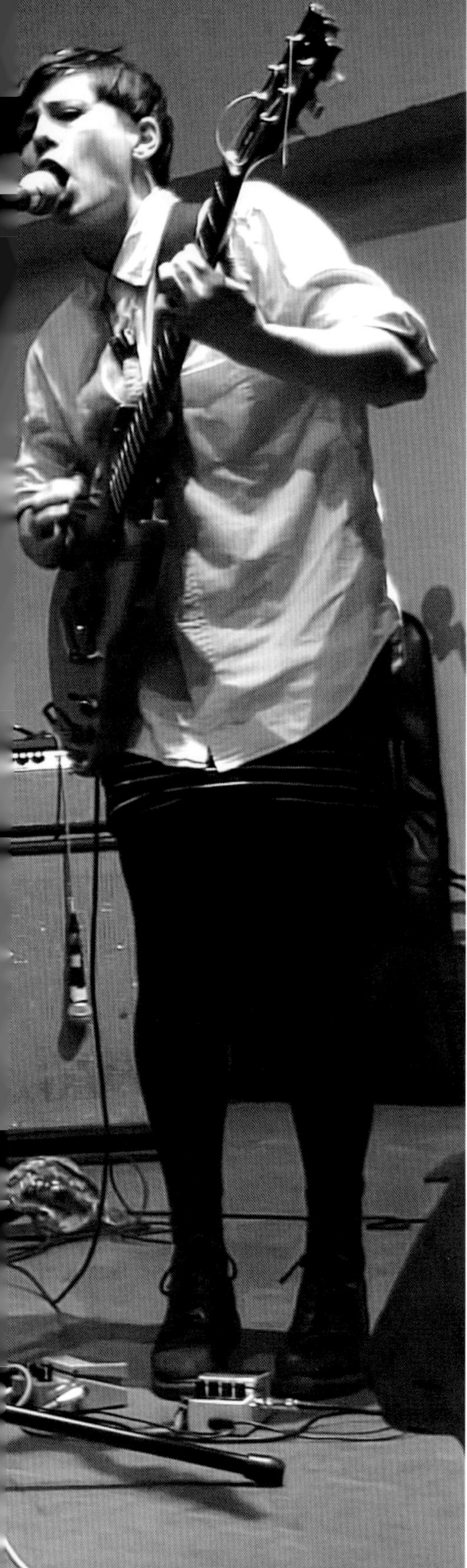

KATY OTTO

I wouldn't be the person I am if it were not for the DC punk community. At seventeen, two things happened: I started playing drums and I stumbled into my first Fugazi show. I had been playing for a little bit when I began to realize I lived in a city at the perfect moment in time, with vibrant art and activism. We built community. We engaged in political education. We organized and resisted—and music was always part of it. Playing drums to me is like clapping along—for your bandmates, for a better world, for the crowd. I like playing this role musically, and in DC, I was able to see tons of other women making music, making art, engaging in resistance work, and running labels from a very early age. Not only that—they were always open and inviting, welcoming me, mentoring me, encouraging me. It meant, and means, the world to me. It helped me to truly see and feel my own power to make things happen.

Positive Force DC was a place where I learned some basic organizing skills and forged relationships with a number of folks. I lost some of my initial shyness and began reaching out to ask how to do things. My best friend and the first person I played music with, Bonnie Schlegel, decided she wanted to start a record label to put out music she loved. I ended up joining her, as did our other friend Sara Klemm. We were helped along the way by so many amazing women, including Kristin Thomson of Simple Machines and Kim Coletta who ran DeSoto at the time. Our label, Exotic Fever Records, first released an EP by our friend Clark's band the Halo Project. We sold it simply at shows we attended, as they weren't playing out—it was more of a studio project. Sara had founded a DC Books to Prisons project, so we also put out a compilation benefiting this. In our history, we would go on to put out four more benefit comps for Compassion Over Killing, the District Alliance for Safe Housing, Helping Individual Prostitutes Survive, and Vietnam Veterans of America. They included artwork, recipes, and writings from the artists. We also had the honor of putting out an array of bands over the years.

The label is now eighteen years old, which is hard to believe—and it's still going strong. Times have changed and digital distribution plays a critical role in disseminating music. I have always thought it was really important for women and other marginalized people to run record labels—essentially, to own and control the means of production for cultural work. People have sometimes assumed I just put out projects by women—that's never been the case, but it's an interesting assumption.

I think it's powerful for women to make work in public, to take up space in public, and to support one another. I would never have been able to play in bands, go on tour, book shows, organize conferences, participate in demonstrations, and use my voice as much as I have were it not for the amazing women (and men too) who encouraged and mentored me from an early age. I truly want to share the things I have learned and any resources I have with other people, and especially other women.

TROPHY WIFE • CALLOWHILL • BALD RAPUNZEL • DEL CIELO • PROBLEMS • HELSINKI • RAINBOW CRIMES

Katy Otto, Trophy Wife / WDC, 2017

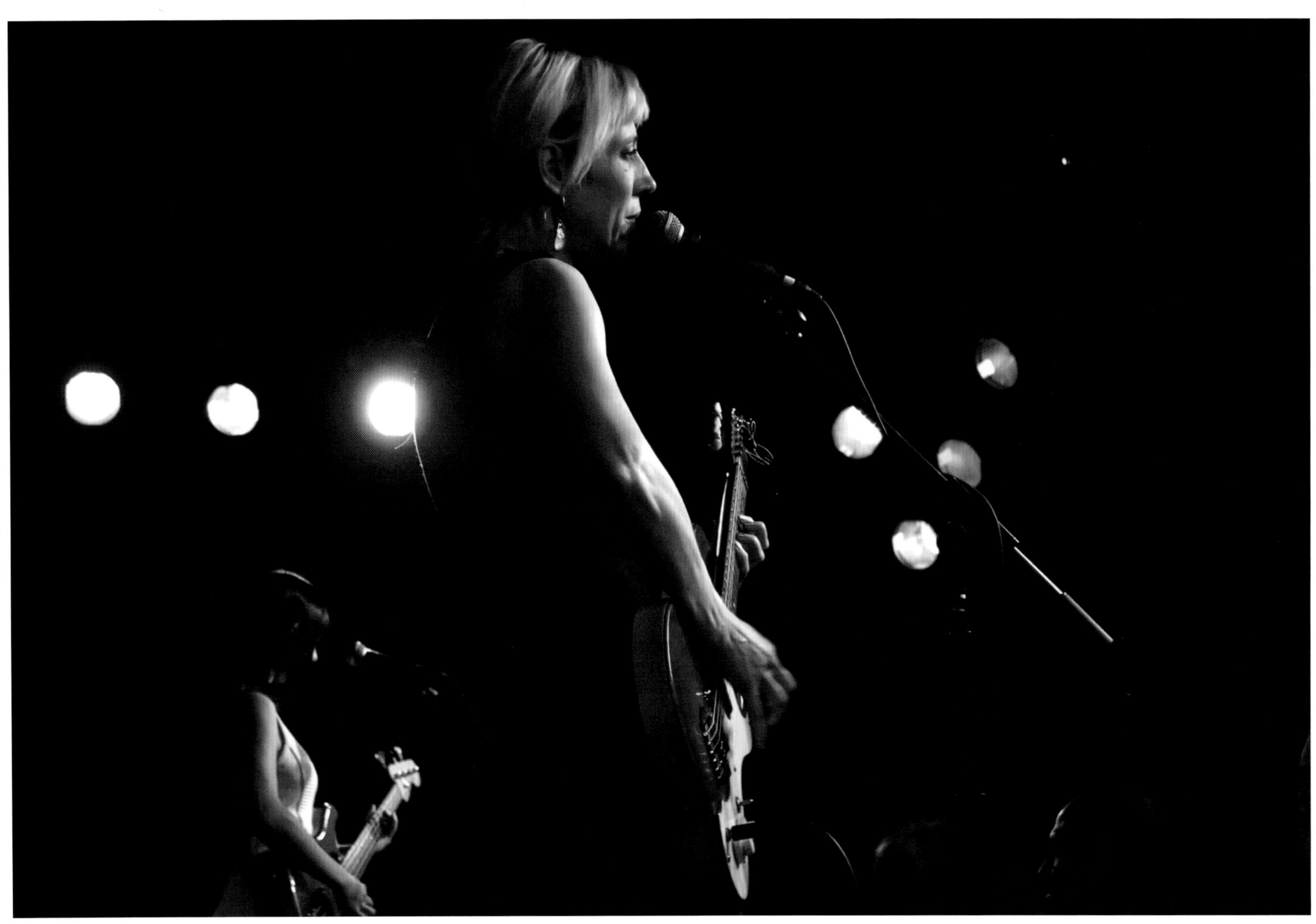

Christina Billotte, While, Black Cat / WDC, 2016

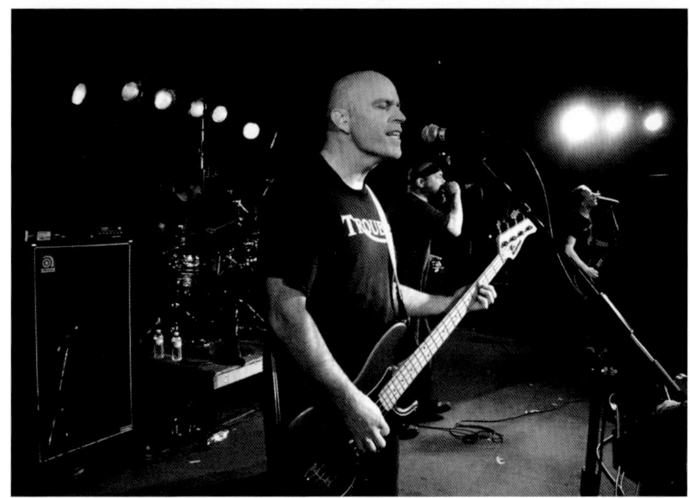

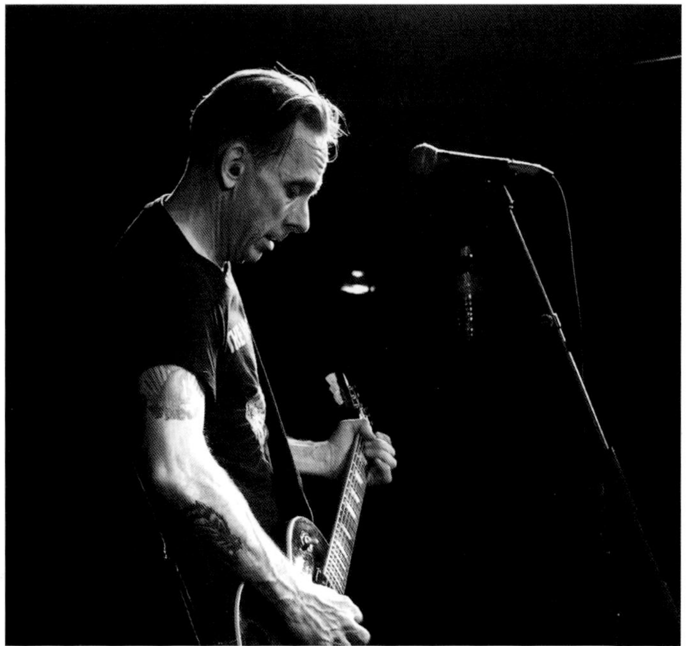

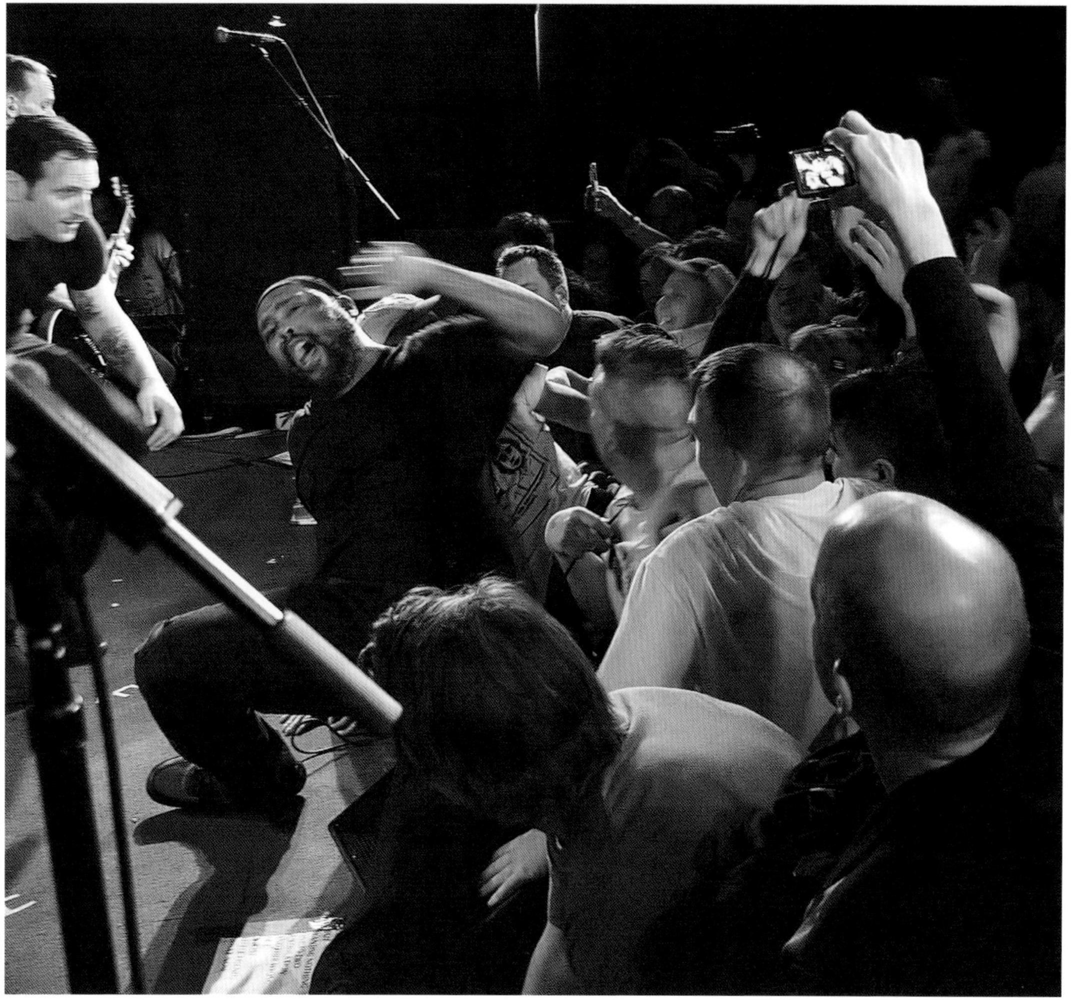

Dag Nasty, Black Cat / WDC, 2016

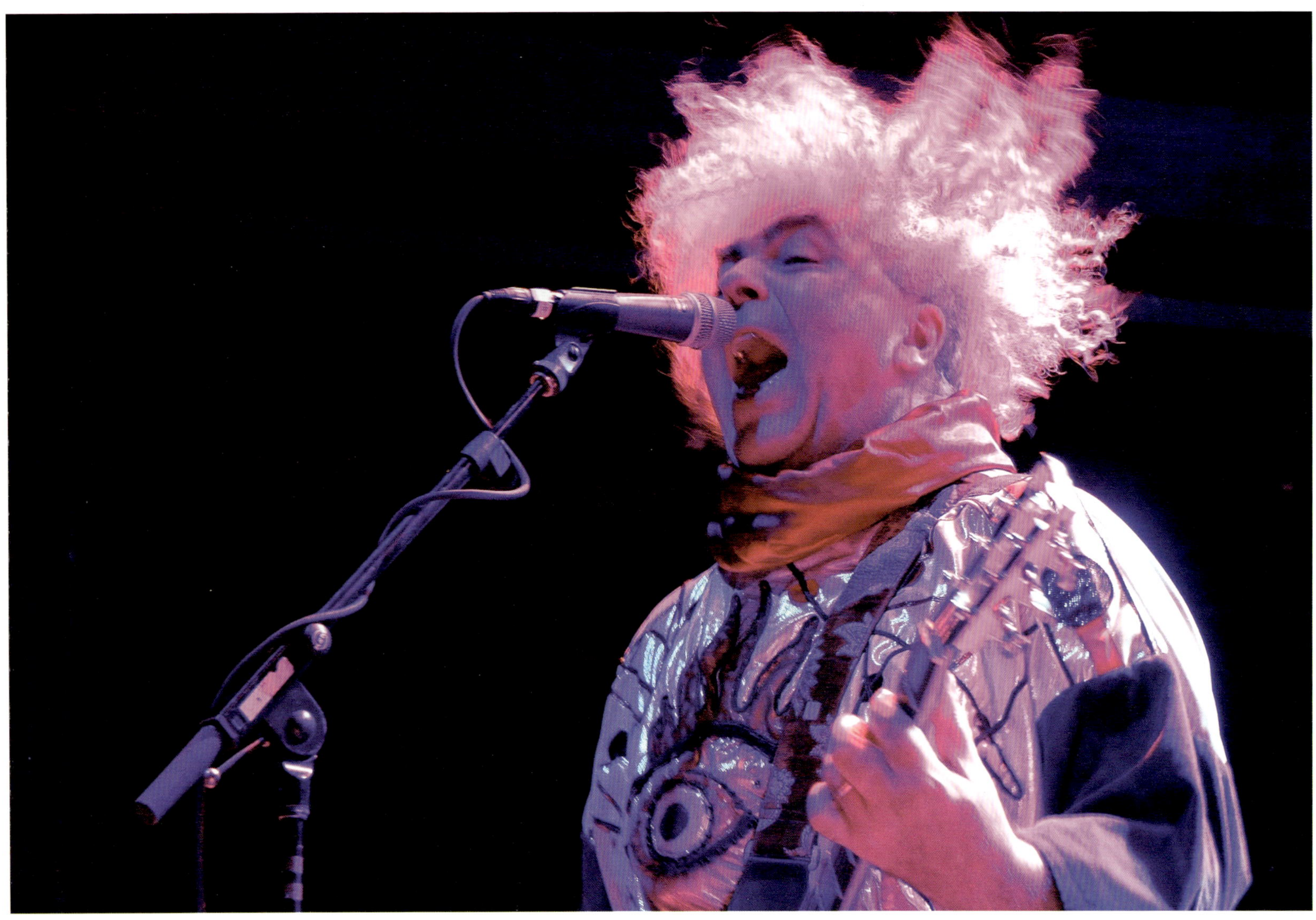

Buzz, Melvins, 9:30 Club / WDC, 2016
Opposite: Alec MacKaye, benefit for Doc Knight, Black Cat / WDC, 2016

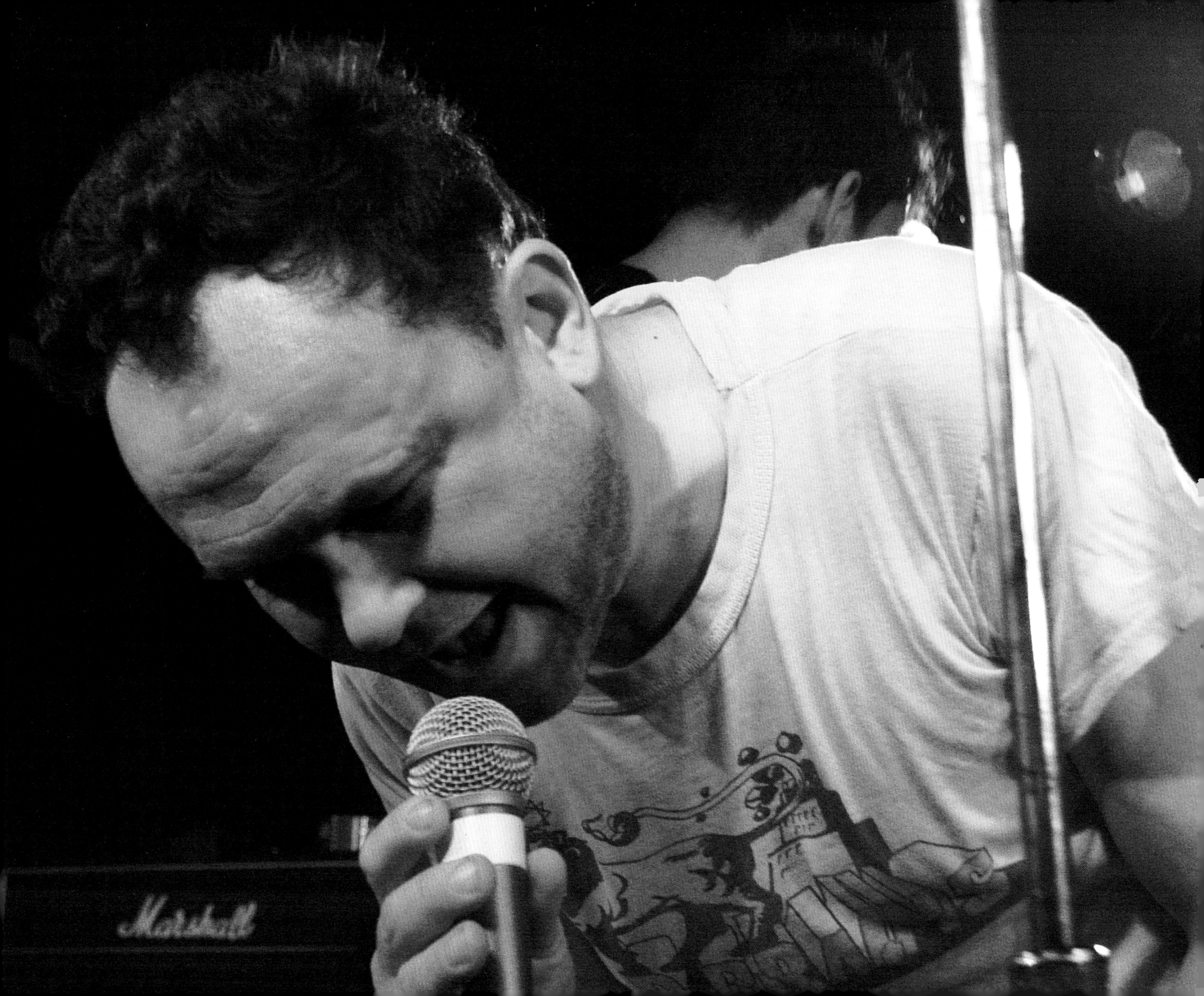
Marshall

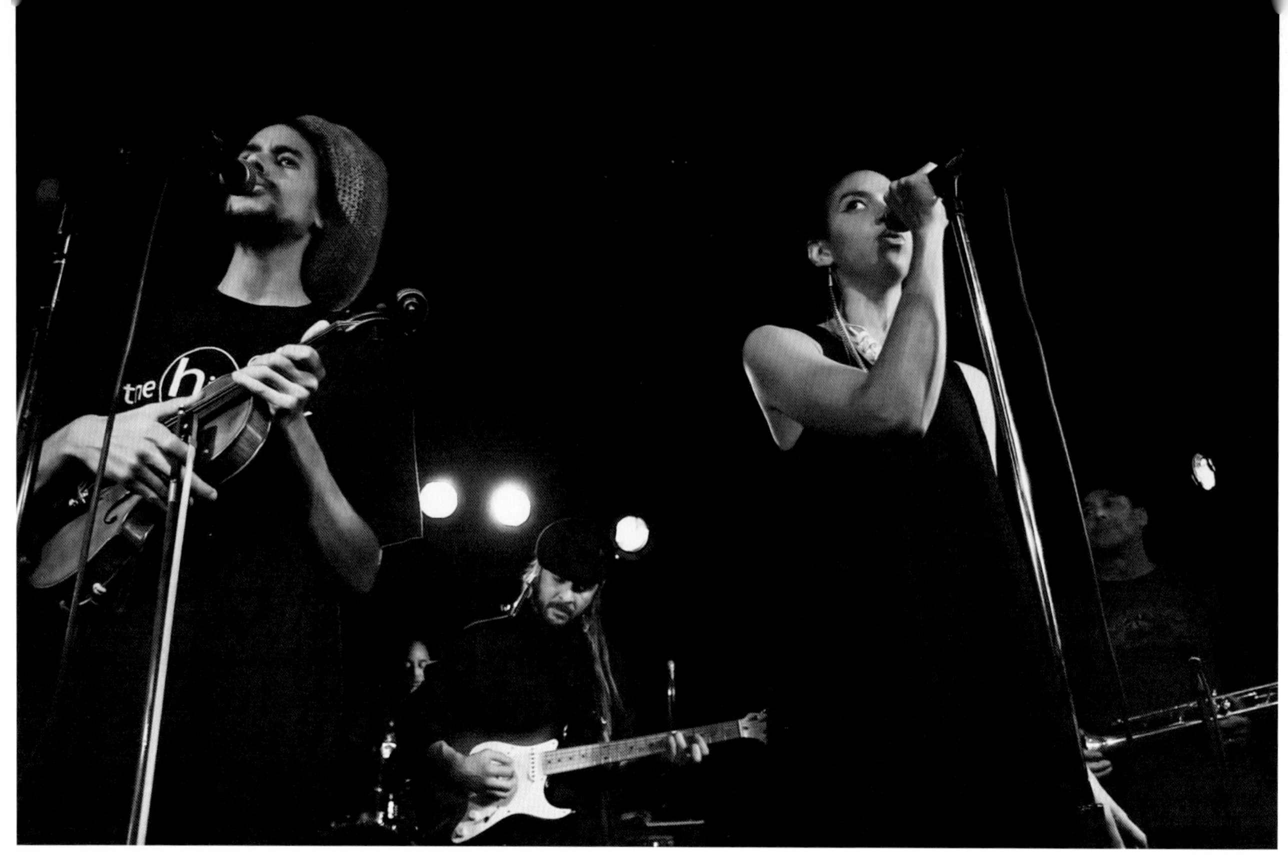

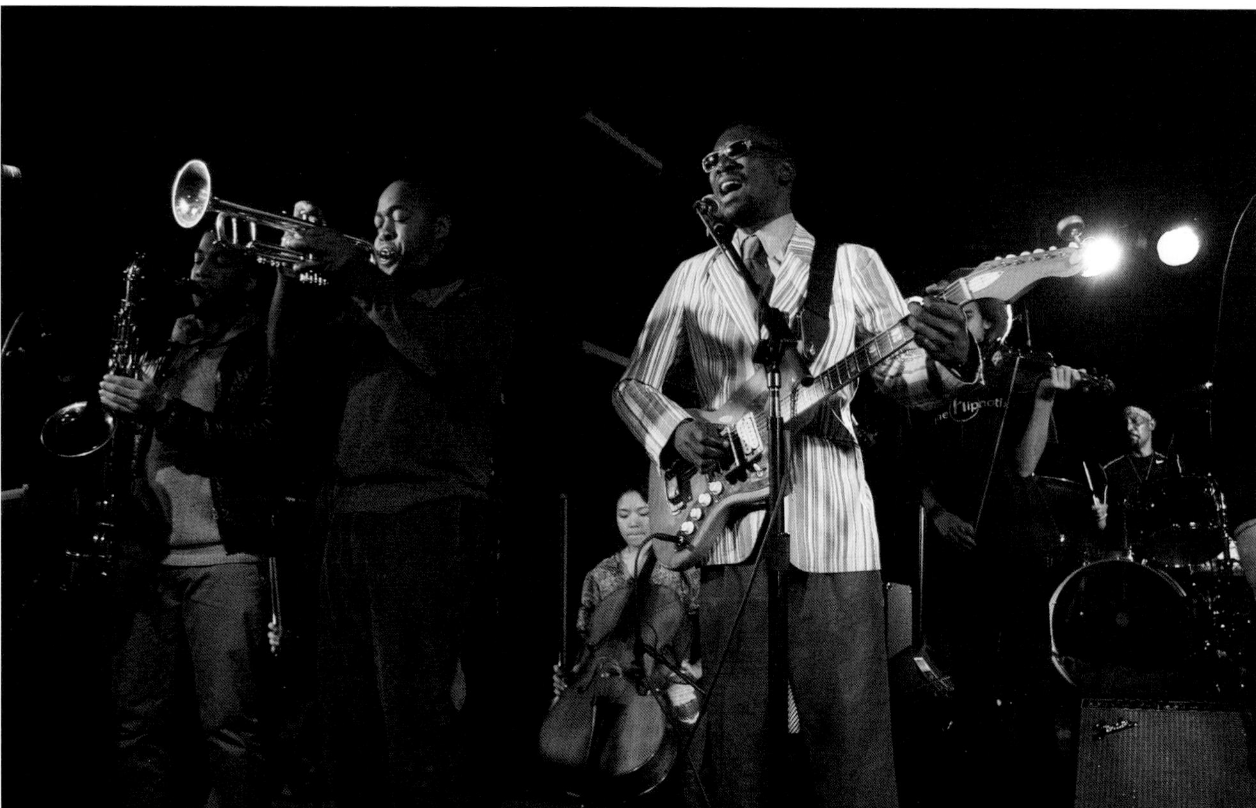

From top: Adriel Iamwills and Sapphirai Williams;
Sitali and Juju, benefit for Doc Knight, Black Cat / WDC, 2016

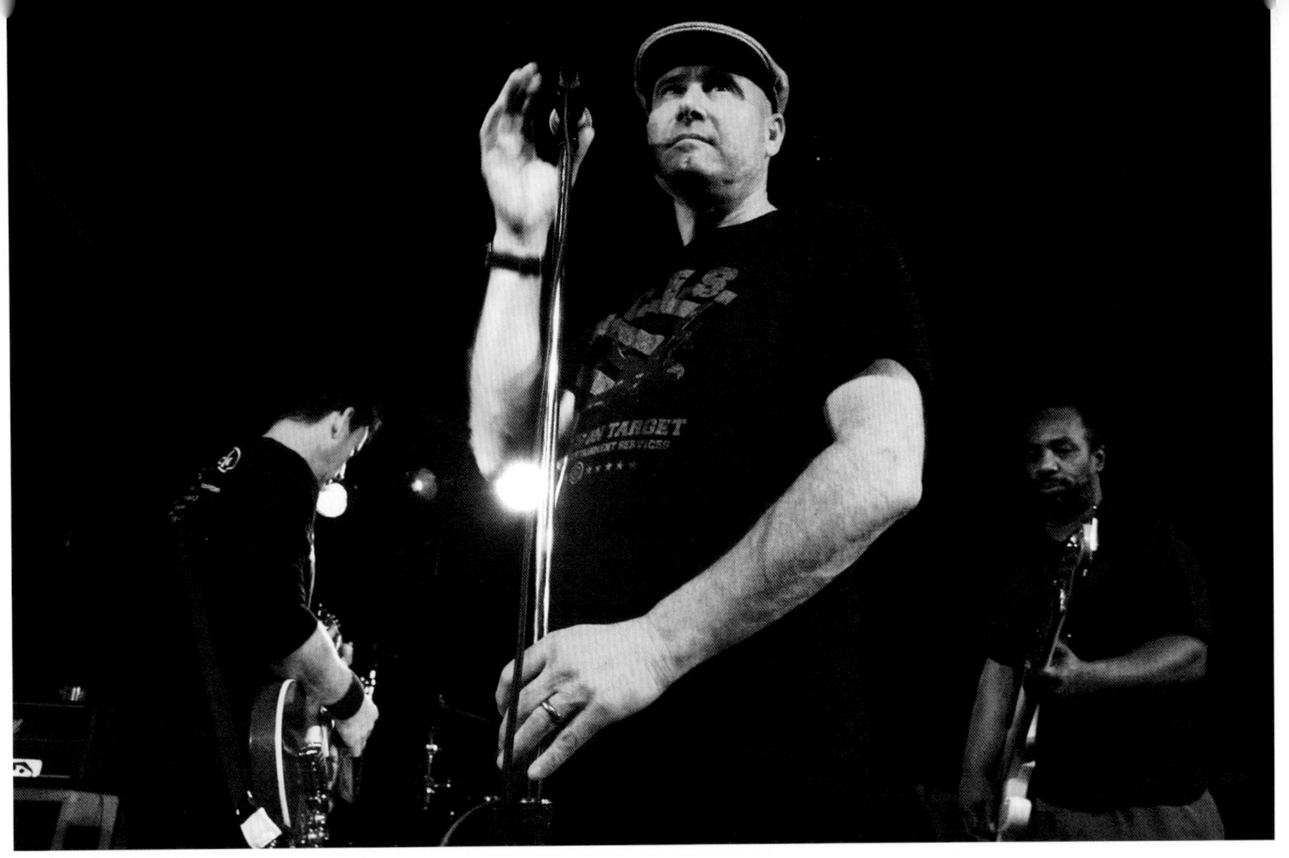

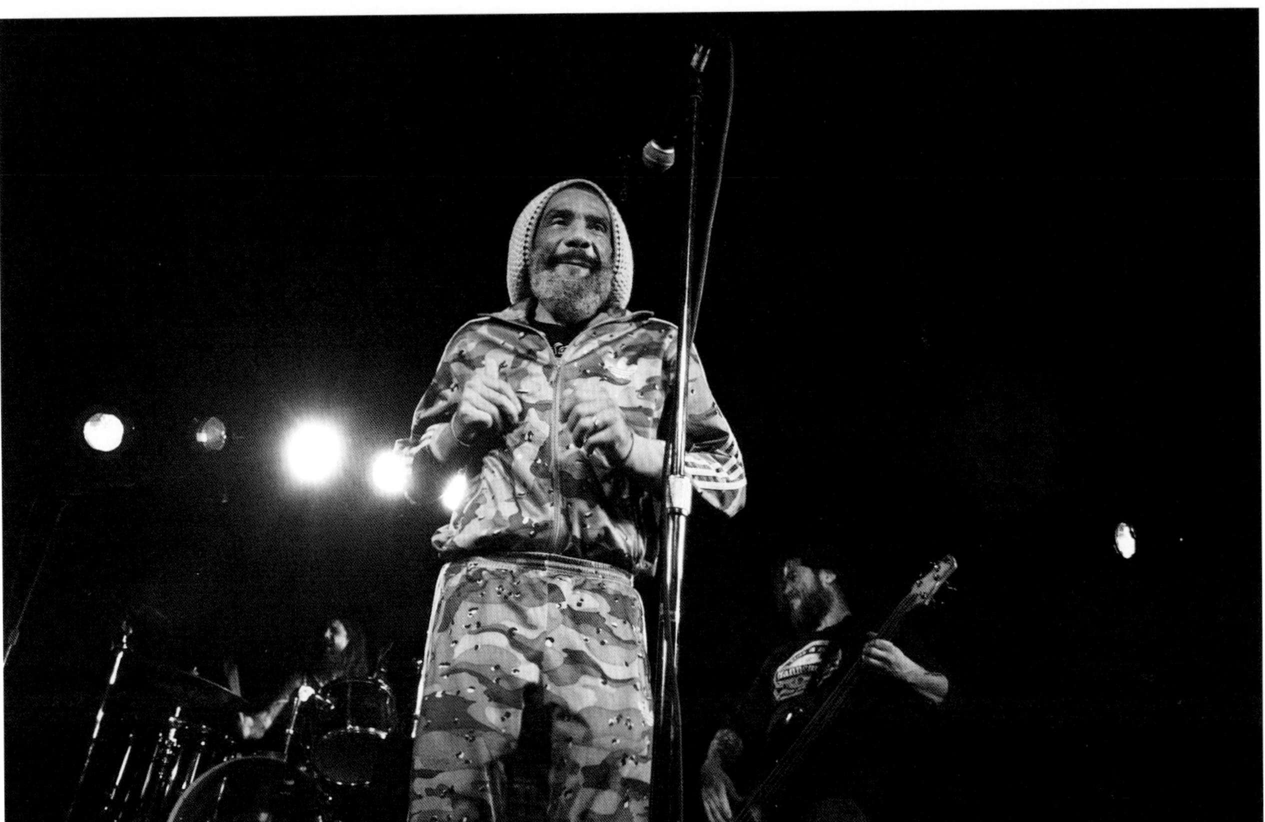

From top: Scream; HR, Bad Brains,
benefit for Doc Knight, Black Cat / WDC, 2016

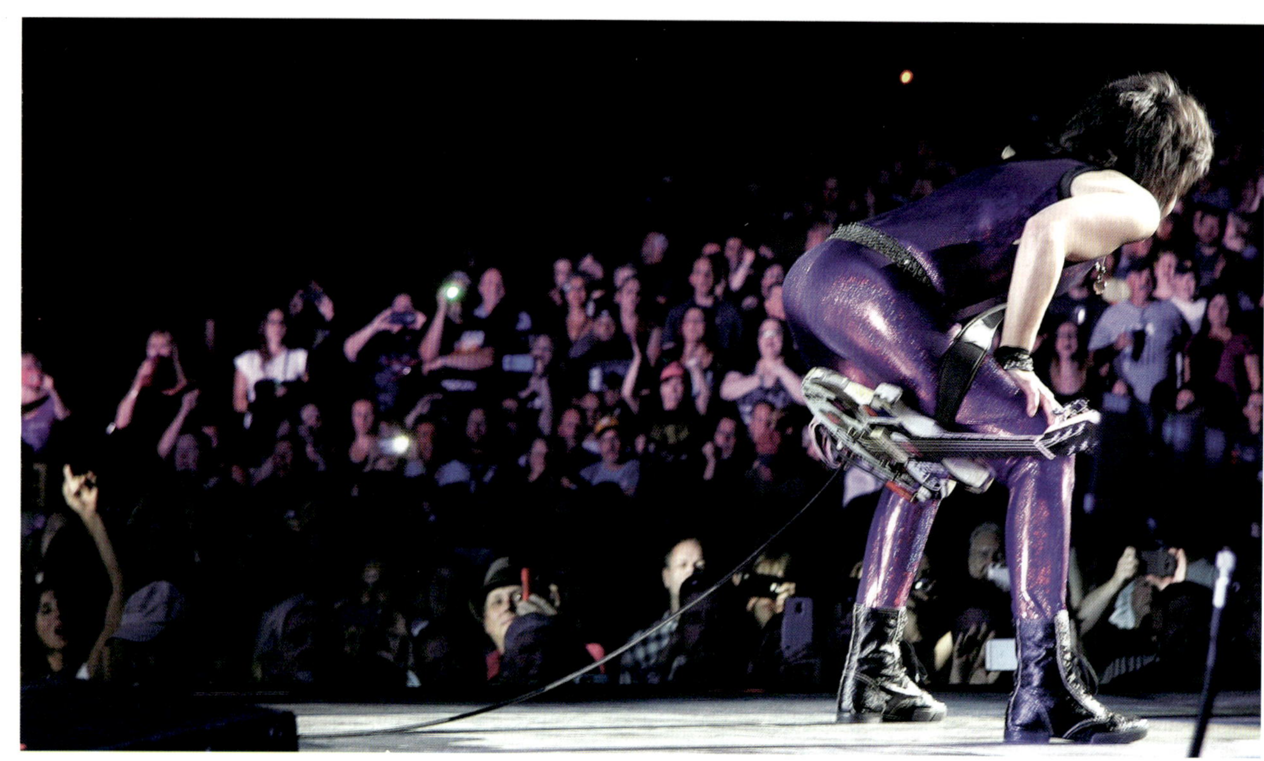

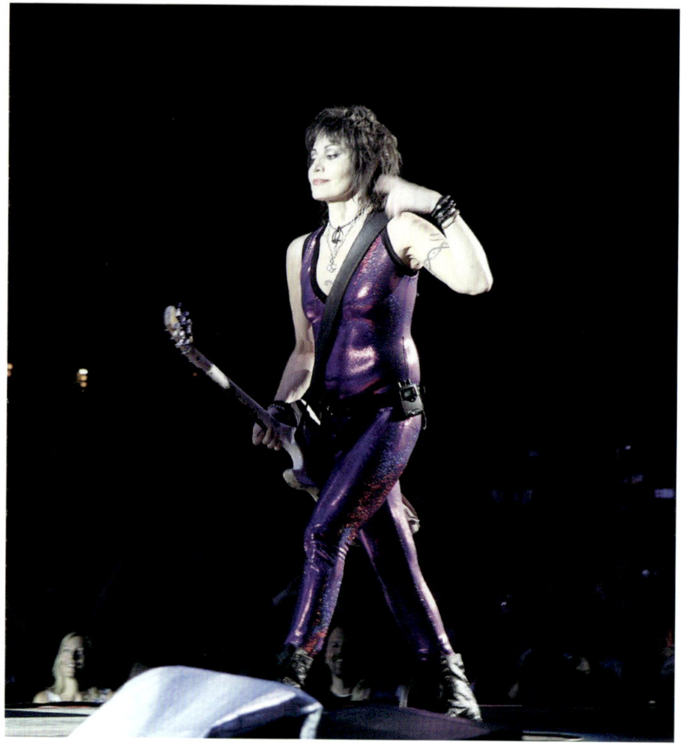

Joan Jett, Jiffy Lube Live / Bristow, VA, 2016

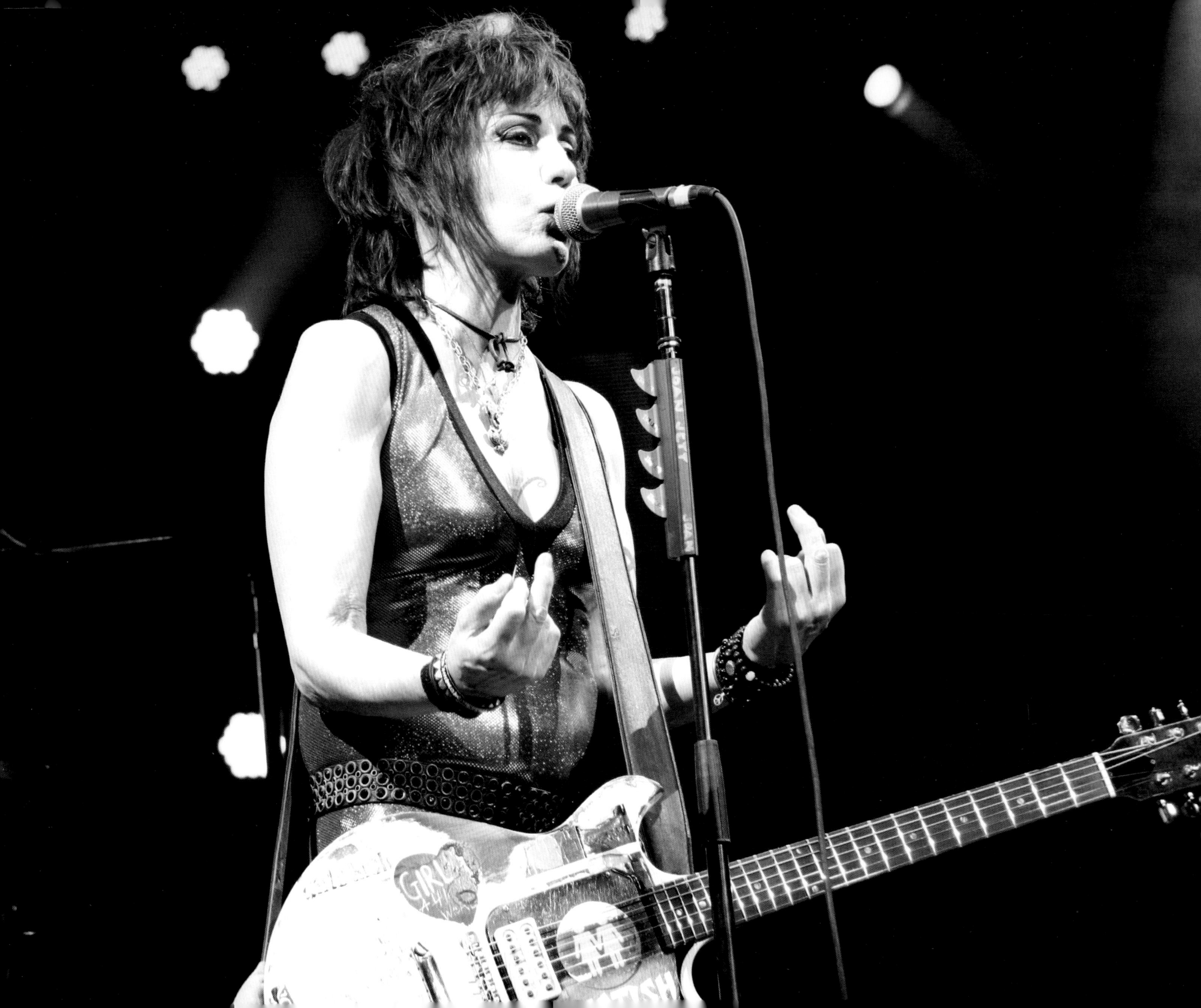

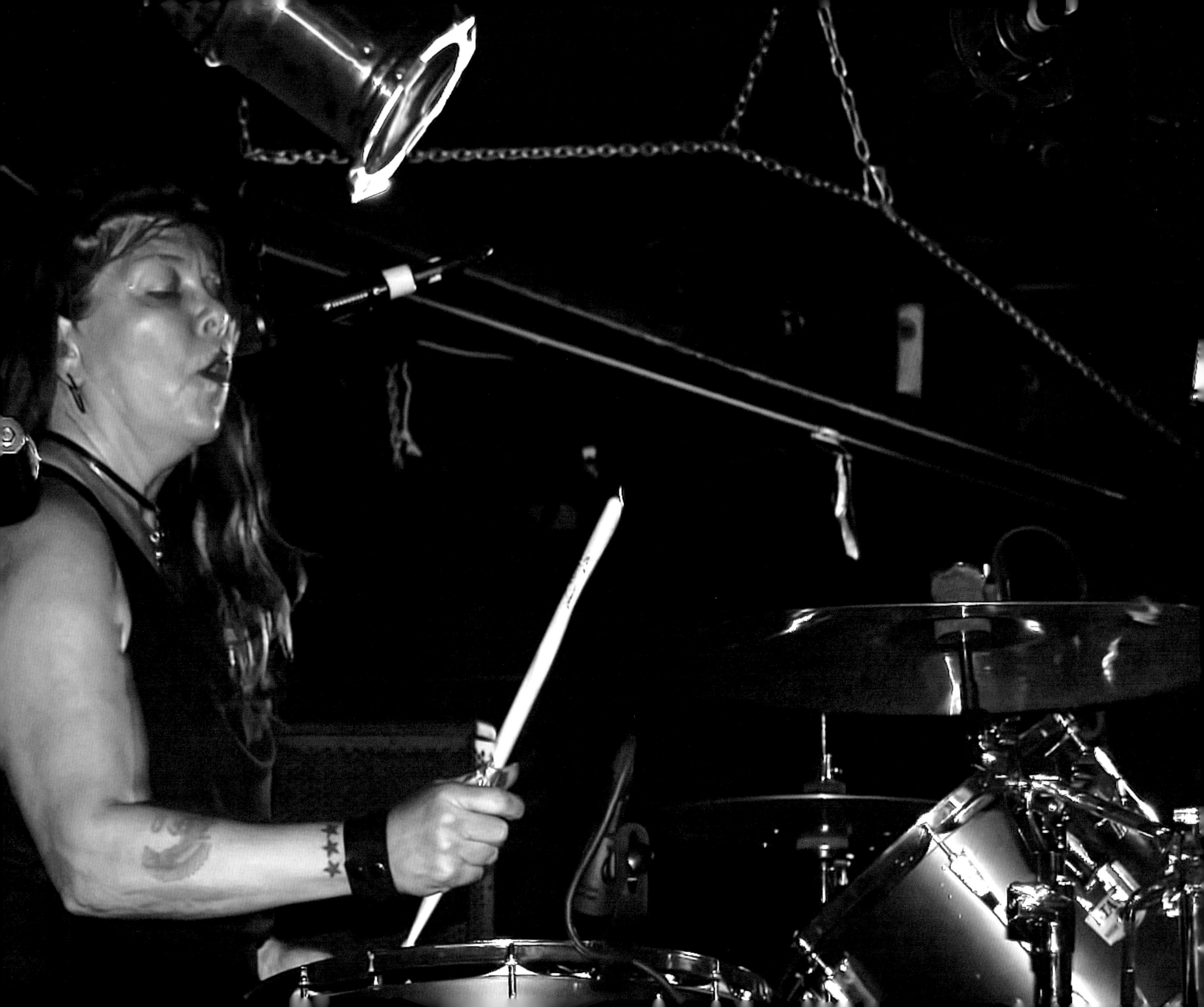

LORI BARBERO

I remember my parents always having the stereo console blaring in the living room when I was a child. They listened to a lot of Fifth Dimension, Sergio Mendes, Gladys Knight, Herb Alpert, and Carpenters. Mom always sang to every song that came on the radio too. My grandmother also gave me quite a few records she received from Columbia House records. So, with all of that, that pretty much planted the seed. Anyway, going to high school in New York led me to hanging out and seeing a lot of bands in the late seventies in New York City. Every time I saw any band perform, I just sat and watched the drummer . . . I finally picked up the sticks at age twenty-six.

I remember in the seventies and eighties, bands just seemed more raw, honest, spontaneous, and edgy. I think now a lot of music is very saturated, soulless, overproduced, and unoriginal. Obviously I care more for the raw music than the overcooked.

Getting behind a drum kit and pounding the crap out of it is the most therapeutic thing for me to do, both mentally and physically. I find if I don't get a chance to play as often as I'd like, my mental state changes. I also love traveling across the States and internationally to perform. All of the benefits that come with that is priceless. Seeing old friends and meeting new ones, going from city to city and country to country, plus the cuisine—the best!

BABES IN TOYLAND • EGGTWIST • THE KOALAS

Lori Barbero, Black Cat / WDC, 2015

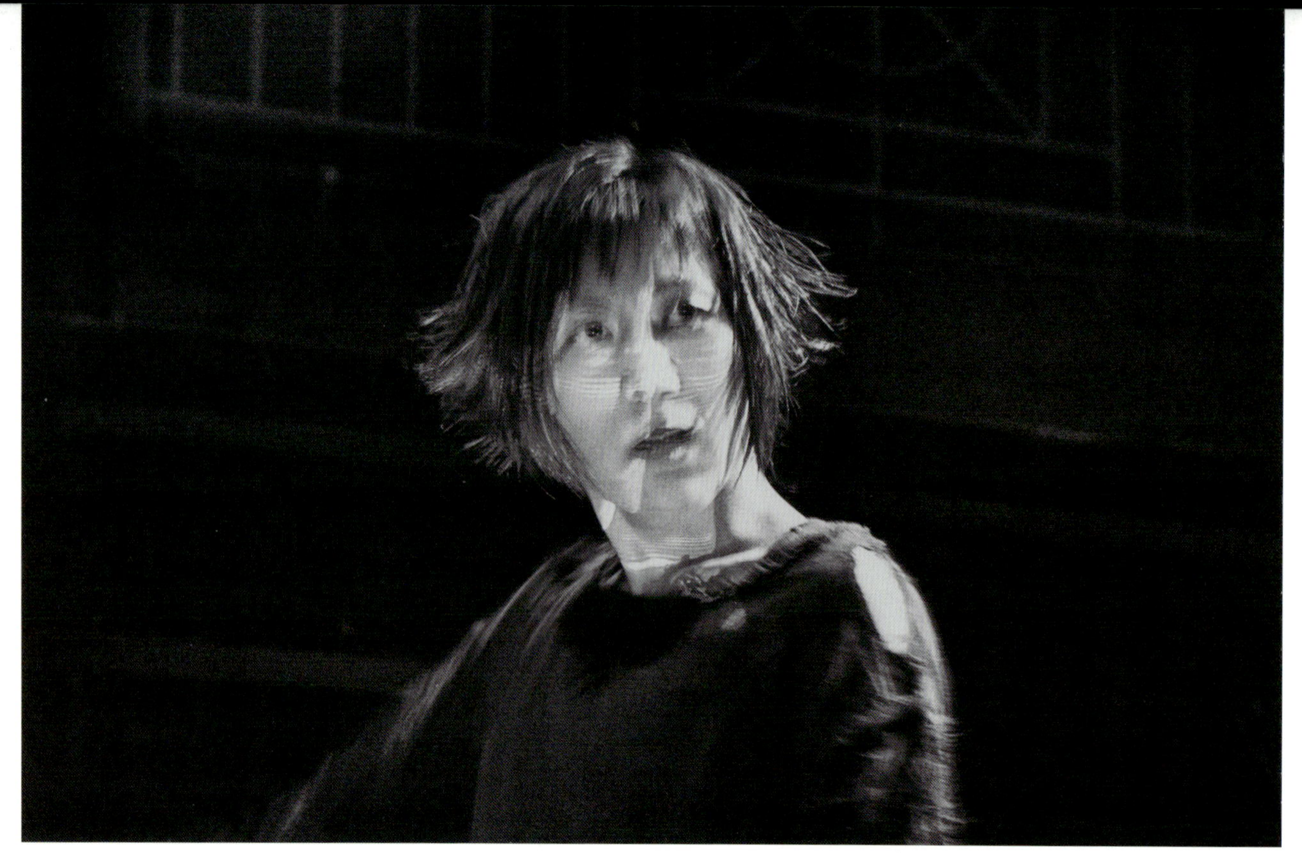

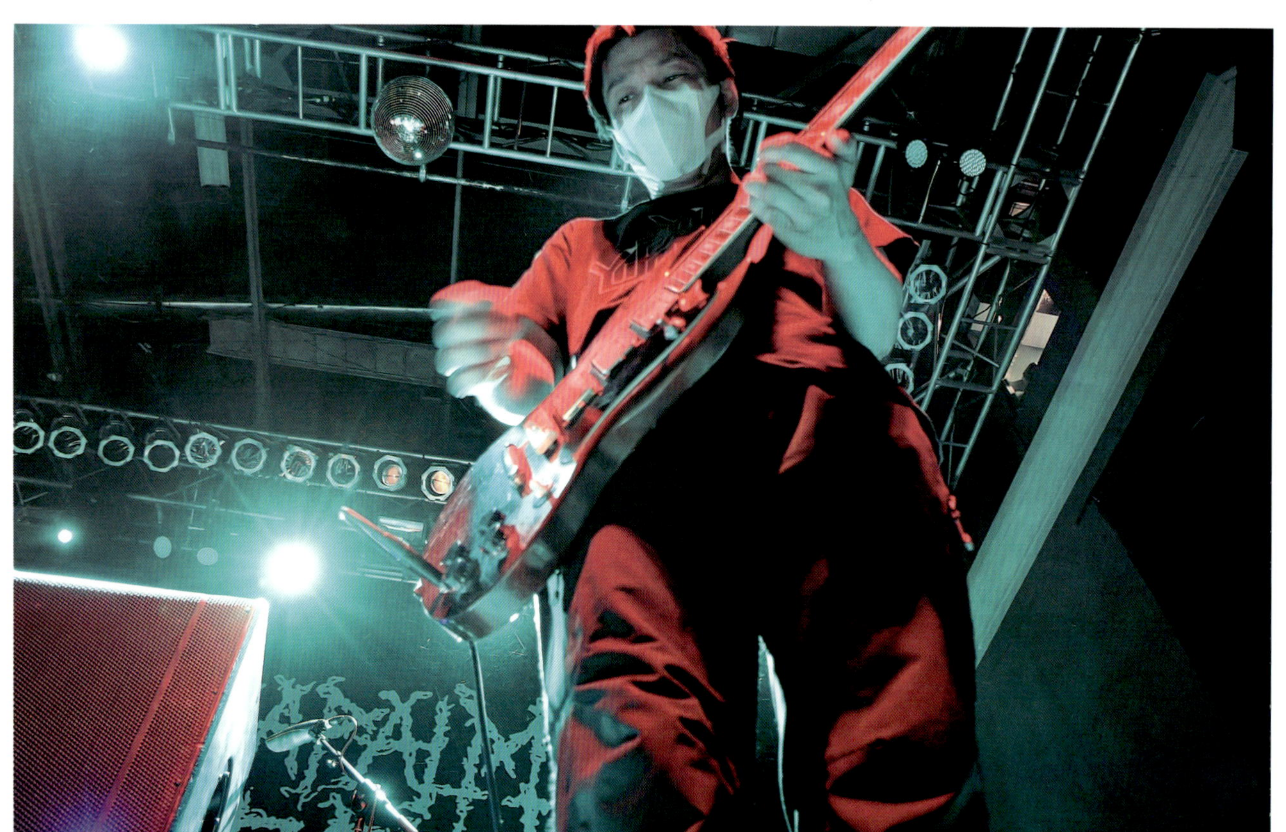

Melt-Banana, 9:30 Club / WDC, 2016
Opposite, from top:
Puff Pieces, Black Cat / WDC, 2016;
Quasi, Rock & Roll Hotel / WDC, 2016

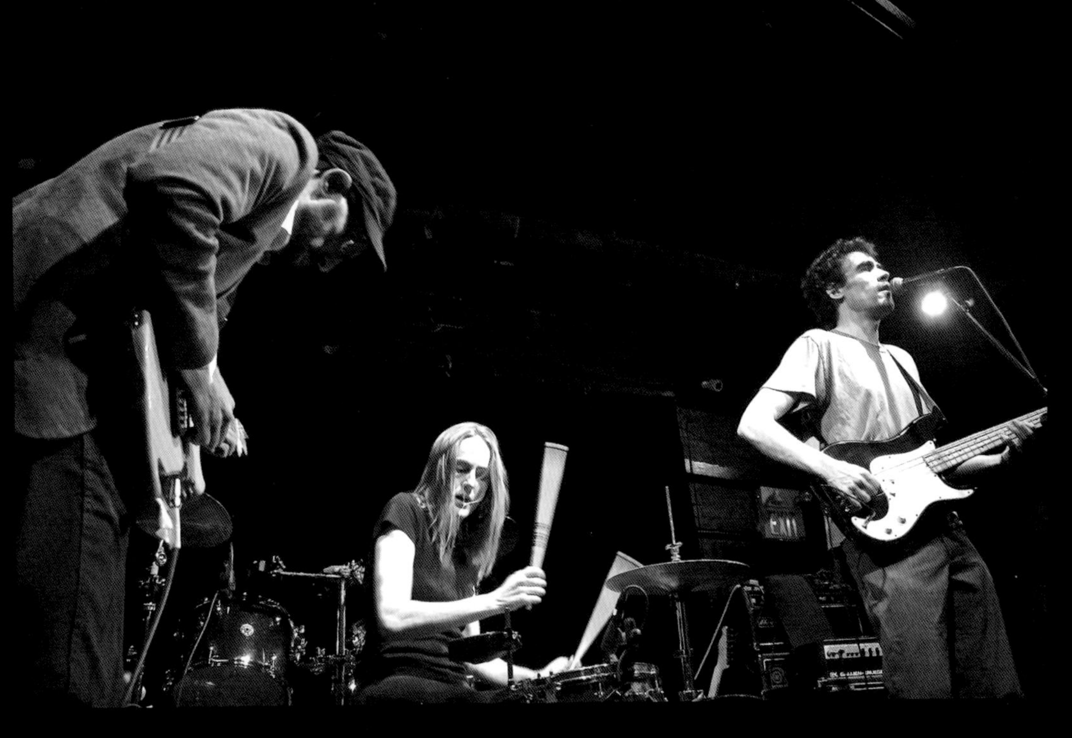

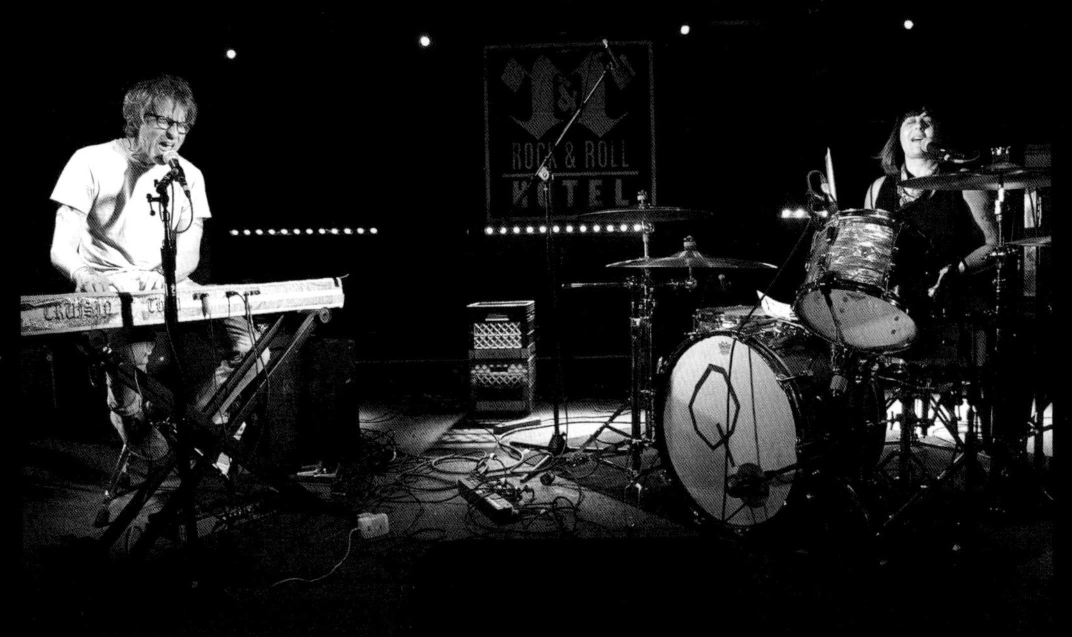

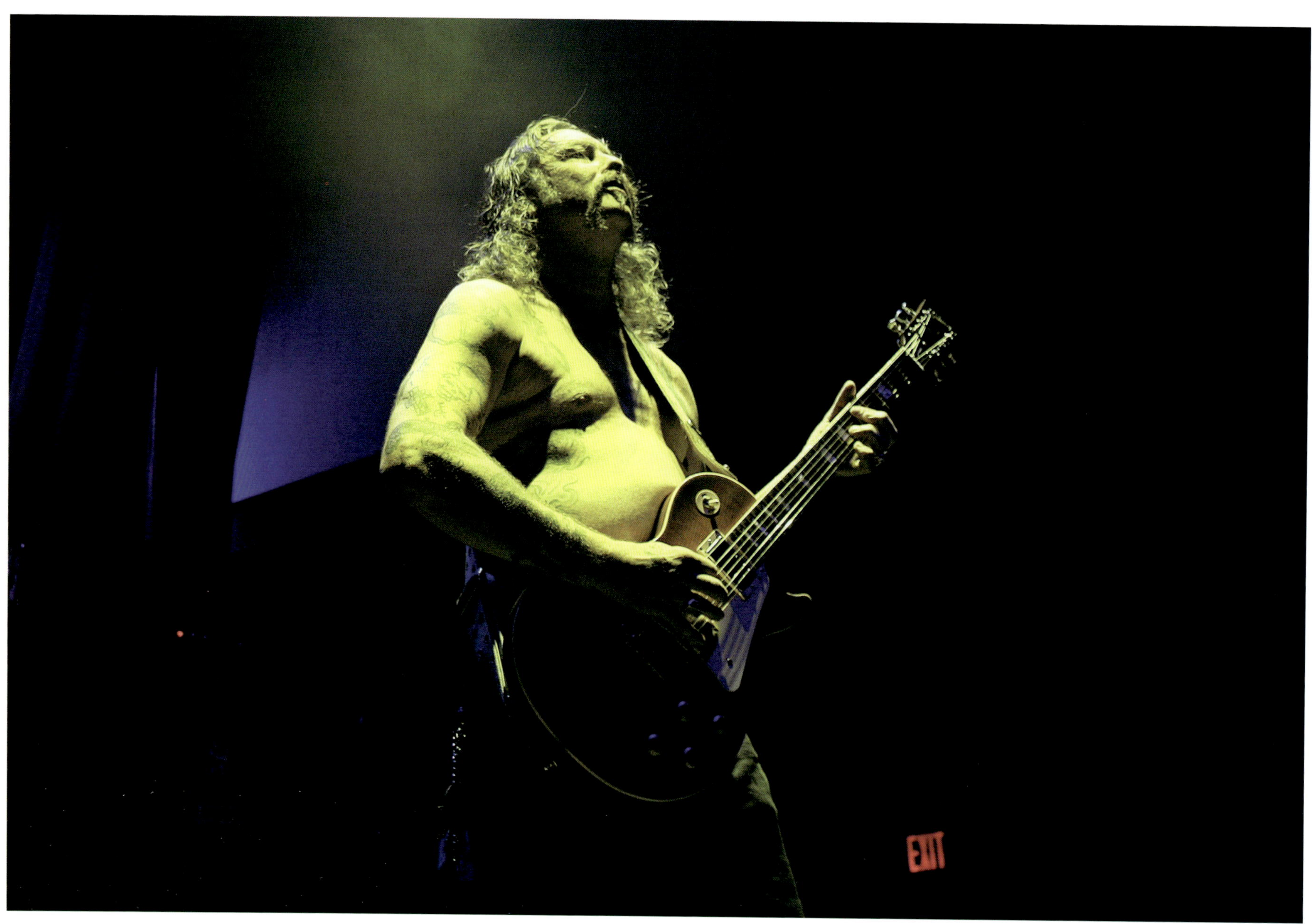

Matt Pike, Sleep, 9:30 Club / WDC, 2016

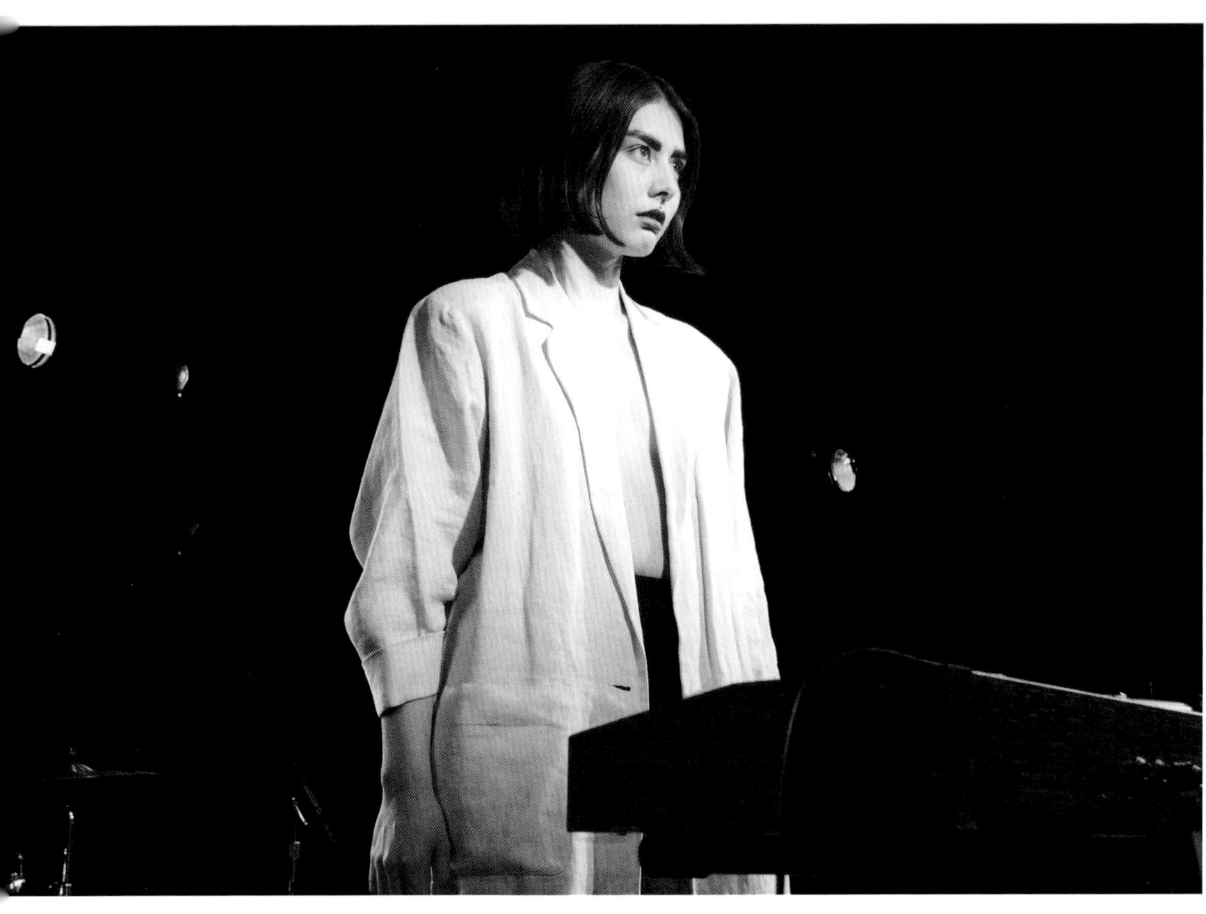

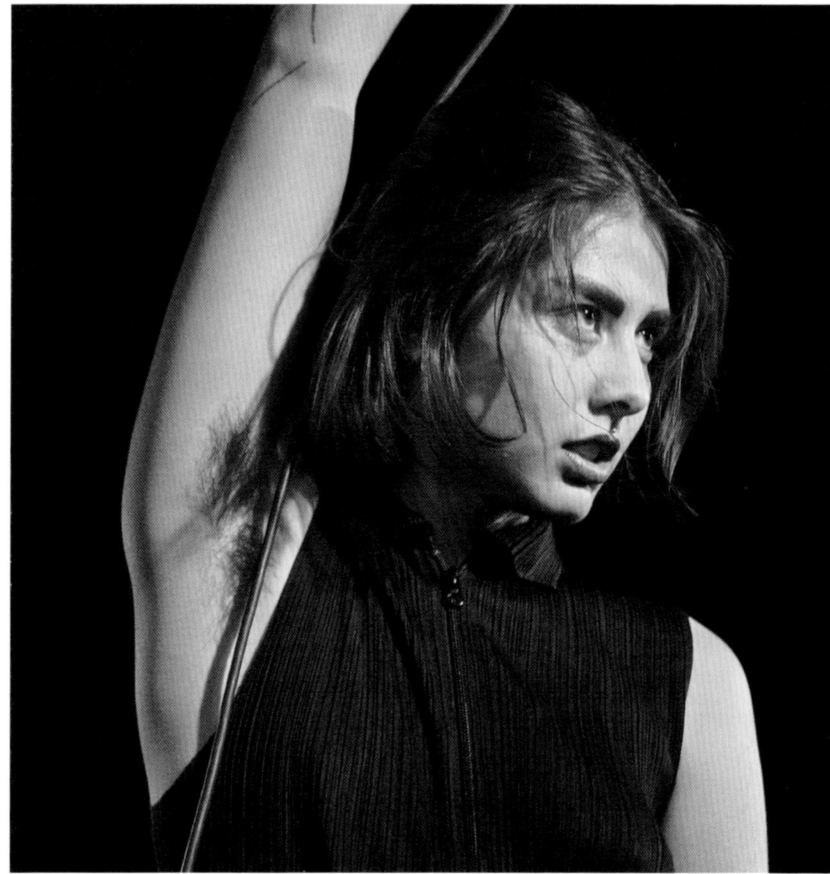

Olivia Neutron-John, Black Cat / WDC, 2016

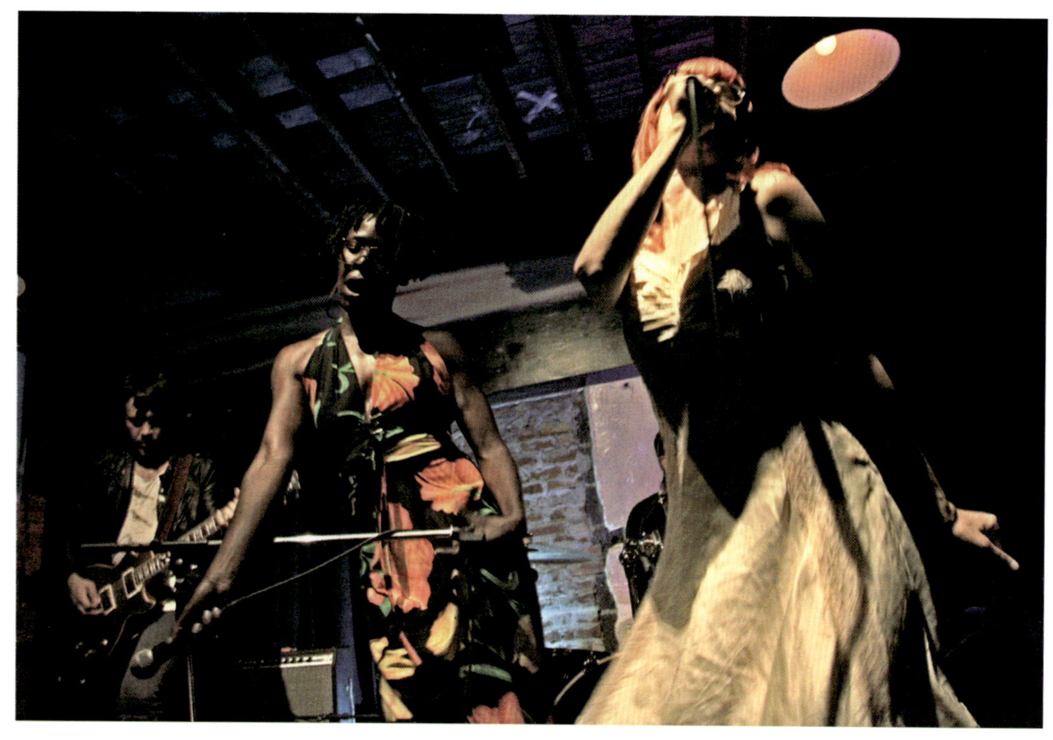

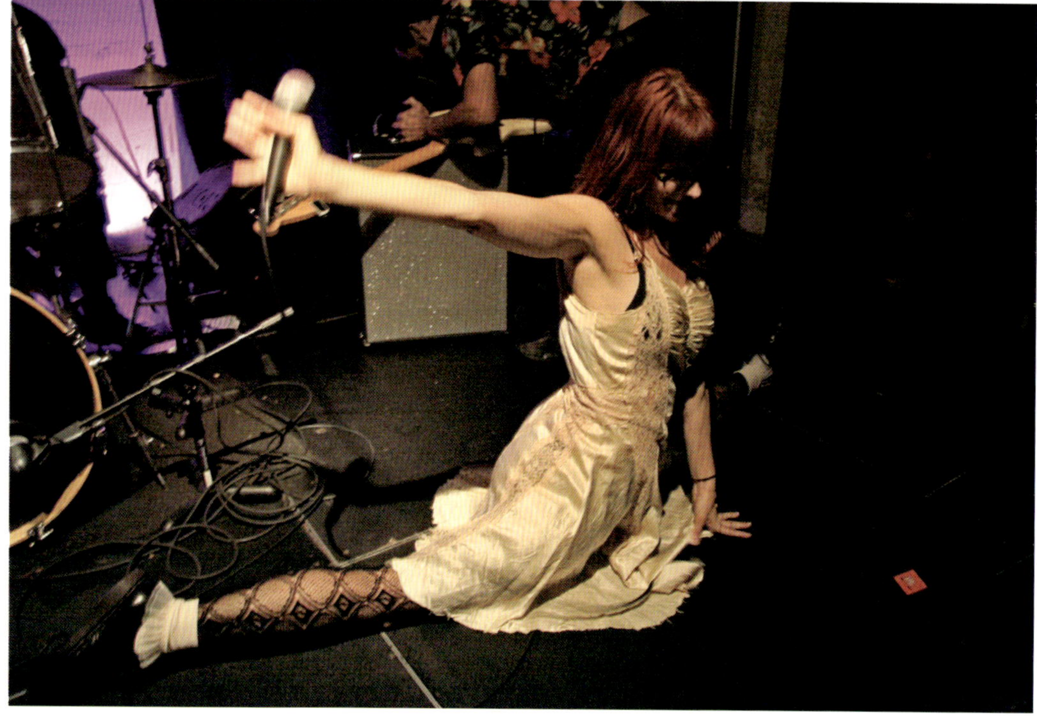

Sex Stains, Comet Ping Pong / WDC, 2016
Opposite: Sistr Mid9ight, Black Cat / WDC, 2016

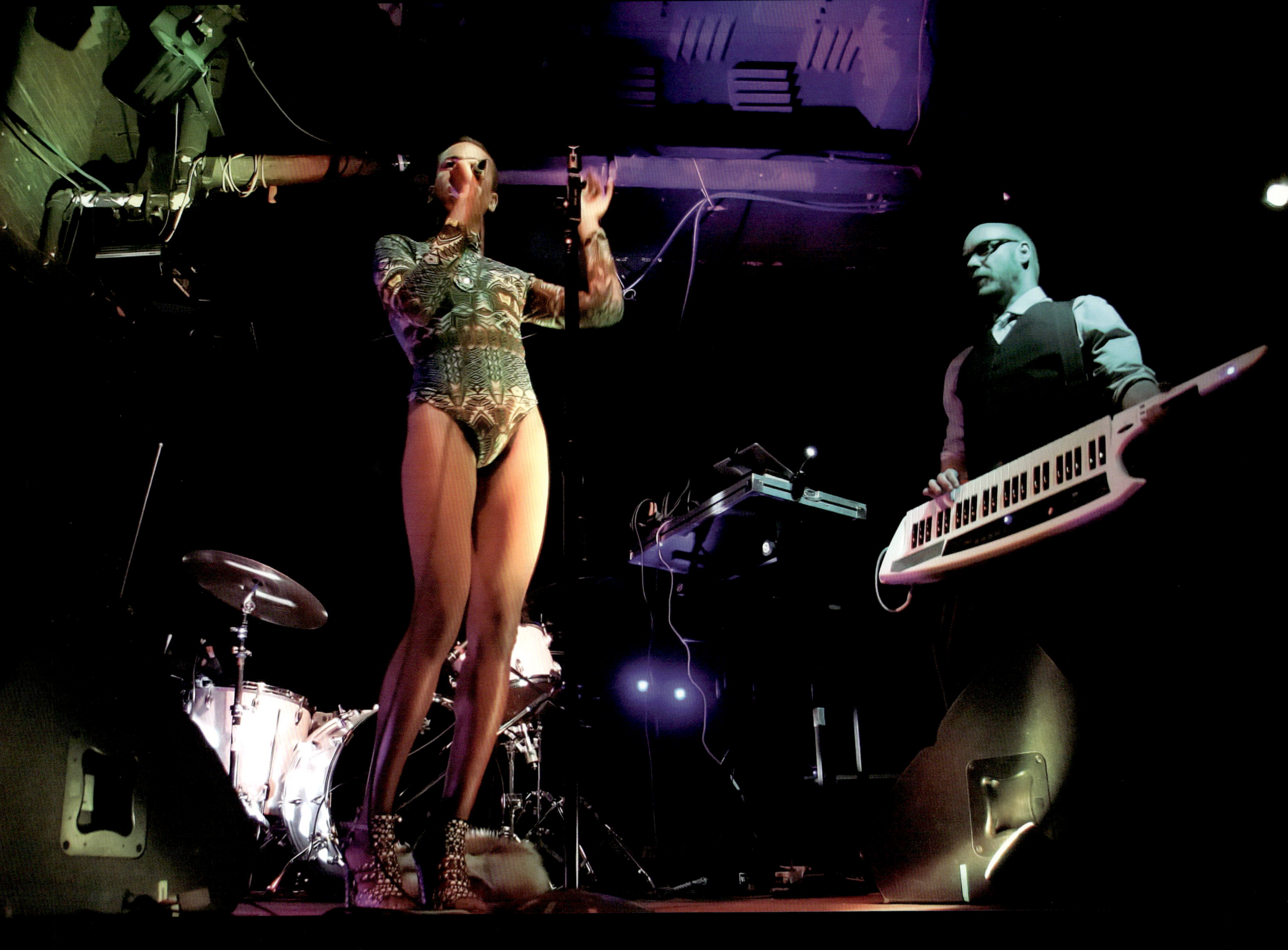

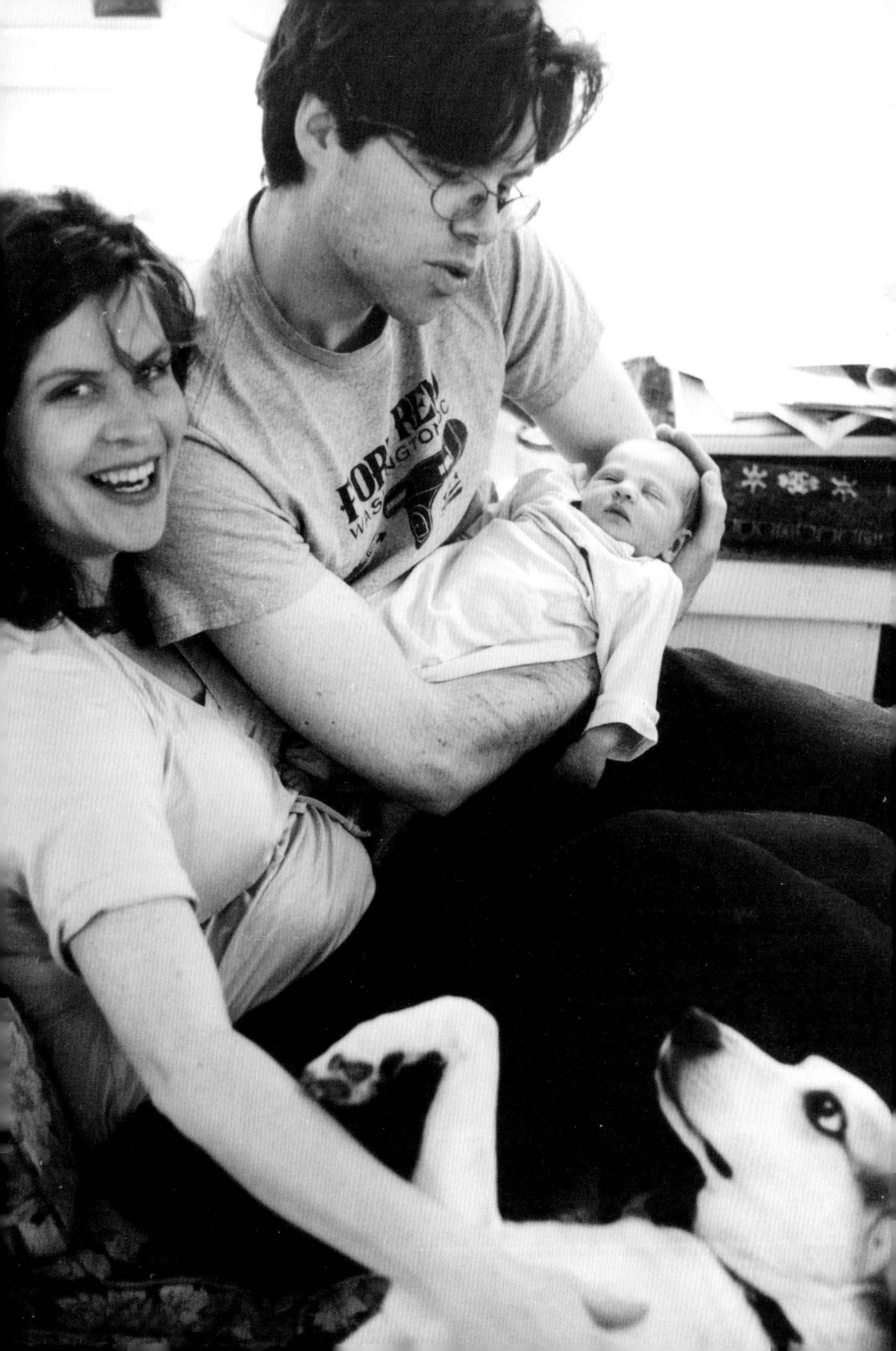

NATALIE AVERY

As a teenager growing up in DC's punk scene, I remember this incredible sense of discovery and possibility as I explored parts of my city I'd never been exposed to. DC in the 1980s, like so many of its counterparts, had suffered from years of disinvestment, its downtown dull and dirty. To so many people, DC was just a boring government town where nothing interesting ever happened.

But here were these rooms, 9:30 club, d.c. space, the Landsburg Center (an empty department store), Space II Arcade, dozens of church basements—sites of some mind-blowing music and life-changing events. So in the rubble of a hollowed-out town, people were building this culture and creating this music, both go-go and punk, that would have such a lasting impact. It all seemed like this huge beautiful secret. The music of that time was important and groundbreaking, but so were the places where I experienced it. It was in these spaces where I thought to myself, *I will be in a band,* where I first questioned things and started to use my voice.

Fast-forward to the late nineties, right at the cusp of an economic boom that would transform DC. I lived in a neighborhood called Mount Pleasant, the heart of DC's Latino community, just minutes from downtown DC and teeming with group houses where bands lived and practiced, people made zines and clothes and threw dance parties. I started putting on shows, only to learn that the neighborhood's restaurants were off-limits because local politics akin to the movie *Footloose* (but with racist overtones) had forced them to forgo having live music and dancing.

This is the time when I was introduced to La Casa, a little Mount Pleasant building owned by a small group of radical people who wanted a place to worship together outside the confines of a traditional church. The owners of La Casa opened their doors to the community and allowed the space to be used by musicians, community groups, activists, youth organizers, and more. And within its walls people ran nonprofits, put on concerts and art shows, and created a community radio station. In contrast to those bent on banning music and culture from neighborhood restaurants, the owners of La Casa opened their doors to their neighbors, allowing hundreds of musicians, artists, and community organizers to create, to perform, to experiment, and to have a free space to organize against some of the dehumanizing forces at play in our changing neighborhood, our city, our world. They asked for practically nothing in return.

Places like La Casa offer some hope in these very dark times. In a city totally reconfigured by what seems like an unceasing development boom, it's that much harder to find and keep the kinds of spaces needed for people to find and raise their voices, to create revolutionary music and art, to resist apathy and hopelessness, and to build the kinds of communities of hope and resistance that we so sorely need.

FIRE PARTY • STIGMATICS • SCARAMOUCHE

Family portrait / WDC, 2002

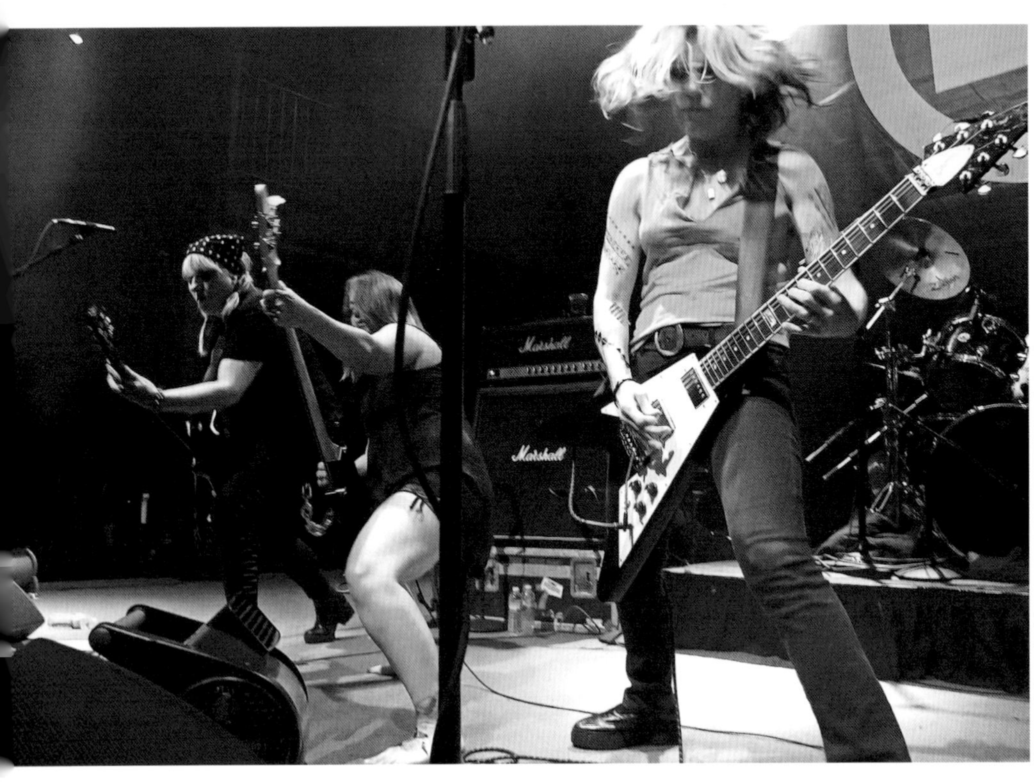

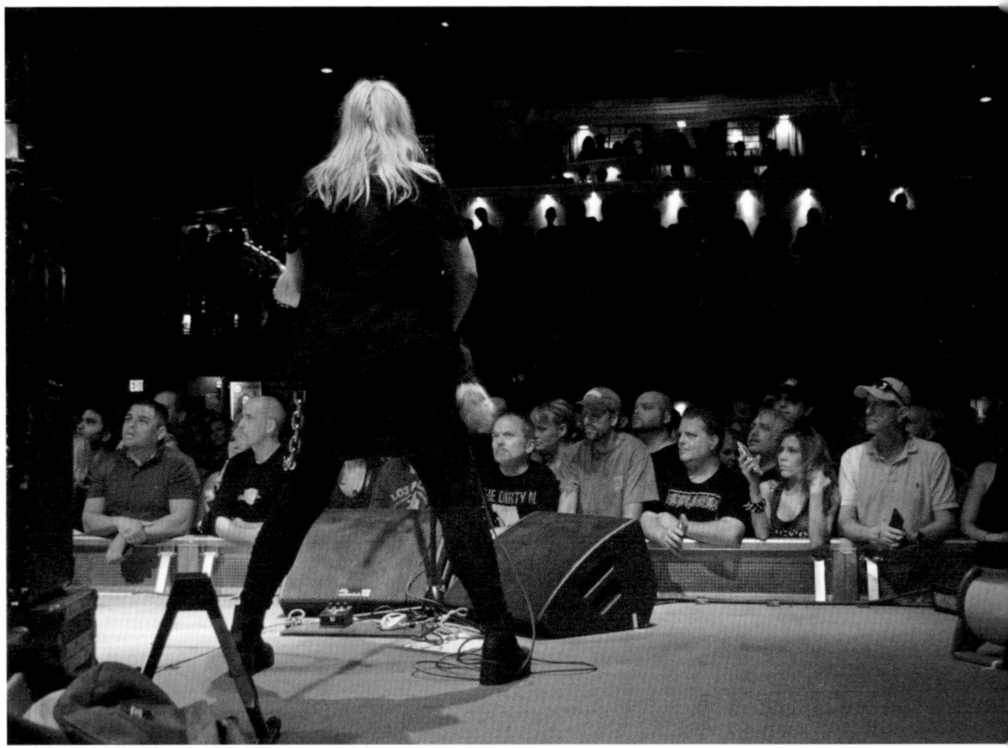

L7, 9:30 Club / WDC, 2016

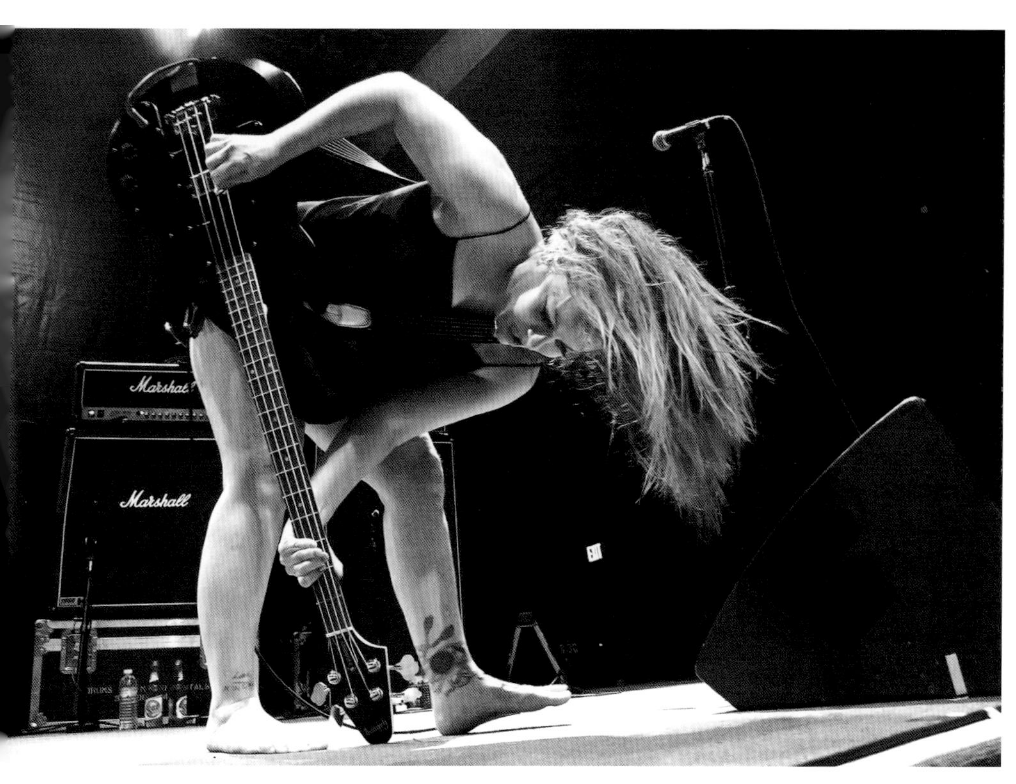
Marshall

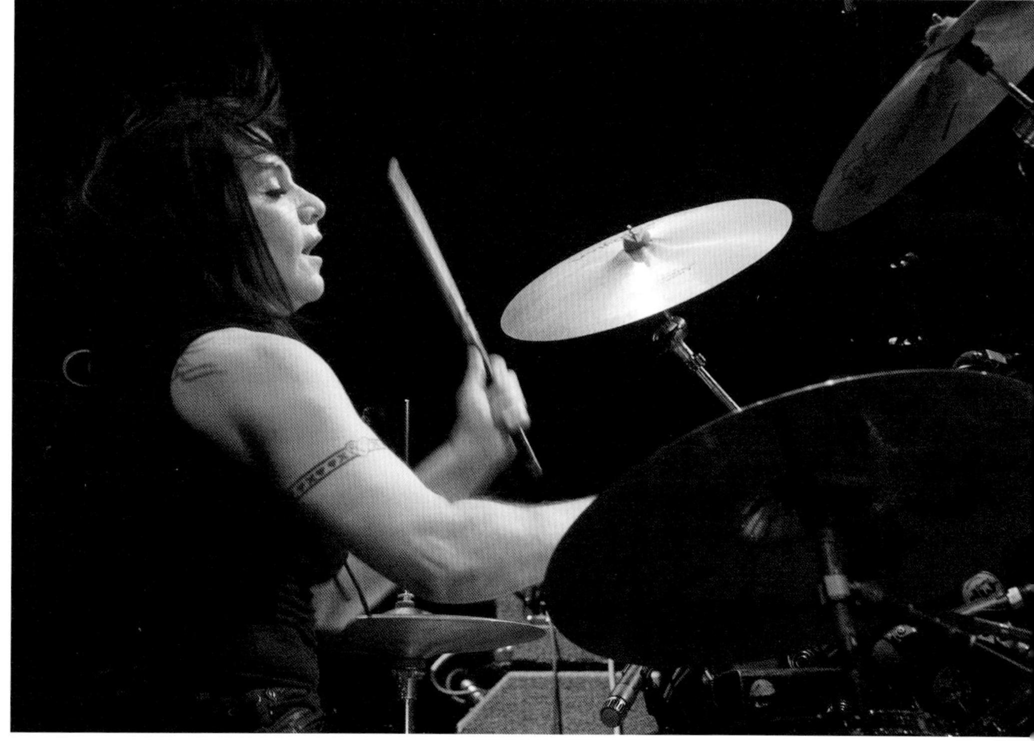

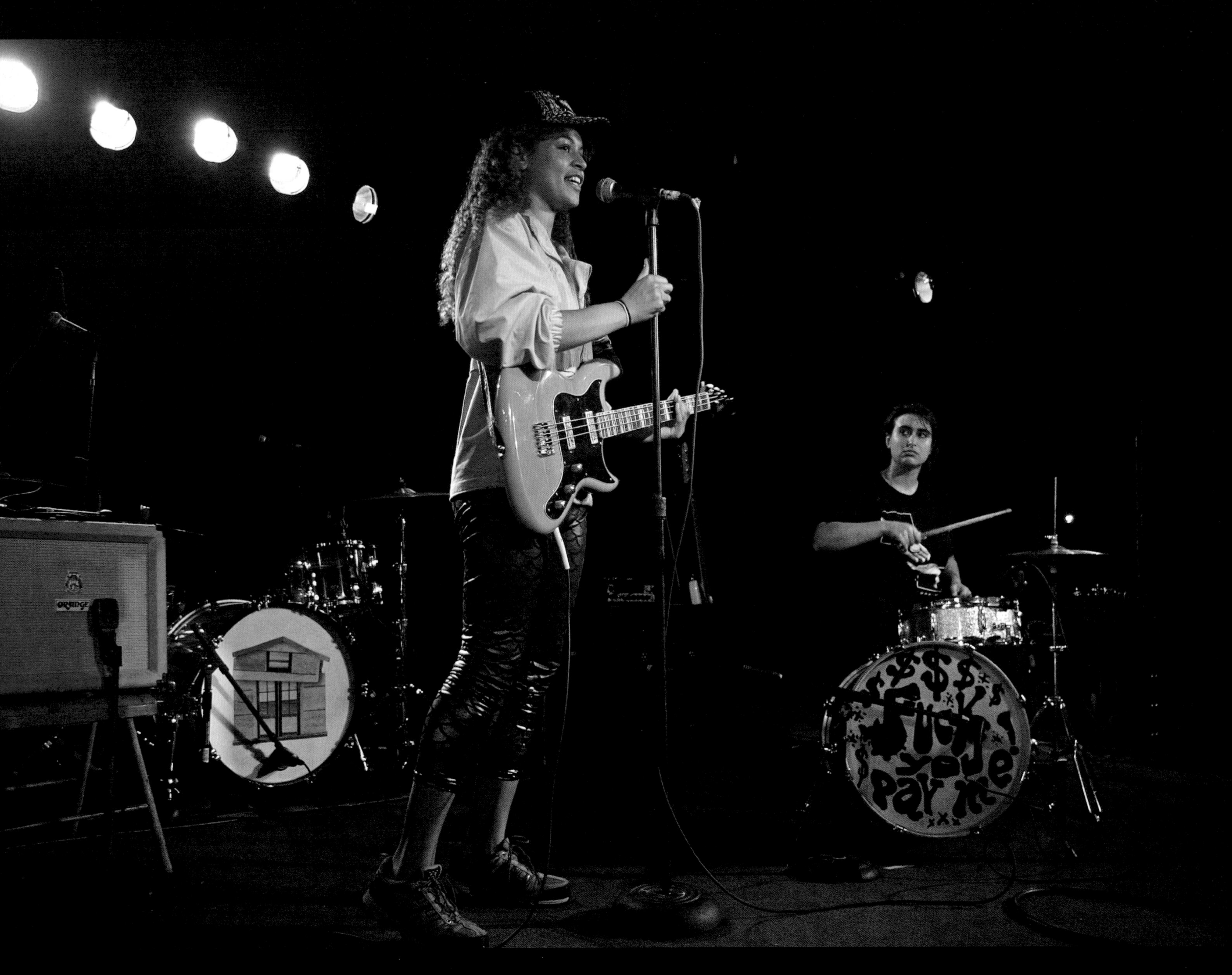
ORANGE
Fuck you pay me!

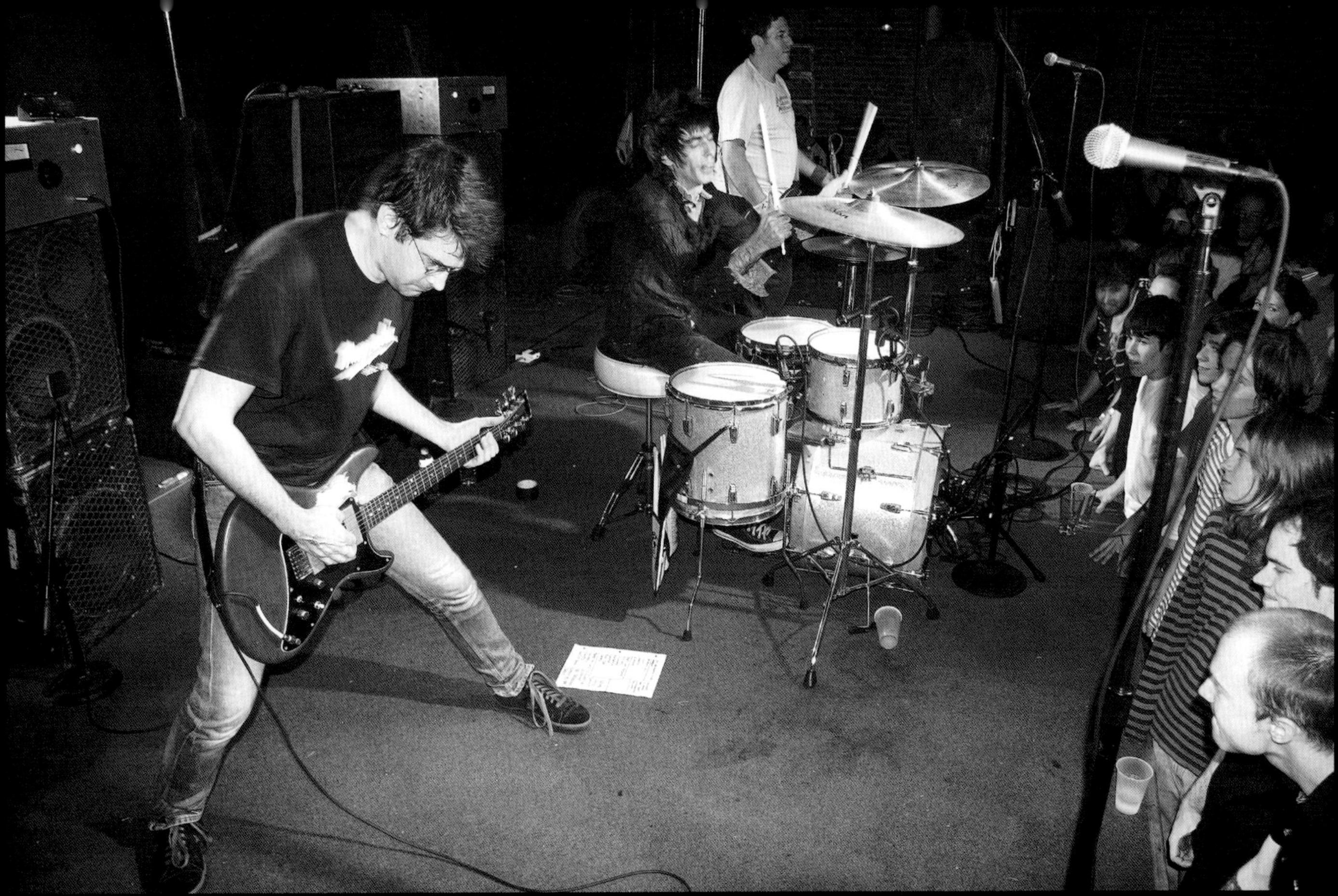

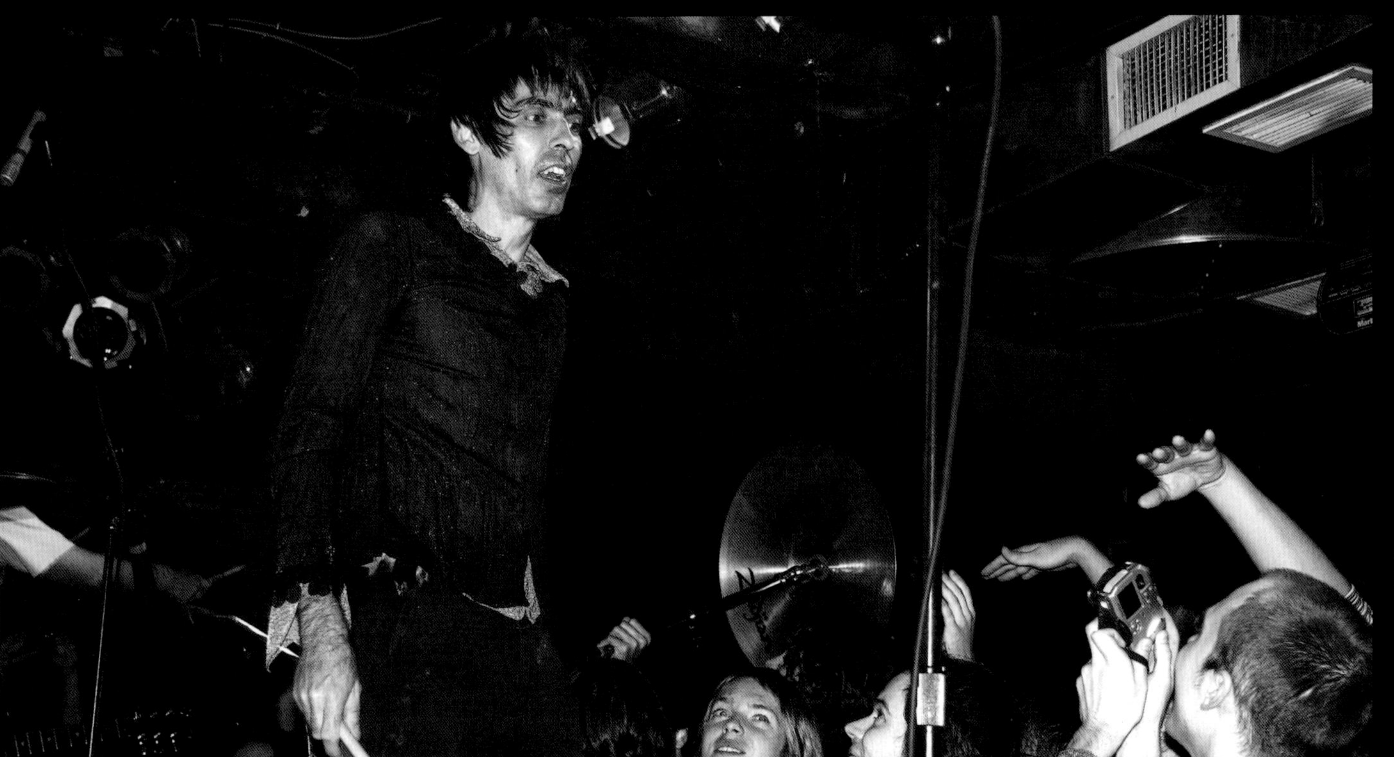

Shellac, Black Cat / WDC, 2016
Opposite: Sneaks, Black Cat / WDC, 2016

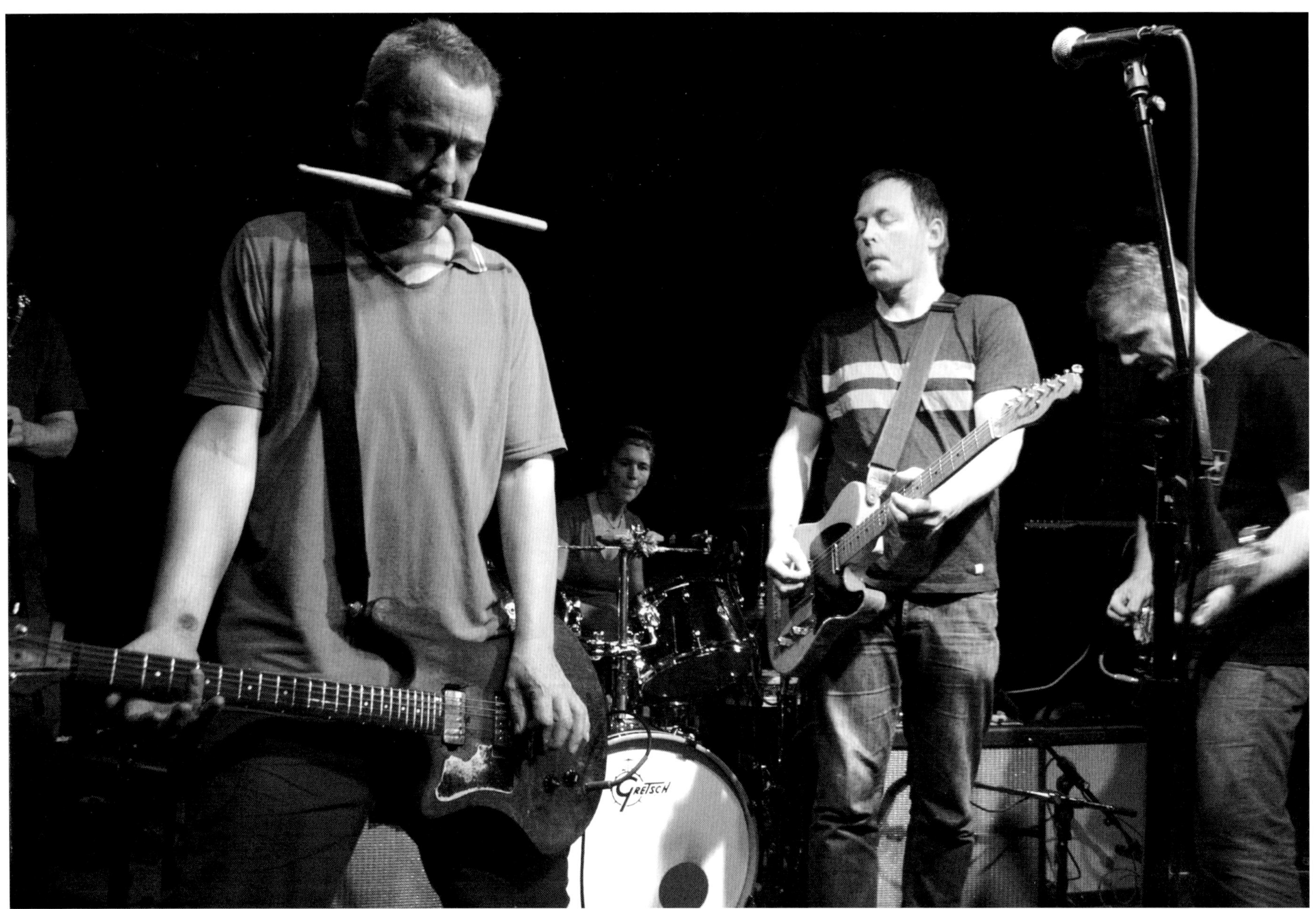

The Ex, Black Cat / WDC, 2016

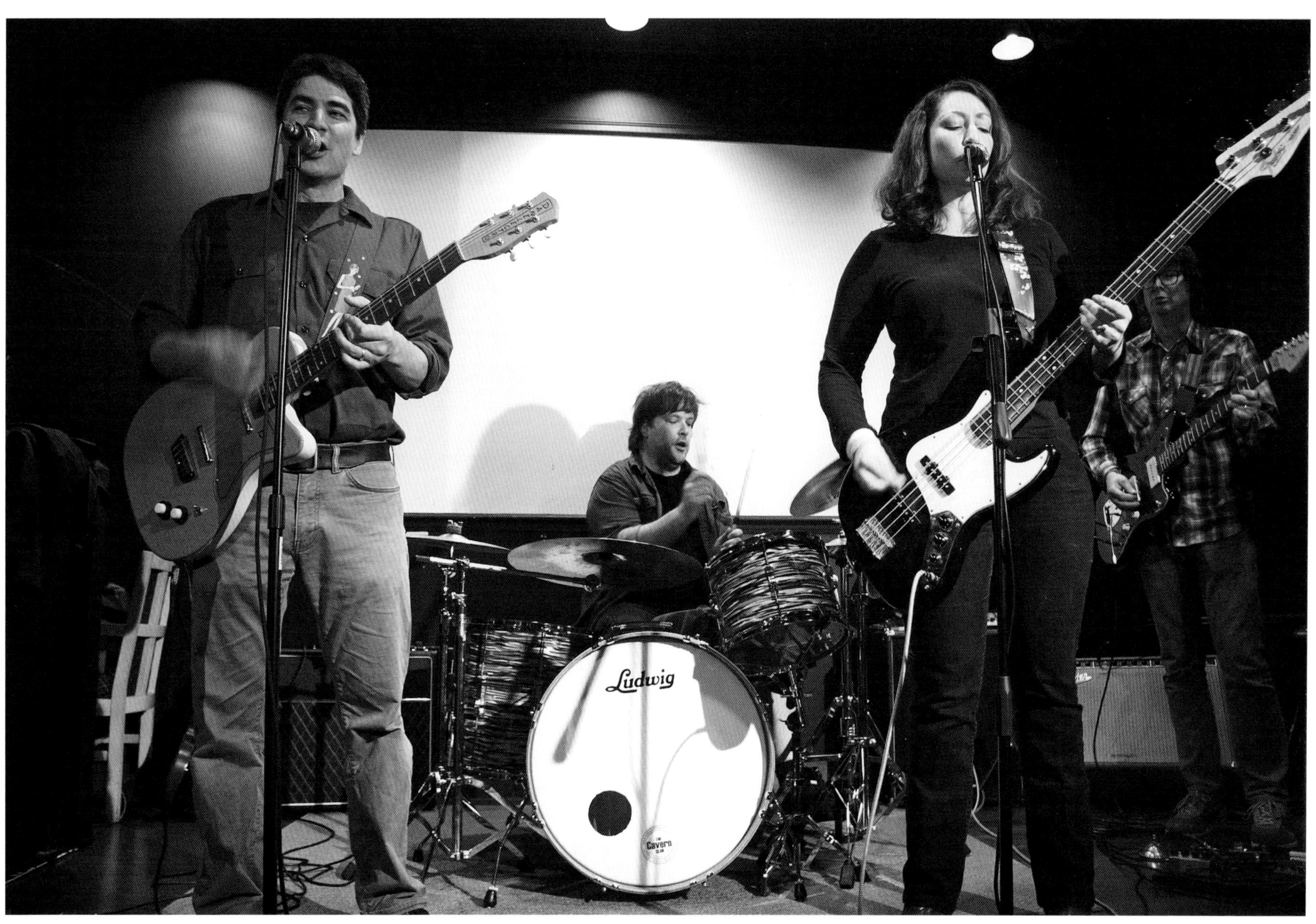

Soccer Team, Busboys and Poets / WDC, 2016

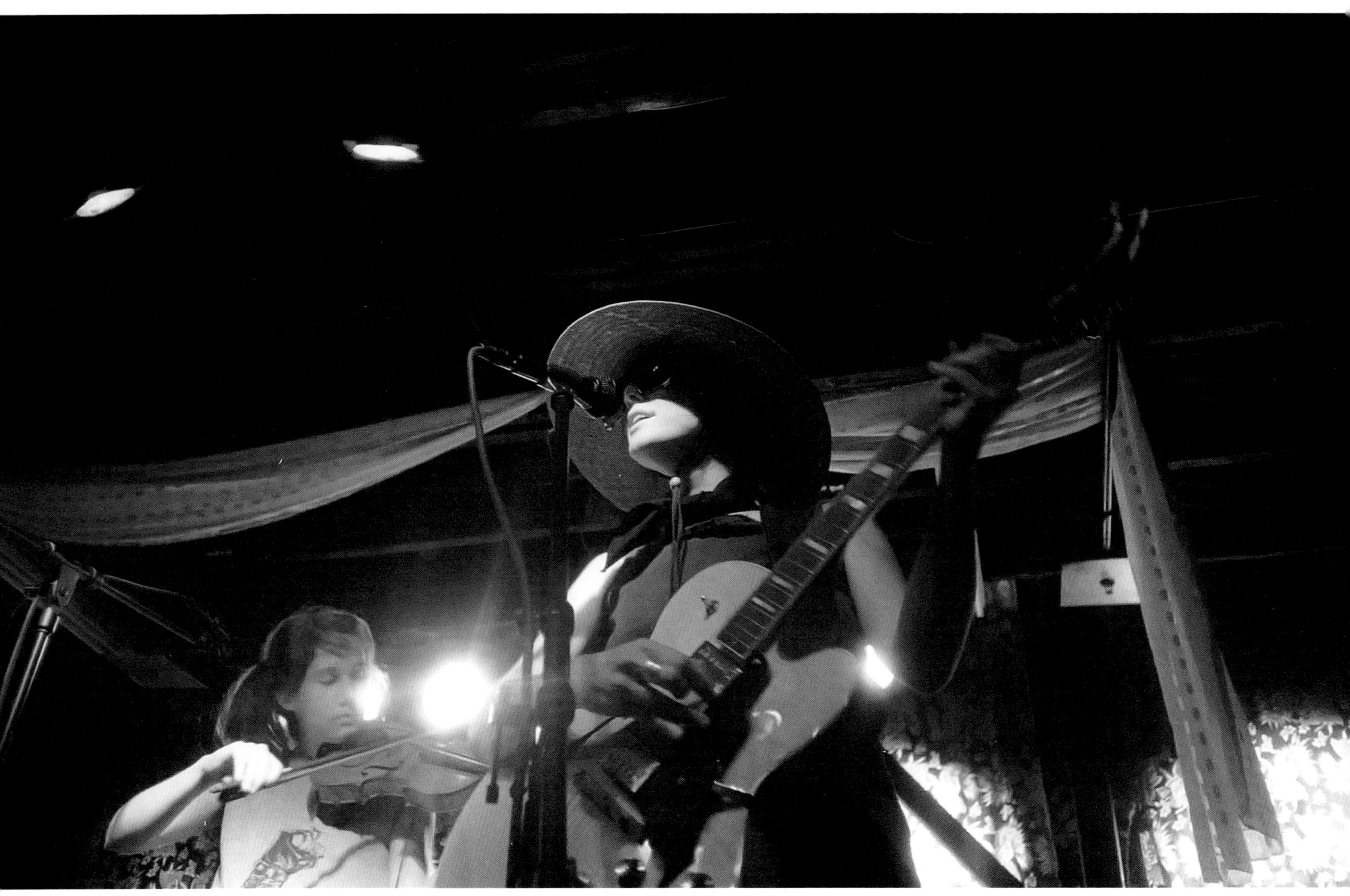

TARA JANE O'NEIL

At some point which I can't remember, I found out that I am music. Just as we are all music. I could step into it with ease and joy. As much as children are allowed to be, children can be genderless, borderless creatures. I was Olivia Newton-John singing, and I was also in love with her. I was John Lennon in the mirror even though I was an eight-year-old girl in Kentucky and he had just been assassinated. In the eighth grade I found myself to be a girl child in puberty with weird shoes when the family moved back to Kentucky after spending the new wave early eighties in Anaheim, California.

Shortly after this move I began my lifelong relation with an autoimmune disease, which affected my everything including my relative wellness, energy, appearance, and unusually early brushes with mortality and illness. My body and my environment were swiftly changing things. As a kid we moved nearly every year. I was a perpetual new kid; Other. My tale of typical teenage suburban alienation is just that. Though my singular bag was able to hold many versions of Otherness. At fifteen I got my own guitar. At some point I found out that music was the key to the realms of refuge that could be found with other people or found in solitude.

At some point I found out that when we move together we can find joy and we can save our lives. In the eighties and early nineties, Louisville punk (generally speaking) was a sparkling and angsty beast, but it wasn't my only nation. I found disparate communities seeking some version of refuge. I found spaces where weirdos and Others of all stripes could BE, in that beautiful hybrid shape we made. I found friends. I found foils. I went to every kind of show and watched and learned how these sounds were happening.

I am not self-taught at all. I learned from everyone I sought out and and stumbled upon. As a woman, and a queer one, in a punk scene, I was Other, inside of a scene made up of Others. But I had chops, so I was accepted. So few were the women playing at that time, so then the women were beacons of light, and beacons of light draw every kind of attention. Playing music came easily to me; the difficulty came in how to bring my self and my instrument out of my room. My friend Jason Noble eventually called me out of that space. How fantastic and how lucky I was to land where and when I did. I've seen music change and save lives in every place I've been lucky enough to visit. Its genie takes many different forms. When a thing can bring you into a positive body experience, into the universal body, into a body of people that makes some kind of sense to you when you are otherwise adrift in seas of alienation and pain, you keep doing it. For communion and joy, and for survival.

TARA JANE O'NEIL AND THE ECSTATIC TAMBOURINE ORCHESTRA • RODAN • DRINKING WOMAN • RETSIN • THE SONORA PINE • THE KING COBRA

Tara Jane O'Neil / Portland, OR, 2005

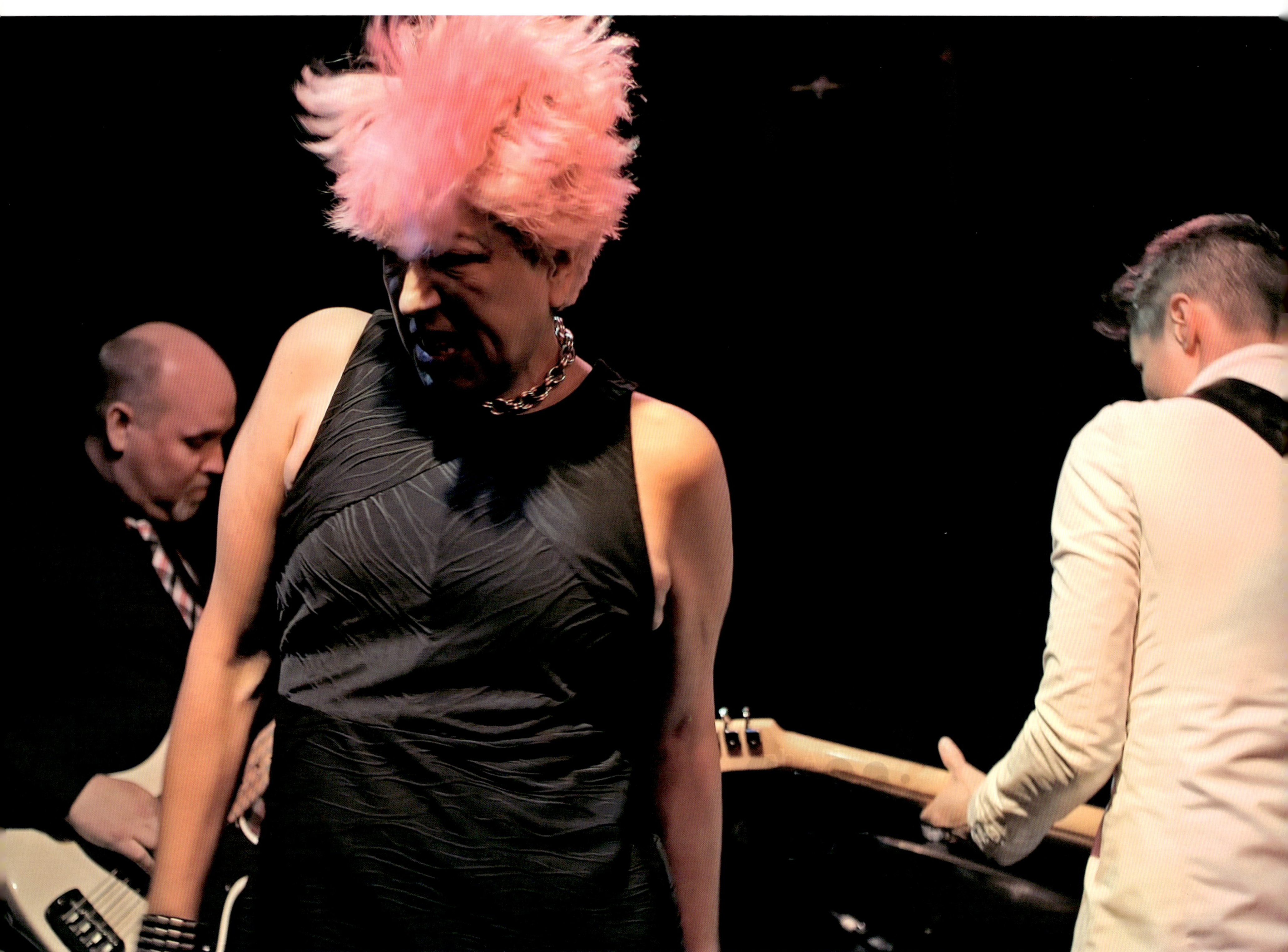

Alice Bag, Black Cat / WDC, 2017

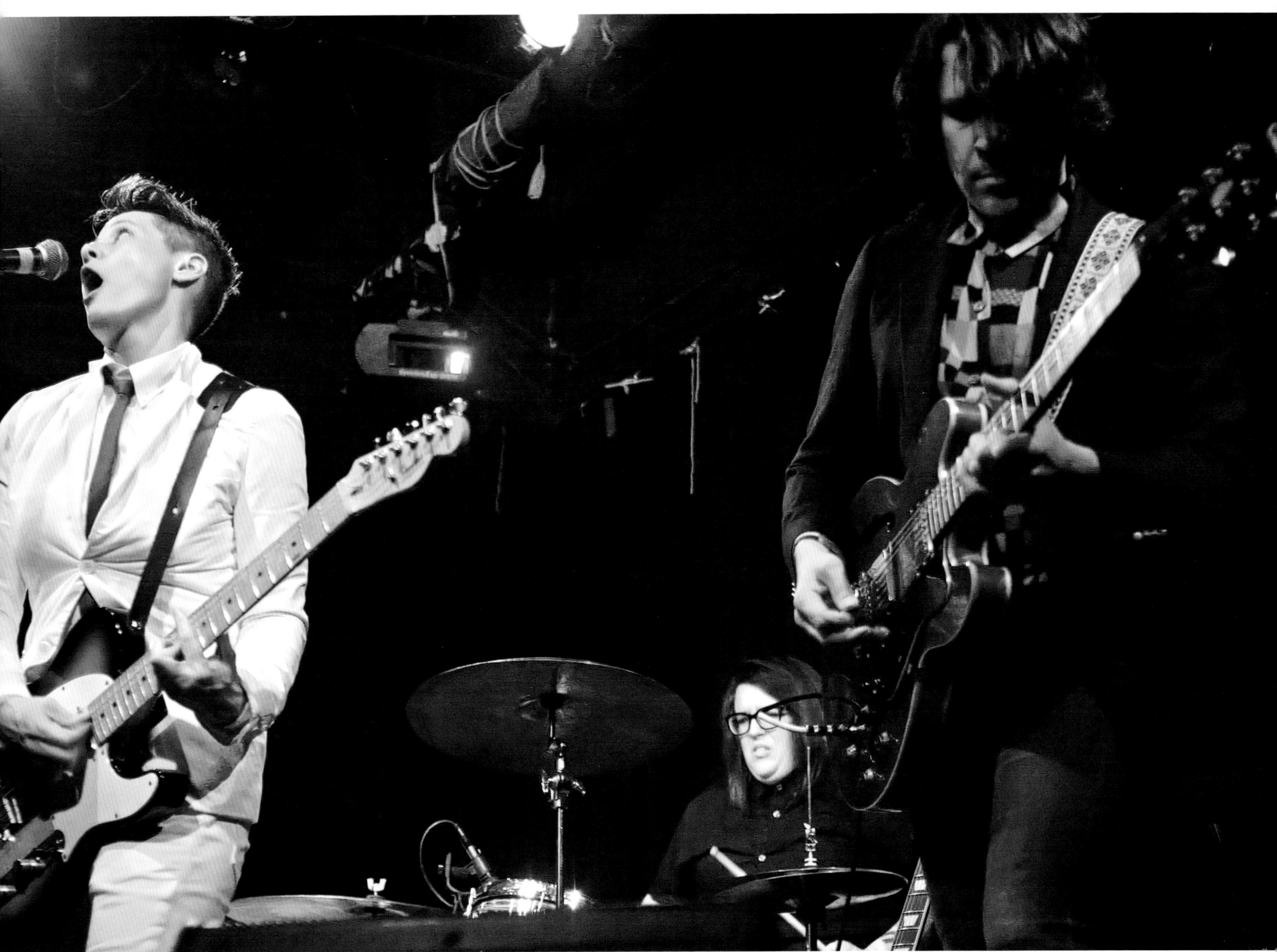

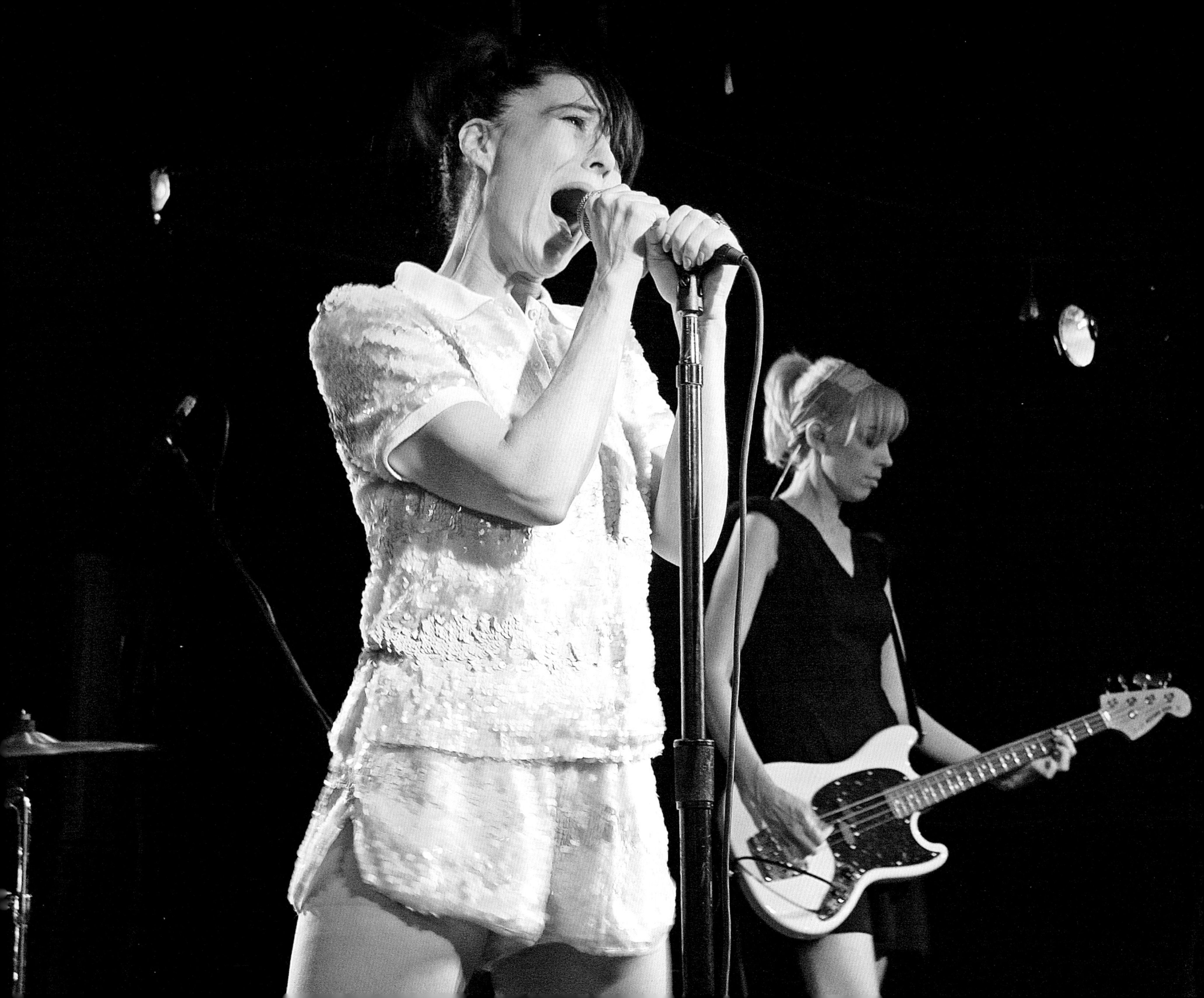

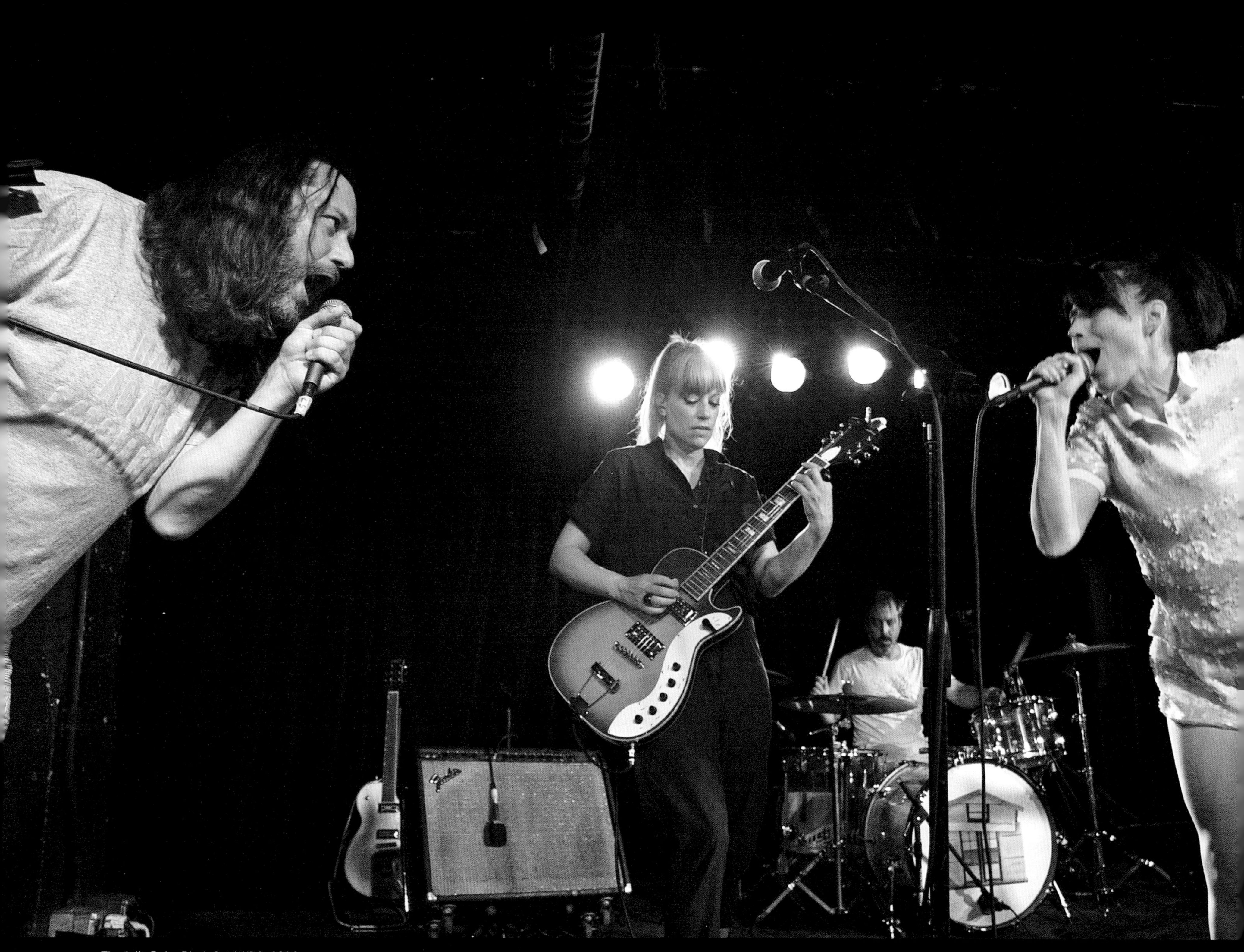

The Julie Ruin, Black Cat / WDC, 2016

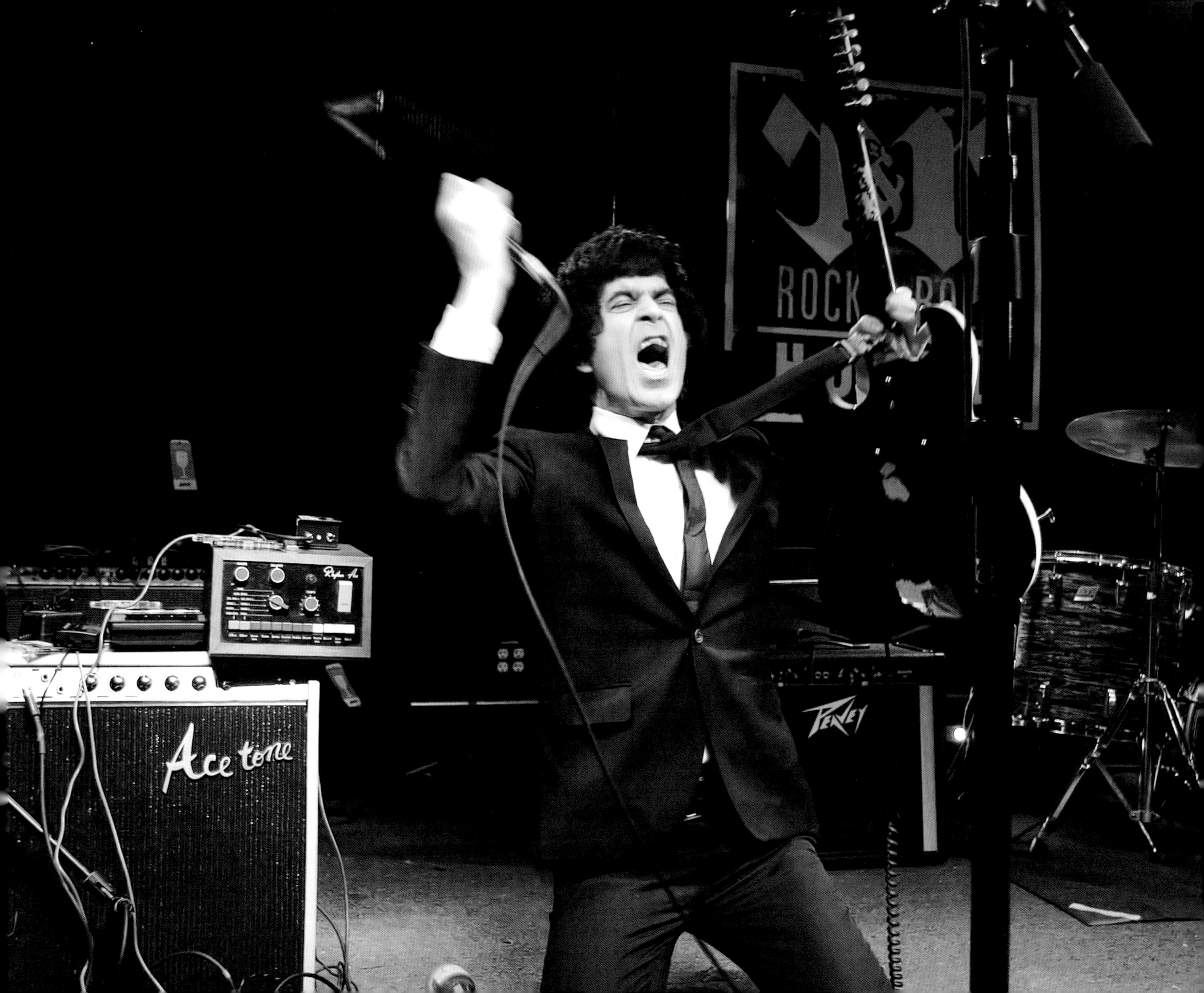
Ace tone
Peavey

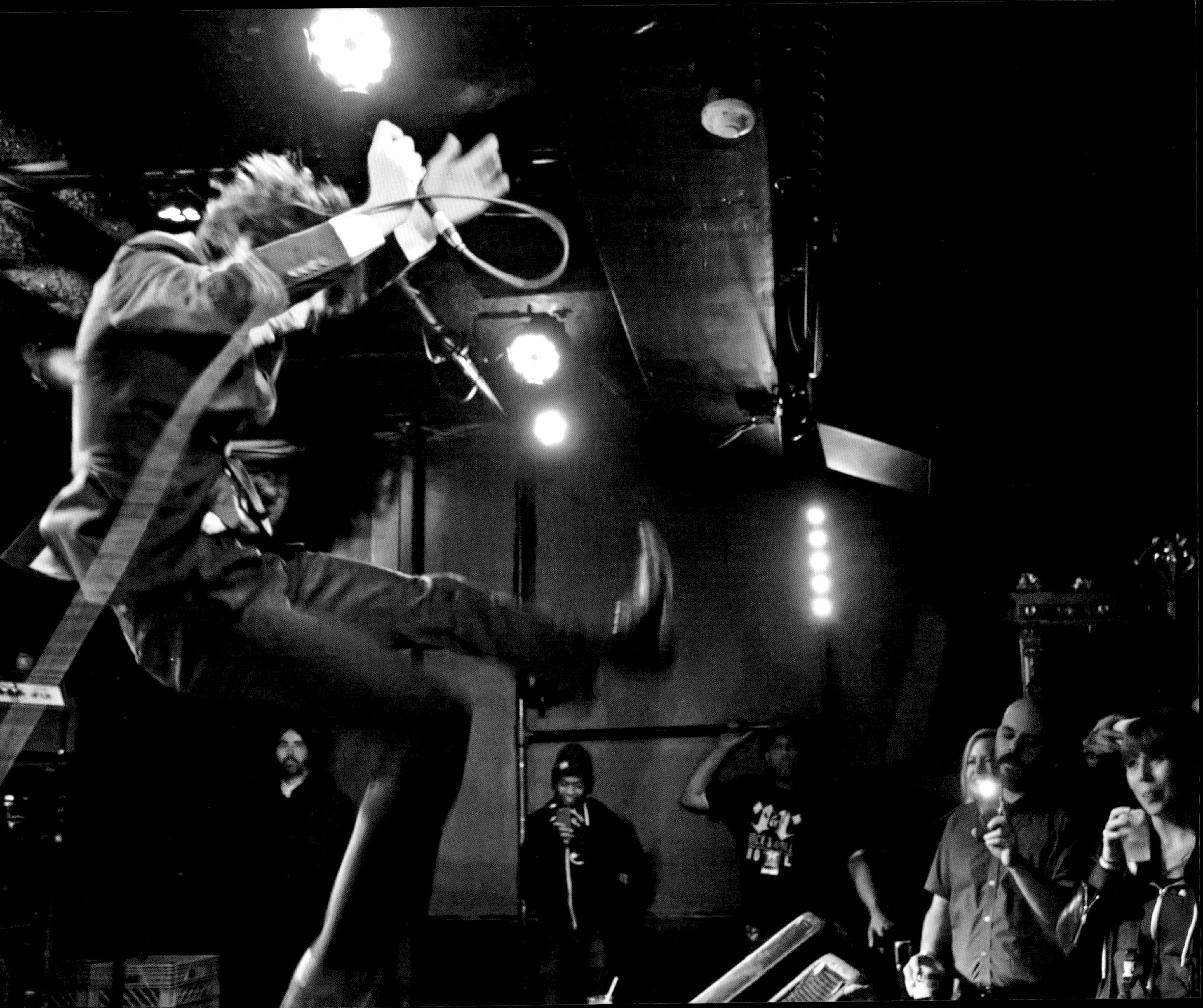

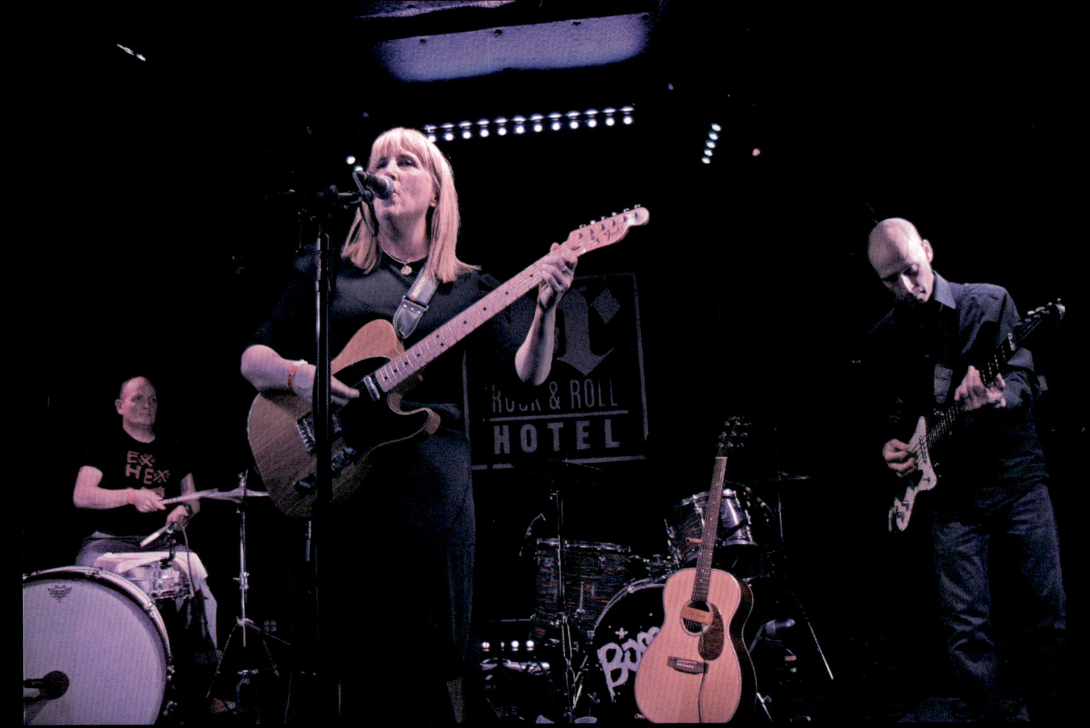

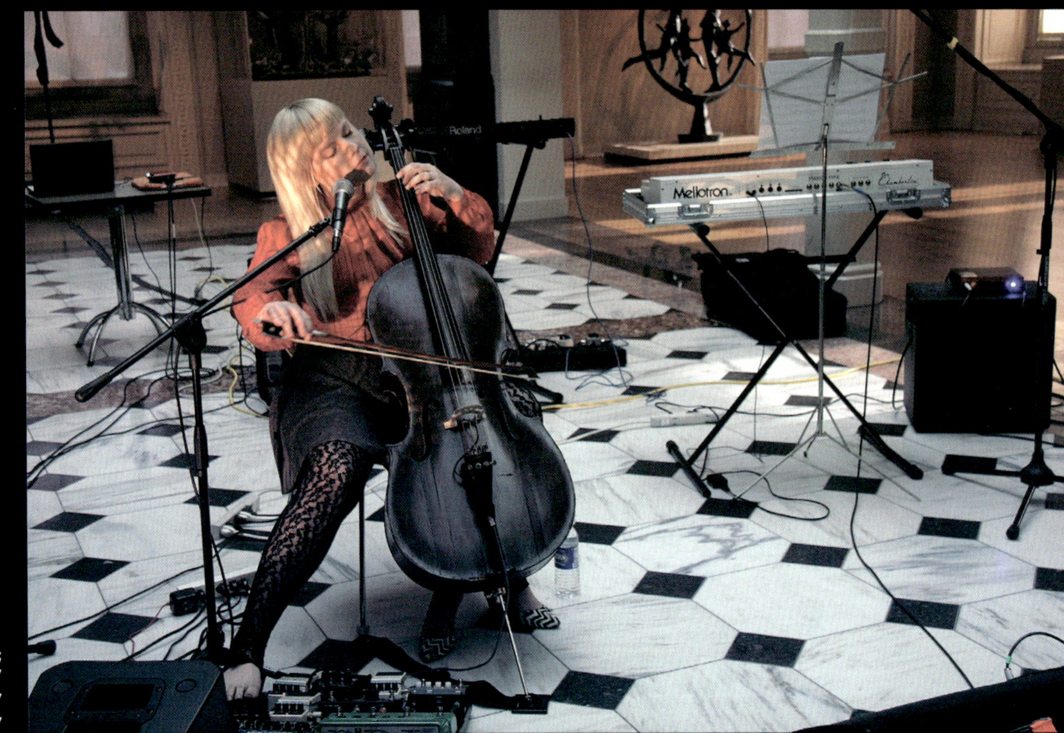

From top: Anna Connolly, Rock & Roll Hotel / WDC, 2017;
Janel Leppin-Pirog, Smithsonian American Art Museum / WDC, 2017
Opposite: Last basement show at the MLK Library / WDC, 2017
Previous page: Escape-ism, Rock & Roll Hotel / WDC, 2017

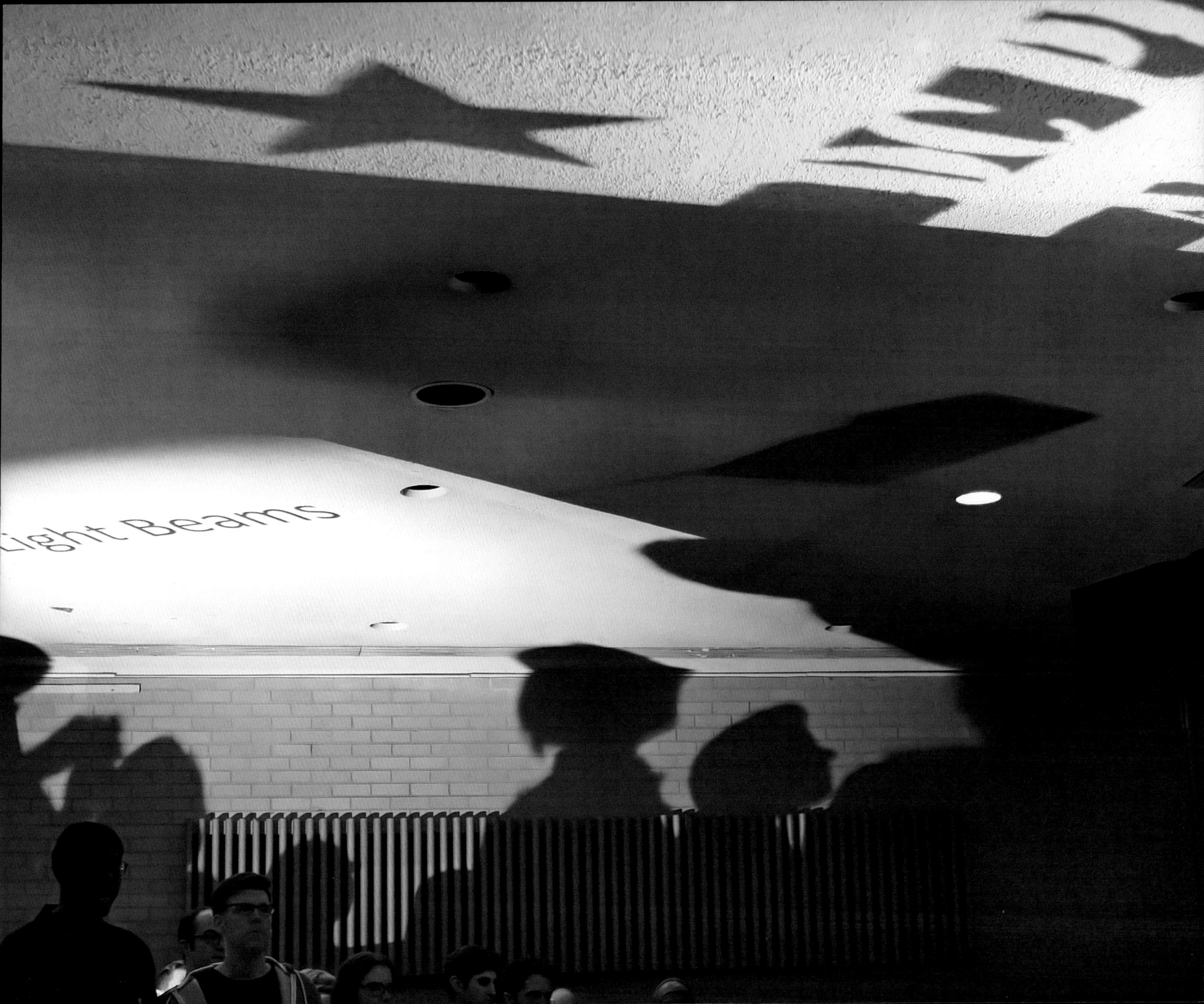
ight Beams

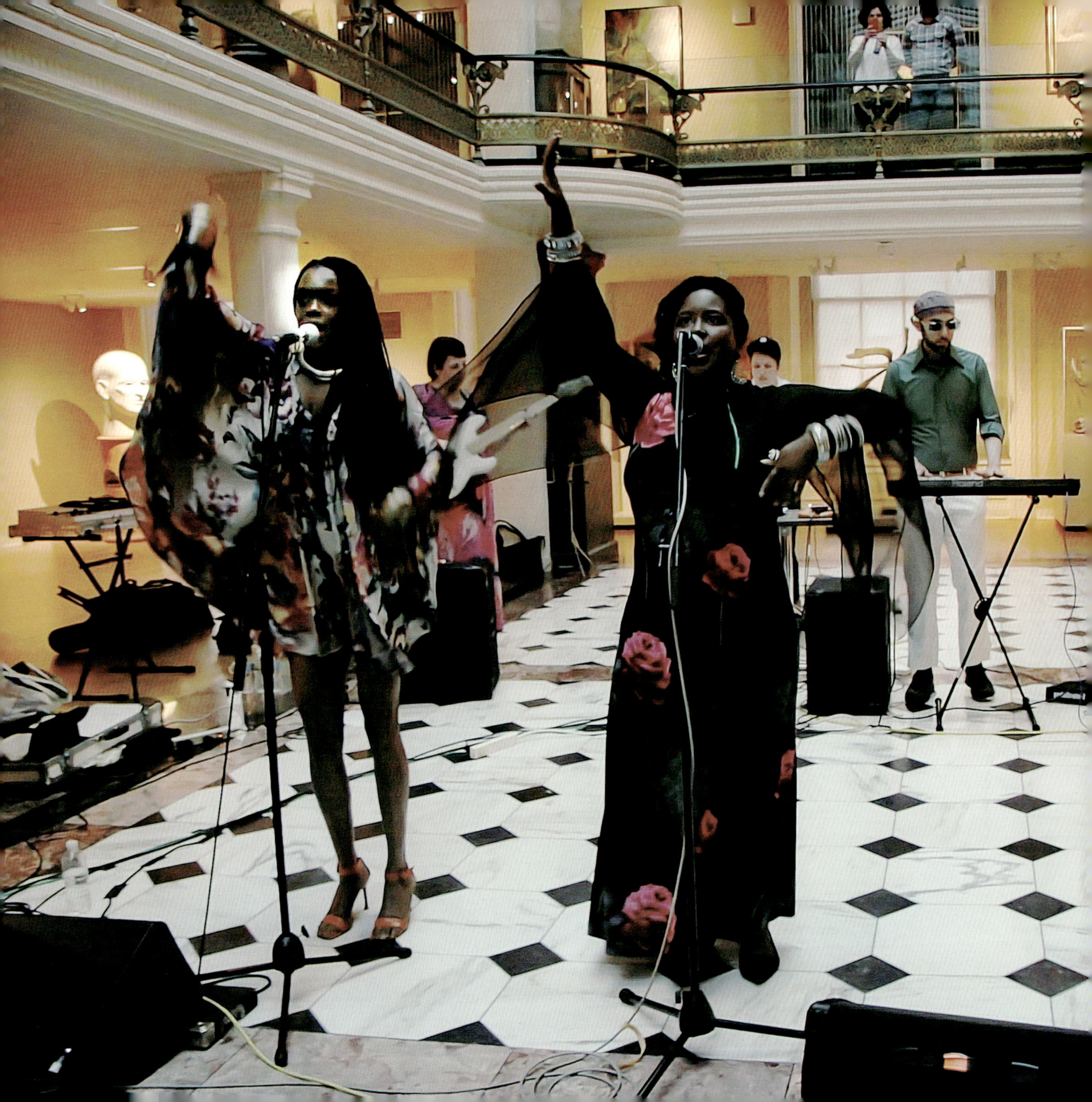

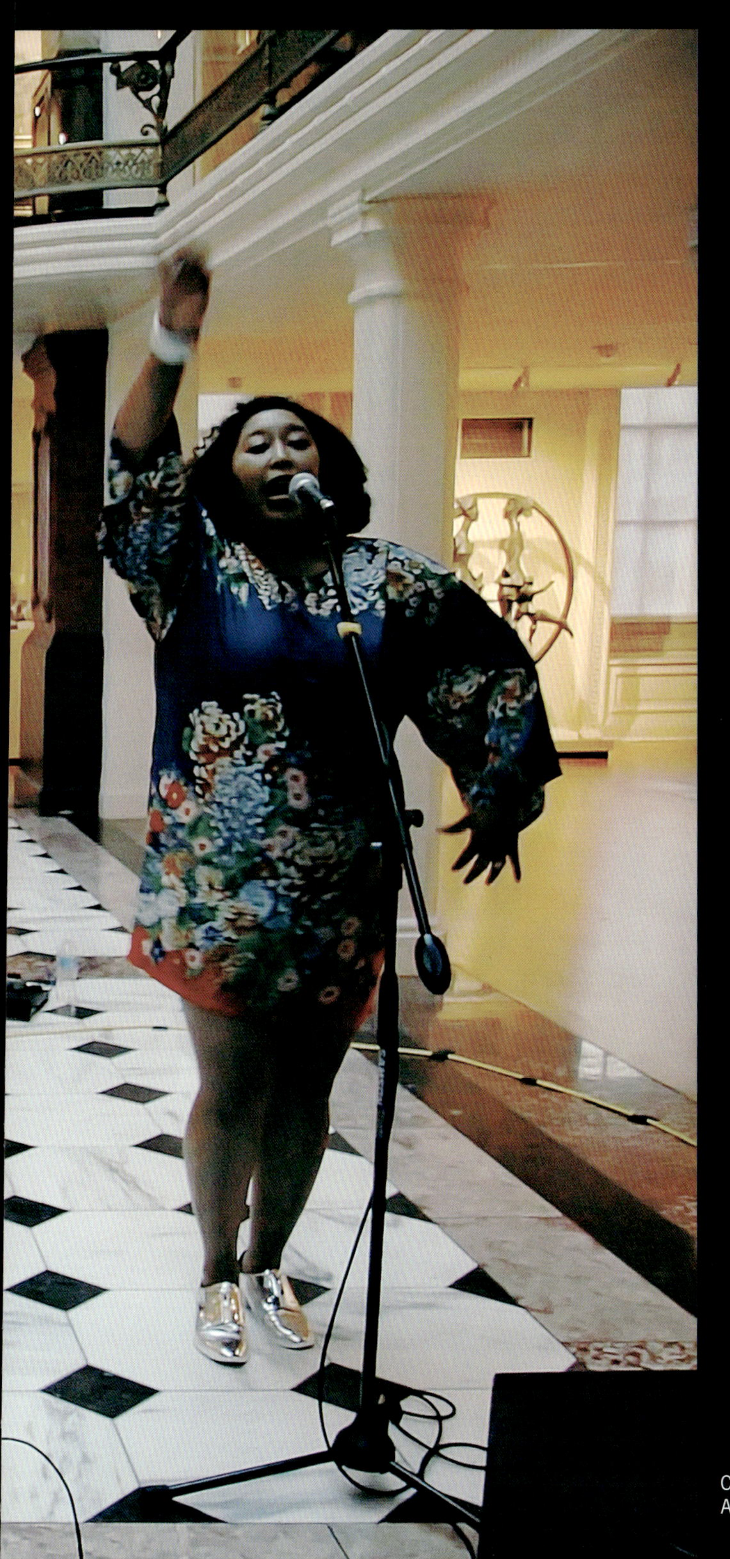

Coup Sauvage and the Snips, Smithsonian American Art Museum / WDC, 2017

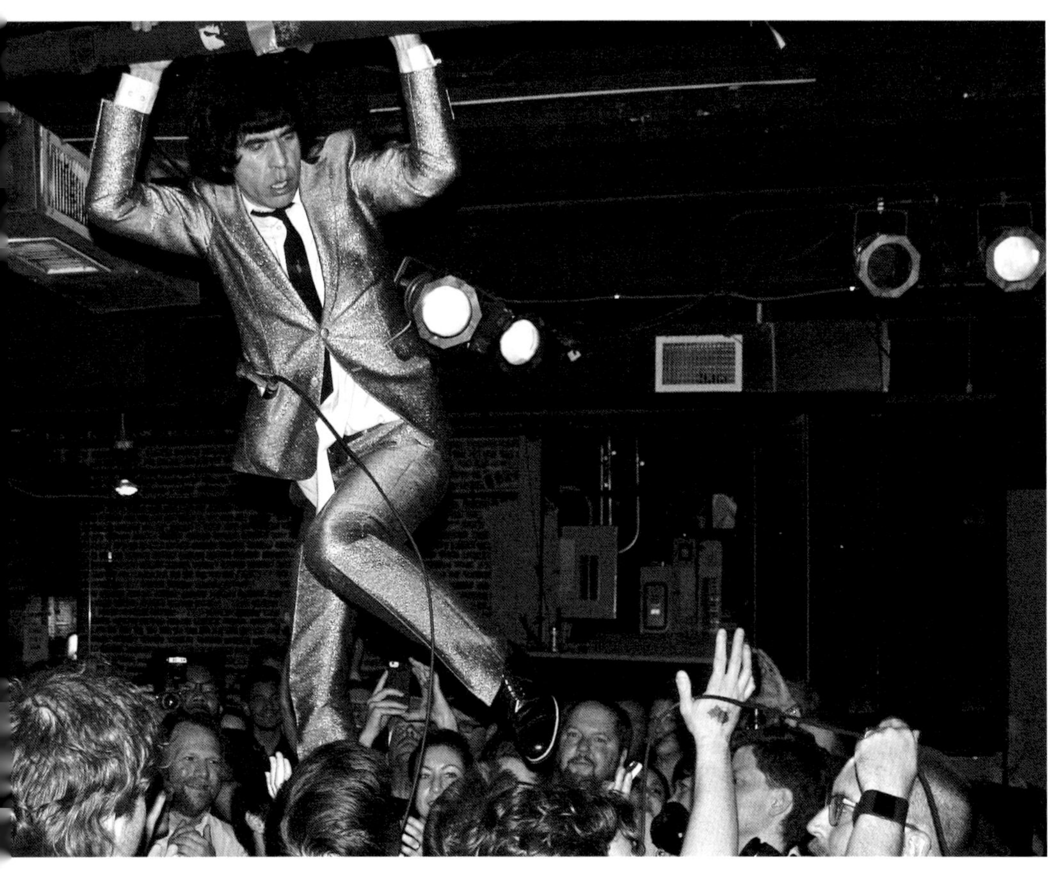

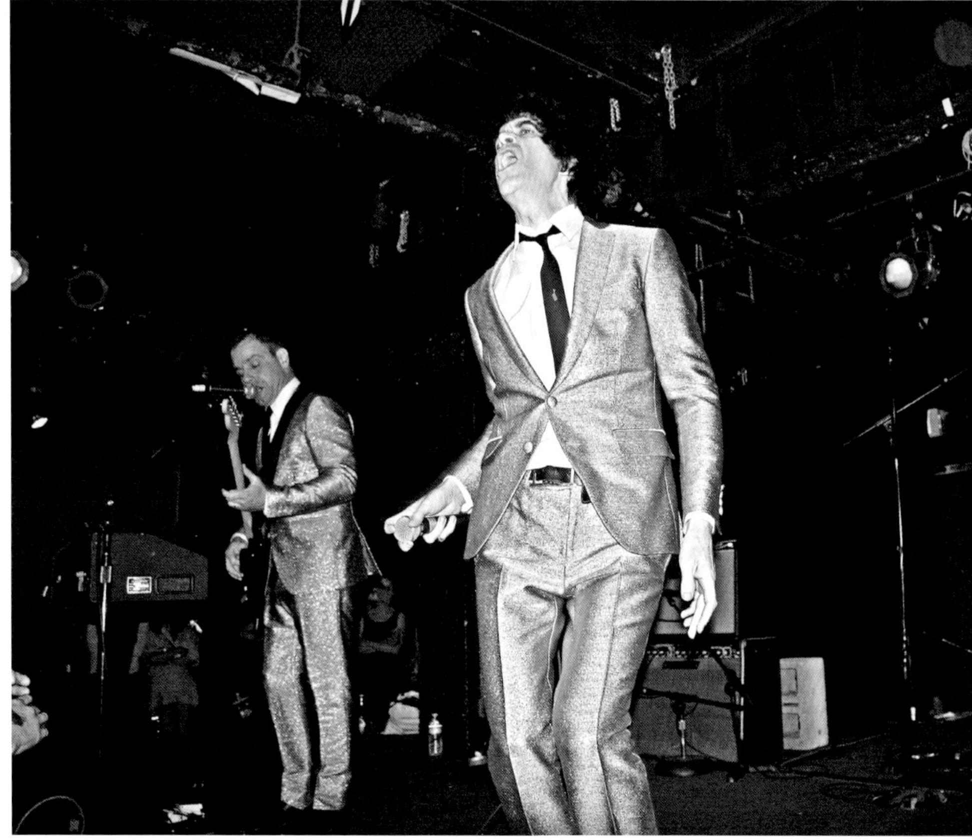

The Make-Up, Black Cat / WDC, 2017

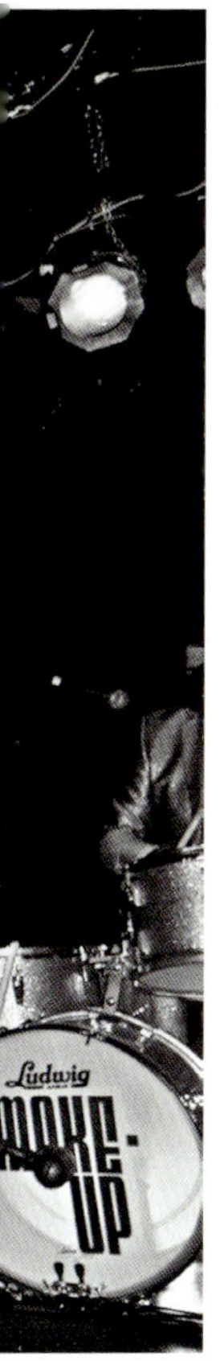
Ludwig

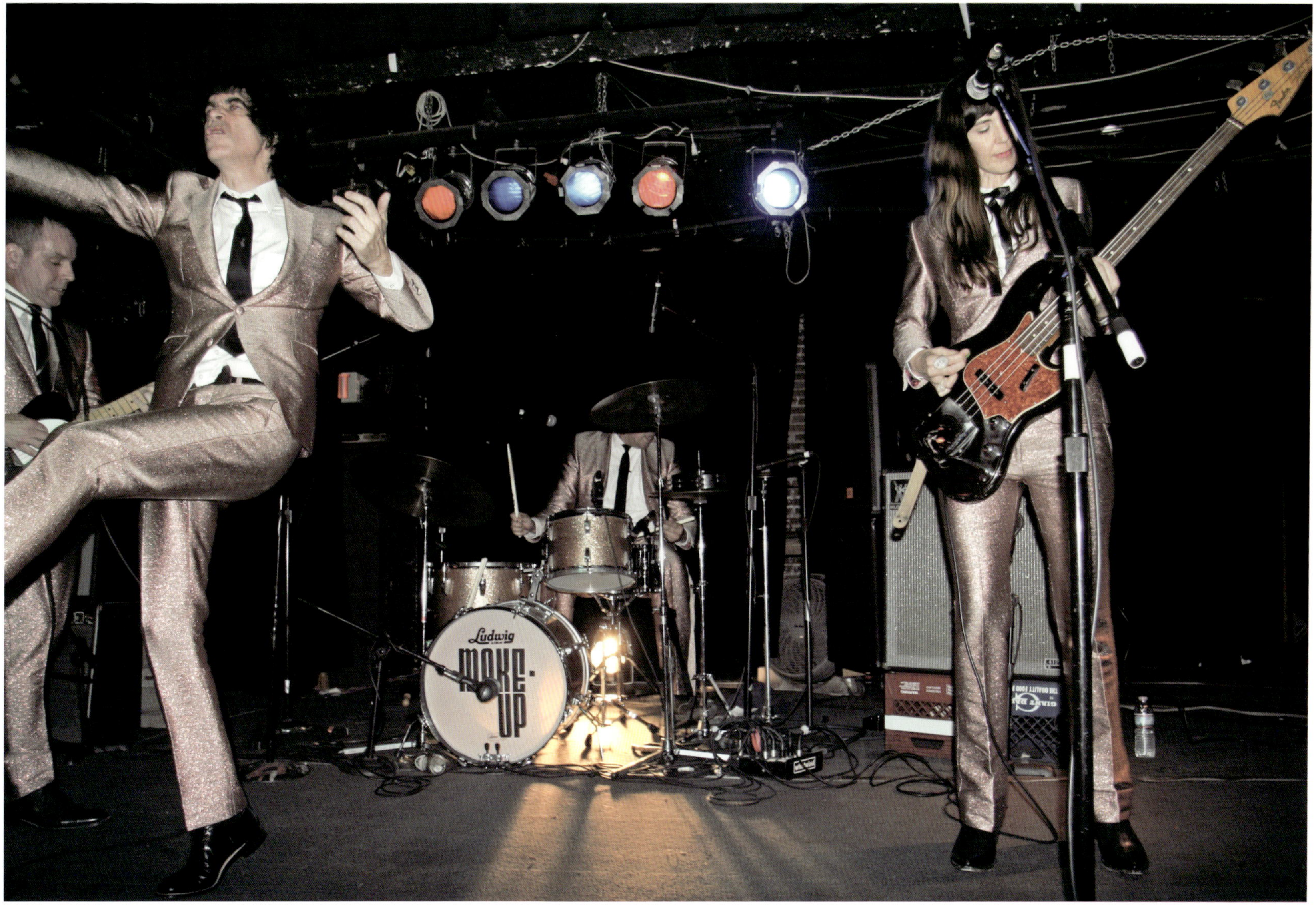

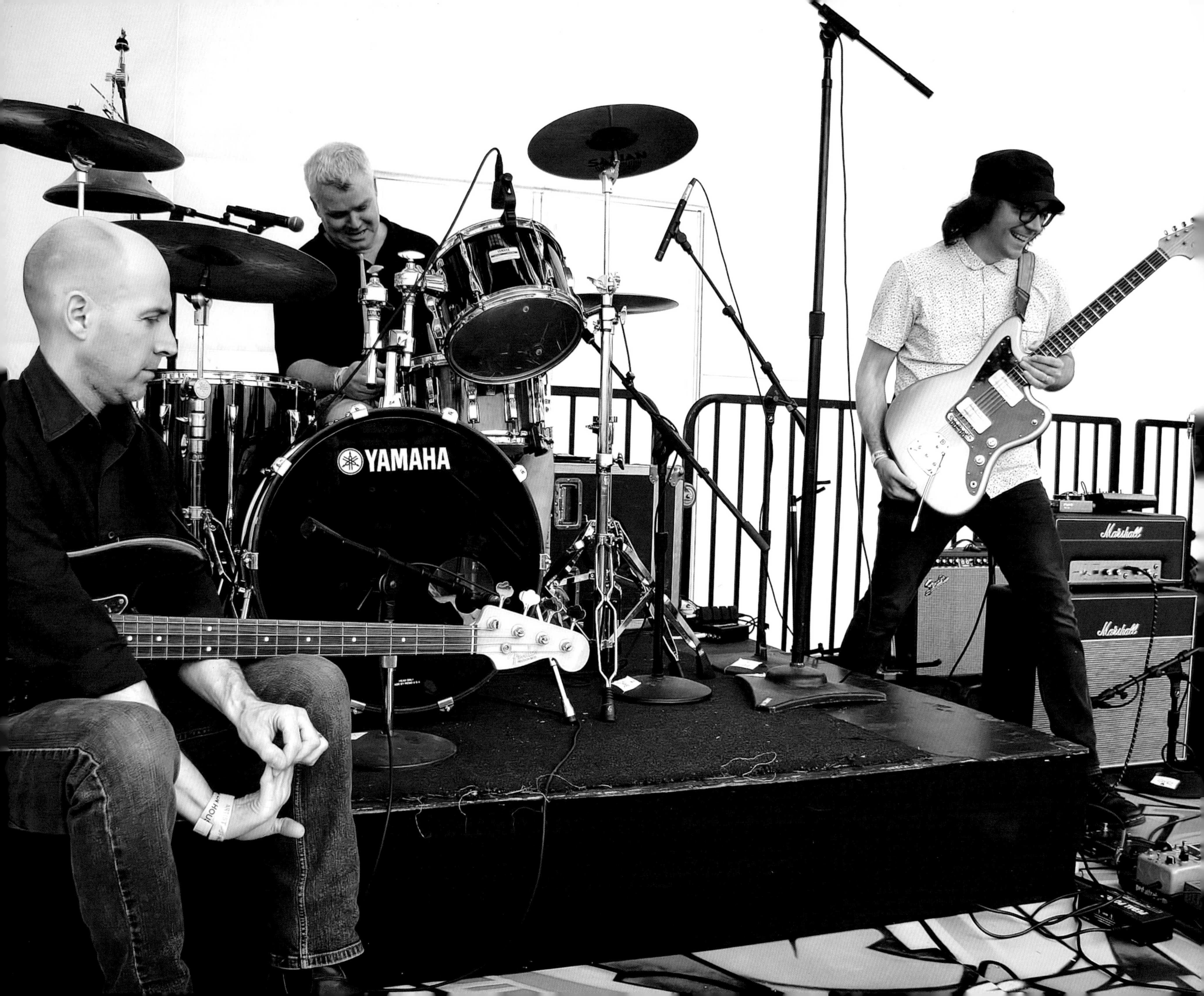
YAMAHA
Marshall
Marshall

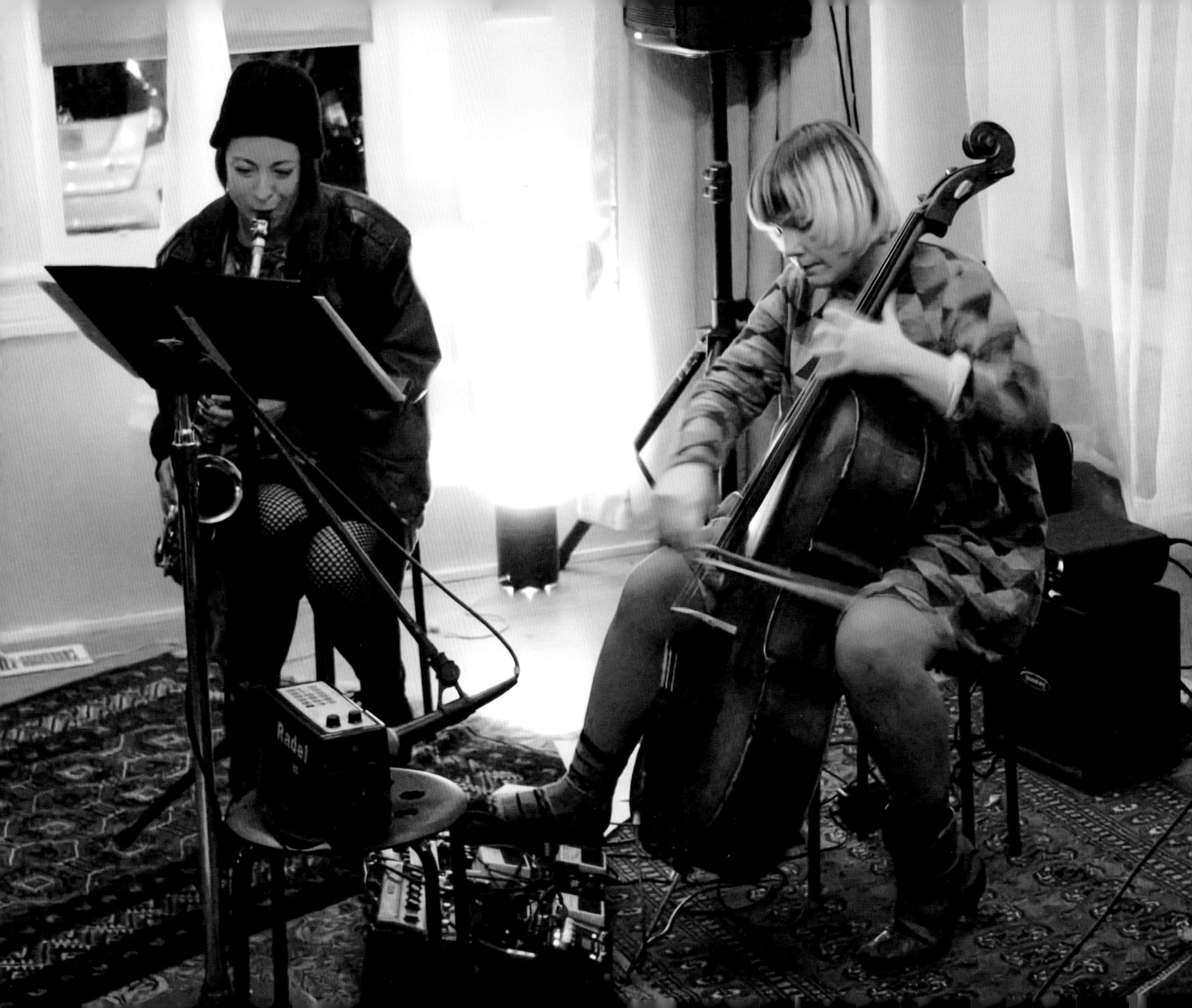
Radel

LELY CONSTANTINOPLE

Looking at these photographs reminds me of when I first met Antonia in the mid 1990s. She had just moved to DC and was having a hard time communicating in English with new friends. We were both photographers so we started sharing work to get to know each other better. One set of images stood out: portraits of objects found on walks—seedpods, dead leaves, acorns—rephotographed close up on stark white or black backgrounds. They were abstract, intimate, and raw. They revealed much about Antonia's approach to her work.

Antonia loves anyone who creates something with a full heart. The photographs in this book make that plain. When I watch her take pictures at shows, I am struck by this: she comes early, picks her spot in front of the stage and stays there, allowing events to unfold around her. Other photographers chase down shots, but Antonia stands patient, ready, and present. She is spectator and participant, simultaneously observing and taking part. Her relationship to and with music (and its creators) is a conversation, an exchange of energy. Musicians make records, and Antonia's photographs are live records capturing the power of the moment.

Lely is a photographer, photo archivist/editor, and teacher.

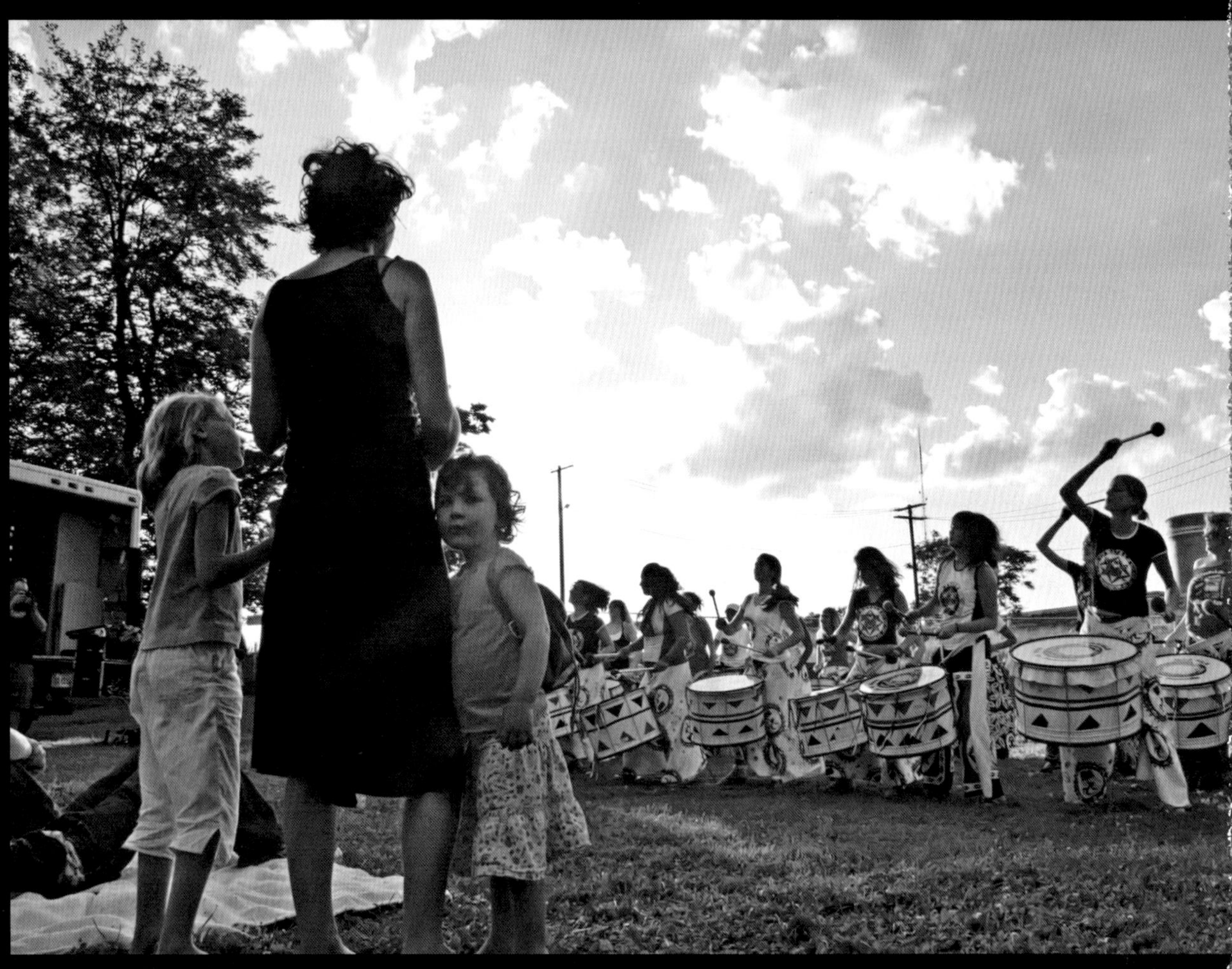

Batalá Washington, Fort Reno / WDC, 2009
Previous spread, left: The Messthetics, John F. Kennedy Center for the Performing Arts / WDC, 2017
Previous spread, right: Sarah Hughes and Janel Leppin, Rhizome DC / WDC, 2017

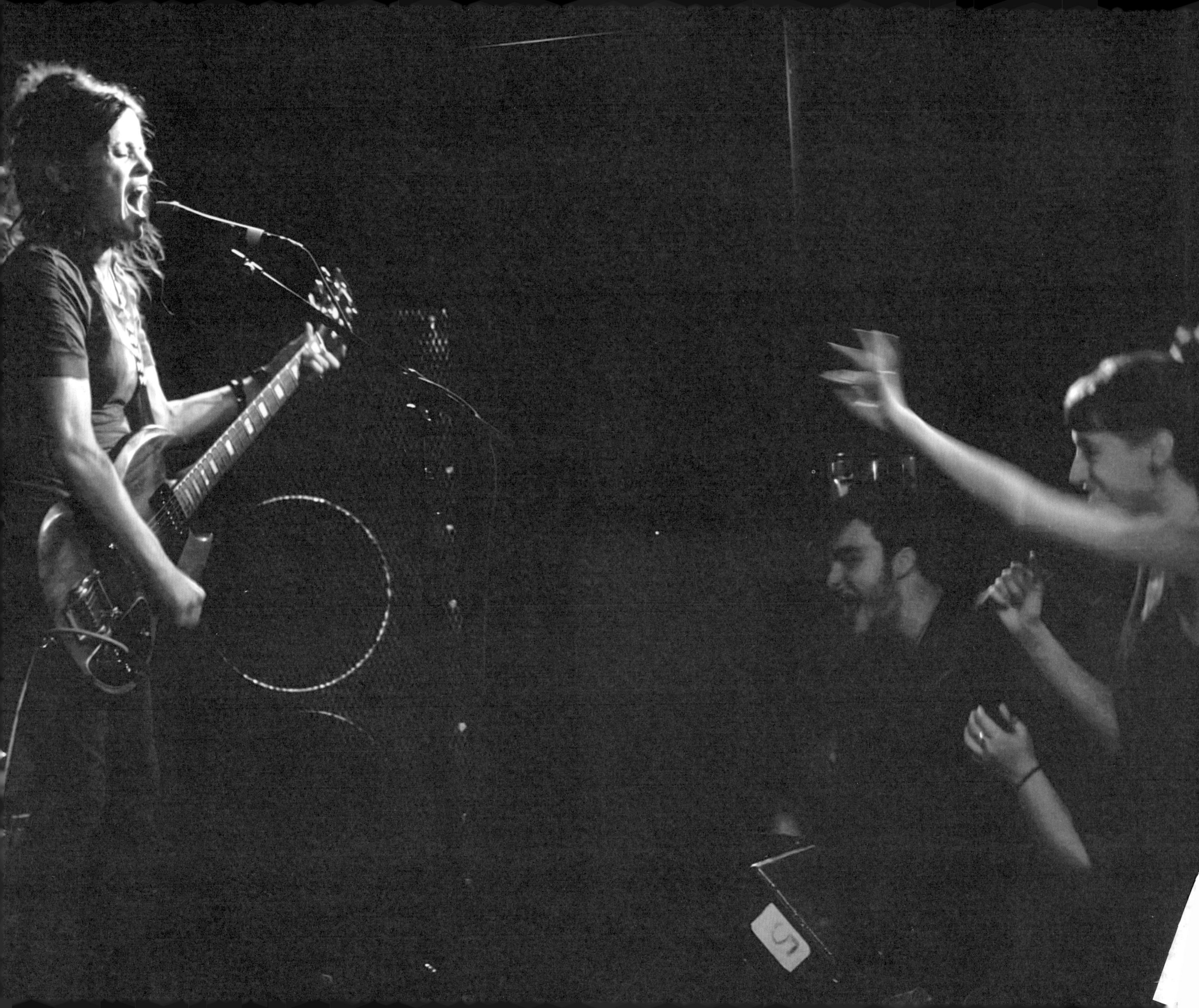